D1547131

The White Light Within

The White Light Within

A Political Spy Thriller

THOMAS and
MARY MARTZ

This is a work of fiction. The characters are both actual and fictitious.
All incidents, descriptions, dialogue and opinions expressed are the product of the author's imagination and are used fictitiously.
They are not to be construed to be as real

Cover photograph © by the estate of Mary Martz
Cover and interior design by David Ter-Avanesyan/Ter33Design

This book is dedicated to two Marys

Dr. Mary Chamberlin
Without whose answer to "the question" this trip
would never have been taken
and
My Mary
who insisted we write our story.

June 2019
Lebanon, New Hampshire, USA

Tom and Mary Martz sat in the hospital room, anxiously waiting for a response.

Dr. Chamberlin broke into a big smile and said, "Absolutely. There is no reason that Mary cannot go to Paris. I highly endorse the idea!"

1

Friday, June 21, 2019
Paris, France

NINA

She emerged from the metro at the Concorde. Nina took the 12 metro from Abbesses, the closest metro stop to the apartment where she lived at 10 Rue Garreau. From Abbesses, she would metro to either Assemblée National or Concorde. The Assemblée National was the choice on rainy, cold, snowy, or a combination of all three, days. Paris had those in the late fall and early spring. Days that couldn't make up their mind between rain, snow, or both. Those days were always one thing . . . cold. Today was none of those. Today was a perfect Paris day. Bright, sunny, with a just-right warm temperature.

This was the kind of day to walk the last 1.5 kilometers to the gallery. Nina loved this walk. Up from the metro station at Rue de Rivoli along the border on the east side of the Place de la Concorde and the Obelisque. East through the Jardin des Tuileries. The crunch of the small stones on the walkway always felt and sounded good; the kind of ordinary sound that your mind could get lost in. Each step was a hypnotic melody. France and particularly Paris did walkways through parks well. Much better than most European cities, though many of them had learned the art from Paris, and certainly much better than the few she experienced in America.

Walks in America always seemed to be one of three things; ugly, black, hotter than Enfer in the summer, and asphalt; hard on the feet and too bright for the eyes on sunny days and concrete; or mud . . . dirt that turned into a gooey consistency with the least amount of water added.

She liked aspects of America. She certainly had enjoyed her time in Miami learning English as a second language. She and the other foreign students had wonderful times on the warm evenings out in the Miami nightlife. The beaches were sandy and full of life, though there seemed to be a lot of older people on the beach. She and the other female students had found it hard to find any beaches in Florida where you could go topless. It's much different from the South of France and most European beaches, where it was almost an expectation for a young woman to be sans top. No one seemed to give it any notice except for the foreigners, mostly Americans, who haven't normalized this in their country.

Nina had her fair share of stolen glances and stares from men and not just Americans. Many of her boyfriends had said she was "perfect". However, like most young women, she never felt "perfect". She was happy with how she looked. She had been asked to model a few times. She was a bit skeptical about this but had done some fashion shots. Occasionally, she was asked under false pretenses and she in no uncertain way let the guy know what she thought of him. She had studied some self-defense at university and had no objection to using some of it, if necessary, to ward off an unwelcome touch. Fortunately, most of her young men had been nice guys. Only one or two salauds ever had to experience her quick kick or sharp elbow, and they had learned.

Not big, though standing 5 foot 8 inches tall in her flats, some would say she was definitely on the slender side. She was in shape and proud of being so. Running 3 to 5 miles every other day, cycling with friends on weekends, and of rollerblading kept her that way. She loved the Pari Roller rollerblading every Friday night and was able to join in most evenings right after the iSPY Gallery closed.

From the iSPY Gallery she made the quick, gliding warm-up down to the starting location at the Montparnasse. If running late closing the gallery, she could join the group at Cafe de Flore near the Mabillon metro stop or, if she was really late, just wait for her friends to skate by on Rue Voltaire right in front of the gallery, midway through the outward bound part of the 14-mile skate.

Nina had considered staying in the US when she finished her English coursework. There were many opportunities with US corporations for multilingual speakers, and not very many Americans were bilingual. With her being able to speak French, English, and Russian, she was in a good position to be recruited.

Art, math, and writing were her interests, history too. That is why she studied them at the Russian State University for Humanities. Just as she was contemplating staying, this incredible thing happened. A call from a distant relative, Evalina, asking her to come to Paris and talk with her about a job, a life living in Paris, and working at Evalina's gallery, iSPY Gallery!

She continued her walk through the Tuileries, remembering the day she was contacted. At the time, she was in the final semester of her studies in Miami. She was studying in one of the common spaces in the academic building when Marta, one of the lead instructors and head of the school came up to her.

"Nina, there is a long distance phone call for you in my office. It is someone in Paris who says she is a distant relative of yours. Someone named Evalina. Do you know her?"

Nina thought for a few seconds but could not think of anyone named Evalina in her family. Evalina was a common name in Russia, particularly in the history of Russia, but no one in the family came to mind. Besides her maman and papa, she didn't know too many other of her distant relatives. Living in the country had kept the family isolated from very many people.

"No," Nina replied, "no one comes to mind. Did she say why she was calling?" Had something happened to papa or maman, she wondered?

"She said something about perhaps offering you a job at her gallery in Paris. She said she owns a gallery that specializes in Russian artists." Marta, staring at her, asked, "Do you think something like that would be of interest to you? Otherwise,

I can tell her that you have no interest in talking with her."

Intrigued by this strange happening, Nina said, "Yes, I think I would like to talk with her. Ironically, I have dreamed of living in Paris and only thought of it as a dream. She says she is a relative? How interesting. Yes, I will talk with her."

Nina and Marta walked down the hallway toward the offices. They entered the office and Marta picked up the phone, pushed the small flashing button and spoke.

"Evalina, this is the headmistress. I have Nina with me, and she wishes to talk with you. I'll put her on."

Marta held the receiver to her head, nodding a few times, and then spoke once more. "Yes, she is a delightful young lady. From your description of your need for the position, a perfect fit. I'll put her on and I'm sure you will notice that from just talking with her. Here she is."

Marta handed Nina the phone and exited, closing the door behind her.

Nina sat down on the chair in front of the desk and spoke a bit hesitatingly. "Hello, this is Nina here."

"Bonjour, Nina," Evalina said. "Since you are studying English, how about we talk in English? Is that okay with you?"

"Certainly," Nina responded. "How can I help you?"

"Actually, it is perhaps I who can help you and in return meet a need for my gallery. Did the headmistress tell you about why I am calling?" Evalina asked.

Nina replied with what she knew so far.

"Well," Evalina said, "let me tell you a bit about the position. How I know something about you already, how you might fit well in this position and with the staff. I will be happy to answer any questions you might have. If this is okay with you and you find this of interest, I would then like to bring you to Paris to talk with me in person, see the gallery, meet the rest of the employees, and work out the arrangements. Does this sound all right?"

Nina replied that it sounded fine.

Evalina began, "I learned of you from a cousin of my father's. I think that would make him my second cousin. This person, Yuri, have you heard of him? No, well that's not a surprise as he is also a cousin of your grandfather's, I think. Your grandfather and Yuri met in Bolkhov, a small village not too far from your parent's home. Anyway, your grandfather proceeded to tell Yuri about the family and you. You know how older Russians are, talking about family. Somehow distant relations came up in the conversation and my father learned from Yuri that a grandniece, you, were studying English in the USA. He knew you already learned French and that you had studied humanities at the Sorbonne in Paris following your studies of the same at the Russian State University for Humanities. Is this accurate so far?"

Nina nodded and said, "Yes, this is all true. How strange that a distant relative would know all this about me."

Evalina responded, "Nina, with Russia's history, there is a lot that the old Russians know of each other and of all the decedents. It is less important how he knows, as it is that he knows the facts. This is what has connected me to you. You see?"

Nina replied she did.

"So, let me tell you about the position and why all of this information was interesting to me."

• • •

As Nina walked past the second of the round ponds in the central walking path of the Tuileries, she realized she was more than halfway through the park. She had been dodging the occasional walker and runner who were unaware of other pedestrians also sharing the gravel path with them. Realizing she had been so wrapped up in her memories of that fateful day, she was absentmindedly walking and was close to her Seine River crossing. The gravel continued to crunch beneath her shoes as she made her decision. She would cross the Seine River at Pont Royal today instead of Pont du Carrousel. In just about a tenth of a kilometer, she would turn right on Ave. du General Lemonnier. It would take her to the Pont Royal and across the Seine to Quai Voltaire and the iSPY Gallery.

In those short minutes, she remembered how Evalina told her the position required someone with good language skills in Russian, French, and English. Russian because of the Russian artist the gallery carried; French because they were in France and many of their customers would be French; and English, much the same, many clients would be American or English.

She would have to travel quite a bit with the job. Her travels would take her to Russia, mainly to escort the artist and their artwork to and from Paris. Travel to the United States, Great Britain, and on occasion, to Australia if shows were arranged in those locations. In addition to these responsibilities, next to Evalina herself, Nina would be the chief spokesperson/host at the gallery openings for the artist.

How exciting this sounded!

Then, Evalina told her that she would be well paid and would be provided with a furnished apartment at 10 Rue Garreau, but with one very small catch. On the extensive travel days when Nina was out of the country, the apartment would be rented to tourists on Airbnb. There would be very large and extensive lockable closets for Nina to store her personal belongings in. Was that okay with Nina? Absolutely! Not a problem!

Nina opened the door to iSPY Gallery precisely at 10:00 am. Evalina was already there. She smiled at Nina and said, "Nina, great news! We have just had an invitation to have a major show to be scheduled in September for LADA's work. It will be in Washington, DC, near the capitol building. I will need you to go to Russia in August to choose the works we wish to show of LADA's. How does that sound to you?"

"Good," Nina replied. She loved the old artist LADA. This would be fun. The trip to Washington, DC, would be fun too. A few of her old classmates from her Miami English as a Second Language days were now working in Washington. Perhaps she could catch up with one or two of them. This could be exciting!

2

Friday, June 21, 2019
New Hampshire, USA

THE MARTZES

Since March 21, 2001, the first day of spring that year, when Mary and Tom Martz were married in Notre Dame Cathedral, they had been back to Paris 14 times. They went multiple times in some years. They had even looked for, and nearly purchased, an apartment in the 16 ar, close to where Tommy had lived with his family at 55 Rue des Belles-Feuilles in the mid-1950s.

On this trip, Air France was their airline of choice, as it was in most cases. They purchased their tickets directly with Air France leaving Boston Logan International Airport the evening of September 2 and arriving the next morning at Charles De Gaulle International Airport outside of Paris. Their stay in Paris would be 7 days, including the day of departure at 1:45 pm on September 9, 2019.

With airline arrangements now made, all they needed was a place to stay. They would have lots of fun planning all the things they wanted to see and do to just relax.

"Darn!" Tom exclaimed, looking up from the laptop. "We just received an email from Francoise, Catherine's friend. Catherine's apartment has a long-term renter. Actually, so does Francoise's apartment in the same building in the 5$^{th.}$ However, Francoise says she will be on holiday and will rent her current apartment in the 15th near Montparnasse to us for the time we will be in Paris. She is on the 16th floor with a view of the Eiffel tower! She sent some pictures. Want to see them?"

Mary replied with mild disappointment, "Sure." She walked over to the dining room table where Tom was with the laptop. It did seem like a nice spacious apartment, perhaps bigger than Catherine and Francoise's apartment. Still, you had to take an elevator up. They liked using the stairs. Good exercise. And it was a new apartment in a high-rise. Hardly the same experience in an old French apartment building like a Haussmann.

“Let’s think about it for a day or so then we can let her know. I’m just not sure I want that to be my last experience in Paris.” That comment from Mary made Tom sad, but he was not about to let on to her how he felt. He never wanted to believe that Mary would not be with him on future trips in just plain old day-to-day living.

“You know,” he said, “our old favorite sites for looking for apartments, New York Habitat and Paris Attitude, seem to have all gone to long-term rentals. No rentals for just a week. What is the rental site that Cath and Jason are using?”

“Airbnb,” Mary replied.

Tom typed Airbnb into the computer. The website popped up but as usual, with Tom and technology, he struggled. “It appears we have to create an account or something before we can do much. Do you think Cath could come over and help us with this?” Mary chuckled to herself and said, “I’m sure Cath would love to help. Let’s text her.”

Arrangements were made with their daughter, Catherine, to come to their home the next day and have her guide Mary and Tom through the techniques of using Airbnb.

And so it happened that the next day, as Nina and Evalina closed iSPY Gallery after scheduling Nina’s trips and putting the apartment on Airbnb for rent, Nina skated off to join her friends for Pari Roller. At the same moment, nearly 4,000 miles away, Tom and Mary rented an apartment for that September at 10 Rue Garreau . . . Evalina’s apartment and the one where Nina lived when she was not on one of her trips.

3

Monday, September 2, 2019
New Hampshire, USA

BON VOYAGE

The flight was booked. The Dartmouth Coach from Hanover Inn to Boston Logan Airport was booked. Evalina's apartment was rented. The trip was on!

They boarded the Dartmouth Coach at the bus stop between the Hopkins Center and the Hanover Inn. After finding seats and pulled up the website of Evalina's apartment. "I can't believe we found an apartment that in so many ways looks like what we would have done with decorations if it was ours. Look at all the paintings." He zoomed in on a few.

"Look at this interesting one between the two front windows." Tom handed the phone over to Mary who was sitting by the coach window.

"I've seen something like this before. It may be a famous portrait of a young nobility. It reminds me of someone. And look how the young woman is holding the mask. And behind her was the young man-like figure with either a mask or blindfold on. It is definitely making a statement!"

"Do you want me to try to email this owner, Evalina, and ask about it? Might be fun to know. Let's see, it's 11:15 am here. Six hours difference in Paris. It would only be 5:15 pm there. Still the middle of the day for a Parisian," he said with a smile. "Let's try it."

In the email, he wrote,

Hello Evalina. We are on our way to meet our flight in Boston. We are so looking forward to meeting you in Paris at the apartment. We love the way it's decorated. You have many beautiful paintings. Mary and I both paint and also collect art. We like several of the pieces you have. There is one that is particularly interesting. It is of the young woman in red. The painting of her is between the two front windows. She is holding a mask in her right hand and there appears to be a young man standing behind her. It is very intriguing. Does it have a story? See you tomorrow. Tom and Mary.

"Well, hopefully we'll hear something. If not, we can ask her tomorrow." Mary smiled at him and took out a Louise Penny novel, her favorite writer, and began reading, still smiling and chuckling silently about Tom.

Less than an hour later a small ping could be heard coming from Tom's phone. Gazing at the screen, he said, "I'll be darned. Evalina has replied!"

"What?" Putting her book down, Mary said, "What does she say?"

"I'll read it to you."

"Dear Tom and Mary, it is good to know that you are safely on your way. The apartment is ready for you. I think you will have a nice time here. It is easy to access the metro. It is in a very fun part of the city. And, as you can see from the pictures, the apartment is very bright and open.

You asked about the painting of the young woman in red. She is one of my distant ancestors. An aunt from long ago. It is not for sale but some of my paintings in the apartment are. If you find something you like I will be happy to talk with you about a price.

Sadly, I will be unable to meet you at the apartment tomorrow. Unfortunately, I have had to unexpectedly travel out of the country on business. My close friend and colleague, Natalya, will be meeting you at the apartment. Here is her cell number.

Text her the moment you arrive at Charles de Gaulle Airport and she will meet you at the apartment. I most likely will not be back in Paris until after your departure. Perhaps we can meet the next time you rent the apartment. Sincerely, Evalina"

"Well, shoot. I was hoping we would meet Evalina," Tom said.

"Yes, so was I. Interesting, her friend Natalya also sounds Russian. I think I've heard you talk too much about the spy books you read, but it is interesting. Two Russian women. One has to leave the country unexpectedly. The second one will meet us at the apartment once we land. I think we are into a spy mystery of our own. What do you think?" she said, smiling at Tom and silently remembering the episode with the "Smiths" several years ago.

"I think you're reading too many Louise Penny mystery books myself," he said with a smile back. "Still . . . it is interesting."

They arrived at the airport having suffered no delays on the Dartmouth Coach. They checked their bags and received their boarding passes. Going through security was almost easy with their "known flier" status.

They really weren't sure what had allowed them to have that status other than the one embarrassing trip in 2014 when Mary had to explain to the TSA security people about her mastectomy and her faux breast. They suspected that the TSA didn't want to be confronted again with such an embarrassment for the flier . . . or for themselves. Other flyers hearing the situation had not shown much approval of the tactlessness of the agents. They expressed their disapproval with each other loudly enough for the agents to know how they felt.

"What do they do with a young woman who has implants?" One woman asked. "Does that give them a legal right to grope her?" Several other women agreed angrily.

Boarding the flight had the same standing in line, inching forward, trying to sneak in with the earlier boarding groups, being told that you must wait until your group is called, showing your passport and boarding pass, and scrambling to find overhead luggage space above your seat. Those tasks accomplished, Mary squeezed into her seat next to the window. Tom likewise squeezed into his seat, his six-foot frame bent in unusual contortions with his knees nearly up to his chest.

Now any man traveling on an airline can tell you the worst thing that could happen is to be seated in the middle seat with two men on either side of you. The old saying, "If man was meant to fly, God would have given them wings" is only partially correct. The true saying should be, "If man was meant to fly, God would never have given them wide shoulders!"

Men's shoulders, arms, legs, and other assorted body parts were never meant to be crammed into a metal tube with three of them side by side. Fortunately for Tom, though still not in a comfortable position for the flight, he had Mary beside him. The worst that could happen now was that another man, a full-figured woman, or worse, a very full-figured man would sit beside him in the aisle seat. Luck was seeming to be with him!

The aisle seat next to Tom remained open. A good sign. Perhaps it was unsold. Who would choose the last seat . . . even an aisle seat . . . if the other two seats in the row were already chosen? And it was almost the end of boarding. Most people were already settled in their seats, earplugs on, books out. A good sign. But his luck was about to change.

Walking down the aisle, two women suddenly appeared. The first woman, a very attractive 40- to 50-year-old looking at the seat signs on the overhead baggage compartments. She looked down and right at the seat next to Tom. She turned to the young woman behind her. The young woman was incredibly beautiful and had to be 6 foot 4 inches tall! The first woman said something and the two of them continued to walk toward the one open seat.

Unnoticed by Tom, the seat behind him in the next row aisle was also open. The older of the two women settled into it after putting her roller bag in the overhead compartment. The younger woman had a roller bag and a huge duffle bag slung over her shoulder The roller bag may fit above the seats in the baggage compartment, but not the duffle bag. He knew it was destined for the floor below the seat in front of the one she was now claiming next to him. There was no way the bag was not going to spill over into his foot room next to his already cramped space with his own backpack and small duffle bag. And where in the hell was she going to put those incredibly long legs?

Longlegs smiled at Tom as she put her roller bag above. Tom looked over at Mary. True to form, she had already snuggled against the window and had drifted off to sleep. Mary had a knack for doing that. She would sleep most of the flight. Ol' Tom, almost not a wink.

Longlegs now slid the duffle bag partially under the seat with the rest of it laying out in the area on the floor where the young woman's feet would be if the bag didn't take up all the space . . . which it did. At least for now, however, it had not crept into Tom's space.

Somehow, and to this day he still does not understand how, this long slim creature managed to hop up onto the seat, legs folded under her, and curl up into a ball. There had to be no bones in her body. Anyone walking down the aisle would swear that she was only 2 feet tall and not the six-foot-four-inch woman he had seen standing beside the seat.

Could she stay this way the entire flight? Could he figure a way out of the three-seat aisle if nature called? He was, after all, a man over 50. Being a man over 50 demanded some natural occurrences more frequently than it did to younger men . . . and certainly more frequently than it did to women.

"Darn," he thought, "if only Mary liked aisle seats and not window seats, how much easier trips would be!" Somehow, he would figure something out. Otherwise, this would be a long, sleepless, and very uncomfortable flight, as it became.

Longlegs took out a book and began reading. Mary continued to dose. The flight attendants made their final preparations, and the Air France flight was pushed back from the gate. A few minutes later, with Mary now awake watching the ground slip away beneath the plane, they were airborne. Mary looked to her left. Saw her sweet Tom sitting and watching his flight monitor screen. She then saw Longlegs sitting beside him. She nudged him, tilted her head in a way that asked, "So who is your flying companion there, buddy boy?" A small smirk on her face. He did one of what Mary called his "Hoosier shoulder shrugs" and shook his head. She chuckled, took his hand, and laid her head on his shoulder.

The sky outside the aircraft began to turn dark. Tom continued to watch the flight information on the screen. They were flying over New Brunswick now. Mary put her book down. Louise Penny had been entertaining her. Pre-dinner warm towels were handed out.

Longlegs, Tom noticed, had hardly touched her food. Choosing to sip water out of a plastic bottle from her duffel bag, she had at least eaten the peas, mushrooms, and salad. Mary had meanwhile stored both her cheese, Tom's cheese, and the French rolls in Tom's backpack. Those she would save for a picnic.

Mary could reach down under the seats. There was no way his body could bend and work that way. The cabin was beginning to be prepared post-dinner for the darkening of the cabin and the long trip through the night.

This may be his last chance. He turned to Mary, told her he was headed to the restroom, excused himself to Longlegs, and jumpingly fell over the duffle bag and somehow landed upright into the aisle. How he managed to stay upright was a mystery to himself and he was sure to others. He glanced at Mary. She had a big smile on her face and was chuckling. He smiled back, did his shoulder shrug, and sauntered off toward the restroom. The last time available to him until breakfast was served! The truly long part of the flight had begun.

Taking a longer amount of time than the necessary necessitated, doing a few stretches, watching the efficiency of the flight attendants for a while, he now wandered back to find his aisle. It was a bit harder in the dimmed lights in the cabin. He passed by Longlegs, as she was almost unnoticeable in her little rolled-up ball on the seat. She was asleep. The woman behind her was asleep. Mary was asleep. And darn if the people in front of their seats weren't asleep too... with their seatbacks all the way back! Tom wondered if there were any open seats anywhere else on the plane. Realizing that it was a full flight, he had no other alternative than to try to reenact his jumping fall back into his seat.

Scanning the movies for something to occupy his time. Tom selected the Woody Allen movie, *A Rainy Day in New York*. It began as Mary stirred just long enough to lay her head on his right shoulder. She would stay there, using his blanket as a pillow, for the rest of the flight. She was soon fast asleep again. "If only I could do that," he thought.

A few minutes into the film, he suddenly realized he now had another head resting on his left shoulder. Turning his head to his left, there was Longlegs, head resting on his shoulder and fast asleep. What to do?! Any man would be in heaven sandwiched between two beautiful women. However, this was a long flight. The woman on his right, the one he loved. The one on the left . . . he didn't even know! This predicament lasted the entire sleepless trip, through all of *A Rainy Day in New York*, *Rocketman*, some other godforsaken murder movie, and right up until the lights in the cabin came back on.

A sleepy Longlegs, realizing that she had been resting her head on Tom's shoulder, apologized just as a sleepy Mary woke up unaware, he thought, that a strange woman had been "sleeping" with her man . . . well, technically she was sleeping... he had not had a wink of sleep. He was exhausted and both shoulders hurt.

Tom whispered to Mary that he was going to head to the restroom. She told him she would follow shortly. He stood up, Longlegs understanding a sense of urgency on his part stood up and moved into the aisle after lifting her duffle bag from under the seat and placing it on her seat. This made for a much less dramatic exit and with a bit more grace on his part. Tom hurried off to join the toilet queue.

When he got back, Mary was not there. He stayed in the aisle waiting, as did Longlegs who was talking with the woman who had boarded with her. A few moments later Mary returned. They sat back down and held hands.

Breakfast was served and cleared. Final instructions about processing through customs were played on the video screens. Flight information and movies ended. Landing instructions were given by the flight attendant in both French and English. A few people were shooed back to their seats post "fasten your seat belt" signs coming on.

Flaps lowered, wheels came out. All of the regular things that happen on an inbound flight. Then the big bump that comes from the huge steel structure's wheels finding the hard cement runway. Another safe landing in Paris. . . . or the outskirts of Paris, Charles de Gaulle Airport.

Tom and Mary waited as they always did for most of the other passengers to get their bags together, shuffle to the doorways, and exit the plane. Longlegs and her companion got out of their seats, Longlegs offering Mary and Tom to go first. Mary and Tom declined the offer and watched them leave.

"Well," Mary said, "how did you enjoy sleeping with your new friend?"

"What?"

"I saw your little sweetums with her head on your shoulder throughout the night. You don't think a wife whose husband is sitting next to a babe isn't going to keep her eye on them, do you?"

"Look," he said, "I didn't do anything! I was just watching the movie and the next thing I know this strange head is asleep and resting on my shoulder."

Mary, detecting panic in his voice, laughed. "Kidding." She did that all the time to him. She took his hand sweetly, smiled at him, and said, "I saw the whole thing. You were tres gallant for both of us ladies. She was underage anyway. Her mom, the woman behind her, brought her to Paris for her 16th birthday."

"What?" "She's only 16?"

"Yep," Mary said with a chuckle. "They grow them big these days, don't they?" Mary and Tom gathered their bags and proceeded to the exit. "Still . . ." she said, "it was a good thing your hands stayed on the tray table all night where I could see them!" A big smile on her face and a wink.

They exited the plane for the adventure to continue.

4

A BIT OF RUSSIAN HISTORY

Russian history, like the rest of European and Asian history, is complex. The real importance of Russian history for this story did not begin until the mid-1700s. This impactful story originated on May 2, 1729, with the birth of a baby girl.

Princess Sophie Friederike Auguste von Anhalt-Zerbst-Dornburg was born in Prussia. Sophie became the leading figure in a plot, as so often happens in political history, of marrying into a ruling family that consolidated power for a primary family. As a step to ingratiate herself to the Empress of Russia, Sophie joined the Russian Orthodox Church at age 15. Upon her being received as a new member, the church officially changed Princess Sophie's name to Catherine. Thus, on that day in 1744, Sophie became the future Catherine the Great of Russia.

Catherine was an interesting young woman. At the age of 10, she met her future husband Peter III who was to become the future Emperor. He was Sophie's cousin. He swore one day that they would be married. She found him quite obnoxious and quite ugly. But she was also very politically wise. It was that political wisdom that led Sophie to develop a close relationship with Peter's Aunt Elizabeth, Empress of Russia. Elizabeth chose Sophie to marry Peter III, and they were married in 1745. Catherine was 16 and in the heart of royal intrigue.

Catherine and Peter had an unhappy marriage. While Catherine ingratiated herself with the people of Russia by adopting their ways and praising its history, Peter III found everything German to be to his liking. He isolated himself from the people of his country.

Catherine gathered strong political allies while Peter didn't. To say they were opposites would be an understatement. And so on January 5, 1762, with the death of Empress Elizabeth, her nephew Peter III became emperor of Russia. His reign did not last long.

Catherine and co-conspirators staged a bloodless coup the night of July 8 and the day of July 9, 1762. Her husband Peter III was arrested and imprisoned. Catherine became the sole ruler of Russia nearly 6 months after Empress of Russia Elizabeth had died. Eight days following the coup, Peter III died mysteriously.

Catherine earned her title of Catherine the Great because of the transformational effect she had on Russia. She acquired territories often through force but equally through negotiations. She brought the idea of grade schools to the towns and villages of Russia. Her interest in French history and culture led her to transform Russia into one of the cultural centers of the world through the arts and humanities. She even transformed international law with the concept of "Free Ships and Free Goods". Her impact on the culture of Russia would touch the heart of the country and of her family's future generations.

The royal lineage hardly ever follows a direct course. The next significant player in this story is the last Tsar of Russia, Nicholas II, Emperor of Russia until his assassination in 1918 following the abdication of his title and power in 1917.

Until 1613, Russia was ruled under the Rurik Dynasty. In 1598, the last ruler of the Rurik Dynasty, Fyodor I, died. Following his death, Russia had a tumultuous time for 15 years known as "The Time of Troubles". That time ended when a Zemsky Sobor, "assembly of the land," was convened and elected Michael Romanov as the new tsar. This began the 300-year rule of Russia by the Romanov Dynasty. A dynasty that included, through marriage, Catherine the Great and her later great, great, great-grandson, Tsar Nicholas II.

Now Tsar Nicholas II appears to have inherited more of his genetic material from Peter III's side of the family than from Catherine's. Nicholas alienated himself from his people in much the same way that Peter III had alienated himself from the Russian people back in 1762. Nicholas was aided greatly in this alienation by his wife, Alexandra, and of course the questionable holy man Rasputin.

During the night of July 16 and on July 17, Tsar Nicholas II, his wife, and five children were assassinated by Communist revolutionaries. This ended the rule of the Romanov Dynasty.

Distant relatives of the Romanov ruling family escaped the revolution in many ways, most by leaving the country for safer lands. Some family members distanced themselves from the public spotlight of the Romanov name. Those staying in the country went into hiding inside Russia. Many of them kept the love of Russian culture within their hearts but dread for the future and the direction they ultimately saw their country going.

Some left Russia, and some stayed. Some even became players in this story, all because two old men met in a small village and shared stories of the legacy of the family and where that legacy was located. Two of the legacies are now working together in a gallery in Paris.

5

Friday, June 21, 2019
Paris, France

EVALINA

Evalina watched as Nina skated off. A light-hearted, graceful, and truly beautiful young woman. She was fortunate when old Yuri had contacted Evalina's father about the young woman, a distant relative. It had all worked out superbly. Better than Evalina could have expected. Not only was Nina an excellent representative of the iSPY Gallery, but she and Evalina had also become good friends. Perhaps more than that. Evalina was more the older sister to Nina. They enjoyed the same interests. They enjoyed talking with each other. Nina shared with her "older sister" her boyfriend problems. They laughed, smiled, and just thoroughly loved being with each other. Yes, Nina was a great find!

Evalina thought back to Nina's visit to talk about the position. Nina had arrived in Paris for a short week during Nina's last semester spring break in Miami. Though Evalina had seen pictures of Nina, the pictures just did not do justice to the image of the young woman walking out of customs at Charles de Gaulle International airport. She was angelic.

Evalina walked over to her and said, "Nina?" Nina looked at her, smiled, and said, "Yes, Are you Evalina?" "I am," came the reply from Evalina. They stood there for a moment not sure whether to shake hands but then almost instantaneously hugged each other.

Evalina remembered how embarrassed and apologetic Nina had been over the hug. Evalina laughed and said that the hug was mutual and what should be expected of a family meeting for the first time...they were, after all, cousins, even if they were distant cousins. They both laughed and the momentary tension of the first meeting was eased. It continued to be an easy relationship and grew stronger each day over the next two years. "Two years!" Evalina thought. Incredible. How quickly those two years had passed. How much fun. And, how exciting.

From Charles De Gaulle they had driven the near hour to the gallery talking. The time passed quickly as they talked about Nina's experiences in the United States, her interests in the arts, and her desires for her future. Evalina decided to keep much of the story of the gallery until they were actually there before going into the details.

She did tell Nina, in general terms, about the duties that Nina would have should the position be offered to her and should she accept the position. Although neither one said it to the other, in their hearts, they knew the position would be offered and boy would it be accepted! "For sure!" Nina thought.

Parking in Paris is a real problem. However, Evalina had a special place not too far from the gallery that she rented from a small boutique hotel. She pulled into the cobblestone courtyard through an open "horse gate" of wrought iron and parked the car.

"Nina, this hotel is where you will stay for the week. It is also where we house the visiting artist for their openings and shows. I think you will find it very nice. Let's take your things inside and get you settled into your room. The gallery is just a short four blocks from here."

They entered the small hotel. The place appeared to be less than a hotel, as it has a total of six suites converted from an old maison. In front of them in the large entry room was a lone antique desk. Sitting at the desk was a young woman about Nina's age. Behind the woman was a large marble fireplace of reddish stone streaked with white. On the mantle above the fireplace were several antique vases that appeared to Nina to be from the early 1700s or before. The rest of the room, though not full of furnishings, was appropriately decorated for a home that came from the same period as the vases, the mid-1600s to early 1700s.

The young woman looked up, smiled at Evalina and Nina, and said, "Mademoiselle K, bonjour." Speaking French, she asked if this was Nina, the houseguest for the week. Nina was introduced formally to the young woman. Ninette became one of Nina's new friends in Paris and one of her constant companions on the Pari Roller.

The young woman asked them about luggage and was told the only bags were the backpack in Nina's hand and the roller bag she was pulling. Ninette took the roller bag from Nina and led them to the large circular stairs on the right side of the entry room. At the top of the stairs, they proceeded down the hall to the room farthest from the stairs. The room they entered had a beautiful view through large floor-to-ceiling leaded glass windows overlooking the back quiet and restful garden. "This is nice," Nina thought to herself. "I shall be very happy here." And she was.

The two women went back downstairs to the entry hall and left Nina in her room to freshen up after the 9 ½-hour night trip from Miami International. Nina had slept well on the flight thanks to the unexpected fact that the ticket waiting for her at check-in was first class. First class! She had never even flown business class before. This whole thing had to be a dream. A dream she hoped would never end. And so far, it had every indication that it never would. How did she get to be so lucky?

Nina and Evalina strolled the four blocks to iSPY Gallery. The sounds of Paris, though busy, are much quieter than the sounds of New York, San Francisco, Los Angeles, or Miami. Only every so often do you hear a car horn. Occasionally you would hear the "hee haw" of a police car, ambulance, or fire truck. But even those were much less often than in an American city. Still, almost no drivers in the world match the French and particularly the Parisians for their daring and speed. Traffic sped by them as they turned onto the final few meters to the iSPY Gallery on Quai Voltaire. They reached the front of the gallery and entered.

Evalina had moved the gallery to this location in the 6 arr at 1 Quai Voltaire from its initial location in Montmartre near Evalina's home in 2007. Evalina had, at first, lived down the hill from the home she now occupied. In 2007, she lived in the apartment where Nina was going to live. Catherine, Evalina's mother, was 69 at the time of the accident. Crossing a road in Paris can be dangerous. It had been that day for Evalina's mom. Both the home that Evalina inherited, the large maison from her father shortly after the death of Evalina's mother in 2010, and the apartment belonged to Evalina's parents and before them, to Evalina's grandparents.

Evalina's father, a noted Russian Astrophysicist, never recovered from the loss of his love and best friend.

• • •

Fall 1960 in Switzerland
Evalina's parents Catherine and Maxim Meet

Catherine and Maxim had met one day by chance while in Geneva. He was doing research on the quantity of light in the universe, where it goes, and where it is stored, at the famed Swiss Federal Institute of Technology, Lausanne. She was an aspiring Russian artist doing plein air landscapes. She was with her close friend and mentor, another already well-known artist, LADA.

LADA taught at the Ecole des Beaux-Arts in Paris, where Evalina's mother was studying. LADA also spent her time in Russia and Turkey when not teaching. Although 12 years separated them in age, LADA was 33 and Catherine just 21, they were best friends. They laughed and giggled as young women do. Young men often approached them. And they laughed and giggled some more after turning most of the young men down. They had a friendship that was much like the one that would be developed by Evalina and Nina. Perhaps this was the model that became the reality for Evalina and Nina.

They were enjoying a lakeside pre-lunch glass of rose wine on this sunny day. Two young men approached them and were shooed away, quickly. Catherine had rolled her eyes with the attempted pick-up line foisted on them by one of the men. Following their departure, LADA took a more serious demeanor.

"Catherine, at some point we must not keep turning these young men down. If you do not start getting to know some, even if for just a short moment, you will end up like me...an unmarried old hag."

LADA and Catherine both laughed. LADA, though unmarried and a bit older than the perfect age for marriage, was hardly an old hag. She was a very "presentable and stylish young hag," Catherine replied. Again, they laughed.

"You know, Catherine, I have had my share of amusing dilettantes with young admirers. Several lovers. Nothing serious. Just fun. But you, my dear, need something more. It is written in your eyes. I think you will be a successful artist . . . businesswoman, perhaps . . . and wife and mother. Before that, you must have your share of fun, too. So, let's begin finding you some fun!"

Catherine rolled her eyes and said, "You can't be serious!"

"Yes, my young dear, I am quite serious, and we shall begin today. Look to your left. Do you see that young man at the table across the terrace? The one absorbed in reading a book and sipping on a caffe?"

"Yes," Catherine replied with a bit of a scowl on her face. "Why?"

LADA picked up her bag sitting beside her chair and pulled out a sketchpad and drawing pencil. "As your instructor, I am giving you an assignment; you are to go over to this young man, tell him he has a very interesting face and that you are going to sketch the secrets that lay within this remarkable face."

"You must be kidding! I can't do that!"

"Yes, you can. It is an assignment. It's what we artists do. We capture what nature has provided. I think nature is providing this for you. Now do as I say, Catherine!"

Catherine realized her mentor, teacher, and friend was quite serious. With that, she took the sketchpad and pencil from LADA, reluctantly stood up, and began walking towards the young man's table. She looked back over her shoulder at a smiling LADA, frowned at her, and continued on.

Once at the table, she sat down to a slightly startled, quite handsome young man and told him, "I am an artist. I see within your face something of interest and will sketch you!" This was more of a statement than a question.

"Pardon, mademoiselle, you wish to do what?" he asked.

"Sketch you," was the reply.

"But why? There are many interesting faces among the patrons here. Why me?" The young man knew he was putting her on the spot with that question as she looked up sideways from her sketchpad with her left eyebrow raised. Catherine too realized she was on the spot. How could she explain? After a moment, she said to the young man. "Monsieur, do you see the young woman at the table to your right, across the terrace?"

"Oui." He looked at LADA, smiled, and gave her a slight wave that she returned with a smile and wave.

"Well, she is my friend and teacher at the Ecole des Beaux-Arts in Paris. She has given me this assignment. We are here on vacation and for her to give me continued instruction. So you see, monsieur, I have no choice in the matter. You are my assignment."

The young man laughed. Smiling again across the terrace at LADA, he waved a salute to her from the right side of his forehead. She replied with similar actions while pleased to see a handsome young couple...and perhaps the beginning of "the fun". One person, a pleasing and happy young man, sitting with a beautiful young woman who was giving her quite a ferocious scowl. LADA could not help but laugh.

"Well, mademoiselle, if I am your research subject and a class assignment how can I, myself a teacher, turn down an assignment for a student? You may proceed."

He was giving her his approval? She didn't need his approval. She was her own strong woman. Well, he was somewhat good-looking. Perhaps she would overlook this bit of what she perceived as arrogance on his part.

She picked up the pad once again and started sketching and out of the corner of her eye, saw LADA and the young man exchanging smiling humor at her expense. She would get even with LADA for this. "Some friend!" she thought, then chuckled to herself. It actually was a nice assignment . . . and perhaps . . .

Her thought was broken by his voice, "So you are a Parisian? Yes?"

She tilted her head up coyishly from her sketch. This time with a smile on her face. "Non, monsieur, I am a Russian studying in Paris. I am in my last year of study. Are you Swiss?"

"No, mademoiselle, I too am Russian, but I was born to Russian parents in Paris. I am a professor and researcher of astrophysics. I am here in Switzerland doing postgraduate research at the Swiss Federal Institute of Technology. It is located up the lake at Lausanne. I am in Geneva today for the weekend. A holiday of sorts because research on what I study never ends."

"Imagine," she said, "two Russians, who live in Paris, meeting on a lake in Switzerland on vacation. What an amazing coincidence . . . a miracle of sorts, non?"

He chuckled, smiled, and said, "Mademoiselle, have you ever heard of a man named Albert Einstein?"

"Of course," she said, once again just a little perturbed by his perceived questioning of her world knowledge. Then she realized she was doing it again. Putting the feelings she had for other men who unwelcomingly approached her onto him. After all, it was she who approached him and he welcomed her. He was a nice guy.

Noticing a little bit of ire in her reply, he continued, "I mean no offense by the question. As a physicist, I have learned that not everyone has the interest in science as I do. Therefore, I do not want to assume that everyone would know of him. I am a great admirer of him, you see?"

Looking up from her drawing coquettishly, she listened to him.

He continued. "Albert Einstein had two quotes that have great meaning to me. The first is, 'there are two ways to live: one is as if nothing is a miracle. The other is as though everything is a miracle.' I live my life believing the latter."

"The next quote of his that I love is, 'coincidence is God's way of staying anonymous'. So you see, it is physics, God . . . and your good teacher over there . . . who have brought us together." He smiled nicely at Catherine, and she smiled the same way back at him then they turned toward the table across the veranda, smiled, and waved at LADA. That was 58 years ago . . . in 1961, the year it all began.

6

1942
Paris, France

LADA

LADA was born in Russia in 1928. Her parents were both artists. Her father was 35 years old when she was born. At age 22, after completing his art studies at The Imperial Academy of Arts in Saint Petersburg, Russia, he became the "artist de court" to Nicholas II, the last Tsar of Russia. The Academy was formally abolished in 1918 following the Bolshevik revolution; so, too, was his position in the court of the Tsar after Tsar Nicholas II and his family were murdered. Luckily, LADA's father and mother were not killed. Others in the court were not so lucky.

His art, like art by all Russian artists of that time, became more restricted and controlled. They were mandated to paint what was appropriate art for the good of a communist state. It became more restricted under the dictator Joseph Stalin. Many Russian artists were purged, as were scientists, scholars, and politicians during the rule of Stalin.

Her mother, also a gifted artist, was never recognized because she was a woman. Women artists just began being recognized for their talent, skill, and insight following the impressionists. Many of the best works of LADA's father are now believed to have been created by his wife, LADA's mother.

Born of a talent gene pool like this, it was no surprise that LADA was a child prodigy. Both father and mother living under constant fear of post-revolution cleansing decided in 1924 to purchase a second residence in Paris. These secondary residences would serve the parents well and also play importantly into LADA's future, and her political beliefs.

In 1934, at age 6, LADA's family whisked her away permanently to the home in Paris. The time was the beginning of the "Great Purge" under Stalin. The parents lived out the rest of their lives in Paris, until one fateful day. They hoped to ensure that their young daughter, already showing great artistic talent, would one day receive proper art education at the Ecole des Beaux-Arts. The university where she would eventually teach and be the instructor, mentor, and friend to Catherine, Evalina's mother.

The young LADA was influenced by two extremes. The love of her parents for their native Russia and the fear they had of how Russia was changed post-Tsar Nicholas II. Russia became very brutal during the years of Stalin, especially to the educated and creative. She also was in her most impressionable years living in Paris. These early development years corresponded to the "crazy years' of the late 1920s and early 1930s when Paris became the leader in art, music, and literature. That world was dominated by the likes of James Joyce, Pablo Picasso, Ernest Hemingway, Josephine Baker, the Fitzgeralds, Salvador Dali, Jean Cocteau, Colette, and other writers and artists.

Life in Paris was upended by the Great Depression in 1932. It finally settled in France after the rest of Europe had already been in its throes. The economic impact on the middle and lower classes of Parisians stuck hard in the young girl's mind as she witnessed hunger and poverty. Exempt from those conditions herself by the wealth her parents had accumulated earlier in her life, she knew that she must find a way to make the world safe and better for everyone. A powerful mission for a young girl not even in her teen years.

As she grew through those teen years and then college, she associated herself with liberal thinkers and equality-minded individuals. She would slip into the underground meeting rooms where philosophical, socialist, and democratic ideals were shared. Even in her preteens, she was a vocal participant. These meeting places were the breeding grounds of the resistance, of which she would become an important participant. There she found a purpose for her painting!

Her thinking was not met with enthusiasm from her parents, who had been part of the aristocracy in Russia during the Tsar Nicholas years. Still, they had raised her to be a strong, independent woman. They wanted her to have advantages and opportunities that women of her mother's age had not had. If she were to have political and social views that differed from their own, so be it. They would continue to love, support, and believe in her until they no longer could and she was left on her own.

On June 14, 1940, Nazi Germany began the occupation of Paris. LADA was barely 12 years of age. Although young, she continued meeting in the underground spaces sharing information about where the Nazi troops were and what they were doing. A young girl was assumed to be unthreatening to the German soldiers. She often wandered the streets unaccosted. Although others feared for LADA, being fearless herself, she proved to be a great asset gathering information. This information was passed on to the men and women of the resistance and aided them in arranging sabotage and guerrilla warfare against the occupiers.

Her parents tried to talk her out of this involvement and considered moving to the south of France. Their decision to make that move came too late.

One day while LADA was in one of the underground hideouts of the resistance, unbeknownst to her, her mother and father were rounded up in the "Vel d'Hiv Roundup " on July 16 and 17, 1942. LADA was 14 years old. On that day, 13,152 Jews were rounded up, including more than 4,000 children. Although LADA's father was not Jewish, her mother was a Russian Jewess and therefore the whole family was "contaminated". Had LADA not been meeting secretly with her resistance companions she would have been part of the Roundup.

The people taken during this "cleansing" were moved to the Velodrome d'Hiver. Suffering in extremely crowded and unsanitary conditions, after a short period, these luckless human beings were loaded on cattle cars and shipped to Auschwitz. There they faced their mass extermination. LADA never saw her parents again.

The underground resistance became her parents. They cared for her and for her safety. She had great difficulty at first, sad and without hope but filled with hatred for the Germans. She soon focused her emotions on helping her colleagues defeat the occupiers who had destroyed her family.

The resistance learned they could use her art as a means of transmitting information out of Paris to the Allied forces in England. Her canvases were treated with gesso, a glue-like opaque white substance, so coded messages could not be seen through the backside of the canvas. Then a thin acrylic paint, the same color as the gesso, was applied to the canvas to cover the coded message. Acrylic paint, fortunately, had been created in 1934. A fast-drying polymer emulsion tinted with pigments, LADA would paint over the canvas with oil paint in what became her familiar impasto technique . . . still in use by her today, 77 years later.

The paintings would be hurriedly dried in ovens and smuggled out through various underground networks. Each coded painting grouped with nine other paintings she created but did not have coded messages under them. If ever these paintings were intercepted and someone took the time to remove the paint, they would have only a one in 10 chance of uncovering the painting with the coded message.

LADA became a fast and accomplished artist. Many of the other nine paintings still exist and are quite collectible. The ones that were coded no longer exist. Once the paint was removed and the code deciphered, the canvas was destroyed. It was impossible for the enemy to determine how the information was being provided to the Allies.

It is thought that LADA produced over a thousand paintings from 1942 to 1945. Of those thousand paintings, nearly 100 conveyed the important messages that helped defeat Germany and rescue France and Russia from the Nazis.

This same painting and coding process she continued to use allowed a most important message to be conveyed from Russia to the President of the United States, John Fitzgerald Kennedy, in July 1962.

7

Friday, June 21, 2019
Paris, France

PARI ROLLER

Nina skated the four blocks over to the hotel where she had stayed two years ago. Her friend, Ninette, still worked at the hotel. She loved it. She was paid nicely. The position allowed her to meet interesting guests. They also provided her with a beautiful suite of rooms on the top floor. They had been the servants' quarters long ago but they were hardly that today. The suite was just as elegant as the guest's suites. And it was hers!

On Pari Roller nights, she and Nina would meet at the hotel and skate off to Montparnasse to meet up with the nearly 35,000 other rollerbladers. The 14-mile skate began at exactly 10:00 pm. Following the finish back at Montparnasse, they would find friends for late-night clubbing, dancing, and a little drinking. They would end the evening back at Ninette's suite for the night, usually after 2:00 am. But tonight would be different.

Leaving the hotel at 9:15 pm, the fastest way to get to the departure location for the Pari Roller was to skate through the back streets. This they did effortlessly. The crowd of skaters was already growing. Most would be at the starting location, Rue du Depart, 15 minutes before the start. Nina and Ninette would wait to see how the crowd grew before determining where to join the flow of the human sea.

Ninette packed a small picnic dinner, leftovers from the hotel kitchen. The hotel had limited food for breakfast: baguettes, croissants, marmalades, fruit, and cheeses. While approaching stale, the baguette and croissants smeared with soft cheese satisfied them until the end of the skate. You didn't want to eat too much beforehand.

To avoid the crowd, they skated over to the small triangular pocket park. Almost alone there, they ate their quick picnic with only water to drink. Alcohol and wine might come later with friends. One needed to keep their wits about them when skating with 35,000 other skaters . . . some near beginners . . . and some quite accomplished.

Neither the beginners nor the accomplished did you have to worry about. It was the ones who thought they were accomplished, weren't, and took chances with themselves and with others. Those were the ones to watch out for and most of them of were young men. What is it with men that they must prove themselves all the time? This skate should be for exercise and fun. That is how Nina and Ninette viewed it.

It was a quarter before the hour when Nina and Ninette looked for the right place to join the throng. They did not want to be in the front. That is where the really accomplished and the "accomplished" wished to be.

The middle of the pack was fine. However, you had late joiners who would weave in and out of the packed group. This too could be dangerous. No, if you were like Nina and Ninette, interested in exercise and fun, the end of the pack was a good spot. That is where they often joined in the skate and where they decided to join this night.

The group started moving right at 10:00 pm. Nina and Ninette started skating almost at 10:15 pm exactly. What normally would be a nearly two hour skate had begun.

From Rue du Depart you flow on to Rue de Rennes then to Boulevard Saint-Germain. From there, you skate down two quais bordering the south side of the Seine. Eventually, you cross the famous river four times during the skate. The third crossing is from the left bank or south side to the right bank or north side on the same bridge Nina had walked to iSPY Gallery that morning, Pont Royal. It's a one-way bridge heading to the north bank.

As Nina and Ninette made the turn, they became separated from a lot of the pack. Perhaps as much as 20 feet between them, the people in front, and the same with the people behind. Approaching the center of the bridge with Ninette on the right side closest to the bridge railing and Nina on the left, Ninette happened to look behind them. Approaching fast and straight at them was one of the police escort cars. She quickly grabbed Nina's right arm and swung her hard to the curb. Nina, caught completely by surprise and without understanding, tried to keep her balance. Her left skate toe hit the curb and she flew towards the stone railing, landing on her kneepads and the palm of her hands. Her head missed the railing by inches. Out of the corner of her right eye, she saw Ninette hit hard into the railing and fly in what seemed like slow motion over the railing and nosedive toward the water. Unseen by Nina, a fast-moving police car with lights flashing made the north bank of the river and instead of turning east along the skate route, it headed west and then north at high speed.

With bloody hands and knees, Nina stripped her backpack from her shoulders, unlaced her skates, slid them off, and looked down into the water. She saw her friend apparently unconscious and sinking below the surface. Climbing atop the stone railing, she jumped off the bridge into the Seine River 89 feet below. Other skaters were screaming, some were dialing 112, the emergency number in France. Others saw the oncoming river dinner cruise boat heading for the bridge from the left side. Those people began yelling and signaling for the boat to stop. At first, not understanding, the captain waved to them from his boat's bridge. Then, realizing that they were signaling a problem, he quickly ordered a reverse of the engines. The dinner guests, having finished dinner, were having cocktails when this happened. The luckless passengers who were standing fell forward all over themselves and others. What was left of the food and drinks did not slow down with the boat but flew through the dining room. One passenger on deck was almost pitched over the bow and into the water.

A boat this size cannot stop quickly. It continued to slide under the bridge, its left side scraping the support arch. That slowed it down but not enough to stop it, and it continued to drift toward the opening on the other side and to where Nina was fighting to keep Ninette above water.

Police cars began arriving. An elite squad of Brigade Fluviale, armed police, divers, and medics were dispatched and raced northward along the Seine River. They passed the Notre Dame Cathedral, Ile de Cite, Pont Neuf, Pont des Arts, Pont du Carrousel, and finally to Pont Royal. They would have arrived too late.

Nina hit the water feet first, toes pointed downward. Still, the force of the impact was tremendous. A fall of over 89 feet stung her legs, arms, and chest. She continued down deep in the cold Seine water. She began kicking her legs, moving her arms downward in an effort to pull herself back toward the surface. Finally, she felt the loss of acceleration and the beginning of the movement upward. She broke the surface and tried to locate Ninette in the dark.

Laying on her back, legs below, Ninette's torso began its slide below the surface. Nina swam a painful five meters, her legs aching and deadened. She grabbed hold of her unconscious friend and kicked her own legs, treading water, in an effort to keep them both on the surface.

Above the girls on the bridge, two other skaters, young men, also dropped their backpacks and took their skates off then jumped off the bridge. Two more men did the same.

Nina knew she was losing the struggle to keep Ninette afloat. She was fighting the downward pull that Ninette's backpack and skates were causing. Just as she thought she had lost the struggle, two strong arms grabbed Ninette. Two more joined those arms and then two more grabbed hold of Nina.

The boat bow slid out the east side of the bridge. The captain shined the huge searchlights onto the commotion in the water, turned the boat's wheel hard to port. The long glass-covered boat continued scraping along the bridge support. It came to a stop short of the people struggling in the water.

Two of the emergency inflatable rafts were launched and crewmembers maneuvered the inflatables towards the group in the water just as the Brigade Fluviale boats arrived. It all happened in less than five minutes after the first call had gone out to the police squad.

Divers from one of the Brigade boats jumped into the water. One held an inflatable neck brace. He quickly began to secure the brace around the unconscious Ninette's neck. The other had a backboard. With the neck brace in place, the two officers began sliding the backboard under Ninette while attaching her to the board with its straps. A difficult procedure with the water current pulling them downstream. They had done this many times before. People had often attempted suicide from the height of the Parisian bridges. Some had been successful.

With precision that came from many practice training exercises and real-life events, they successfully attached Ninette to the board. Other members of the Brigade, assisting them from the boat, carefully pulled Ninette's backboard onto the inflatable craft. Each saying a prayer to themself, "This young woman we are not going to lose!"

The other Brigade team helped a struggling Nina onto the second inflatable. Young men who had assisted in the rescue, some of them in pain from their own jump, were loaded onto the inflatables from the tour boat and trailed after the two police boats headed toward waiting ambulances.

Ninette was unconscious. Her right leg appeared to be broken midway up her thigh. Her left leg too was obviously badly injured, scraped, bleeding, and swollen. Bruises began showing all over her body.

On the other boat one of the police medics looked after Nina's bleeding hands. Just then Nina realized the force of striking the water had literally ripped her shorts and t-shirt off. Her undergarments were still intact but barely. A 50-mile an hour plunge into cold river water will do that to you.

The boats maneuvered as quickly as possible toward the boat launch ramp. Ambulances and paramedics were already waiting for Ninette and Nina as they arrived. The medic on board Ninette's rescue craft who worked on her and assessed the damage had already sent a report. It was not good.

The police medic working on Nina's hands said to her, "she is your friend, yes?" Covered now with a thermal blanket, Nina nodded and said "oui". "She is lucky to have such a brave and good friend as you. You both could have drowned. Can you tell me what happened?"

"I really don't know. Suddenly, Ninette grabbed my arm and slung me onto the sidewalk. I fell and out of the corner of my eye saw Ninette hit the stone railing and fly off the bridge. All I knew was I had to save my friend!"

"Well, mademoiselle, you did a wonderful thing. I hope your friend will be okay. We will need to ask you some questions when we reach the shore. Will you be all right with that?"

"Yes, but I would like to go with Ninette in the ambulance to the hospital. I want to know if she is okay. Will I be able to do so?"

"No, mademoiselle, I do not think that will be possible. They will need to concentrate all their efforts on her in that ambulance. There is a second one waiting to take you to the hospital. It will take you to the same one so that you will be close to her. Will that be all right? It will be the best that we can do"

Nina, crying, shaking almost uncontrollably due to the shock of what had happened, said softly, "Yes, that will do." The medic pulled out another thermal blanket and quickly spread it over her.

Ninette's boat reached the ramp and a stretcher was wheeled close to the boat. Six large police officers lifted her backboard onto the stretcher. One paramedic taking vitals and the other one talked with the police medic from the boat to get his assessment of the patient while slowly pushing the stretcher toward the ambulance, allowing the boat with Nina to land. Two paramedics wheeled another stretcher from the second ambulance down the ramp. With the aid of the police medic, they lifted her onto the stretcher.

The police medic went to his team and told them he was going to ride with the patient to the hospital. As he turned to join the paramedics pushing Nina's stretcher toward the ambulance, a plain-clothed police inspector came over and talked with him. Their conversation lasted a few moments, leaving a questioning look on the medic's face. He listened intently. Finally, they shook hands and the inspector walked away. The medic joined the other paramedics in the ambulance. The ambulance with Nina secured in the back raced up the ramp to the quai, on its way to the same hospital that Ninette was being taken: Groupe Hospitalier Pitie Salpetriere. They had the best trauma center in Paris and Ninette needed it now.

The ambulances raced the wrong way east on quai Voltaire. During the race to the hospital, the police medic asked quietly, "Did you know a police car tried to run you down?" Startled, she asked, "What. Why? That's impossible! No?"

"According to several of the witnesses, a police car turned left onto the Pont Royal Bridge coming the wrong way from the west. As you made it to the middle of the bridge, it sped up coming straight at you. That must have been what your friend . . ." he paused trying to remember her name.

"Ninette," Nina said.

"Yes, Ninette. She must have seen this. That is why she did what she did. Throwing you out of the way. Unfortunately, she could not make it safely out of the way herself. Witnesses were pretty clear and constant in their observations. You were the intended target of the driver. Do you know of anyone who would want to do this thing?"

Very confused, Nina shook her head no and said the same, "No! This cannot be true?"

The police medic replied, "I'm sorry, mademoiselle, it is true."

At the hospital, the officer told her he would go back to his unit. He would check on her through the night and perhaps the next day. "You should expect a police detective to stop by sometime over the next couple of days with more questions."

With that, he got out of the ambulance and said, "Be careful, mademoiselle!" leaving Nina in a more bewildered state than before.

Ninette was rushed into the trauma treatment area and received an immediate CAT scan of her spinal column and head. Her leg was stable in a temporary splint. Based on the bruising on her back, they felt she had to have internal bleeding or perhaps a ruptured spleen. She must have landed flat on her back in the water. Perhaps that protected her from a broken neck. They soon would know.

Meanwhile, other trauma doctors in a room down the hall were looking at Nina. Her injuries consisted of a sprained left ankle; badly scraped and bruised hands, legs, and arms; and total emotional exhaustion. Nurses brought her hospital scrubs to wear. Her attending physician suggested that she stay at the hospital for observation. She agreed to do so in order for her to stay close to Ninette.

Then she made the call to Evalina.

8

Friday, June 21, 2019
Paris, France

THE ESCAPE

While the ambulances raced through the city on the way to Pitie Salpetriere Hospital, the faux policemen in the stolen police car, having turned slightly left off the Pont Royal Bridge and then north on Avenue du General Lemonnier disappeared into the underground parking of the Jardin du Carrousel. Taking a ticket from the automatic dispenser, the driver let it drop from his hands to the garage floor. The arm of the gate lifted, and he sped down the ramps to the lowest level. Few cars parked at this level.

Finding an out of the way spot, he parked. The two men exited the car and headed to the stairs. Knowing that there were security cameras throughout the garage, doubting a wide-awake guard was monitoring them, they pulled their caps low over their foreheads, and covered their faces with their hands. Inside the stairwell, they quickly pulled off the police jumpsuits and threw both these and their caps under the bottom stairs. They were sure these would not be found for some days.

Climbing the stairs, they made it to the first underground landing. Exiting the stairs at this level, they proceeded to walk quickly through the garage onto the street above. At street level, waiting for traffic to clear, they dashed across the street to the main garden and walked a diagonal path to the garden's north exit. Reaching that exit, they made their way to the Tuileries Metro. It was now 11:00 pm. On Pari Roller, the metro ran until 2:00 am. Plenty of time to make several transfers to their end stop northeast of the central city.

With the sounds of the ambulances and police cars screaming "Hee Haa Hee

Haa," the two perpetrators walked casually down the stairs to the metro knowing they had successfully made their escape.

9

Saturday, June 22, 2019
Paris, France

A CHARMED LIFE

At 3:00 am, Nina began to fade. The extensive examination, CAT scan and X-rays, and sedatives left her exhausted. She made her phone call to Evalina.

Evalina, awakened from a deep sleep, took a few moments of repeated questions to realize her good friend was in the hospital following a mysterious accident during Pari Roller. She told Nina she was on her way despite Nina's assurance that it was not necessary.

Evalina hastily put on some clothes. They were what one would describe in the United States as "sweats". Totally not French, but quick to pull on. No makeup, hair a mess, she raced out the front door of her home and into her car. Finding it difficult to breathe, she sat in the car for a few moments trying to calm down. Her best friend was seriously injured and it was all her fault!

Breathing easier now, she backed the car out of her driveway and into the dead-end street on the side of Montmartre. During the 20-minute drive to the hospital, she thought about how she got Nina involved in this. She was very conflicted. They were wonderful friends that grew out of the work offer to Nina two years earlier. Now, because of that offer, this lovely young woman was nearly killed and might continue to be in terrible danger. Was this related to the work?

When Evalina's mother, Catherine, had told her the truth years ago, it all sounded exciting. She couldn't see how anything could happen. They were just transporting paintings and artists back and forth between Russia and Paris. How would anyone know that there were coded messages under some of the oil paintings of a sweet older woman named LADA? Had they found out?! Is that what this is all about?!

Her maman had told Evalina the romantic story of how LADA assigned Catherine to sketch the young man, who would become Catherine's "fun" and Evalina's father. The three of them, Catherine, Alexei, and LADA, had spent the rest of the summer together. They talked about art. They talked about physics and light. They talked about purpose and the meaning of their lives.

LADA began sharing with her best friend and her best friend's lover how she had lost her parents in the Holocaust. She told them how she served in the French underground as a young teenager and how she found purpose in her life. Her life and art would be used to protect the less fortunate and to help provide for a safer and more equitable world. She explained how her paintings were used to send coded messages out of France and she, through her paintings, had significantly played a role in defeating Nazi Germany. She had helped save France. She had helped save the world. She had helped change history!

Evalina arrived at the hospital. Parking the car on the street, she walked into the hospital grounds, an old gunpowder factory transformed to a hospital in 1634. It was the premier teaching hospital in France covering all specialties, especially neurology, the reason that Ninette was rushed there.

At the information desk at the Urgences Generales, she learned that Nina was in a patient room for observation. Her friend, Ninette, was in neurology surgery due to the head trauma she suffered in the accident. Evalina was given the room number for Nina and was told visiting hours would begin in five hours. After several minutes of heated discussion, an attending doctor was called into the discussions. Hearing the pleas from the distraught woman, Nina's only relative living in France, the doctor allowed Evalina a short visit with a sleeping Nina.

Evalina was escorted to Nina's room. Outside the door, an armed police officer was seated. The doctor explained the situation to the police officer. Evalina was required to leave her driver's licenses and purse with the officer. He did a quick pat down of her clothing and told her the door must be left open for him to observe. He then let Evalina into the room.

Nina had several bags and IV tubes pumping fluids into her. These were electrolytes, a mild sedative to relax her, and a mild painkiller for the pain from her sprained ankle.

A nurse came into the room to check on Nina and to assure that the bag's drips were continuing to flow. The nurse asked, "You are her relative?" Evalina replied she was. "You have a very brave and fortunate relative, madame. That police car could have hit her. She could have died from that jump. She could have drowned from the water. And, the river cruise boat could have run over her and her friend. This Nina, she must live a very charmed life! Oui?"

Nina had said to Evalina, once the offer was made to her for the job at iSpy Gallery, "I must live a very charmed life!" Interesting how the coincidence of the term "charmed life" could apply to the exciting offer of a new job in a city where you dreamed of living and could be applied to having narrowly escaped death in four ways in one night! Wait, what?

"Nurse, what did you say? A police car nearly hit her?" Nina had told her quickly about the car but had said nothing about it being a police car.

"Oui, madame, that is what we have heard. A police car suddenly came up the road on Pont Royal. As it approached their position on the bridge; it accelerated to a high speed and appeared to aim right at this young woman, your relative. The other young woman grabbed the patient just in time to hurl her onto the sidewalk. Unfortunately, the car did hit the other girl and knocked her over the guard wall and into the Seine. We understand she is undergoing neurological surgery right now to relieve some bleeding on the brain."

"They thought she might have suffered a broken neck and back, but no. From what is being said in the hospital, somehow the backpack she was wearing and the things inside acted like a shield for her neck and back. Hard to explain, but true! She does have a broken right leg and lots of severe bruising. But other than the bleeding on the brain, she is okay. Hopefully, the surgery will cure that. We pray!"

Evalina, looking at Nina, could only shake her head and cry. "How could this have happened?" she thought to herself. The nurse finished her work, handed Evalina a tissue from the container near the sink, and said, "You must be very proud of this young woman, Nina. She is truly a brave girl. She will be sore for a few days and must wait for the bruising to heal. But she will be fine. She is strong. And she did not suffer any long-term injuries. Be safe, madame." The nurse walked to the door and left.

The police officer entered the room and said, "Madame, I must ask you to leave now. You will have to wait in the waiting area downstairs. Patient visiting hours will be in just a few hours and you can visit her again."

"Merci," Evalina said to the officer. As Evalina got up out of the chair, Nina's eyes opened slightly. A small smile appeared on her face. She whispered in a strained and soft voice, "Evalina, thank you for coming," and then her eyes closed and she was back asleep.

Evalina walked to the door and looked back at Nina. She smiled at her as she wiped more tears from her eyes and said, "Sleep well my little dear, sleep safely." She walked out of the room and sobbed. The police officer took her by the hand and said, "Madame, I will make sure she is safe. My colleagues and I will see that nothing more happens to her. Rest assured!"

10

Saturday, June 22, 2019
Paris, France

THE ESCAPE CONTINUES

The two perpetrators boarded the #1 metro heading west. At the Concorde stop, they got off and proceeded to the #12, heading south. Two more train changes put them on #10 east to Gare d'Austerlitz station. Directly above them at Gare d'Austerlitz, exactly one hour after their attempted murder of a young female skater in Pari Roller, the two young women were being treated.

The two men below ground changing metros yet again couldn't care less. Their mission, they were sure, had been a success. Neither of these young women could survive that fall off the bridge!

The #5 metro took them to their last stop. Exiting at Bobigny Pablo Picasso, they found their car nearby and drove to a safe house in Reims, part of the Champagne region, which was what they would drink in celebration.

Arriving at the safe house at 3:00 am, it was too early to report in. Popping the champagne cork, they began the celebration of their success. It was hard to wait the four hours before being able to call, but they did not want to upset the commander with an early call, even with good news. He was a rough man and easily brought to anger. The news would be too good to have spoiled. Drinking champagne would have to suffice. Not as good as vodka, but it would do. These two men's names are unimportant. They would soon be totally forgotten.

11

Saturday, June 22, 2019
Paris, France

GOOD NEWS

At the precise moment the two men made their phone call to the commander, Nina's doctor walked into the emergency waiting room. He had good news.

"Madame K, good morning. Come with me to my patient's room, Nina? She is asking for you. She will be released today. All her tests are good. She will be sore for a few days and need to rest. She is a strong young woman."

Nina looked up as they entered the room. Evalina walked over to the bed. Nina took Evalina's hand. Both women started to cry.

"Nina, Nina, what were you thinking? We could have lost you, Angel."

"Evalina, she is my friend. I had to try. Now, I learned she saved my life. You would have done the same, too, yes? If it were me and you and I fell off the bridge?"

Nodding her head yes with tears still coming, Evalina said, "Yes, my dear. Like you. With no hesitation!" Both women smiled at each other.

"I have more good news," the doctor interjected. "The other young woman . . . your friend," he said, looking at Nina. "She came through the surgery well. She had a hematoma in the right side of her head." Looking seriously at Nina, "She was lucky she was wearing a helmet. That probably kept her alive."

"The injury required emergency surgery, as you know. The surgeons performed a craniotomy." Both women, frozen with apprehension, listened intently. "They remove a portion of the skull. The procedure was successful. Her skull portion was only temporarily removed. It has been replaced. She will be staying here for several days and then transferred to a rehabilitation center, perhaps for several weeks. But she will be fine, assuming no more bleeding."

He smiled, "More good news. Her broken leg is a simple fracture and will not need surgery. She will be in an upper thigh to toe cast, however. She will need to wear this for a few months, perhaps as many as three or four. It will be fine. And there will be no surgical scar." Both women smiled with this news.

"She does have multiple deep bruises, primarily on her back and the back of her legs. There is no internal damage to any organs, the spleen, liver, or kidneys. Unbelievable for the fall she had!" he laughed. "Somehow her backpack seems to have protected her. We are considering researching the effects of carrying a backpack with croissants and baguette for the safety of our military paratroopers!"

"All in all, a very lucky young woman." Looking at Evalina, "And, she had your relative here..." turning now to Nina, " . . . as an angel watching over her, to thank!" "Both of you are very lucky!"

"I must get on with rounds and check on my other patients. You both have a good day. Perhaps a quiet celebration, oui?" Smiling he said, "But no dancing!" Looking now at Nina, "I think it will be too hard on that ankle of yours, mademoiselle." He turned and left the room.

12

Saturday, June 22, 2019
Paris, France

THE PHONE CALL

As the good news from the doctor was being delivered to Evalina and Nina, so too were the assassins delivering their good news to the Commander. The Commander, head of the district of France (France, Belgium, and Netherlands), Russian SVR (Foreign Intelligence Services) picked up the phone. The voice from the phone said in a slurred voice, "The first phase of the mission is accomplished, Commander. The young woman has been eliminated!" Silence from the other end.

"We are preparing to perform the second phase on the old artist. She will be eliminated shortly." More silence!

Now in a booming voice, he heard, "What the fuck are you saying? ELIMINATED!!!"

Stunned, the agent said softly and fearfully into the phone, "Yes, eliminated . . . as you ordered." Silence but more deafeningly. Silence continued.

Then, a voice shaking with anger held the criminal's attention. All the man could do was bob his head up and down in what appeared to the second agent as a sign of the wonderful things in store for them once the mission was completed. The head bobbing continued. Had the second man not been so drunk he would have realized how ashen his partner's face had become, how drawn with lines of worry too. This continued for several more minutes. Finally, he put the phone down.

The second agent, excited, wanting to hear about the good news, couldn't restrain himself. "Will we receive big bonuses . . . rewards? What kind of honors? Will the stories of us killing the spies be in the paper? Will we be given summer dacha on the beach? Tell me all the good news, my friend! What did he say!"

Turning slowly, lower lip trembling in fear and anger, he said to his drunk partner, "You fool! We were not to eliminate the young woman and the old artist!"

"What?" his partner said.

"We were not ordered to ELIMINATE the two women, the young one and the old artist! We were to ELIMINATE THEM AS SUSPECTS as a means for the spies to deliver information!"

"But . . . but the Commander said 'eliminate them'. I heard him say so."

"You never listen well. You are always interested in violence! You play too many of your foolish video games! Then you play them in real life! You expected him to order their elimination. What he wanted was for us to follow them. If they were the means of information passing, to learn how it was done! You fool!"

The partner's face now also became ashen. "Does that mean no bonus? No dacha by the sea? No medals?"

Shaking his head "no" and trembling with anger, the first man said, "We are to leave this place immediately by car. We are to drive to Dunkirk. We are to wait until dark and steal a fishing boat. We are to sail 20 nautical miles out into the North Sea. At precisely 2 am tomorrow morning a submarine will appear. We will be loaded on that ship and brought back to Russia. Then, we will be taken to a military base and flown to Tempa!"

"Tampa? We are going to Florida? In America?" A bright smile appeared on the second's face.

"No, you fool! We are going to TEMPA!!! The weather station on Kotel'nyy Island Novos Sibirskiye Ostrova!!! (New Siberian Island). We will be guarding that weather station for the rest of our miserable lives thanks to you!"

In Moscow, the Commander was trying to figure out how to "cover his own ass," as they say in America. Not only did these fools botch their assignment, but they had also alerted the French and US operatives that the Russians were onto the passing of information. They also nearly attacked a Russian artist who the Russian President adores. He collects LADA paintings. He has some hanging in his home at Cape Idokopas on the coast of the Black Sea. He has a couple in his office in the Kremlin. The Commander had seen them there.

The Russian President laughed that he had LADAs in his office just like that US President John Kennedy did when he defeated that fool Nikita Khrushchev during the Cuban Missile Crisis. He used them as a statement of how he is defeating that fool in the American White House now in 2019, 57 years after the missile crisis. Such political fools! No intelligence to play this game of international strategy. Both of them are fools. One Soviet Russian, the other American.

The commander considered what to do now. For now, he would pull back his people. That would give him time to think of a new strategy. He would also have his people in Paris observe how the French and Americans react to this situation. Were they alerted? How were they responding? Would life still be normal for this LADA artist? Would they hide her? What happened to this young woman, Nina? Was she killed?

What about this Evalina person? Now there is an interesting woman. He would learn more about her, her father, the former astrophysicist, and her deceased mother. And more about how this young woman, Nina, became part of this iSPY Gallery, which is an interesting name for a gallery . . . especially one thought to be passing Russian information to the French and Americans. Who would be so audacious to include the words "I Spy" in its name? Is this a case of "hiding in plain sight"?

Yes, answering these questions would take time. Lying low for a couple of months would be good idea!

13

1961
Paris, France

A WORLD CHANGED

A lot was happening in Paris during the post-WWII years through the early 1960s. Much like the world today, the war had not ended conflicts worldwide; it had not brought the peace in the world that was hoped for following two wars that were to end all wars. And it has not brought prosperity to most of the world's citizens. Those who were rich seemed to be becoming richer, while those who were poor seemed to be becoming poorer. Just like today.

A big difference was how this was all reported. There were no 24/7 news reports on biased cable channels. "Film was at 11". The news was handled in 15-minute and eventually 30-minute broadcasts by true journalistic pros like Douglas Edwards, Edward R. Murrow, John Cameron Swayze, Walter Cronkite, Chet Huntly, and David Brinkley. When Walter Cronkite ended his CBS News Broadcast with "and that's the way it is" you knew that was, in fact, the way it was! No other agenda, just deliver the factual news.

Those years in Paris, 1945 through the early 1960s, were tough times for Paris where LADA and Catherine lived. They made frequent trips to be with Alexei in Lausanne and in his somewhat mysterious appointment at a research institution in Limoges, France. This institute was doing research in sending light through bundles of something that would be termed optical fibers in 1963 by a British investigator in this new process.

A Dutch scientist first demonstrated this process in 1953. Alexei and this scientist had worked together on the project both at Lausanne and in this secretive research facility in Limoges. A veiled side of the French Government funded the work in Limoges. Alexei and this man also collaborated with the scientists in London, funded by the British Government's GCHQ (Secret Intelligence Agency).

Their work there was to use these processes to transmit images. Although the institute remained secret, in 1968 it became incorporated into a new multidiscipline University, the University of Limoges. In 2019, much of the research going on in this institute continued to be highly classified and secret. A good deal of it is the result of Alexei's theory of the storage of light using what is now called "black matter".

As LADA introduced Catherine and Alexei more and more to the social problems in the world, they gained a greater understanding of the socialist movement. They met with LADA's artist friends, many of whom were strong members of the socialist party. These discussions centered on all people's responsibility as world citizens to help make change for the better . . . for everyone. The three became aware of the issues caused by the Soviet Union in keeping freedoms, people's rights, and economic advancement from happening. Stalin had been a terror to the Russian people. When he died in 1953, LADA had hoped for change. His predecessor, Nikita Khrushchev, was not much better, she explained. They and others must do their part to see that change could happen for the good of the world.

One evening in the late fall of 1961, Alexei came home to the apartment but was obviously disturbed about something. All evening Catherine and LADA tried to get him to open up about what was troubling him.

"Alexei, I am your friend and lover. LADA is your friend too. We want to help you. Tell us what is troubling you. You are no fun tonight; you are making your ladies sad . . . and mad!"

Letting out a long sigh, he said, "Catherine, today I ran into an old friend of mine at EPFL. He is a physicist and engineer who deals in the field of rocket thrust and propulsion. He and I had lunch together. I am not really sure why he is in Lausanne. The institute does not seem to have any relevance to what he works on."

Alexei struggled for the right words. "He is at the Soviet Space and Missile Research Institute in Moscow. We talked about his work. What he could share. He told me much of his work was secret. Not unlike mine. However, he was quite concerned. He said that he had learned through talking with others at the Institute and finding documents telling of an effort underway to move Soviet missiles to the island of Cuba, just off the shore of America."

The other two waited for him to go on. "Georgo, that is his name, he thinks that this will be a real escalation in the threat of retaliation by America on the Soviet Union. He really seemed worried. Right now, America and their president do not appear to know anything about this plan. He is afraid if this plan goes forward that it could end in a nuclear war!"

LADA, silent during all this, asked quietly, "Alexei, do you think this man could provide you with proof? Perhaps one of the documents?"

"Why do you ask that, LADA? This man told me all this in complete confidence. He seemed very scared. Scared at the knowledge he is now keeping and scared that others will find out that he has told someone. No, I do not think he can provide us with such a document. What would we do with it anyway?"

"I still have my connections, Alexei. I think this information needs to be shared with our French government and with our friends in the United States. Will you be seeing him again?"

"LADA, I am very troubled by this. We are talking about betraying our homeland by providing this kind of information even if we had it. I am not comfortable with this!"

"My friend, what would be worse? To alert the Americans to what will be on their doorstep to avoid a nuclear war in which no one would win . . . no one would benefit. Everyone would lose. Or, would it be better to help our homeland and the rest of the world remain alive? I would choose the latter. What about you?"

Alexei shook his head back and forth, appearing to try to clear his mind. He then got up and left the room saying nothing to the women.

LADA looked at Catherine, "I'm sorry, my dear one, for upsetting your love. He is a good man. He is very troubled by this. But I have seen the results firsthand of people who did not tell what they knew was happening. It resulted in horror. We cannot let a horror take place if it is within our power to alert others to the horror."

"But LADA, if we had such a document, how would we get it to the Americans?"

"I have a group of paintings that will be shipped to the United States early next year. They are for a show in Washington, DC, near their White House. It seems this young President Kennedy likes Russian art. He actually owns a couple of mine already. They are in his office in this White House."

"If we had documented proof, I could put it on a canvas and paint over the document with an acrylic paint as I did during the War. Once the painting and document is in the US, I can direct their government agency on how to remove it unharmed from under the oil painting. The process is simple. Acquiring the proof is quite another. Alexei has to try."

Alexei was gone for several hours. After a long walk and thinking by himself, he decided to head home. Back at the apartment, he told the women of his decision to try to find Georgo the next day. Alexei would ask him for a document that verified what Georgo had told him. "I am still very troubled by this decision but in my heart, I know it has to be done."

The women both kissed him, each on a separate cheek. He said quietly, just loud enough for them to hear him, "Let us pray that we are doing the right thing and that God will protect us." To which the women both silently said to themselves, "Amen!"

The next day, Alexei found Georgo. Seated by himself outside the dining facility overlooking Lake Leman, Alexei walked over to Georgo and asked his old friend if he could sit.

"Yes, sure."

They talked for a few minutes about the beauty of the Swiss mountains and lake. They talked about the strange fall weather allowing them to sit outside and enjoy this natural beauty. After what Alexei felt was an appropriate amount of time, he asked the fateful question.

"Georgo, the papers you told me about yesterday, the ones that frightened you so. Do you have them with you? Would you share them with me?"

Georgo looked stunned. Then he asked, "Alexei, what would you want to do with these papers? Yes, I have them. I am trying to figure out how to destroy them! I'm sorry I ever acquired and read them. Why would you want them?"

Trapped by the question, realizing the only thing he could do, Alexei began, "I have this friend and she has connections…" Alexei began telling LADA's history during WWII. The discussion lasted well into the afternoon. At the end, Georgo reached into his satchel beside his legs, pulled out a 12-page document, and handed it to Alexei, telling him, "You must swear never to tell anyone other than your friend how you acquired these. Do I have your pledge, my friend?"

Alexei nodded his head "yes" and said, "You have that pledge, Georgo. You are a brave and good man. Yes, I pledge this to you!"

Georgo stood looking down at his friend he said sadly, "Alexei, this will be the last time we will see each other. You must never try to find me again, nor I you.

What we are doing is dangerous to us and those we love. Be careful, my friend! Our lives are trusted to each other." He walked away.

Alexei whispered, "Goodbye, old friend." He too stood up and walked away to a new work he had never considered before.

Over the next several days, LADA prepared the canvases with the documents and then hastily but beautifully painted the Swiss countryside paintings. The three then used her old drying technique on the oil paint and aged the paintings slightly. Alexei stayed in Lausanne. Catherine and LADA loaded the paintings into shipping crates and escorted them by train back to Paris.

In Paris, she contacted her old associate at the Directorate-General for External Security. She told him of a group of paintings she must get to the United States immediately. She must go with the paintings.

Her associate was reluctant at first and told her he would get back to her. He did, several days later. The arrangements were agreed to under one condition: he must escort her to the United States. He must be involved with the discussions regarding this information with his American counterparts. LADA agreed and was greatly relieved that he would be going with her. She could trust this man. He was a man who could take care of any situation that might unexpectedly happen. He could be ruthless!

On the morning of February 3, 1962, LADA, the man, and 30 paintings were loaded onto a Boeing 707 flight from Paris to New York. Three of these 30 paintings each contained four pages of the document beneath their oil paint surface. The paintings were transferred to another plane in New York at LaGuardia airport for a flight to Washington, DC. There, four men met the plane on the taxiway in a large van. They loaded the paintings, LADA, and the man accompanying her into the van and transported them to a new secret location for the CIA. It had just been created in late 1961 and it was called "Langley".

The documents below the paint surface described in detail the Soviet Union's plans to build missile silos just 90 miles from the US shore. These documents, the first clues of the Cuban Missile Crisis, would be confirmed by aerial photos in October 1962 by Air Force pilot Richard Heyser from his U-2 aircraft. The documents described the new propulsion system, which Alexei's friend, Georgo, had helped develop. The papers also said this system would allow missiles and their nuclear warheads to reach anywhere in the continental United States from Cuba.

Therefore, on that day in February 1962, the three close Russian/French friends helped prepared the world to step back from the brink of nuclear war and total world destruction. No one other than LADA, Catherine, Alexei, the Frenchman, the four men from Langley, and a young President of the United States, John Kennedy, would ever know of the impact these three friends had made toward world peace. One of the 30 paintings, from that most significant trip, still resides in the White House.

14

Tuesday, September 3, 2019
Paris, France

THE ARRIVAL

Passing through customs in Paris was always much easier than passing through customs in the USA. Why was that? Mary and Tom always checked their roller bags and carried on a small duffle bag each, along with Mary's purse. It meant they had to wait for the baggage to be unloaded. Even that seemed to be smoother and take less time than in the USA, which was good because Tom was exhausted after that uncomfortable flight.

Actually, the only hold up they had was when the French customs agent wanted to try the new fingerprint-reading device on Mary and Tom. Mary went first and it couldn't read her fingerprints. After three tries, the agent gave up on Mary and it was Tom's turn.

Many years ago, one of Tom's weekly chores was to burn trash in a brick trash burner. It had a metal grate on top that looked like a grill grate for a Weber grill. Tom, who was usually conscientious about things, forgot that he had already burned several loads of trash and absent-mindedly reached down and grabbed the grate with his fingers.

He didn't feel any pain initially, but there was a sizzling sound. Suddenly, the pain hit, and he dropped the grate and ran for the hose. Too late. Grooves from the metal grate were burned into all ten digits' fingertip pads.

After his mom did what she could to take care of the burns, it was off to the doctor for proper treatment. His hands were wrapped and would remain that way for a couple of weeks. The good news was he had to stop taking typing class. Yes! The bad news: for several years he had lost his fingerprints. Even in college when he was in ROTC and they needed his fingerprints for his military ID card . . . you guessed it . . . no fingerprints!

Perhaps that's why on almost every international flight he had taken, up until just a couple of years ago, he would be pulled aside and either frisked or the metal wand was used to scan his body for hidden things. Perhaps someone who has had questionable fingerprints is on the international "watch list".

Did this fingerprint history cause the French new fingerprint system to fail with Tom? Nope, piece of cake. Identified on the first try and off he and Mary went to retrieve their bags.

Knowing how tired Tom was from taking care of his two ladies through the night, though she still kidded him about that, she suggested they take a cab directly to the apartment. No argument from Tom. He texted the number Evalina had sent him for Natalya and let her know they would be getting a cab. They should be at the apartment in a little over an hour. The text reply came quickly letting them know she was already at the apartment and would be watching for their cab to arrive.

Almost immediately upon reaching the designated location for cabs, one was signaled over for them. The driver was a middle-aged French woman. After pleasant "bonjours" all around, Tom handed the driver the address that Mary had prepared on a piece of paper before arriving in Paris.

The driver said in very good English, "You are American, oui?" Both Tom and Mary replied "oui". "I know of this street. I grew up in Montmartre. We should be there quickly unless there is construction or deliveries to shops. That can create some traffic problems in the narrow and winding streets. We shall see."

The time was now 8:30 am, just a little over an hour and a half since the wheels of their Air France flight had hit the runway. They would be at the apartment sometime between 9:30 am and 10:00 am.

Holding hands, excited to be back in Paris, big smiles appeared on both their faces as they looked at each other. Unnoticed by them, the driver had witnessed this through her rearview mirror. Smiling to herself, she thought pleasantly, "They are a happy couple. So good to see." And she drove them safely to the apartment.

• • •

As the driver was unloading the roller bags from the trunk, a young woman in her late 20's opened the door to number 10 and said, "Madame et Monsieur Martz, bonjour. Je suis Natalya."

Tom and Mary both said, "Bonjour Natalya."

The four then began to say simultaneously that they don't speak much French. They all laughed. Natalya pulled out her iPhone and spoke into it in Russian. She turned the screen to Tom and Mary and the translation from spoken Russian appeared in English writing on the screen of the device. It told them that if they spoke English into the phone, it would translate it into Russian for her to read. Not quite as easy as if they all spoke the same language but it certainly would do.

They entered the building and proceeded to the third floor. Mary and Tom would prefer to be on the sixth floor for more exercise, but three flights would do. As with all Paris apartments, this one had a digital code lock for the front door. Natalya showed Mary and Tom the key to the inside door to the stairs off the small entryway. A door straight ahead of them in the entryway would have taken them into the service area of the small but, according to Evalina, good restaurant that was attached to the apartment building.

The apartment opened to a small entry area. On the walls were assorted small mirrors and nick-nacks. One wall had places to hang coats and an umbrella stand with a couple of umbrellas in it. Those could come in handy as the rains do come fairly frequently in Paris. However, this summer and early fall of 2019, not so much. In fact, France and particularly Paris was in a very deep drought. This was quite evident to Mary after Natalya left as she usually tried to rescue the dried-up geraniums in the window planters. She was successful. Before Tom and Mary left Paris just a few days later, the geraniums were in bloom.

To the right of the entryway was a small "American Cuisine" kitchen. Why small kitchens in Paris were called "American Cuisine" baffled Mary and Tom. Had the French never seen a true American kitchen? Heck, the American refrigerators were almost as large as the entire French kitchens!

Straight ahead and slightly to the right was the door to a very nice size but somewhat dark bathroom. No external light. The bathtub was a good size. All in all, this would do nicely.

To the right of the bathroom door was a door that led into the only bedroom. It too was a good size for a French apartment. A large queen-sized bed and nearly floor to ceiling double-paned glass windows allowed them to look out onto a small garden, and beyond that, a pocket park with kids playing.

One of Mary and Tom's favorite pastimes in Paris was to sit in pocket parks and watch children playing. This they would definitely do while in the park themselves or sitting on the bed in the evening and watching the kids play from the apartment. How wonderful!

Straight across from the bedroom on the other side of the small entranceway was a good size living room with a small dining area. Although it was a good size, it was filled with two large white leather sofas and several white leather dining chairs, two of which were at the small table and two of which were on the right side of a beautiful white marble 1800s fireplace.

Those chairs were also tucked away beside one of two of the floor-to-ceiling

French door windows that were on the front of the apartment facing Rue Garreau. Between the two sets of windows was the large painting of the mysterious young woman in a red gown with a mask in her right hand. It instantly caught Mary's attention once more. "We are going to figure this out!" she said to herself.

It wasn't until Natalya left and they explored the apartment further that they found all the Napoleon dishes and the number of books and magazines on Astrophysics written by one Dr. Alexei K, a distinguished professor of Astrophysics.

Natalya continued to show them around the apartment and explained which of the large floor to ceiling closets contained additional linens for the bed and towels for the bath. Most of those were kept in one closet on the right of the bed as you looked from the foot to the head of the bed. The other closet was locked. It was explained they contained the personal items of the permanent resident of the apartment. Mary and Tom assumed that it was Evalina. They would find out later that no, it was the personal things of Evalina's friend, Nina, who worked for Evalina.

The same was true of all the built-in cabinets that surrounded three walls of the living room. Other than the display cases with the Napoleon dishes and astrophysics books, the cabinets were locked. Again, Natalya told them that they contained the personal items of the person living here full time. This was quite normal to Tom and Mary as it had been the case in other apartments where they had stayed.

Most people in Paris tended to be minimalist. A couple of sets of nice items and then multiple accent pieces. Whoever lived here had lots of nice items and lots of nice accent pieces and much more.

Natalya finished giving them a tour of the apartment. She told them on departure to leave the keys on the dining table and just to lock the automatic lock as they leave as she had a spare key and could let herself in. She also checked with them to make sure they had her cell phone number programmed into their own. She told them through her phone app that if there was a problem to text her and she would take care of the problem right away. It was a nice warm friendly greeting to their stay. The only thing that would have been better is if they had met Evalina herself. Maybe next trip. . . .

Natalya left and Mary could tell Tom was beginning to fade. She thought they had better find food quickly. "Let's find food and let him nap. I can explore the apartment and use the computer Evalina provided to search the internet. I have an idea who the woman in the painting is."

"No argument from me," was his reply. Locking the doors, off they went on their first adventure in Paris that trip.

15

Saturday, June 22, 2019
Paris, France

JOSEPHINE BARKER

Evalina pulled into her driveway. "What time is it?" she wondered.

Looking at the dashboard clock, she saw it was almost 12:00 pm. She had been at the hospital for nearly 8 hours. She was exhausted. She needed a bath and food. Mostly she needed rest.

She walked up the limestone pavers to the front door. It was unlocked. She knew she had locked it when she left for the hospital. Hadn't she? Was this the day of the housekeepers? Puzzled, she called out, "Hello, is someone here?"

A male voice coming from the living room, replied, "Hello, my daughter. It is Papa." She walked down the entryway hall to the living room. There sitting in his favorite chair was Papa. Sitting in Alexei's lap, his miniature black poodle, Josephine Barker III.

After the hit-and-run car accident that killed Catherine, Alexei could not stay in the house. It had too many memories and he was getting too old to roam the entire big place. Six bedrooms was more than one man needed. The guest-house had two bedrooms and was a perfect size for him. The family home for four generations was now Evalina's. Alexei moved into his new home, the guest house. Perfect!

He had his favorite chair in the house and he occupied it now. With a concerned smile, he asked, "Are Nina and her friend okay? It is all over the news this morning. I thought of calling you on your cell phone because I knew you must have been notified. I thought better of it. If there was something I should know, I knew you would call me."

Evalina smiled back at him and sighed. Then she told him all she knew. She gave the medical report on both the girls. With a deep sigh, she said, "Papa, this is all my fault. I never should have brought Nina into this dirty stuff."

Alexei studied her for a short while letting her angst settle down. As Alexei rubbed Josephine's ears, he asked, "Evalina, did Catherine and I ever tell you why our poodles have all been named Josephine Barker, even though none of the three had ever truly been a barker?"

"You told me once that they were named after that African-American singer and dancer of the 1920s, Josephine Baker. I assumed because these poodles all kind of prance and they're black. Is that why?"

"No dear Evalina, that is only part of the reason. Our first Josephine Barker had been the companion for LADA. She eventually realized having a companion required more responsibility than she could accept. Her travels and painting required much of her. She loved the dog and asked us to keep her. The real problem was much deeper. Having Josephine with her everyday brought back the memories she was trying to forget . . . the loss of her parents in the terrible way she had lost them."

"You see, when word came to the underground about the roundup and how LADA's parents had been taken, there was, at that location, an exotic black woman. This was the dancer and singer, Josephine. Josephine was a very kind and sweet woman. Your mother and I were sorry you never had the opportunity to know her. She died in 1975, just three years before you were born. We considered naming you Josephine after her. However, family history called, and we felt we should name you Evalina instead."

Evalina laughed, "I could have been named after a dog?"

Alexei laughed and said, "No dear one, you would have been named after this beautiful exotic woman, Josephine. Let me tell you the whole story."

"Here was this broken-hearted little girl, LADA, inconsolable by any of the other people at the safe place. Josephine, who was still allowed to travel all over Europe to perform, she was a darling performer for the Nazi's as they saw her as a performing animal . . . less than human . . . but very entertaining. Much like the way they viewed the great American track star of the 1938 Olympics, Jesse Owens. They were mesmerized by their talents."

"Josephine happened to be at the location when the word came. She walked over to the small sobbing LADA, took her in her arms, and held her close to her bosom. She let the poor girl sob and sob. She didn't try to quiet her or try to use words to console her. She just held her close."

"LADA told us she didn't know how long she was held crying like this, perhaps a couple of hours or more. Finally, she stopped crying. She looked up into Josephine's beautiful face and saw tears flowing down the woman's cheeks. And in her eyes she saw true love for LADA!"

"Now Josephine was married to her second husband at the time and was unable to have children naturally. She looked at the little waif and told her, 'I can never be a replacement for your Maman, sweet one, but you now have a new mother . . . and that is me."

"LADA and Josephine never told anyone else of this other than your maman and me. We felt deeply privileged to know. That is why you were nearly named Josephine. After this great and wonderful friend of LADA's and eventually ours. This beautiful woman, who loved our friend so much."

He smiled at his daughter. "You know what? After the war, Josephine Baker eventually adopted nine children. They were of various races, ethnicities, and religions. She called them her "Rainbow Tribe". There was a woman who loved. She is like LADA . . . and your mother, my Catherine. And it is no wonder. She taught LADA how to love. LADA taught your mother. And, now my sweet daughter, you are teaching our Nina."

Evalina saw the tears in her father's beautiful old eyes. She too began to tear up. Feeling the need to lighten the mood, she asked, "But why Barker and not Baker for little Josephine I through III? You and Maman couldn't spell? A play on words perhaps?"

Alexei replied, "Yes, a play on words. Not the one you are thinking of. It is because dogs bark, though very rarely do French Poodles. The play on words is that the bark is the warning sound made by a dog. It is the way warning messages are relayed. The play on words is that of the warning messages that Josephine Baker, and then LADA, and now us, send out. In that way, we are all 'barkers'. You see?"

As usual, Evalina saw. Her father was not only a very gifted astrophysicist, but he also was a very wise man. She understood that this conversation was much more than just him telling the whole story of the naming of the dogs and the "adoption" of a child by an exotic performer and beautiful woman. It was a message from him to Evalina, of the importance of their lives' avocation. Their passion.

"Evalina, it is true. This horrible thing that has fallen on Nina and her friend Ninette may well be because of this work that we are doing. As others have done, my sweet daughter, we cannot turn a blind eye to how we must go forward. Perhaps we must be more cautious. Alerted now."

"Josephine Baker taught LADA how to use her art to send the important alert "barks" to where they were needed. She told LADA how she smuggled coded messages of what she had learned about Nazi troop movements from the parties where she entertained them. The messages were written in invisible ink on her music sheets. She wrote them in her underwear, as she knew, because of her special position, no one would look there" "

"She and Josephine came up with the idea of coded messages below LADA's oil paintings. Josephine was a good friend of Pablo Picasso. She knew of a French chemist who mixed all of Picasso's oil paints. Picasso, who had stayed in Paris during the war and had close ties to the underground resistance, had introduced her to him. This chemist, Henri Sennelier, was approached by Josephine with the idea of painting over messages on canvas."

"He knew the problem was much more complex than Josephine realized. Having something under oil paint that would not be destroyed by the solvents removing the paint . . . impossible!"

He set to work on it, however, and came up with the secret technique. That technique is still only known by LADA, myself, you, and Nina. We must make sure it always stays secret."

The depth of her emotional tiredness hitting, Evalina said they should discuss this further when her mind was clear. Should they continue to send these messages? Right now, she was exhausted.

She looked at the handsome old man and thought "no wonder my maman fell in love with this person." She said to him, "Thank you, Papa. This talk was needed. We will have to continue it later. I have so much more to ask of you. Right now, I need rest."

"They will be sending Nina home this evening. I am going to have her stay with me in this house until she is better. Once Ninette can come home, I want her to stay here too, until she is fully healed. Do you think this is all wise?

He looked at his "little girl" and saw someone much like Josephine. "Yes, my sweet. I think that is a wise idea. Very wise! Josephine and I will leave you now to rest." He placed the little dog on the floor, got up, and headed for the door. A little Josephine Barker, prancing her dance walk after him.

16

Saturday, June 22, 2019
Moscow, Russia

ORDERS

The Commander picked up the phone and answered the blinking line. His new senior agent in charge of the mission clearly understood his orders: follow the young woman, Nina, and the artist LADA, and watch them. Do not hurt them. Do not let them know you are watching them. Avoid violence at all costs. Learn everything about them. Keep the Commander informed.

"The young woman, Nina, is to be released from the hospital this evening. The other young woman who was with her when the accident happened is in much worse condition. The report is that she will recover but will be in rehabilitation for several weeks."

He continued to give a complete report on both the girls' medical conditions. The line at the other end had remained silent the entire report and he began to believe he had lost connections on the "secure" line. Finally, he heard a gruff but reasonably pleasant reply from the Commander, who was not known as a pleasant person.

"This is good! Keep an eye on the young woman, and the old artist. Also, assign someone to watch this other young woman. We don't know if she is involved but I would rather be sure than to slip up for the President again. Do you understand?!"

The question said it all to the agent. "Do not slip up on this mission like your former colleagues did or you may not have a submarine waiting for your stolen fishing boat!" He understood. No one would ever goof up again. Not on the

Commander's watch.

"Yes, Commander, all is understood. Perfectly! We have also secured monitoring the phone lines at the person Evalina's residence, her father's residence, and the iSPY Gallery. We are tracking the cell phone calls of all the individuals as well as their computers. We can bug these locations too. Do you wish for us to do so or to monitor their conversations with bionic ears?"

"No bugging of the places at this point. I want time to pass before we do anything intrusive. We can wait on that. Use the bionic ear. The monitoring of the electronics is fine. Just do not get caught! Understand?!"

The phone call ended.

The Commander sipped his vodka-laced coffee, thinking. Standing back and watching was the best plan. The agent assured him the team was hard on the research of the people in question. If it is them, how are they doing it? His team would find out. Then, he will have to reveal it to the president. If he has to report that it is something...God forbid! The president will not be happy! This president does not like being taken for a fool. Unfortunately, the messenger is often at risk in the process too!

He picked up the communique from the submarine Captain and reread it. Coming through to his office at 15:30 it confirmed that the submarine had its assignment. Be at the 20 nautical mile location off Dunkirk at precisely 3:00 am tomorrow morning. Observe the fishing boat for an hour and half. Let the fools think they have been forgotten. Then raise the sub nearly on top of them. If you smash the boat,no big deal. Let the two men on board drown. If that doesn't happen, load them on the submarine; lock them in quarters with a guard. Don't let them come into contact with any other personnel until they are safely unloaded upon docking in Russia. If you feel the need at any time to shoot them . . . fine!

The Captain receiving the communication from the SVR Headquarters in Moscow, at first thought it had to be a joke. Then he saw that it was signed by the Commander and he knew this was no joke. He acknowledged the orders and did what was asked. He didn't want to be on the Commander's bad side. One had a habit of disappearing should one do that. Not this Captain.

The communique was sent back with the understanding how the operation would proceed. Early the next morning it proceeded like clockwork . . . a very slow clock for the two men on board a "forgotten fishing boat" . . . until the water exploded nearly below them. Loaded onto the submarine and secured in quarters they were off and headed to their new and not nearly as pleasant lives. How cold can an island off the coast of Siberia really be? They were destined to find out.

17

Friday, June 21, 2019
Paris, France

THE INVESTIGATION

Although the two perpetrators thought their parking late at night in the underground parking garage at the Jardin du Carrousel would go unnoticed, they were wrong. The security guard saw the police car enter the garage, take a ticket, and let it fall to the ground. He followed them on each floor's video monitor as they sped down the ramps to the lowest floor, drive to the most inconspicuous spot, and park the car. He watched them, with caps pulled low suspiciously placed over their faces, hurry to the stairway. Then saw them emerge in civilian clothes from the stairs, on the floor one level down from the ground floor, walk up the car ramp, and head for the Jardin de Tuileries. There he lost sight of them.

While he was watching their antics on the video monitors, his television was tuned to a late-night soccer match and was interrupted with breaking news. The TV showed the scene of a terrible accident during Pari Roller. The TV reporter interviewed a young female witness to the accident. The woman described seeing this police car apparently trying to run down these two skaters.

Instantly, the security guard called the French emergency police number. He described what he had seen on his monitors. He was ordered to lock the entrance and exit ramp gates and not let anyone into or out of the parking garage. Investigators were on their way. Do not touch anything or let anyone else touch anything. The guard hit the switch that activated the emergency locks on the gates and proceeded to monitor his screens for any activity.

A few moments later, three unmarked sedans with flashing blue lights and sirens arrived. He opened only the incoming gate and walked from his office to the place where the ticket machine was located. He told the investigators what he had seen. One bent down with gloved hands, picked up the garage ticket, and placed it in a plastic bag.

Two inspectors asked him to escort them to his office so they could view the security tapes. Meanwhile, two of the unmarked police cars drove down to the lower level and to the location where they found the stolen police car. A forensic team in a van arrived shortly.

As the two officers with the security guard reviewed the tapes, the police investigators in the office described to the other investigators on the lower floor what they were viewing. Those investigators listening to the description began to reenact what they were hearing. In no time, they found the police uniforms. Shortly after that, the forensic team had them bagged and on their way to the lab for analysis.

At police headquarters, an alert to all public transportation modes was sent out. It ordered that they begin monitoring their video screens. Special note was to review the landing platforms at both sides of the Tuileries, Concord, Palais Royal, and Chatelet metro stations. A description of the two suspects was sent to these monitoring security locations. It was also sent to all taxi companies operating in Paris. Most of the buses had stopped running at 8:30 pm. Those that were still running received the police announcement.

Live monitoring of the stations continued as some security tapes were reviewed at the metro stations between 10:45 pm and the current time of 11:30 pm. It didn't take the agents long to spot the two suspects on the westbound ramp of the Tuileries station platform. Those agents alerted the agents at the Concord station. Now, the following of the suspects was in real time as the agents were able to track them from station to station and change of trains.

Police, dispatched to each of the stations where transfers took place, picked up the security tapes and inspected the platforms and trash containers for anything that the perpetrators may have left behind. They found nothing at any of the stations. However, with the parking garage ticket, the clothing, and the car, there was enough forensic material to identify the suspects.

Any time an event happened in France and particularly Paris in which it appeared there may be terrorism or foreign espionage involved, the Directorate-General for External Security (DGES) as well as the Directorate-General for Internal Security (DGIS) were alerted and involved. Even though this appeared to be a singular event, both agencies began to take over command of the investigation and resulting activities.

The agencies monitored what was happening with the Paris Police investigation. By 12:00 pm, the police and the two agencies had the names and nationalities of the two suspects. They also had the name of the intended assassination victim and of her association with iSPY Gallery.

This was no accident. Russian intelligence was involved, and it was important to learn what they knew, how they knew it, and why they had ordered this attempted murder. The operation was now totally in control and headed up by the two agencies, the DGES and DGIS. The police would be used only as back up. Decisions on action? Those would be determined by the two Directorate-General agencies.

When the two Russian suspects boarded the number 5 metro heading northeast from Gare d' Austerlitz, two plain clothed agents boarded with them. When the train stopped at Gare d' Nord, they were replaced by two different agents. Two more agents joined those two at Stalingrad station. As it appeared that the suspects were headed for Bobigny Pablo Picasso, a full team of six agents was waiting for the metro to arrive. Their duty was to follow the suspects and to monitor their activities. Neither the DGIS nor the DGES wanted to alert the Russians that they were on to the activities of the Russian agents or that DGIS and DGES knew the Russian operative's location.

The train pulled into the last metro station. As the two suspects departed the metro car, one was bumped by a heavyset old drunk. The bump allowed the heavy set drunk to deposit a small electronic device into the coat pocket of the Russian agent. The drunk said, "Pardon, monsieur," then he asked the Russian agent if he had any spare change. The agent pushed the drunk aside and huffed off, saying, "Spare change! You old fool; you are lucky I didn't shoot you or break your damn neck".

This was Russian agent number two. The more violent and video playing of the Russian agents who was not known for his smart thinking as it proved out.

With the electronic device in place, the two agencies followed the signal to the safe house location. Surrounding the house, they watched and listened with long-range optics and audio devices. The two Russian agents became drunk on champagne.

When the French agents overheard the phone conversation from the Russian agents to the Commander and the Commander's apparent response to the report, the DGES and DGIS agents fought to keep from laughing. They finally burst into full laughter when they heard the first Russian agent tell his partner what the Commander had said and where the two Russians would end up.

Drone video caused further hysterics for the French agents as they viewed the Russian submarine nearly capsize the stolen fishing boat. That was followed by witnessing the Russian agents being hauled unceremoniously onto the submarine for what would prove to be the most unhappy ending to their story.

A happier conclusion awaited the captain of the stolen fishing boat. Just over the horizon and out of visual sight of the fishing boat, a French coast guard cutter was patrolling. It just happened to be in the general area, perhaps. It waited until the submarine departed before it sailed to the location of the fishing boat. The agencies wanted to do further assessment of any materials that might have been left behind by the drunken and despondent Russian agents. They also wanted to return this most valuable asset to the French fisherman. After all, this was France:

"Liberté, Egalité, Fraternité".

In Paris, the DGIS agency alerted two other international agencies of what had happened. Those agencies were the British MI6 and the American CIA. Soon, two CIA agents, a man and a woman posing as a married couple working for the US Embassy, would be involved. They were the "Smiths" and they had met Mary and Tom Martz once before. They came into contact with Tom and Mary Martz once again that fall with the Martz's rental of the apartment where Nina lived.

18

Tuesday, September 3, 2019
Paris, France

FIRST ADVENTURE

"I know what we should do," Mary said looking at her half-awake man. "Let's go to the little market Natalya told us about just a block away. We can get a small baguette, some cheese, some fruit, water, and perhaps a small bottle of wine there. We can take it to the little pocket park we see out the bedroom window of the apartment and have a picnic watching the children play. We can go out to one of the restaurants this evening for dinner and get other groceries then. What about it, Angel?" Angel was Mary's pet name for Tom and her pet name for all she loved, her kids, and grandkids too. Tom's pet names for Mary were "doll" and "babe". Doll was fine, but she never thought she was much of a "babe". But if Tom thought she was a "babe" in his eyes . . . so be it . . . . "babe" was good. Actually, to many men's eyes in her younger years Mary was a "babe". Tom was always quite pleased to see the number of men's eyes that would follow Mary in the rooms where she entered. And this woman had chosen him. How lucky was he?!

"Sounds good, babe," was his reply, and she smiled and took his hand.

The small grocery was on the opposite side of the street a block to their right as they exited the outside door of the apartment building. Directly across the street from the grocery was the small dead-end street that led to the pocket park and to Evalina's house, though they did not know this about Evalina's house. They thought she was the occupant of the apartment at which they were staying.

They entered the grocery shop and said, "Bonjour, Monsieur," to the shopkeeper.

He appeared to be of Algerian heritage. He politely said "Bonjour, Madame et Monsieur," back to them.

The baguettes were set in a small basket beside the counter. Just beyond them were the assorted fruits that were not on the stand outside the door. There were apricots, which they chose. There were beautiful dark cherries that they took too. Mary grabbed a small soft herbed cheese and a glass bottle of "Perrier" lime flavored water.

She chuckled to herself as she picked up the bottle remembering that time in Alabama. They were on a road trip from Tuscaloosa where Tom worked at the University of Alabama. They were heading for their escape home (occasionally one just had to escape "the deep south"!) in Bloomington, Indiana. Stopping at an interstate gas and minimart, Mary picked up a bottle of Perrier water and took it to the register. The woman at the register had no idea what the price of the water was as not too many of their clientele ever drank such fancy waters. The register woman in her loud southern voice yelled through the store microphone to someone named Clint, "Clint wha'sa price on the Pee er water?" He yelled back, "The what water?" She again yelled, "The Pee er water." Everyone in the store and down the block had to know that this was water that someone who urinated had to be drinking. Not so in Paris.

"Darn, we forgot a knife for the cheese, let's be heathens and eat with our fingers!"

"Should we get the wine?" Tom asked.

"Nope. You would be asleep with your head on my shoulder!" She smiled. All he could do was shake his head and laugh. And she would be right.

Crossing the street and heading up the hill behind the apartment building half a block, they came to the gated entrance of the small pocket park. It had a dirt play area, a large sand area with slides and seesaws, and strange animals to ride that perched on long metal springs. Park benches surrounded the sand play area and many beautiful big trees provided dappled shade to the children and mothers or nannies watching the children playing.

Looking at the back of the apartment building, Mary and Tom could easily pick out the apartment where they were staying. It had planters outside the large floor to ceiling windows with dried up looking geraniums in its planters. Those Mary would rescue. To the left side of the playground was a large fenced in space. The fence was on all sides, including covering the top. They would learn that evening this space was used for "caged soccer" played by the teenage boys. Every now and again, a teenage girl might join the play. It was rough. Exactly what one would expect from teenage boys.

They sat on a bench in the shade to eat their picnic. A few of the parents and nannies' eyes would glance at them wondering who this strange older couple was, perhaps the grandparents of one or more of the kids. But most of the parents knew most of the kids. They played here all the time. No, this was a new couple. Nevertheless, they seem pleasant and are enjoying the kids' play. The parents went back to talking with each other and not paying any attention to the nice couple picnicking.

Mary and Tom learned that at various times during the day different children would be the primary users of the park play areas. During the mornings and early afternoons, the play areas were mostly used by preschool children. In the early afternoon, the majority were primary school aged children. Late afternoon would see the park turned into mostly preteen and teenagers, except for the sand play area, which remained primarily used by small children. The small children were the ones that Tom and Mary found most entertaining.

On this day, two small children, one boy and one girl, were the ones that caught their attention. The boy, perhaps four or five, was racing around the play area acting as an airplane. With arms outstretched and watching how they sailed around, the boy did not see a three-year-old girl sitting on the ledge to the sand-box area. As the imaginary plane dipped its wings and started a circle, the plane crashed into an obstacle on the ground. The boy pilot did not realize why the crash took place. He landed in the sand. The ground object, the little girl, fell flat on the sand, face down. In a bit of shock, it took her a moment to realize that she was the object of this crash landing. Suddenly, her lips started trembling. Her eyes got bigger. The tears and wailing began. The boy pilot was trying to gather his wits and start up his engine again. However, seeing the crying girl he stood there and watched.

Two women from opposite sides of the play area approached the two children. Neither was upset by the occurrence. Both were ready to assist the two young crash victims to regain their composure so that all could go back to what they were previously doing. It only took a moment. The boy's mother held out small French pastries to the two children. The mother of the girl offered the little girl some water. Crisis over!

Mary turned to Tom and said, "Boys!" Tom replied, "She shouldn't have been playing in the airfield." She punched him lightly in the arm and asked, "How you holding up, buddy boy?" Tom replied that he wasn't, and the quick decision was made to head back to the apartment for his nap, and though he was not aware of it at the time, her search for the answer of who the mysterious lady of the painting was. She took his hand and off they went.

19

Saturday, June 22, 2019
Paris, France

NINA'S VISITOR

Nina hung the hospital room phone up from the call she had just made to Evalina. The doctor would be releasing her from the hospital in about an hour. Evalina told Nina she was on her way.

A rapping on the door took Nina out of her focus on the memory of the last 24 hours. There, standing in the doorway, was a young man in a police uniform. He was tall, dark haired, muscular, and handsome. Even from a distance, she could see his deep blue eyes. An incredible blue unlike any she had seen before except, in the recesses of her mind, the boat rescue the night before! It was the young medic from the rescue boat!

"Bonjour, Mademoiselle. You are looking better than I saw you last night. Certainly, much dryer." Nina, laughing, said, "Bonjour, Monsieur. You too are looking much different than I remember. Much less worried. Please come in. I must thank you and the others for taking care of my friend Ninette and me. Please come in and sit."

The officer moved to the chair beside the bed. "I checked with the hospital. Your friend did very well with the surgery. They said she has been awake on and off today. She does not remember much at all, as would be expected. They have her sedated and without pain. Overall, they think she is going to do very well. Have you been able to see her yet?"

"No, not yet. I'm to be released in about an hour and hope that I can visit with her then. I feel so bad for what she's going through. Do you have any more information on why someone tried to kill us? Why would some police officers do this?"

"Mademoiselle, I do not have more information that I can share with you."

What an odd statement he just made, "that I can share with you." Why can he not share information with the victim? "Please, you may call me Nina if you like."

"Fine," he replied, "and you can call me Etienne. Etienne Michel. I am a Captain with the Brigade Fluviale, and I am one of the medics, as you learned firsthand." He smiled. She smiled back.

"I'm sorry I don't have an update on the incident. It's been removed from police hands. Beyond that, not only do I not know more, but I am also under orders not to know more at this time."

There it was. Complete confirmation in a circuitous statement. This attack was a result of her work with iSPY Gallery, Evalina, LADA, and Alexei.

"It's a puzzle to me too, Mademoiselle, as I am sure it is to you. All of us on the rescue team would like to understand what and how this happened. All of the Paris Police want to find these two perpetrators. After all, they used the guise of the police to try to do this to you. Still, I have told you all I know." He smiled again.

With a sly smile of her own, Nina asked, "So, if you cannot tell me more about the incident, why are you here?" She raised one eyebrow. "For what purpose?"

Just as Catherine had been caught by Alexi's question all those many years ago, Nina now had the policeman cornered!

He broke into a laugh and said, "Nina, it is not often that I get to pull a beautiful woman out of the Seine after she has plunged from 27 meters and most of her clothing has been ripped away. My purpose? I wanted to see you again. And not for official business. But to know you are okay personally and well…"

Nina interrupted him, "No need to explain, Etienne. I am glad for this personal visit too. It is sweet of you to be here." She smiled and continued, "Perhaps when my friend Evalina gets here you can assist us getting me to her car?" She could see his disappointment. "Oh, you are on duty and have to go back to the station? I'm sorry to have presumed you would have the time."

"No, no problem. My 24-hour shift is over now. I am off duty. I was hoping that I might give you a ride home is all."

She smiled at him, thinking to herself, "I like where this is going!"

"Well, when Evalina gets here then maybe you could follow us to her home. I am staying with her for a few days until I am fully recovered. I know she would not mind if you would stay for dinner. Would you do that for a 'half-clothed rescue girl'?" They both laughed.

"Yes, I certainly can do this."

Just then, there was a slight rap on the door and Evalina began to walk into the room. Looking at Nina and the very handsome young police officer, she said, "Pardon me. Perhaps I should come back in a few minutes."

"Oh, Evalina, don't be silly. Come in. I want you to meet one of the wonderful men who saved my life last night. Evalina, this is Captain Etienne Michel of the Brigade Fluviale. He is the paramedic who worked on me last night."

Evalina was much too wise and knew that something more was happening. She decided to play with Nina and the Captain a little.

“Oh, he is the good-looking young man you told me about last night?” Evalina looked the young captain up and down. “You’re right, Nina, he is very cute!”

Nina blushed. Evalina continued her teasing, “Then he is the one who covered you with blankets after your dive into the Seine had ripped off all your clothes. Certainly, a memorable way to meet a young woman, right captain?”

“EVALINA!!” Nina exclaimed.

The captain played along. “Oui, Madame, tres memorable!”

Even with bruises all over her body and face, Nina began to turn red.

“Captain, if I might be presumptuous to ask, do you think you could assist me in getting Nina to my car when the doctor releases her? And, if it is not too much to ask, could you follow us to my home? Nina will be staying with me for a few days until she is fully recovered. And, lastly, if it is not too much to ask, could you stay and have supper with us just to be sure Nina doesn’t have a relapse? Just in case mouth to mouth resuscitation is needed?” Evalina smiled at the young couple and began to laugh.

Nina and Etienne looked at each other and began to laugh too.

“Oui, Madame, this is quite possible. In fact, I would say it is my sworn duty to do so!” They all continued to laugh, talk, and wait for the doctor.

20

January 7, 2005
University of Limoges, France

ALEXEI'S THEORY

The Eureka moment came on January 7, 2005, at 4:33 pm in Alexi's secret laboratory at the University of Limoges, France. At that precise moment for the first time in human history, the permanent storage of light took place within a fiber optic thread smaller than the thickness of a spider's web silk, which is 20 times thinner than a human hair. This particular thread of fiber optics contained a central core of "dark matter". Dark matter is an exotic particle that interacts strangely with the other particles, protons, electrons, quarks, and the nearly two dozen other subatomic particles.

Alexei's work looked at the idea of dark matter being a non-baryonic matter called "Weakly Interacting Massive Particles," or "WIMPs". Until his discovery, WIMPs were believed to only have the ability to interact with other energy through gravity. If this were the case, then as the compaction of the energy would take place the energy would fall "inward" and create a substance, such as planets, stars, and black holes.

Alexei did not think this was how the matter worked. As the fall inward would take place, energy would lose energy. Alexei's theory was that it was just the opposite: it could increase energy through absorption. That is, the dark matter energy would absorb the other energy and not make a substance, but instead would increase the total energy of the dark matter. In his particular work, the dark matter energy absorbed the light energy into its own. That is why, he theorized, the universe stays dark. All the light energy transmitted by stars, galaxies, and even your flashlight are absorbed into the dark matter energy. In effect, light becomes dark matter. Instead of being called "dark matter", perhaps the more accurate term should be "dark energy"!

His intent in doing the research was to see if there was a way to "capture" dark matter and create a "light battery". Somewhere to store light, such as sunlight, and release it when needed. This had multiple practical purposes, the most important being the end to relying on fossil fuels to manufacture electricity. There would be no need for massive electric power stations; even hydroelectric dams would be obsolete. Salmon and other fish could now swim naturally and unobstructed to their spawning grounds. Air would become clean. Smog in California, China, and India would be a thing of the past. The ozone layer would heal. World temperatures would stop rising. Much of the world's pollution problems would end. Except for the production of plastic. That was another problem to solve!

He also theorized that if information could be stored in light stored in dark matter (energy) and it took the place of computer chips, perhaps there was a way to use dark matter to process information and manipulate it as an electronic computer does. If that were possible, the entire universe could become a large data processing computer through use of all the dark matter.

A big problem he discovered was the cost of dark matter. Some experts predicted in an edition of *Popular Science* that one ounce of the material, based on the current abilities to search for it, would cost "one million trillion trillion dollars per ounce".

Those experts were not aware of the work that Alexei and his team had already developed eight years before the article was published.

Alexei and team, though not capturing an ounce, which would be a huge amount of dark matter, had been able to capture enough of it and for a lot less. They could continue to do so. The storage space was the filament of very tiny fiber-optic threads.

On this day, the small thread fiber of the dark matter he had managed to gather absorbed the light waves he transmitted with information coded into the light. The dark matter then maintained the coded energy without any loss of energy. Most amazingly, through his manipulation of energy pulses, the light energy was released in exactly the state it was first transmitted into the fiber with all the information retained. It had stored it. And, as he continued to learn, stored it indefinitely!

Although he was unable to perfect a "light battery" before his retirement, he was able to perfect a more interesting and perhaps equally important use for his research. He found he could use the very tiny threads of light information to store coded messages. Over the next few years, he continued to perfect the process. By the time Catherine died in 2010, these threads were being woven into the canvas used by LADA. No longer did she have to paint over hidden coded messages. The messages were now woven into the canvas.

In the fall of 2019, some very important messages under LADA's paintings, using this process, were delivered to a "special person" in Washington, DC. Sometime in the future, these messages would be revealed and at that time change the history of the US and the world!

21

Wednesday, September 3, 2019
Paris, France

THE WOMAN IN RED

Mary and Tom arrived back at the apartment and Tom headed for the bedroom, pulled the window curtains shut, and laid down on the duvet. The windows were open to let in the breeze. He heard the children playing in the pocket park, but he was asleep almost instantly. In the dining room, Mary sat down at the computer and began her search for what she felt she already knew: who the young woman in the painting, dressed in red, with mask in hand, was.

Mary grew up in a small town named Wardsville. It is located a few miles from the state capital of Missouri in the USA. Today, it would be called a "bedroom community" of Jefferson City. In the days of little Mary Markway, Mary's maiden name, it was just a crossroads of Missouri State Road 8 and county road W. One of her uncles owned a small store that had some groceries and assorted other things. Little Mary and her siblings, all 10 of them, would pick up soda bottles and cash them in with her uncle for candy. Mary was the second oldest of the 10 children. Her brother Marc was the oldest. Right behind Mary was her brother Dennis. Dennis was her best friend as small children until the brothers both learned that she "ran like a girl" and threw a baseball "like a girl"! "Well, I am a girl," she thought. "Get over it!" Still, it was sad for her when she lost Dennis as her best buddy.

What most people didn't know about Mary was that she was one of the smartest and well-read people you would meet. She never displayed it. In fact, you would probably think she was just a really sweet and wonderfully nice person. That, of course, was also true. However, Mary had two real loves as a child. Art and reading. Reading expanded her imagination and knowledge. Art expanded her understanding of life and spatial understanding. Combined together, you not only had a gifted artist, but also a most intelligent and knowledgeable person.

Wardsville in the late 1940s through 1960s while Mary lived there was too small for a library. Once a month, the county library van would drive to the four corners of the crossroads, at the uncle's store. The kids of the area could check out a certain number of books for the month and return them for more the next time the van came to town a month later. Mary always checked out the maximum number of books. She read them each at least one time.

Even in 2019, Mary was a voracious reader. She had read Louise Penny, her favorite writer's books, three times each. How many people do you know have read the entire Encyclopedia Britannica completely, cover to cover, as a child? Or how many people do you know who have read Emily Post three times as a child? Mary Markway had. And she read anything and everything she could get her hands on. History and art were her favorite subjects.

Today on the computer in the apartment on 10 Rue Garreau, Mary was on a search for a history about an image in a painting on the wall of the apartment . . . a piece of art . . . with a history!

It didn't take long. She found several facial likenesses of the young woman in other paintings in art museums. One of the ones she found, though the person in the painting was a few years older than the woman in red on the wall, was in a painting in The Hermitage, St. Petersburg, Russia. This portrait was done by Jean-Marc Nattier in Paris, France. Jean-Marc Nattier was one of the most successful artists at the Court of Louis XV.

The picture on the wall of the apartment at 10 Rue Garreau was, just as Mary suspected, a portrait of a young Catherine the Great of Russia.

Wait until Tom wakes up and finds out! She knew there was a story there. Evalina is a great niece of one of the greatest women of all time. How cool is that?"

Mary had no idea how really cool "that" is!

22

Friday, June 21, 2019
Russia

THE PRESIDENT'S SUSPICIONS

The Russian President was born in 1952 in the city of Leningrad, now Saint Petersburg, Russia. Educated with a law degree, he joined the KGB and served as a foreign intelligence officer for nearly 16 years before leaving the service to enter politics. In 1996, he briefly served as the Director of the Federal Security Service (FSB) until being named by President Boris Yeltsin as Prime Minister. When President Yeltsin resigned in 1999, he appointed him to be acting President, and four months later, he was elected president. He served on and off in the Presidency and Prime Minister posts until being elected under a constitutional amendment that allows for four consecutive terms as president rather than two. Expect the Russian president to be around until 2036.

Even as an intelligence agent back in the 1970s and 80s, he knew there was a sieve of information being smuggled out of the Soviet Union. That sieve continued in 2019. He was witness to the fact that the French, British, and Americans were aware of Soviet and Russian actions as they were planned well before the actions were implemented. How was this information leaking?

Russian security had found many of the source leaks, moles within the Russian spy ranks, as well as identified foreign espionage officers. That was the easy part. The question he pondered was how was this information being passed? If they could figure that out, they could not only stop the leaks but also feed them false information if desired.

As he sat in his office on that morning in June, he speculated if the artist whose art he loved and collected, LADA, might be involved. He was not a sentimental man. Somehow this old woman reminded him of his mother. They were about the same height and size, and one could tell that as young women they both were probably quite attractive. His mother died in 1998 at the age of 87. LADA at 91 was still vital and active in 2019. She was funny too, and he liked that. He liked a sense of humor, mostly his own, which he never displayed to anyone but his closest friends, of which he had few.

Still, he knew that LADA had been part of the French Resistance during the Second World War and was suspected, even as a young girl, of somehow aiding resistance fighters to smuggle information out of France to the British and Americans. How was always the question. That she did it, less so a question. That appeared to be a fact.

There was the information that had leaked about the 1979 Invasion of Afghanistan. The French, British, and US learned about the perestroika and glasnost before they became public to the people of the Soviet Union.

Information also leaked about the Chernobyl disaster. The three countries offered to give the Soviets, battling the disaster, advice even before most of the Soviet leadership had been informed about how dire the situation was. In 1991, information was passed about the fact that the Soviet Union would dissolve due to a failed Communist Party coup that would lead to President Gorbachev's resignation.

In 1994, France and its two allies knew of the Russian troop plans to enter the breakaway republic of Chechnya. The Chechnyan people were alerted and prepared. Although 100,000 Chechnyan and Russian troops died, the 20-month war would end in a compromise agreement. Chechnya would retain some of its independence. There were Russia's movements into Crimea, part of Ukraine, in March of 2014, which were somehow known by the three countries prior to the surprise attack.

No direct links to LADA. However, it was funny how often she came back to her native country to be inspired to paint. She would return to France with the finished paintings just days before the apparent information got out. His own moles inside the French, British, and American spy services fed him information on the timing as they learned it. It wasn't until his old KGB mind jumped in that he noticed how often the coincidence was that his friend LADA had been in the country and returned to Paris. He put down on paper the approximate dates of her visits and when his people learned the information leaked out. There was a vague correlation . . . not always . . . but certainly enough to trigger his alert.

Most troubling was the knowledge the three countries had of the hacking of the Democratic National Committee's computers in the US in 2016. He, with his old KGB straight face, would deny the obvious. How were these three countries getting this accurate information so quickly? What else did they know? How might it be used against him or one of his puppets, especially that one in the American White House. Better yet, how might he use the leaks for control?

His old friend LADA had been in the country just a few months before the hacking accusations came and around the time that the incidents had taken place. As he looked at the two timelines, now written on separate pieces of paper before him, he wondered, "Could it be her?"

He called the Commander into his office and gave the man the direct order to be discreet but learn as much as possible about LADA, her associates, and their actions. He wanted them followed to ensure that the artist was not a part of this effort to reveal secrets.

Although many of his day-to-day plans and actions were considered by moral people to be highly questionable, he felt no moral shame and would continue to act as he chose. This could be her excuse for her actions. She was the most ethical and honest person.

Still, one cannot have a relationship with someone who is disloyal to you. Even if his loyalty was not always returned. That unintelligent fool in Washington had at least learned that from him. It was funny how many people, followers, that guy stabbed in the back after they served his deeds. Otherwise, the man was . . . well, no other word . . . a fool.

That morning, he had no idea that there would be a major misunderstanding of the orders the Commander gave to his people and that there would be a future attempt on a young woman's life. Nor would he learn of a potential attempt on LADA, which was prevented. The Commander hoped that none of this would ever be known by the president. Fear mandated that be so.

23

Saturday, June 22, 2019
Paris, France

OUR NINETTE

The doctor stopped in Nina's room just before 3:00 pm. He told her that she could be released but that she would have to be wheeled out in a wheelchair, as was hospital policy. Since Nina's ankle was still sore, that was not a problem for her. As the doctor was about to leave the room, he turned and told them that he had checked on Ninette with her doctor. He had learned that Ninette was awake, on and off, but that she was able to have visitors.

Ninette's room door was shut but as they approached, a nurse was exiting. They asked her if Ninette was awake, and the nurse confirmed she was. Nina's doctor suggested that she be the only one to go into the room initially.

Tapping lightly on the door, she opened it just enough to stick her head inside. Lying covered on the bed was a lump of sheets and blanket. At the head of the hospital bed was a round object looking like a head but wrapped completely with bandages, except for the eyes, nose, lips, cheeks, and chin. Dark rings were around the eyes, splotches of bruising all over the exposed face, but it was not hard to see this was her good friend Ninette.

Softly, Nina said, "Hello, Ninette. It's me, Nina."

The round wrapped head turned slowly toward Nina and said, "Nina, it's you!"

Having trouble not crying, Nina replied, "Yes, Ninette. It's me. I wanted to check on you. I've been so worried about you."

"Nina, you saved my life. They told me what you did. I don't remember any of it!"

Nina explained slowly how Ninette had saved her life first and how the rescue of both girls played out. Ninette was obviously going in and out of total awareness.

Finally, Nina said, "Evalina is here too and so is the young captain of the rescue team. They came to see you."

Nina went to the door and opened it, inviting the other two in. The three stayed with Ninette for another fifteen minutes, answering questions about what had happened. Finally, they saw that Ninette was growing sleepier. It was time to leave.

Assuring her that they would be back to see her, Nina bent down and kissed her lightly on the exposed cheek. "Rest well, Ninette, my wonderful friend."

She smiled and Ninette smiled back and said, "I'll be here!" Ninette then indicated with her finger for Nina to move closer. She softly said, "He's cute! Don't throw him back in the Seine! He's a keeper!!" Then she smiled, closed her eyes, and fell asleep.

They quietly slipped out the door and Evalina and Nina looked at each other and chuckled. Etienne, caught off guard by the chuckling, said, "Have I missed something? What's funny? She looks like she went through hell. How can this be funny?"

"Etienne, we're sorry, you do not know Ninette as we do. When she said, 'I'll be here,' that was our Ninette speaking. It was her joke. Where else would she be? Of course she would be here. We were chuckling because to us that is a really good sign. Our Ninette is going to be okay!" Neither she nor Evalina wanted to tell him the rest of what Ninette had said, not yet anyway.

Helping Nina into the wheelchair, he began pushing her down the hall to the hospital front doors. Evalina retrieved her car and then Etienne followed them to Evalina's home for the continuation of Nina's rest and recovery. Of course, Etienne would be there for any need of mouth-to-mouth, which of course was practiced later that evening in the privacy of Nina's bedroom, and most days thereafter.

24

2008
University of Limoges, France

NEW TECHNOLOGY

Work progressed in 2008 on the storage process of light information in dark matter energy. Working with another laboratory in the secret facility of the University of Limoges, Alexei used the technology that lab had developed to nano-size his light pulse device.

This work had begun as early as 2001 in collaboration with Alexei's laboratory at Limoges and its sister university in the USA, the University of North Carolina at Charlotte. UNC Charlotte was a leader in the study and development of nanotechnology. The two institutions secretly had developed the microtubule filaments that held Alexei's dark matter and the device to generate the information-carrying light beam impulses into the filaments.

The UNC Charlotte laboratory had developed the nanochips for the device. Each nanochip was the total size of a dust mite or smaller. When combined, the pulse-creating device was smaller than one's pinkie fingernail. Its size made it easy to transport the device completely undetectable. It acted as a light reader and a camera, which transferred light pulses into the fiber optic thread. All one needed to do was set the device in front of a light source, such as a computer screen, TV monitor, projector screen, or other source of light and let the device capture the image and transfer it to the dark matter where it was absorbed. The data in that light, an image, would stay in the dark matter until the reverse pulses energy stimulation allowed it to be freed. It then would flow out of the thread back into the device for traditional projection onto a computer screen, TV monitor, or projector.

LADA's first canvas was tested with this technology in 2008 by transferring information of the Russian decision to back Georgian separatists. This effort, by Russia, escalated into war with Georgia. Russia and the separatists drove the Georgian forces out of South Ossetia and Abkhazia resulting in Russia recognizing both as independent states.

Although this information was received in advance of this action, as well as later acts of Russia stopping the gas supplies to Ukraine and ending the fighting against rebels in Chechnya, the NATO nations remained, for the most part, silent.

However, France and England were now aware that the new technology of data transfer worked.

25

2010
Paris, France

THE ACCIDENT

Catherine, Evalina's mother, had started the gallery, now called iSPY Gallery, in 1985, three years after Evalina was born. She, like LADA, had a twenty-year career of painting. Her paintings were much appreciated and collected. Once little Evalina came along, however, it became more difficult to paint.

Although Evalina showed the same interest in painting as Catherine had as a child, she was still a child. Trips with French easels to the countryside became more difficult. Oil paints left out in the studio became spilled, smeared, and dropped. It was time to turn more to a new profession involving painting, especially dried paintings, that of owning and running a gallery. The first artist she represented was her good friend, mentor, and teacher LADA. Her gallery specialized in Russian artists as they tended to be overlooked. The gallery would give struggling and established Russian artists a venue in a country and city known for its arts.

The gallery was at the top of the Butte Montmartre not far from the Place du Tertre located on Rue Norvins just as that road turned north to become Rue des Saules. That turn marked the beginning of the old Montmartre Village area. This area was home to struggling artists of the 1800s and early 1900s. It was home to many of the Impressionist and post-Impressionist painters, called the Fauves. Among these artists were Amedeo Modigliani, Claude Monet, Pierre-Auguste Renoir, Edgar Degas, Henri de Toulouse-Lautrec, Camille Pissarro, Vincent van Gogh, and Pablo Picasso. They all had studios and apartments on the Butte. It was the perfect location for a new gallery in 1985.

It was a three-story building situated on the northwest side of the street, as Rue des Saules joined Norvins from the north and attracted many tourists. Her gallery curved around the corner on the ground floor of the building and had large windows on both streets, allowing people outside to view the art displayed inside. Today, it houses Galerie Butte Montmartre. Catherine's gallery was quite small compared to the new iSPY Gallery.

Although the Butte Montmartre became a tourist attraction, the gallery had ambiance and the lure from the history of the art created on the Butte, which gave it a certain verve. For Catherine, it had been perfect. It was an easy walk each day from Alexei and her home on Rue Burq.

Each morning about 9:00 am, Catherine would leave her house, heading south to Rue Durantin. Durantin turned south but Garreau continued east at that point. It was at that intersection that number 10 Garreau stood. They had purchased the apartment at #10 to house the visiting artist Catherine represented. When Evalina became old enough, at age 17, the apartment became hers.

That day started much like any other day. Catherine and Alexei had croissants and cafe au lait on their back porch. From the porch, they could look south down the hill to the small pocket park where children played. Just beyond that park, they could see their daughter's apartment. Although they were separated from her by the distance of perhaps 200 yards, it was comforting to know that their daughter was close.

The large floor to ceiling glass windows of the apartment bedroom would often open at 7:00 am. A smiling Evalina would lean out over the white wrought iron railing and wave. Catherine and Alexei would smile and wave back. A comforting ritual for parents of an only child. This day she wouldn't open the window, lean out, and wave. She was on a trip to Moscow with LADA to bring back paintings that LADA had painted. Catherine would make the journey to the gallery without her pal, gallery partner, and daughter.

The day was a typical overcast morning. It started raining at 8:30 am, a half an hour before Catherine started walking. The rain was the typical Paris mist. Many Brits thought that Paris copied this rain from England. They were wrong. Paris had created this method of rain. All one had to do to prove that was true was look at the street scenes painted by the great artists Gustave Caillebotte and Albert Marquet or view the movie *Midnight in Paris* by filmmaker Woody Allen.

"Actually, Paris is the most beautiful in the rain," said Gabrielle from *Midnight in Paris*. Rainy wet streets scenes are synonymous with Paris. Fog and smog are synonymous with London.

At precisely 9:00 am, Catherine left her apartment, umbrella raised and wearing her light raincoat.

Although she had not been worried about it, she did tell Alexei and Evalina that on occasion, as she walked, she felt as though someone was watching her.

"Funny that you say that, Maman. I too have felt eyes on us as we walked to the gallery. And sometimes elsewhere."

Alexei joined in, "It is not unusual that two such beautiful ladies as mine would have men's eyes on them."

He said this but did not share his deeper thought of concern. Perhaps he should keep closer eyes on both of them. Perhaps he should be watching for eyes on himself too. This conversation had been several weeks ago. Neither of the women expressed any continued concern. He did not notice anything out of the ordinary either. However, ordinary for a place like Montmartre is by definition unordinary. Still, after that conversation, they all felt a little uneasy for a few days. Over time, the concern ebbed, and a more carefree feeling took over. A feeling of the way life always was: joyous and to be savored and lived!

Catherine passed by #10 and momentarily wished her Evalina was there and would join her. She paused only for a moment and looked at the building and the third-floor windows. The geraniums were starting to bloom. She should water them later today as Evalina had been gone for nearly a week. "On my way home, I'll do that," she thought.

As she reached the short stretch of Rue Lepic that joined up with the cut through of Rue Clement, a speeding car missed the turn of the street to the north. The car slammed into Catherine, throwing her body through the air and down the embankment into the trees and bushes.

Catherine was killed instantly the doctors, who did the autopsy, assured Alexei. She did not suffer. A very small consolation for the heartbroken man. His life as he had known it was gone. It would take him several years to accept his Catherine was no longer with him.

Witnesses said a drunk homeless man wearing a hoodie had fled from the disabled vehicle. A Volvo that had been stolen the night before from a location in the 16th arrondissement. No fingerprints could be found. That was unusual.

The witnesses' descriptions of the man were like so many descriptions when someone sees an accident or crime. He was 5'10" tall, some would say. No, he is 6'1" others would say. He was a big man weighing over 200 lbs. He was slight and frail. About the only part of the description that matched was he was a man and he wore a hoodie. He wore old ragged jeans. And he wore old 'baskets,' black basketball shoes or some type of nondescript sneakers.

Evalina and LADA, notified of the "accident" while in Moscow, canceled the rest of their trip. This included the special dinner LADA was to have with the Russian President who was just presented another of LADA's paintings by a "close" friend of the president. He understood why she could not be at the presentation. He personally expressed his condolences to both ladies by phone.

He also wondered to himself, "Was this an accident or one of his rogue agents?"

If it was, he would find out, and that person or persons would soon learn of his justice. He didn't like anyone messing with people he liked . . . unless he told them to mess with them.

26

Tuesday, September 3, 2019
Paris, France

MONSIEUR X

Opening his eyes and stretching, feeling groggy, Tom swung his legs off the bed and planted his feet on the floor. How long was he asleep? Looking at his watch, which he had set to Paris time upon takeoff from Boston, he saw that it was now 4:30 pm. Subtracting six hours, he figured it was 10:30 am West Lebanon time. He had been asleep for about five hours. Not enough to make up for a whole night of lost sleep. Added to that the time that he and Mary had traveled and been awake for breakfast . . . when was it? Nearly two days ago? He had not slept for eighteen hours. Five hours wasn't enough, but it sure helped.

He opened the curtains to the windows and watched for a few moments as the children and teenagers played in the park. Loud deep gruff voices came from the fenced in "cage soccer" field. A little high voice from the sand and swing set area. A kind of a contrast but it seemed to work. Everyone in their respective places, playing their respective games. Tom sighed. When, he thought, would he ever have that kind of energy again. Then chuckling, he said to himself, "Not in this lifetime, buddy boy, buddy boy!" A cup of dark coffee might help, however.

He opened the door to the bedroom, crossed the small entryway, and entered the living room. There he found Mary going through the open cabinets and bookshelves.

"Well, look who is finally up. How are you doing, buddy boy?"

"Pretty good. Who are you? And where am I?"

"That bad, huh?"

"Well, I'm sure by the time we are headed home in what...9 days...I should finally be adjusted to the time change. Let's just hope there are no more long-legged women sitting beside me blocking the aisle!"

"You mean little girls," she said laughingly.

"Right. No more little girls. What do you think of upgrading to business class?" They both laughed knowing that would never happen.

"How about I share with you what I have been doing while you were getting your 'beauty sleep' and then we can go out and find a fun place close by to eat dinner?"

Tom replied that it sounded like a good idea. Mary had him sit at the computer and said, "Let's look at some pictures. I think they will reveal a secret to us." She opened a website and began scrolling past several images that looked not unlike the painting of the young woman in red on the wall. She then stopped on one particular image. It was the one in the museum in St. Petersburg.

"Darn!" Tom said. "That's her!"

"Yes and look at who it says it is on the description under the painting."

"Catherine the Great of Russia? You're kidding! How did you find it? How did you know?"

"Well, being an art major helped. But reading the Encyclopedia Britannica cover to cover was actually the main guide. I had read about her in the encyclopedia when I was about ten or twelve. It had this picture in it. I remembered it." Tom looked at her with amazement but not so much surprise. She always amazed him with things she knew and read.

"Really? That is really, really cool. Catherine the Great! I wonder what that makes Evalina. How many generations do you suppose? Three or four?"

"More like five or six."

"What do you think the painting is about? I mean, it's kind of strange. Catherine is dressed in a ball gown. She is holding a mask in her right hand. But look at the mask; it is of her head from the lips up. In the mask her eyes are open wide. But on her face in the painting, it's as if they are blank spaces. Just white...unless they are turned sharply as if looking far to the left of her. And the young man looks as though his mask is more of a black blindfold over his eyes. It appears a little of the blindfold has slipped up and he can just barely see out of the bottom of it. Her lips are colored bright red. She kind of looks cunning, doesn't she?"

"Yes, you got it. I think this is a painting displaying the cunningness of her in arranging for the arrest and imprisonment of her husband, Peter III. He was killed mysteriously three or four days later and she became the Empress of Russia, the longest female ruler of Russia and one of the longest of any country in history! She was responsible for bringing education to the children of Russia, much like our public education system in the US, but a couple of hundred years before we did. She also brought culture through the arts, visual arts like painting and drawing, music, and literature. Catherine was also known to have quite a "Great" and ferocious sexual appetite. We can discuss that later tonight!" Mary said with a wink.

Mary got up from the table and walked to the bookcases behind her. "And look at what else I found." She then began showing all the astrophysics books by Alexei as well as the magazines and articles by him, all in Russian, but still impressive. "Look at all these ornate dinner dishes, full sets of gilded, hand-painted dishes. All of them are of Napoleon. Why? There is some story here for sure!"

Mary moved across the room and opened the front door. "Feel like a walk? Let's go find a place for dinner. The one next door doesn't open until seven. I'm hungry now," she said. "We can discuss my findings some more over dinner." And out the door she went with Tom close behind.

Tom quickly caught up with her and grabbed her hand. She smiled at him, and he smiled back. "Which way do you want to go?" she asked.

"We went west a block on Rue Durantin to the small grocery and I didn't see anything that way. We know that the restaurant adjoining our apartment doesn't open until 7:00 pm. I don't see anything more that way. How about we walk south on Durantin until we find something we like? That way we get a walk in too."

Mary, who was quite directionally challenged, replied, "South. How the heck do we know which way is south?" She was still smiling but Tom's complete confidence in directions drove her crazy sometimes . . . well, that's a figure of speech. However, she drove him crazy sometimes too with her telling him to try to spell a word during their occasional Scrabble games. Those games didn't happen often and she had to play him by herself, being both herself and him. What annoyed her then was he often won the games; imagine that!

"Two ways to tell," he said as they headed south on Durantin. "First, we know the Seine River is south of the Sacre Coeur, right?" She nodded yes in reply. "We know that the Sacre Coeur is on the top of the Butte Montmartre. We also know that water flows downhill. If the Seine is lower than the Sacre Coeur is, walking down the hill must be south. Durantin at this juncture with Garreau splits off and goes downhill. That must be south-ish. Also, it is late afternoon and early evening and the sun is to our right. That must be west because the sun is in the east in the morning and the west in the evening."

"Too much information. I trust you. Let's go! I'm hungry!" Still smiling but slightly annoyed at the length of Tom's answers . . . and often in what she called, "Indiana slow," how she described his speech pattern from growing up in Indiana.

Durantin ended at the corner with Rue Ravignan. Turning slightly right, they continued downhill to where Ravignan ended at Rue des Abbesses. They walked past the triangular park at Place des Abbesses. They would use this metro stop often as it was the closest to their apartment, but it had many, many stairs to climb as you came out of the tunnel and up the inside staircase of the hill.

Not finding a restaurant that seemed to have food that was calling to them, they turned right, yet again at the intersection of Rue Durantin and Rue des Martyrs. Mary had shared a book she once read with Tom called *The Only Street in Paris, Life on the Rue des Martyrs* by Elaine Sciolino. Since it is a book about the 18th arrondissement and the Butte Montmartre, Tom had read it just before their trip. He was happy and amused that she had used a postcard he had given her for birthday a few years before. The postcard was the Eiffel Tower in the setting sun with pink and purple hews in the sky as the sun cast its closing light on the tower.

In French, he had written in ballpoint pen:

Ma belle femme, Marie
Vous allumez ma tour d' Eiffel!!

Avec amour la plus profond et désir pour vous,

Vôtres pour toujours dans la grande passion

In English, it translated into:

My beautiful wife, Mary

You light my Eiffel tower!!

With deepest love and desire for you,

Yours forever with great passion

And he signed it,
    Monsieur X

He used that pseudonym often with love notes to her. He was her Monsieur X for sure and always.

At Boulevard de Clichy, a major thoroughfare, they turned right once again. Somewhat disappointed and becoming increasingly hungry, they had turned westward and on a flatter part of the beginning of the 18th arrondissement. They crossed Rue Houdon. The walk was becoming much longer than they had anticipated. Finally, they reached the Place Blanche metro station. Another metro station they would use often. Heading back up the hill toward their apartment was Rue Lepic. Long ago, they had looked at apartments on Rue Lepic as it crested the Butte. It was familiar to them.

"Let's turn here," Mary said. "If nothing else, the restaurant next to the apartment building will be open now."

Again, they turned right and headed back up the Butte. At the corner of Lepic and Abbesses to their right was a cute little restaurant just across Rue Tholoze . . . Le Nazir.

"This is it! The perfect little cute French sidewalk cafe! And look, they have Confit de Canard!"

And so they grabbed a table on the street and both ordered the duck leg and thigh roasted to perfection, with baby roasted potatoes in the duck fat (a recipe that Tom would later perfect at home in West Lebanon as a special treat for he and Mary). This would be a restaurant that became one of their two favorites on this trip. The other one would be much closer to their apartment but would also be touristy. However, it would have an incredible view of the city below. For now, they just savored the crunchy roasted skin of the duck and the perfectly roasted and seasoned potatoes. The small side salad was perfect too.

And let's not forget the crème brûlée. As Mary once said about life, "Life is like a crème brûlée. If you don't crack the crust, all you are doing is licking sugar!" Think about it!

27

Friday, July 12, 2019
Paris, France

THE CAPTAIN AND THE LIEUTENANT

Three weeks had passed since the "accident". Nina was now fully recovered and enjoying a wonderful start to summer with Etienne. Was this perhaps love?

Ninette, bandages removed, hair starting to grow back . . . a kind of burr punk rock look . . . but attractive, was well on her way to recovery. She would continue rehabilitation but was regaining all of her faculties and physical abilities except for the cast on the darn broken leg. It was healing well too, however.

Ninette was being released today to continue recovery at Evalina's home. Nina had moved back to her apartment at 10 Rue Garreau. The suite she had occupied on the ground floor of the house had been converted into Ninettes's rehabilitation suite. Occupational and physical therapists would each come by on alternating afternoons to "give her a workout." This would be exerting but fun!

Since the suite was on the ground floor, there were no stairs to climb and as she grew in strength, she would have the full range of the ground floor to stroll.

All this would happen in the next few days. For now, Nina and Etienne were headed to Ninette's room to assist her with being released.

The door to the hospital room was already open. A good sign. Nina slowly walked in with Etienne a couple of steps behind. As Nina cleared the small corner, she was met with a surprise. Etienne, not realizing Nina stopped short, banged into her from behind.

"Umph!" Nina groaned.

"Sorry! Why did you ssss . . . oh."

There sitting beside Ninette's bed was another young police officer.

"Capitan, bonjour!" he said and stood at attention. He was about the same size and height as Etienne.

"Lieutenant Guenard. What are you doing here?"

"Well, sir, it is like this. . . " He began to tell the story about how he had been concerned for the young woman he had worked on in the first boat of the rescue. He was the medic on that boat and second in command of the Brigade Fluviale to Etienne.

They usually worked different shifts. Etienne preferred the night shift as Paris was so beautiful from the water at night. Lieutenant Guy Guenard preferred the day shift. He was working a double the day of the accident as one of the other paramedics was in bed with the flu.

"So you see, I thought I would check on Ninette the next day. And, well, I guess we just kind of hit it off and I continued stopping by . . . and well, here we are."

Etienne and Nina looked at each other and started laughing. That took Lieutenant Guenard by surprise until they told him how the same thing had happened to them.

Ninette laughing too and said, "Nina, you see, I didn't want to throw him back in the Seine either. Don't you think he is cute too?" The girls both looked at the men and said together, "Oui!"

"Wait!" Ninette said while looking at both young police medics. "You mean neither one of you knew that the other was looking in on each of us?"

"Well, oui," responded Etienne.

"Why not?" Ninette asked.

"As for me, I did not want anyone else to know as I was unsure if it would be breaking police policy. That of fraternizing with someone who is part of an ongoing police investigation."

Ninette jumped into the discussion. "Yes, but neither of us is a suspect. We are the injured parties. Surely that would not be true for us, as you say, you all are not 'fraternizing' with us?"

"I'm sure that is probably true. I did not want to officially check, as I felt better about not really knowing. Playing it safe so that I could continue to see you now, Nina, and not wait."

Now Guy added, "Yes, that is true for me too. Better to plead ignorance than to miss out on seeing Ninette."

Etienne asked the two women, "What about the two of you? Did you both know about each of us seeing each of you?"

"Of course I knew that Nina was seeing you, Etienne. I told her not to throw you back," she smiled. "But I did not tell Nina that I too had a cute policeman coming to see me. I guess I didn't think it was necessary at the moment. I wanted to wait and see if Guy would continue to visit. And he did!" Looking at Guy, she said, "He makes me happy. He has checked on me every day." Guy took her hand and smiled. He added, "She makes me very happy too!" Now all four young people were smiling. What had started as a horrible attack had transformed itself into a surprisingly happy outcome. The thought of an outcome now hit Nina.

"But what about the ongoing investigation? Doesn't that still worry you both about seeing us?"

"Technically, we have never been involved with the true investigation. Our role was to save your lives. The investigation fell into the hands of the significant crimes investigation team. A police detective from that unit has questioned me on a couple of occasions about what you might have told me in the boat and in the ambulance on the way to the hospital. But that's all. I had no more information helpful to him."

"That is true for me too," Guy added.

"And, as I told Nina," Etienne said looking at Ninette, "for some reason even the significant crimes team has been somewhat suppressed in what they could not continue to do and what they can tell us. It seems for some unknown reason the investigation has fallen into the hands of the "internal and external" terrorism teams from the Directorates of Internal and External security."

This was news to Ninette and Guy. Nina had heard some of this before, of course, but the term "terrorism" was never used. The three of them looked at Etienne, and Guy asked, "Really? Do you know why this move has taken place?"

"You three now know as much as I know. We are all in the dark on any more answers of why."

Nina had her suspicions, but this was not the time to tell all of the complexity of LADA, Alexei, Catherine, Evalina, and iSPY Gallery. She would wait. For how long, that was unclear to her.

Just then, the door opened and a nurse rolled a wheelchair into the room. In her left hand, she carried a clipboard and documents.

"Your doctor has signed your release orders, Ninette. You are free to go. Would you like for me to call an ambulance to take you to the place where you will complete your recovery?" Looking at the two fit young men, Lieutenant Guy Guenard in uniform, she added, "Or do you have your own medic team here to help you home?"

Smiling, she laughed and added, "You know, you two young ladies have brought us hospital staff some fun romantic speculation. Two beautiful young women being visited by two very handsome young policemen, and medics too. Lots of the female staff are very envious of you ladies!" She added, "And lots of the male staff are extremely envious of you gentlemen, though none have the courage to make a challenge as you are both very fit . . . and armed!" They all started laughing.

"I suspect I will hand the hospital's patient over to her new medical team now. Ninette, let me give you the instructions on your medicines and on your care."

She began the instructions. The two police medics listened carefully and fully understood the medical terms. Nina and Ninette? Well, they were happy that medically trained people were with them, as the instructions seemed somewhat complicated and filled with those medical terms. They were happier, however, that now all four of them could be open with each other and could enjoy fully being together, for the most part.

Of course, there was Nina's secret and soon it would be Etienne's too.

28

Monday, July 22, 2019
Moscow, Russia

THE TRANSFER

Nearly five weeks after the "accident" Nina and LADA left for Moscow. The trip would last four days. On July 22, Nina would return to her apartment for six weeks. She, LADA, and Evalina would prepare the final materials to be shipped to the US. Nina and LADA would depart for the show of LADA's work in Washington, DC, on August 29, 2019.

Nina's apartment would remain unrented until September 3, 2019, when Natalya would open it up for Tom and Mary from West Lebanon, New Hampshire. They would be staying at 10 Rue Garreau until they departed on September 10, 2019 . . . 7 days later. Much would occur during this time frame.

The drive to Charles de Gaulle Airport seemed uneventful, as did check-in. Neither Nina and LADA nor Evalina were aware of the black Mercedes that followed them. Most sleek current model Mercedes would have sped past them showing off their powerful engines. Not this one. It and its three occupants were perfectly satisfied to stay unnoticed. The passenger who exited the car at the departure gate level would continue to be unnoticed.

He was in no rush, as his intelligence agency already knew on which flight the two women would be. A seat was reserved for him on the same flight a few rows behind them in business class. The women were in first class. No Russian intelligence officer would be permitted to fly first class unless it was absolutely necessary. Business class would have to do. Besides, they already knew the hotel the two women would be staying in and which rooms. Those had already been set up with surveillance electronics.

He and his Moscow associate would be staying in the suites on either side of the two women's adjoining suites. The orders of the "higher ups" were to observe but under no circumstances interfere and remain undetected.

What was unknown to the two men was that Nina would disappear for a couple of days to meet up with her father, her father's cousin Yuri, and a third man who was another distant relative. She would be carrying only two things on this short departure from LADA's side. She would have a special canvas among some others. The special canvas had unnoticeable micro-threads woven throughout. She also carried a small device the size of her little fingernail on her left hand. In fact, if one looked at the nail, they would not notice that it was not real and could be removed from her finger.

A few hours later after an uneventful flight, still under the careful eye of the Russian agent, Nina and LADA landed in Moscow and took a cab to their hotel. That evening they ate in the hotel dining room. The next two days would include working on a special project. It would mean each heading in a different direction and being very careful.

Nina's ability to slip off by herself came somewhat serendipitously. LADA decided to go to Konstantin Palace twenty kilometers from St. Petersburg, one of eight homes of the Russian President. It was once owned by the Romanov family. She thought this would be an extremely appropriate subject. LADA took her drawing materials and watercolors to do preliminary sketches. She would begin the finished painting in the hotel suite. Those she finished when she was back in Paris before they left for the USA. She was gone for the two days that Nina disappeared.

The next morning, the two ladies left by cab together to go to the airport. Two agents were assigned to keep track of the women. One of the Russian agents stayed monitoring the hotel rooms. Both women were headed to the same place, they thought. The second agent followed them in a taxi. This was the first of the agents' mistakes. Only LADA was catching the airplane to St. Petersburg. Nina was not. She would stay in the taxi and not return to the hotel. Instead, she instructed the driver to take her to the train station.

As LADA got out of the taxi with Nina, Nina kissed the old woman's cheek and to the shock of the agent exiting his taxi, Nina got back in the taxi and sped off. The agent realized the mistake. They should have had three agents. One assigned to each woman and one to remain at the hotel. Damn! How to tell this to the Commander? Perhaps nothing should be said. The two agents would have to figure that out later. For now, the agent scurried to catch up with LADA and find which flight she would board. Damn, she moved fast for an old woman!

Inside the train station, Nina bought a ticket to Mtsensk, the nearest train station to her father's village. Nina purchased a cheap disposable cell phone and calling card in the gift shop. She made a phone call to her father letting him know she was catching the 8:47 am train to Mtsensk, leaving in 15 minutes. Her father told her that he and his cousin Yuri and another man would be at the Mtsensk train station waiting. A quick "I love you" from both ends of the phone call and Nina went to claim her seat on the train. In her hand she clutched a small overnight bag and the bag containing canvases, one which would become LADA's most valuable and important painting ever created.

The second mistake that the agents made was following LADA, whom they thought most important; they were wrong. The agent with LADA witnessed her sketching and painting with watercolors for two days. Had he followed the unimportant young woman he might have observed her meeting with three men, all of them watching computers, monitors, film screens, and playing with the removable little fingernail of the young woman. The Russians had thought of her as only iSPY Gallery help. Someone who had been "accidentally" nearly killed by a couple of the Commander's lesser agents. Not ones as skilled as he and his partner.

At the check in agent stand, LADA purchased an open-ended round-trip ticket to St. Petersburg on the 9:00 am flight, 45 minutes away. The agent did the same thing at another ticket agent's counter. She didn't notice, he was sure. What he didn't know was that this crafty old "Resistance fighter" had noticed him. She had picked him up on her radar as soon as he exited his cab. She decided to make sure he had an extensive and boring two days in St. Petersburg! She was sure no one followed Nina in the taxi when it left the airport. They had followed the decoy. Just as she expected they would.

The agent hoped this old artist would spend one night in St. Petersburg. He had packed one extra pair of undershorts. The silk kind that women like, though it had actually been some time since he had been with a woman…other than the ladies of Minsky's. Heck, for the right price they would approve of him in anything, except for those tight white things that some Americans wore. He liked style. He liked to hang free! He felt he was a true Russian man! After all, he carried a gun, two if you count the natural one. That always pleases the women. Natural and steel. A real man. A true faulty male ego but one he would never understand. Male egos are that way.

Nina's train left the station in Moscow right on time. The countryside flashed by quickly as the train exited the suburbs of Moscow. It only made four stops along the four-and-a-half-hour trip. Between Moscow and Mtsensk was the typical southern Russian country. The trees, mostly evergreen and white birch. The land, pretty flat. Lots of small ponds and swampy ground. Villages of mostly farmers. An occasional industrial plant. Countryside that you could find in many European countries. Places once devastated by the Second World War were now revitalized by modern Russia.

Still, there was poverty, shanties, and other signs that life was not equal for everyone. There were "have and have nots," just like in most countries. In the countryside of Russia, the have-nots were very visible. Farm town people scrapped by. Nina's parents seemed to be farm people who did that. This was part of the reason that they as a family remained safe and secure. No one suspected their history. No one knew who they really were or what they and their young Nina now did. Was that changing? Were they going to continue to be safe and secure? Was their daughter, Nina, safe? Now that the accident had happened, her maman and papa were unsure. That was unsettling to them.

As with its departure, the train rolled up to the beige building trimmed in white, right on time. It, like the Moscow station, looked clean and well kept. She learned from her parents that services were limited, however. You could only purchase tickets three hours a day and often those times were not followed. Good thing she had purchased the roundtrip ticket at the Moscow station and in cash. No one could use her credit card information to find where she had gone. No one could link her to a visit to her parents, hopefully. She did not want that to happen. She wanted to ensure they would remain secure.

Meanwhile, LADA arrived at her hotel in St. Petersburg. Although she was not a practicing Orthodox Catholic, she thought a bit of quiet reflection would be good for the agent. She headed out with her art supplies for St. Isaac's Cathedral, the largest Orthodox Basilica and the fourth largest cathedral in the world. Here, she sketched for a couple of hours and made life boring for the agent. She had great fun and had some good sketches to work on paintings from this trip to Russia.

Later that afternoon with the setting sun, she did similar preliminary works on the Konstantin Palace. She returned to the palace the second day around the same time to complete her preliminary work. This was after having spent most of the day painting River scenes of the Neva River. She smiled to herself thinking how frustrating this was for the agent, watching an old woman paint.

As Nina stepped down off the train, she saw the distinguished blond-haired man of nearly sixty years smiling at her. He was indeed handsome. He was tall, like his daughter. Blue eyed, like his daughter. Blonde, like his daughter, though his hair was starting to thin in the surprising way that it made a handsome man even more handsome. Standing beside him were two other men. One was a man about her father's same age. The other man, perhaps ten years younger. Which one was Yuri? She all but ran to her father, dropped her luggage to the ground, and leaped into his arms. Hugging each other and kissing each other's cheeks, they finally relaxed. Still in his arms, he held her back just a bit and looked at her. Beautiful as ever, he thought. And then said, "Your Maman and I were worried about you. What you told us about the accident was . . . how should I say this to my daughter . . . a bit understated! We read about more of it in the Paris newspaper, Le Monde. Others who had access to more information briefed us. Are you sure you're okay?"

She smiled at her papa. "Papa, I am fine. It was scary. The friend who saved me received the worst of the injuries. She is doing all right now. She is at Evalina's home resting and rehabilitating. She will be fine, just as I am."

Letting her go, he turned to the other gentleman and introduced them to Nina. The man about her papa's age was indeed Yuri. The younger man was introduced as Daniel. No last name was given. He was the one who was providing the information to be transferred to Nina.

They headed out of the station to the silver 2014 Hyundai Solaris. It was small but large enough for the four of them. Cars needed to be small on the side roads of Russia as they are only wide enough for one car. Most European side roads are that way.

Nina opted to sit in the back with her scrunched-up father. Back seat sitting was not made for a man who was 6' 2". He would put up with it, however. Yuri, the smallest of the men at about 5'10", sat in front of her father and drove. The third man, Daniel, constantly searched around them watching for something out of the ordinary while sitting in the front seat beside Yuri. Convinced that there was no one following them, Daniel told Yuri to begin the drive. Daniel kept monitoring the mirrors as they drove from the station and out of Mtsensk.

They headed to the forests outside of a much smaller village and to an old stone house some miles from anything. It had its own power supply from a good generator, which was hard to find in Russia. It was mostly "off the grid," totally self-contained and efficient.

They wound through the Russian countryside, past evergreen forests and seemingly going ever more uphill. As good as Nina was with directions, she was totally lost at the direction they were headed. That was good, she thought. If ever anyone wanted to get the location out of her, she would have no idea what to tell them. It was a mystery to her.

The trip took well over an hour, perhaps two. No one in the car said a word. Daniel was ever vigilant. She suspected under his jacket he was armed. Actually, she suspected that of all three men, even her father. What they were doing had serious consequences. They all knew it, including Nina. For some reason, however, she was not worried or afraid. She knew what they were about to do was important. Important for the future of Russia and more important for the future of France, England, the United States, and the world.

Finally, they arrived at the small stone farmhouse. Inside was an open living area, including a small kitchen with wooden dining table that could seat six. There were also six chairs that went with the table. An old cloth-covered couch and similarly covered chair and a coffee table were the extent of the furniture, except for the cupboard, which had old chipped plates, metal cups, and a few pieces of silverware. Everything was woodsman primitive. Probably hand made by the person who owned the place, if he was still alive.

The cabin had three small bedrooms. One for Nina with a twin bed. One for Daniel with an army cot. Lastly, one that had two more army cots for Nina's father and his cousin Yuri. Looking at the bedding on all the beds, Nina knew she would be sleeping fully clothed tonight. In fact, she probably would be using her overnight bag or purse for a pillow. Shower or bathe in the place . . . no, not really. There was a small stream a few hundred feet from the shack that had crystal clear water for bathing, unless you just wanted a short rinse with the large enamel pan by the stove and bucket beside it to fill with water. Nina thought if this stretches into two nights, perhaps she'd use the stream; otherwise, she would wait to clean up at the hotel suite the next evening. A bath there would be welcomed!

The men all began their work. They set up equipment, laptop computers, and monitors. Really, the monitors would be useless as the thirty hours of video, twenty hours of audio tapes, and five thousand pages of documents had already been digitized onto several flash drives.

The drives could have been used to transfer the data to the recipient nations, though they would have to use many. The chance they would be intercepted was high. The ability to intercept, play, and understand the data loaded into the dark matter in miniscule threads on a canvas under a painting. Impossible! The threads of the painting held an astronomical amount of data. Much more than even the best contemporary hard drive, which would be too large and easily detected.

Each flash drive was loaded into the USB port of the laptop. As it downloaded the data through the laptop, it passed into a second flash drive device. That was only a shell. That device was merely an adaptor that allowed the small thread in the artificial fingernail to receive the data. After the thread was attached, the fingernail was slid into grooves on the inside of the larger part of the flash drive holding the fake finger in place.

The information passed from one flash drive to what appeared to be a second flash drive. No data actually entered the hard drive of the computer. It only acted as a pass through. Attached to the back end of the fake flash drive, a second small hole allowed one special micro thread from the canvas to be inserted. To do this, Nina had to use special jeweler glasses to insert the thread. Once that was done the hook up for data transfer was completed.

As the data flowed from flash drive to canvas, the screen of the laptop shined bright white. As long as it stayed white, the data was flowing at the speed of light. If one could pause the data, the screen could show the video images. It was impossible to do with the equipment they had. It would take the equipment back in Alexei's Limoges lab to be able to release the data light in a fashion to be viewed as other than bright white light. The total time to store the material in the canvas took only a few hours. The most time-consuming part of the operation was putting the flash drive into the machine, taking it out, and putting in the next.

It was good that the images were unable to be viewed by the three of them, Daniel thought. Some would be particularly hard for Nina and her dad to see together. The video images not only were of "high level" meetings of the two most powerful men, but they also contained very disturbing sexual fetish materials in which the American one participated.

The Russian had made sure the compromising material was exactly what he wanted. This was his ultimate leveraging material. The meetings and audio recording of phone calls? Those were just supporting materials. The videos. Powerful!

The Russian knew all he had to do was figure out exactly when to let the American know he had them and how he was going to do that. He wanted it to be at the most vulnerable time for the American. That man was now fully owned! This took place in 2015, 2016, and 2017. So in 2016 and 2017, knowledge of the videos were allowed to start leaking out.

He timed the release to hacks into important American, German, French, and British websites. The hack into the one in America caused the most positive result for the Russian. Pre-November 2016 seemed to be the best date to begin the leak. That's when he allowed it to start, that summer and early fall.

Of course, there existed stuff on the American and hacks on American websites even before this. None of that material had the same potential as what was assembled over the last three years. All of this recent stuff was carried out by the Russian's former KGB associates, now in important SVR positions. They owed their loyalty to the Russian and their lives. He wouldn't ever let them forget that. The old Soviet Union was dead? No, it had just been sleeping. He was re-erecting it. Feeding it was his own kind of Viagra! His Russian male ego liked that analogy. It was the perfect image. The Russian Erection!

What the Russian didn't know is that now all of this information was in the hands of the team with Nina. Soon this information would be shared with the French intelligence MI6 German intelligence and perhaps the CIA. If the Russian thought that he alone owned the American, he and his SVR associates were vastly mistaken.

While Nina and the team were doing the transfer, LADA was finishing her first preliminary sketches and watercolors of the Konstantin Palace. In the early evening, the light beige building took on a hue of soft terracotta, almost dusty pink. The shadows played marvelously with the white architectural accents on the cornices and window trims. The clouds rippled with alternating pinks and purples. The sky told of a later stormy night. Should she add rain to the scene when she finished the oil version of the painting? Well, perhaps.

She packed up her watercolor paints and paper and headed back to the main entrance of the drive. The taxi she had arranged would be there at 6:30 pm. It was already 6:25 pm. She would have to scurry. "Let's see if my friend can keep up," she thought. "Oh, yes, that's right. He will have to run." He left his car in the parking lot outside the front gate. She chuckled to herself. A run would be good for keeping this agent in shape. His large gut was showing.

The transfer of data to the canvas was completed by 11:00 pm. Nina realized it was too late for the treacherous drive down the narrow, curvy, and dark dirt, gravel, and paved road. They would leave the house first thing in the morning. Sleeping fully dressed was the only option. She would have a shower or bath once she returned to the hotel in Moscow.

She stored the newly loaded canvas with the four others she was carrying. On two, she had sketched pencil outlines of forest scenes viewed on the long drive. Her cheap cell phone had provided enough photo images to allow her to imagine fake scenes. She did not want any actual scene to be reproduced just in case she was caught. She also eliminated the photos from her phone. There was no "cloud" backup for these photos.

While she had done the sketches, her father had put together a quick and simple meal for the team. Hard bread and soft cheese, a piece of fruit each, and a bottle of wine and water to share. No one wanted to drink too much, Daniel and Yuri particularly. They shared the watch through the night. Nina and her father offered to serve their own share. The two men refused this. They would be fine.

Nothing happened that night nor the next day as they drove Nina back to the train station. All their work had been accomplished without a problem.

Nina and her father got out of the car at the station. He helped her carry her bags to the station platform. She could have easily done this herself. Her father wanted time alone with her, however. As they stood together, her father took her close in his arms and spoke quietly to her.

"Nina, maman and I have decided that this is the last we are doing this kind of work. Your accident has caused us great concern for you and for us."

Nina tried to interrupt but her father continued, "We have decided we too are going to leave Russia. We are going to move to France too. We are doing this next week. It will look as if we are going on vacation, but it will be a long and most needed vacation. Daniel and Yuri already know of this decision, and they are supportive of us. They too realize we have done all we can do to save Russia. Until that man is no longer in control, it is not our Russia…the Russia we love."

Nina looked at this strong man. She knew her father. His decision was made. She suspected her mother was set about this too. It will be good that they were through with the struggle to help their country to be all that it could be.

"Will you move to Paris?" she asked hopefully.

"No, sweet one, we will find a place in a small town in the north of France near Normandy. Close enough to visit you from time to time. Distant enough to not interfere with your own life. Cool and not unlike the weather we are used to. We think we could vacation in Paris and the south, but we will never live there."

"You know that I would love to have you close to me. Paris is large. We can find enough separation there."

He smiled, "Yes, but the life of a farm couple serves us well. We can talk more about it once we are in France. For now, let's get you on the train and on your way. I see it now."

The train rolled quickly into the station and stopped. Passengers departed and then Nina and a couple of other travelers got on, but not before a long embrace and kiss on both cheeks. They smiled. She was off to finish the mission.

How had it all started two years ago for her? How did she not know what her father and mother really did? How did she not imagine the interesting and full life she would lead? How much longer would she be involved with this work?

Both women returned to the hotel that day. LADA with enough sketches and watercolors to begin oil paintings. Nina returned with the data-loaded canvas and three others with preliminary sketches of fictitious landscapes. LADA used her imagination to complete final oils on those canvases back in Paris. On the data-filled one, she thought about what image she would paint once back in the studio. Another painting of the Tsar's Palace, copied from her watercolors and sketches? No, something more meaningful. Something symbolic. Then she decided!

She decided to do one other painting. It would be a future gift for the Russian president. It would be the scene of the Bolshoi Theatre, the president's cultural pride and joy. Sure, he didn't like opera. And the dancing was for sissies. Give him a white Tresky horse to ride bareback any day. Shirt off, of course.

She knew he would enjoy this painting. She would too. It would be LADA's final gift to him. The audience applause she would paint would not be as he thought for the musicians and performers. No, she would be painting applause for the ruse that had been played on him. And for her performance all throughout his presidency.

As soon as Nina arrived at the hotel, she drew a long bath to soak off the feeling of the small stone cabin and what must have grown there. Warm, relaxing, and refreshing. LADA arrived a few minutes after she was out of the bath.

When LADA and Nina kissed each other on the cheek at the airport, LADA had quickly whispered that only one agent had followed them. It was important that Nina come up with a cover story of where she had been that night. Their hotel room was most assuredly bugged. LADA would play along with whatever the story Nina invented.

"How did your painting go? Were you able to find some pleasing subjects?"

"Yes, I am most pleased with the color of the sky at the Konstantin Palace. I did some landscapes, riverscapes, and a preliminary sketch from memory of the Bolshoi for the president!"

"LADA, I picked up those additional canvases you wanted. They are by the closet door."

"Thank you. I will sketch my preliminary thoughts before we go out to dinner. What was your night like last night without the old watch dog?"

"You are not an old watch dog. But, still, some things a young woman should keep secret, especially from an old watch dog." She smiled at LADA. "I'll tell you more at dinner. Where should we go?"

"I made reservations for us at my favorite place, Cafe Pushkin. They are for 7:00

pm. That will give me two hours to begin the President's painting. I must get my first coat on quickly." She winked at Nina. Nina understood. If someone were to think an important painting was suspicious, LADA's comment would lead them to suspect that painting. The really important one would only have a preliminary sketch on it like the rest of the canvases.

LADA took out her small tabletop easel and oil paints. She put a small 12" by 16" canvas on it and wrote her secret message and then a quick coat of the special acrylic paint she used on smuggled messages. Then she quickly sketched over the acrylic after copying the draft sketch she had made of the Bolshoi Theater the night before. The sketch completed, she began a light wash of oil paint leaned out with solvent to the near consistency of watercolors. She began the first fat layer just before leaving for dinner. Good thing they made odorless solvents now. Turpentine and other solvents were terribly smelly. She loved the smell of the oil paint, however. Nothing smells better than that linseed oil . . . no perfume . . . nothing!

The first coats finished, the women dressed and headed out the door. The taxi got them to the restaurant right on time. The agent was already there and seated close to their table. He was a different one than the one who had followed them to the airport.

The women knew their room would be searched while they were at dinner. LADA had set small trap alerts to let them know what had been searched. A strand of hair here. A piece of paper with another corner of a paper pointing to a specific letter of a word on the other paper. Tricks she had learned in the resistance long ago, though really the traps weren't needed. They knew their suite would be searched. Heck, almost every room in Russia was searched these days.

Dinner was wonderful as usual at Cafe Pushkin. LADA had identified the follower immediately and indicated secretly at which table he was seated. They made small talk. Nina told the made-up story of the one night stand with a man she only knew as Peter. LADA, of course, chastised Nina for being so foolish but asked for details, which Nina refused to tell.

Convinced that the agent had heard every word of the false tale, following an incredible dessert and wonderful meal, the women headed back to the hotel to subtly check their traps. As expected, all had been tripped. Someone had indeed searched their room.

As suspected, special attention had been made of the President's painting. A small smear revealed that. LADA would have to repair that once they were back in Paris. She didn't want to alert the agents of her knowledge of the search. She and Nina suspected they were being monitored by a video camera. It was a bit disconcerting to the women to know strange men's eyes might be watching their every move. Very disconcerting! Good thing their flight left Moscow mid-morning. They didn't want to push their luck much further. Returning to Paris couldn't happen soon enough.

29

Monday, July 22, 2019
Paris, France

THE ASSIGNMENT

While Nina and LADA were in Russia, Etienne was requested to attend a meeting in the office of the Préfet de Police Headquarters at Place Louis-Lepine. At the meeting were three other people: the Director-General d'Armee, Director-General of the National Police, and Director-General for External Security. Etienne wasn't sure if he should be worried, but he certainly was confused. The Director-General d'Armee spoke first.

"Captain, it has come to our attention that you have a 'special relationship' with a young woman by the name of Nina. Is our understanding correct?"

Etienne considered the question. Surely, these three important leaders could not be gathered to discuss the potential infraction of an officer fraternizing with a victim. That would be insane. He still wasn't sure that this was really in violation of rules. This had to be about something else more serious. Be honest and direct he told himself but lost as to where his answers might lead. He answered honestly.

"Yes, this is true. We are friends." He saw the look on their faces and added, "We are close friends, special friends."

Realizing Etienne's uncomfortable position, the Director-General d'Armee replied, "Good, that is what we hoped!" Now Etienne was completely confused.

"Pardon?"

"We hoped you would say that you were in a special and close relationship with Mademoiselle Nina, as we need your assistance, and so does she."

Etienne's confusion mounted. "But why? For what purpose? Is she in danger?" His thoughts went back to the accident, to the conversation with the detective, and with the removal of the police from the investigation.

"This has to do with the 'accident,' no? She is in danger, yes? And this has national intelligence concerns! Otherwise, the three of you would not be here. Yes? How am I to help?"

"We need to activate you to your military position as captain in the army intelligence and assign you to the division of external intelligence. That is why my colleague is here. You will report directly to him. Your assignment is to stay close to mademoiselle and will lead a team to protect her. Your relationship gives you a natural cover. Eventually she will be informed of your assignment so there is no confusion. You will also be part of the team to protect this artist LADA. Do you know her?"

Etienne replied that he did.

"You are to accompany both women to the United States for an art exhibition of LADA's works. This is a cover for a mission to deliver top-secret information to two US Government agencies, the CIA and the FBI, as well as a Special Prosecutor. You will be fully briefed shortly. First we need your acceptance of this mission. Do we have that acceptance?"

Are you kidding? Will I accept protecting Nina? Without hesitancy! "Yes, you have my acceptance!"

"Good. You can choose two other members for your team. You will also have a member of the CIA, a member from the FBI, and one each from French Intelligence and British MI6. In total, seven members of your team. You will be the team leader. The other six will report to you.

“Each agency will give you a full briefing over the next several days. We suggest you choose your other two members within two days. Your team briefings begin in three days. The team should be assembled by then.”

“You will leave on the mission in three weeks. Some team members will be in place in the US by that time. Is this clear?” Etienne replied it was.

“Good. Thank you for your willingness. Hopefully, this will not be a totally unpleasant assignment.” Small smile. “If there are no further questions and no one of the other directors has a comment, we will adjourn the meeting.” He surveyed the table of members. No one motioned they had a question or comment. Satisfied he said, “Meeting adjourned.”

The other members got up and left the room. The Director-General d’Armee motioned for Etienne to stay for a moment.

“Captain, congratulations! You are working on perhaps the most important assignment of intelligence of the twenty-first century. The young woman and her companion will be carrying information that will change the world in the coming years. It involves damaging information on the Russian President and his counterpart in the United States. It is imperative that it is kept safe.

I wanted you to stay for a moment so that I could give you information on your two American team members.” He handed Etienne the first of two 8 ½” by 11” envelopes.

“Let me first tell you about the artist LADA and her importance to France. It started in World War II . . .” he continued to fill the captain in on the history of LADA and how she had helped to save France, England, and the free world through coded messages under the paints of over a thousand paintings. Then he proceeded with information on the first members of Etienne’s team.

"The first one is a member of the FBI. She is a woman that Mademoiselle Nine already knows. She is the primary head instructor at an ESL school in Miami, Florida. Mademoiselle has no idea that her instructor is actually an FBI intelligence operative. She is highly skilled in martial arts and in weaponry. You will find all of the specifics of her qualifications in the documents inside the envelope. Her work at the ESL is to help us locate good field agents for the US agencies, the British, and ours. The whole story about how Nina was chosen you will learn over time. She does not know the whole story."

He looked at the captain to see if there was any question. He added, "Two of your team are women. The FBI agent and this second one." He handed the second envelope to Etienne.

"Her name with the CIA is Mrs. Smith. She is part of a supposed husband and wife team of agents who go by the last name Smith. Not very original, for sure. She, like the first member, is extremely gifted in hand-to-hand combat and all types of weapons. Both these ladies served on the American Olympic pistol team at different Olympiads. They won either gold or silver medals a couple of decades ago. You can be sure that they will be strong members of your team. Mrs. Smith operates out of Paris and will join up with you in the US around the time that the art show begins.

You will meet them both at the first briefing in three days. Until then, I suggest you familiarize yourself with the details in these two vitas. Please begin immediately your selection of the other two who you wish to serve with you. Any questions?"

"No. Okay, congratulations again, Captain. You will do France and the world proud."

Etienne saluted the Director-General, who saluted back. Etienne pivoted sharply and left the room, wondering when he would breathe normally again.

30

Tuesday, July 23, 2019
Moscow, Russia

NEVER ALONE

Nina and LADA didn't waste any time getting to the airport. The two wet paintings were specially packed in plastic-covered trays. Spacers ensured the paintings were kept from smearing then packed in hard cases with the other canvases. All were taken aboard the Air France flight as carry on items. LADA's remaining painting supplies had to be left behind with the hotel manager.

The case had to be opened passing through security. It was all handled very professionally. LADA had made this same trek many times. Most of the security agents knew her. Her screening didn't take long, not nearly as long as Nina's. LADA suspected the security agents just wanted to spend more time with this lovely young woman, even if it caused the young woman discomfort, which of course wouldn't advance the agent's efforts to get to know her. "How dumb men can be," LADA mused.

They were at the airport early and tried to act normal. LADA could not detect who or where the watchers were, she just knew they were there. Perhaps they were using the airport security cameras. It was important to act normal. Eat a small breakfast in the Air France Club after checking out the duty-free stores. Neither one purchased anything.

When it was time to board, they were in line with the other first-class passengers and boarded quickly. The time spent in the plane as all the passengers boarded and the luggage was loaded seemed to take forever. Finally, the cabin doors were closed and sealed. A few minutes later, the Air France flight crews gave their briefings, and the plane was pushed back from the gate.

The engines took over and the plane moved ever so slowly. Finally, it was "next for takeoff". The engines revved, and the plane started moving forward down the runway. Faster and faster. The nose of the plane lifted slightly, a feeling of the earth letting go of the wheels, and suddenly they were airborne. Climbing slowly at first and then steeper, a slight turn left. Now a steeper climb and continued left banking turn. The airport disappeared behind them out the window. The plane continued its climb to cruising altitude at 35,000 feet. It was a safe and non-turbulent flight. An hour later, they crossed out of Russian airspace. Nina felt like she could fully breathe again.

LADA subtly checked out all the passengers in first class. They really couldn't see much of the area in business class from their first-class seats. LADA smiled and winked at Nina as she noticed the younger woman watching her. Nina, for her part, was watching out of amazement. Here was this 90-year-old woman under complete control, using the skills she acquired as a kid over 75 years ago, to ensure their safety. What a woman! "Could I be like her?" Nina wondered. "Will I live to be 90?"

LADA didn't tell her until after they landed and headed to the gallery that she had spotted four agents all sitting in first class with them. This surprised and concerned Nina. LADA told her that two of the agents were French External Security agents that she had known for some time. The other two agents were a man and woman, probably CIA. They learned at the first team meeting these were the Smiths. Overall, she told Nina, it appeared they were in good capable hands. This also meant whatever information had been loaded into the canvas was much more important than they had realized!

Back at the gallery, Nina and LADA put the nearly finished painting of the Theater into a small valis. LADA took it home to her studio to finish. Eventually, it would be hung in Nina's apartment until the appropriate time for LADA to present it to the Russian president. She would let him know in advance that she had painted something special for him. If he only knew how special its meaning was. It was a painting that caught Mary and Tom Martz's attention too in more ways than one.

The rest of the paintings were taken to the back of the gallery. LADA worked on them over the next few days in a small studio she had there. Those paintings would be sent on with them to the US for display at the show. Among these was the one with the stored information.

Unbeknownst to the two women, the French intelligence was already monitoring the studio, gallery, and the surrounding area to ensure that the pieces would remain safe. This was true of the President's gift painting too. It would be monitored in Nina's apartment. Ultimately, that fact would prove to be a significant problem for the Russian Intelligence Commander. Too bad it was protected by the French. Someday the Russian President might actually learn of the message it contained.

31

Tuesday, July 23, 2019
Paris, France

ETIENNE'S TEAM

It didn't take Etienne long to pick the last two members of his team. One he had known quite well for some time. The other, he had met briefly. He arranged for meetings with the two men separately. They met at the same conference room where he had met the three director generals, the Préfet de Police Headquarters at Place Louis-Lepine.

His first meeting was with Lieutenant Guy Guenard. The briefing to both men was the same succinct one he had received. At this time, he really didn't know more. What he did know was that he trusted the lieutenant. He liked the man. And he knew that Guy was very capable with weapons, self-defense, and medical knowledge. Etienne hoped none of those skills would be necessary. Still, it would be good to have his second in command from the Brigade Fluviale with him.

Guy showed up with the same perplexed feeling that Etienne had. He didn't know why they met at a place other than their own headquarters on the Seine. He also found it mysterious, and a little troubling, when Etienne was unwilling to share with him over the phone the purpose of the meeting. Etienne was his friend and was also his commander, so he trusted that the meeting was not going to be a hard one for him...he hoped.

Etienne was in the conference room when Guy arrived. It was a small conference room used for squad meetings. The table only had eight chairs around it. Etienne was seated at the table as Guy entered. He stood up and offered his hand to Guy, smiled, and indicated for Guy to take a seat. Nothing unusual, though Etienne was not in uniform so they didn't attempt a salute. A handshake, less formal, opened the way for a non-threatening atmosphere.

"Pardon, Captain, should I call you by your rank or is it okay for me to call you by name? Eh, Etienne? Capitan?"

Both men smiled. "By all means, Guy, let's use names. I think you will find this meeting as interesting as I did a day ago. But we are friends first and foremost which is not an insignificant reason that I asked you to meet with me."

"Well, now you have my interest really stirred up! What's going on?"

"Guy, this has primarily to do with Nina, though Ninette, as we know, is involved too. It also involves the iSPY Gallery, the owner, Evalina, and her father, Alexei, a very special artist who I will inform you about, and information regarding some misdeeds of two of the most powerful people in the world. Are you ready for this?"

"This all has to do with the accident, yes?"

"Yes, that's part of it. That is probably how we got involved professionally, but there's much more. Let me share with you what I know. I am asking you to be part of an international security and intelligence team I have been assigned to lead. You will attend a meeting of the seven team members and the Director-General d'Armee and others to brief us on our mission. Does this sound of interest to you?"

"Wow, are you kidding? Yes, I'm interested. If I am half as interested in the rest of what you tell me as I already am, you have my unconditional acceptance of being on the team. Tell me what you can."

"Let me begin by giving you a bit of history about this artist LADA and her involvement with the underground during the Second World War. Her story plays into this situation."

Etienne began the story of LADA and the loss of her parents, her adoption by the underground, and especially the singer-dancer Josephine Baker. He told Guy how the underground used LADA's paintings to send information on the Germans to the Allied commanders in England. How the French, British, and American intelligence agencies still use her paintings to deliver important information regarding the Russians. He then told her of the link to iSPY Gallery through Alexei and his wife Catherine, and how Catherine had been killed in 2010 by a speeding drunk driver similar to the accident that occurred with Nina and Ninette. He told of Evalina's ownership of the gallery and how Nina became involved.

Throughout their mission, they would not learn of the fiber optic thread of dark matter and the light energy information it stored. They were left to assume the information was on the canvas in the traditional way it had been done since LADA and Josephine Baker had invented it.

Etienne shared with Guy the vitas of the two female members of the team, both American, one CIA, the other FBI. He told him that two other members at the big briefing in two days were a member of French External Intelligence and the other a member of the British MI6. There would be seven members in all, including Etienne and Guy.

"Who is the seventh member?" Guy asked.

"I'm meeting with him later today to give him the same briefing that I have just given you and to ask him to volunteer to join us. I think there is little doubt that he will."

"So, who is he?"

"He is the lead inspector who was in charge Nina and Ninette's case. He was pulled off the case and his operation closed down following the finding that the perpetrators were Russian Intelligence agents. His name is Chief Inspector Marcellus Bonnet."

"What? This is true? About the Russian Intelligence agents?"

"Well, it is just speculation on my part at this point, but all the information I have learned points in that direction."

Etienne explained he came to this conclusion because of the police investigation being closed down and handed over to external intelligence. Then he mentioned the involvement of a Russian gallery, its Russian French owner, the Russian artist LADA, the fact that Nina is Russian, and she and LADA are on a trip to Russia all pointed to speculation of Russian intelligence involvement.

"Etienne, I hate to ask this, but you don't suppose . . . How can I say this my friend . . ."

"That Nina is a double agent?" Etienne smiled and said, "No my friend, I'm sure of that. She and her employer are related. Nina has retold me some of the history of the family, but she doesn't know all of it. She does know enough to say there is no love of the family for the current head of the Russian government. She loves her homeland but the homeland as it was before Stalin, Khrushchev, and now this current president. No, she is not a double agent, of this I am sure. And it's not because she is special to me. It is because of my police intellect telling me so."

Guy smiled back at Etienne. "Etienne, that is good enough for me. I appreciate your asking me to be a part of this important mission, even if we don't know all the facts yet. If it is for France, for the Free World, and my good friends Etienne and Nina, I accept the honor and responsibility. You know I will do everything possible to assist you in seeing this mission through successfully."

The two men shook hands. Even though Etienne was not in uniform, Guy saluted his superior officer. Etienne saluted him back and Guy pivoted and exited the room.

Etienne thought to himself, “If only the next recruiting of Chief Inspector Marcellus Bonnet goes as easy.” And it did. They met later in the day with almost a duplicate briefing by Etienne. The chief inspector was extremely pleased to accept. The team was complete.

32

Friday, July 26, 2019
Paris, France

THE BRIEFING

Three days later, the assembly of the whole team took place. However, this time it was not at the Prefet de Police Headquarters or at the offices of the Director-General d'Armee, the Director-General of the National Police, or the Director-General for External Security. This time the meeting of all seven team members and important guests was held at the Elysée Palace, Rue du Faubourg Saint-Honoré, which was the official office and residence of the President of the French Republic.

The meeting took place in a secure room in the underground second basement of the Elysée Palace. This room, had it not been without windows, would seem like a normal boardroom or meeting space on the main floor used for official functions of the French President. It was nicely decorated, but the walls were treated in such a way that no sound or radio waves could penetrate or leave the room. In some spaces that are soundproof, there is a feeling of almost sickening airlock. The absence of sound is almost deafeningly quiet. In this space, the air management and manufactured sound eliminated that feeling of unease.

The seven members of the team were seated at a large board table. The team included Etienne; Guy; Mrs. Smith, CIA; Marta, Nina's ESL teacher and FBI agent; Rene, the chief inspector; Gaston from French Intelligence; and Jack, MI6. Seated with them were the Director-general d'Armee, Director-General National Police, and Director-General for External Security.

The special guests arrived in their own car to not draw unnecessary attention to the meeting. It was, after all, just functional. Nothing special.

The doors to the room opened and in walked the special guests. LADA was first. Then Evalina, Alexei, and finally Nina. The surprised look on Nina's face told it all. She had expected this to be a rather plain, uneventful, and perhaps boring meeting about preparations for one of LADA's shows. Instead, here were all the uniformed members of the official government law enforcement agencies and several strangers. Wait, that's Madame Marta from ESL, Etienne, and Guy! She wondered what was happening.

The Director-General d'Armee offered them places to sit. As they sat down, Nina, still in shock, the doors at the other end of the room opened and in stepped the President of the Republic. Nina almost fainted. She knew that what she and LADA had done was important, perhaps even dangerous, but she had no idea that it rated this level of importance. Nina smiled at Madame Marta, and she received a smile back. "Guess this explains a lot of the character of this woman," she thought. "FBI? Who would have guessed? Well, perhaps. But, wow!"

The French President greeted them and apologized that he could only stay a few moments. He shared with them his appreciation for what they were embarking on doing. He explained that what they were carrying to the United States was unquestionably the most important intelligence of his time in office. He assured them that everything within the government of France and their allies in Great Britain and the US would be done to ensure the safe delivery of the intelligence and their safety. At that, he walked around the room, starting with LADA, took their hands, and gave them his personal thanks for what they were doing. Then he left the room.

The briefing began much the same as Etienne's first meeting and the meetings he had with the two members he recruited. Then information was provided to everyone that he had not heard before. That portion of the briefing was provided by Mrs. Smith, Madame Marta, and the Director-General for External Security.

The Director-General for External Security began. "This team will be under the leadership of Captain Etienne of the Brigade Fluviale. He has been activated into the role he holds as a reserve officer. He is now currently on duty as Captain in the army intelligence. Lieutenant Guy, you're also being activated in the same branch immediately. Do you understand?"

Guy responded, "Yes, sir!"

"Good, then let me introduce to everyone who we have in the room." Beginning with Etienne, the Director-General proceeded to introduce each person by name, by official position within which organization they belonged, and a brief description of their personal attributes for the team.

Finally, he arrived at LADA, Nina, Evalina and Alexei. He again described each one and the role they played with the project. He spent considerable time talking about LADA and her Second World War history. He then spent an equal amount of time describing her more contemporary work still using her traditional canvas process. He provided the background for Alexei, Catherine, and the work they had done on behalf of the NATO countries. He left out the role those three had played in the Cuban Missile Crisis, as even he was unaware of what they had done. He then described how iSPY Gallery was the pass through for the information carried on LADA's canvases.

He got to Nina. He described how she was spotted by Madame Marta simultaneously as they were becoming fully aware of her from Evalina's cousin Yuri and a team in Russia that included Nina's father and mother. This further astounded Nina of how much she didn't know of her parents. She always had thought of them as simple farmers. God, how wrong she was. Life on that farm wouldn't have been nearly as boring had she known the work they were truly involved doing.
"Now we come to why the team is assembled. We believe that the Russian intelligence agencies are on to the iSPY Gallery, LADA, Evalina, Alexei, and Nina. We believe that they have been suspecting this operation for some time and have recently, under the direction of the Commander for Russian Intelligence who

heads up the operations in France, Belgium, and the Netherlands, attempted to verify this belief. They know they must be 100% accurate or the wrath of their president will come down on them!" He then explained the 'friendship' the Russian President had with LADA. Their services knew he owned several of her works.

"The intelligence teams from MI6, France, and the US have detected that there is a considerable amount of collusion going on between certain top leaders of key countries. Some of this collusion was going on prior to the US election in 2016. It is going on or is attempted in Great Britain and France."

"That is why all three nations are involved in this room. The collusion had its most dramatic impact in the United States. There is information on one or more of LADA's canvases that has been gathered over the last three years. That information documents this collusion and the compromising situation that some countries' leaders have been put in to guarantee their full participation with the Russian President. Knowledge of this information has begun to be systematically leaked out. We believe this is being done by the leader of Russia to ensure that the others know the leverage he has on them."

"I will not go into how this information is able to be coded onto the canvas. It has. We are to keep it safe. It will be delivered to the CIA Headquarters in Langley, Virginia, USA, by this team assembled."

"Here is how we will proceed. October 2021 will mark the sixtieth anniversary of the United States and Soviet Union Missile Crisis."

"Not well known was the fact that a young President of the United States was so enamored with the paintings of a young Russian artist, LADA, that he purchased and hung several in the White House. One he specifically hung was in the Oval Office. It remains there. President Kennedy was elected sixty years ago next year on November 8, 1960.

This special showing of LADA's works in Washington, DC, for the sixtieth anniversary of the Kennedy Presidency will begin this year and continue for a year. It is the perfect cover for the delivery of the LADA artworks that are to be shown there, including a very special painting. Only four people have knowledge at this time of which one of the 250 paintings has the information encoded on it. It will remain that way!"

"LADA and Nina, along with part of the team, Mrs. Smith, Capitan Etienne, Lieutenant Guy, and Chief investigator Gaston, will travel on the same Air France flight leaving CDG on Thursday, August 29."

"Madame Marta will depart tomorrow to go back to her role in Miami with the ESL language school there. You will join the team again in Washington, DC, on August 29. You will be visiting with several of your other former ESL students in Washington and just happen to be staying in the hotel where the other team members are located. The officers here from MI6 and French intelligence will have subset teams both here and in the US ensuring the areas around these four individuals are safe and secure. The two members will join up with the team on the first of September."

The briefing continued for another hour. It dealt with the specifics of the special location in Washington, DC, where the show would take place. The two long halls in the Kennedy Center for the Arts, the Hall of States, the Hall of Nations, and the Terrace Gallery were the locations. The art would be interspersed with history of the relationship between Russia and the United States, including the role each played in the lead up to the current political crisis.

The briefing ended. Everyone knew their basic assignment. The team would meet several more times, all but the four guests, up to the date of departure to ensure logistics were foolproof.

At those meetings, it would be decided that Madame Marta and Mrs. Smith would have an assignment to specifically watch and protect LADA. Etienne and

Guy would be assigned to watch and protect Nina.

The MI6, French Intelligence agent, and the chief inspector would watch over Evalina and Alexei. This group, less the chief inspector, as he would be traveling with the first group, would depart together on August 30 with the materials that Professor K would need to access the messages hidden on the painting. He again kept everyone else in the dark about what and how, except Alexei, LADA, Evalina, Nina, and himself. They would be the only ones who would know the special way the information was stored and accessed.

• • •

That evening, Etienne, Nina, Guy, and a nearly fully recovered Ninette went out to dinner at a small bistro near Etienne's apartment in the 10th arr. Etienne could tell something was bothering Nina.

As they entered the small bistro, he said to her, "Nina, is everything okay? Have I done something?"

She looked at him, lower lip protruding slightly, enough below her upper lip to form the pout she wanted. She replied softly to his question, but with just the slight intended anger to let him know he had screwed up. "Yes! How long have you known that you would be leading this team and didn't tell me?"

"Nina, I just learned three days ago. I was asked to recruit two additional members and brief them. I wanted to tell you. I should have told you. I'm sorry. Please forgive me! I'm so pleased I'm going with you."

Looking at him in the eyes, with less pout but with serious intent, she said, "But you think I can't take care of myself? I need my big strong man to protect me! Right?"

"Cheri, of course I know you can take care of yourself. But I am glad I will be there with you if something happens. I want to make sure we are together for a long, long time. I would do anything to keep you safe, just as I know you would do, will do, the same for me."

Wait! Had she heard Etienne correctly. "Together for a long, long time?" She continued to look at his eyes. They were serious. She was sure of it.

"Wouldn't you?"

"Wouldn't I what?" she asked, coming out of her thoughts and back into focus on his question.

"Wouldn't you keep me safe so we can be together for a long, long time?" He hoped, no he prayed silently, that she would say "yes".

"Etienne, are you saying you want to be with me for a long, long time? Really?"

He cocked his head slightly to his right and studied her eyes closely now. Was she joking? Could she not tell of his feelings for her? Was she playing with him?

He replied, "Yes, of course. Is it not obvious to you, Nina? I love you. I don't want to ever be without you. I want to make sure you are safe. I want us to be safe together. I want us to protect each other from hurt and harm so we can enjoy life together. That's what I want!"

With that, she smiled, pulled him to her, and kissed him hard and deep. She pulled back just enough to smile and look into his eyes and say, "Yes, me too. That's what I want too!"

Then she kissed him firmly and deeply again. Meanwhile, a smiling Ninette and Guy, holding hands at the other end of the small dining room, had watched the whole episode with great pleasure. Both of their own hands firmly gripped the others, released and gripped the other's hand again. A signal that they appreciated what they were seeing. They looked into each other's eyes, and then they smiled at each other.

Later that night, both couples, Nina and Etienne at Nina's apartment and Ninette and Guy at Ninette's apartment, would each share their love with their partner. Until then, Guy had one more mission for the night.

In the back, in an out of the way corner of the bistro, close to the table that Etienne had reserved, sat an old 1957 Gottlieb "Aces High" pinball machine. The art on it was very dated. A sheik with his harem, women dressed in outfits not nearly as revealing as Elvira and other pinball graphics of today. But it was fun to play. The owner of the bistro supplied a box of old 1950s French 25 centimes with which to play the machine.

Both young women were playing the game, laughing and enjoying themselves. Etienne and Guy had wandered over to the zinc-covered bar to refill the four wine glasses with a nice 2018 Chateau Beauchene Grande Reservé Chateauneuf-du-Pape. The wine was better than the usual table wine they typically enjoyed but tonight was different. They were all celebrating "joie de vie". They had much joy! Guy decided this joyous time was the right time to pose the question to the team leader, his friend.

"Look at them over there, Etienne, laughing and enjoying life. You would never have suspected we were so close to losing them that night, my friend. Never having the chance to know them. We are fortunate men, yes?"

Etienne, looking at the two young women, nodded his head, and replied, "Oui."

"And look at how my sweet Ninette is playing that game. She is winning. She is moving with speed and accuracy. All of her cognitive functions are good. Yes?"

Etienne, now realizing he is being set up for something, looked at his friend with suspicion and amusement. "Oui," he said with a longer drawn out "oui".

"I think she is back to almost full normal. A complete recovery. Her broken leg only needs a soft cast now. Soon she will not even need that."

"Oui."

"Well, I have a proposal to make. A suggestion to our plan so to speak."

"And that is?" Etienne asked.

"I think Ninette should go with us to Washington for LADA's show. It makes sense. Two young couples in love," he said, looking at Etienne and smiling, "and sharing a travel adventure together. Much more realistic cover than two single guys traveling with a young woman and an old artist. That is no cover at all. What do you say, my friend…team leader?"

Etienne laughed. Perhaps the earlier glasses of wine were muting his senses, but his friend was making sense.

"Do you think she would go if you were to ask her and tell her the mission, Guy? That there is some danger involved?"

Guy smiled back and said, "Yes, I think she would go. I didn't tell her the whole mission. Just that you and I would be escorting Nina, LADA, and 250 paintings to Washington. I asked her, if I asked Etienne for permission for Ninette to go, would she like to go too? She said yes!"

"All right, my friend. I will seek approval for her to go as part of the team. Your idea makes sense. Then we can fill her in totally and see if she still agrees to join us."

Etienne sought approval the next day and approval was received for Ninette to join the team. The Director-General d'Armee was initially hesitant. Etienne built a strong case. It made sense, though the Director-General was concerned about the closeness of relationships. Then, re-thinking it, it made more sense to him because both Etienne and the lieutenant would have much more to lose if they were not successful.

"Permission granted. She may join the team. Fill her in completely, understand?"

"Oui! Understood! Merci!"

Etienne, Guy, and this time Nina too, explained the whole mission and background to Ninette. She loved the idea and intrigue. Without hesitation, she eagerly agreed. Ninette was added to the team.

33

Thursday, August 29, 2019
Moscow, Russia

SOPHIA

To say she was nervous was a gross understatement. She was scared to death! He was not going to take this well. And she had to be the messenger despite the fact none of it, absolutely none of it, was her fault. Sure, she might have had it more securely guarded. She could have not let it be used that night for the benefit of amusement for her colleagues. She could have made sure every hard drive and flash drive had been personally secured by her. She hadn't. Damn it! Nothing she could do now but to face the fact that she had been trusting and stupid. But who could have stolen it? It had to be someone there viewing, laughing that night. What they had watched was just a small part of all that was missing. No, it couldn't have been stolen that night now that she thought about it. It had to have been stolen at another time! God, it was good she thought this through again before facing him. Still, how it was stolen and who stole it would come down on her. She had better have answers and soon. Damn it!

Walking down the hall, she was glad for two things and that was why her military skirt was so short that day. Her legs were good! Really good. And he couldn't keep his eyes off a good set of female legs like hers, especially as she would cross and uncross them. She would be sure to do that frequently during this meeting.

It also would help that she was nicely formed on top too. The tight military blouse and slight gaps at the buttons would further distract him. At least she hoped! Her choice of bra was very much not a military issue. Everything about her showed through. She had no other cards she could play. Present the facts, present possibilities of how and whom, and then play the female distraction card. It would work. It had to!

Her high heels were loud on the granite floor. Close now, she stopped. She took a deep breath and opened the door.

There on the floor, playing with his white Alina puppy named Verni, which means "faithful" or "loyal" in Russian, was the President of Russia. To call her a puppy was perhaps not quite accurate. The all white central Asian shepherd dog was now a year and nine months old. She still had puppy traits and loved to roll around on the floor with the President. Verni was currently on her back, docile and enjoying her tummy rub. The officer knew that Verni was not the only female the President liked to roll around with on the floor, and not with a kind and considerate tummy rub, though very few people ever witnessed it. Everyone had heard of the episodes. There was believed to be his own tape library of the events . . . struggles.

He was lying flat on his back with a rather spectacular view up the young officer's slim, well-shaped, and tightly muscled legs. He was in no real hurry to get up. "Hello Sophia, what a pleasant surprise!"

"Mr. President, you remember I phoned your administrator regarding an important intelligence breach. Did he not inform you?"

Acting as though the notification just came back into mind and not letting on that his playing with the dog had been part of his plan, "Oh, yes. I remember" he said, raising slowly while still enjoying the view. Now admiring the woman's chest too, with what she felt was a disgusting lecherous smirk on his face. He stood up.

The dog, still eager to play, kept growling and fainting at him. "Let me call her handlers to fetch Verni. One moment."

He knew his kindness to dogs had a certain appeal to the young ladies. Even the military type, not known for overwhelming emotional concern for living things, as most of the female side of the species had. Still, even females in the military seemed to fall for dogs. For the most part, he thought that lack of female traits was a good thing, except when trying to lure a young woman to his bed. And this one was definitely a candidate for that.

The handlers came in and retrieved Verni. "Please sit, Sophia." Motioning to a chair across from him at the coffee table between them.

Immediately, as she sat, she realized that her chair was somewhat higher than the leather chair he chose. He sat down, hips well forward, nearly off the seat, legs spread wide, feet on their heels, leaning way back in the chair, his hands folded behind his head. Normally the power player would have chosen the higher chair. In military terms, "the higher ground". She realized his position was strategically chosen to give him the spectacular view he wanted every time she would cross and uncross her legs. His sitting position was a definite statement of "I've got one! You don't! I'm the dominant. So be it!"

"This breach that you wish to inform me of, what is it?"

"Mr. President, you know the hard drives and flash drives of those 'special' videos, audio files, and documents that we keep safely secure?"

"Yes, go on." He was enjoying her nervousness and her trying hard to hide it. Discomfort was something he enjoyed causing to his adversaries. Individuals he wished to dominate and conquer. This beautiful woman was one. She would fight hard . . . emotionally and physically. This would be fun.

Just then it happened, her first crossing of legs. A flash of color. What color? He was unsure. If he did not identify it by the end of this meeting, he was sure to find out this evening. That was part of the plan.

"You know, as you requested, second copies were all made of the originals."

"Yes," he replied already knowing where this would lead, but loving to watch her squirm. The result he was anxious to see. No matter how hard she was trying to hide it, it was having its effect. As her breathing became faster and the mounds of her breasts raised and lowered with each hard breath, the results became obvious to his eyes and her sense of feeling. He already could see the telltale results through the material of her bra and blouse. She knew he could see it. It brought a bigger hideous smile to his face. She knew exactly why his smile was growing and no matter how hard she tried, could not stop the effect that caused the smile. Humiliatingly, she had to continue and tried desperately to hide her anger. If he knew she was upset, it would please him even more. Try, Sophia, try!

"Sir, it seems the copies have all disappeared!"

"What?!" He said in fake anger and jumped to his feet. The smile was now purposefully replaced on his face with a mask of anger. He loved it. He loved the fearful emotion he was building up in her. No matter how hard she would try to fight it. His lack of conscience and KGB training had ensured his desired goals would be achieved. "How did this happen? Who is responsible? What actions are YOU TAKING, SOPHIA?!" He made sure to yell, assuring her he was putting it all on her. Part of his well thought out plan.

Squirming more and fighting the faster rise and fall of her breasts, she tried to think of a logical answer and course of action to explain to him. All she could come up with seemed stupid.

"We have identified everyone who had access. We are doing extensive background checks on each person even though, as you know, they all had the highest of our security checks already. We are viewing and reviewing all of the security videos of the vault area."

Nearly in tears, which she didn't want to be, she said, "We will find whoever did this and recover the materials. I assure you of that."

He sat back down in his leather chair, taking up the same domineering position he had before. Slowly he let his anger mask dissolve and replaced it with the lecherous smile once again, and with an unsettling evil glint in his eye, he replied, "I'm sure you will do EVERYTHING you can do to make RIGHT this terrible breach of TRUST! Am I correct in that assessment, SOPHIA?"

"Yes, sir."

"Sophia, do you know my dog's name, Verni, means 'faithful and loyal'"?

"No, sir. I mean is that so, Mr. President?"

"Yes, Sophia. That is what it means. Isn't that a good name for a female dog...a bitch?"

Reluctantly and trying desperately to hide her building anger, Sophia replied, "Yes, Mr. President."

"Yes, that is probably a good trait for all females to share...isn't that true, SOPHIA? DON'T YOU THINK ALL FEMALES SHOULD SHARE THE BITCHES' TRAIT? Loyalty and faithfulness? Did you see how eagerly she rolled over on her back for her master's fondling? Didn't she seem to be one happy little bitch?" He looked forward to the answer to the questions the beautiful and pleasingly distraught woman would provide.

"Yes, sir, Mr. President." Hiding her loathing for this animal as best she could and thinking to herself, why the hell did I dress this way? I'm only encouraging his demeaning of me. All the while she was struggling with her feelings. He knew what she was thinking, her internal struggles. His KGB psychology studies had provided that understanding. She is blaming herself for his control over her. She is making it easier and easier! His smile grew. He let a few moments of time pass knowing her treacherous anger to herself was building inside her.

"Good. So here is what I would like you to do, Sophia. I want you and your team to work hard all day to come up with the answers. I want you to uncover who did this. Why have they done this? Find out where the materials are, how YOU will recover them. And, lastly, to whom have they been released. Is this clear TO YOU, SOPHIA?" He emphasized the last sentence to ensure she knew this episode was fully on her shoulders and in his salacious way on all that was beneath her shoulders, from there down her body to the floor. All of it! His trap had been successfully laid. Both his goals would soon be achieved. "Am I quite clear, Sophia?"

"Yes, sir!" The heaving mounds of her chest expressed.

"Good. Then I expect you back here at my office at 21:00 hours with the full, AND I MEAN FULL, results of your findings."

She tried to interrupt him and stammered, "But, Mr. P-"

He stopped her. "You may go now, Sophia! I will see you here tonight! It is always good to see you, SOPHIA. YOU ARE AN AMAZING YOUNG FEMALE!" Emphasis on the female. "I am sure you will have good news to bring me. It will PROVIDE ME GREAT PLEASURE! Of that, I am ASSURED. YOU UNDERSTAND!" Not a question but a profoundly strong statement of future fact. "Please leave now! I have other pressing matters to attend to!"

As gracefully as possible the young woman rose out of her chair, uncrossing her legs, his eyes once again catching the revealing quick flash of color… light pink! She turned and headed for the door. Nice, he thought, light pink! A good color choice. As she began to reach for the door handle, his voice stopped her.

"Oh, and Sophia!"

She turned and replied, "Sir?" Hiding the anger trembling in her voice.

"Sophia, I love my females in uniform, especially when they are dressed in a uniform that fits them as well as yours fits you today." His eyes purposefully traveled up and down her form. "However, I like them even more OUT OF UNIFORM!" Emphasizing the double meaning. "And I also like soft, frilly, and clingy. Since we will meet here this evening after normal duty hours, assure me that you will dress accordingly. AM I MAKING MYSELF QUITE CLEAR TO YOU, SOPHIA?!" Smile firmly in place.

Humiliation building, she, as militaristically as possible, replied, "Everything is clear Mr. President. Quite clear."

She opened the door to leave. Again, he called to her.

"Sophia!" She paused. "I'm sure you will agree with me... Don't you find panty and bra lines disgusting on clingy and revealing material?" He waited for her troubled answer.

Trembling, she replied in an ever increasingly sheepish way, "Yes, sir."

"I'm sure you will find a way to ELIMINATE those disgusting lines! Won't you, Sophia? It will make our deeply meaningful discussions so much more pleasurable and easier. True?"

"Yes, sir," tears forming in her eyes.

"Good, Sophia. I don't want anything in MY WAY for a pleasure-filled evening. Correct, Sophia? You want to bring me great pleasure? Not like this terrible news you brought me today. I'm sure you will do everything physically in your control to bring me this great pleasure. Won't you, Sophia? Am I RIGHT, SOPHIA?" Then he added, "DEEP AND FULFILLING PLEASURE! That is so HARD to find these days. I'm sure YOU CAN AND WILL PROVIDE IT FOR ME! You are a good FEMALE officer who understands her DUTY! Just like my bitch, Verni. Loyal and faithful. Ready to lay down YOUR LIFE for me." His double and triple meanings, very clear to her. "You may go now, Sophia!" He returned to his desk, picked up some papers, and turned on his computer screen.

With that, she left. She closed the door and broke into deep, overwhelming sobs.

He smiled watching the young broken woman on his closed-circuit video security monitor. She could not move. Her shoulders rose up and down with her uncontrollable sobs. What a great view he had of her outside his office. Broken, distraught, emotionally uncontrollable. If only he could zoom in on her broken face more . . . and those heaving breasts! Time for that tonight! Totally in his hands! His hands to do whatever he wished to do to her, to totally and overwhelmingly humiliate her. His trademark approach to women!

He wouldn't have to worry about flashes of color tonight. He had been assured of that. He was always amused at the colors and styles his conquests wore to try to seduce him. Hell, he didn't need their seduction. He just wanted to dominate them. That is why he wasn't going to let her amuse him with flashes of color or style. His total desire today was her complete humiliation and domination. Of that, he was very successful!

The American tried to emulate him in style but was a total bozo at it. Crude and not subtle. He, on the other hand, was the true master and he only revealed it to them . . . the females under his complete control! Humiliation and dominance. His motto, guiding principle . . . his creed.

He also knew with pleasure that she would never be able to answer the questions unless he gave her those answers. He and his former KGB colleagues had assured that was the case. No one but he and the two of them would know that he himself had arranged the materials to pass to the appropriate people and then to the Americans. And his two former KGB associates knew their wealth and health were in his hands. That is why he was the "Most Powerful Man in the World".

He continued to watch her until she was able to gather herself enough to move, trembling. No military bearing left. He laughed at the video picture . . . pleasantly pleased . . . deeply pleased.

He called Verni's handler to bring the dog back into his office. He smiled. He began to work on his more pressing business. He needed to attend to Verni's tummy rub!

34

Thursday, August 29, 2019
Paris, France

DEPARTING FOR WASHINGTON, DC

On the same morning during which a young Russian Military Intelligence officer was being totally humiliated and demeaned by the world's most powerful misogynist, LADA, Nina, Etienne, Ninette, and Guy headed for Charles de Gaulle Airport to board the 1:40 pm Air France direct flight to Washington Dulles International Airport. Both Etienne and Guy were cleared ahead of time to carry their police firearms on board the flight. Additional safety precautions were already taken and in place.

The men arrived at Evalina's home shortly before 10 am. They were driven by one of Etienne's Brigade Fluviale team members in one of the Brigade's special vans. He thought that the five people he was driving to the airport were headed there for a relaxing vacation. He had no idea of the important paintings they would be escorting on this fun and relaxing trip.

Mrs. Smith and Chief Investigator Gaston arrived at the airport in separate taxis. They did not acknowledge or sit near the other five travelers. They did sit with the others, once on board the flight, in the same business class section of the aircraft, both in aisle seats. LADA and Nina sat together in the front row of Business Class, seat A for LADA and B for Nina. Across the aisle from Nina sat Etienne in seat E, with Ninette and Guy filling the remaining seats. Mrs. Smith sat in aisle seat B of the second Business Class row. Chief Investigator Gaston in aisle seat K of the second row. Mysteriously, the remaining two seats in the first row, K and L, remained unused for this flight. Highly unusual.

Trailing behind the Brigade van, as it left for the airport, was a black Mercedes. Two unknown men were in that car. Without their knowledge, another car followed them. The four men inside the second, trailing, vehicle were special members of the military intelligence rescue team. They were heavily armed. They kept their distance from the Mercedes and continued to be unnoticed as the van pulled up in front of the Air France terminal. The car passed on through the departure gate area. Two of the heavily armed intelligence team quickly exited the car. With their uniforms and special identifications, they easily passed into the terminal looking very similar to the other military police guarding the departure gate area. Since 9/11 in the United States and the stadium bombing, concert hall, and restaurant attacks in 2015 in Paris, security has remained high, especially at the airport. The two-armed guards, keeping their distance from the five travelers they were guarding, acted as casual as armed security guards could. Still, they kept sharp eyes out for anything that appeared to be out of order.

Another rather strange event had occurred at Charles De Gaulle Airport overnight when the 8:15 pm flight had arrived from Washington, DC. Normally the plane would be cleaned and readied for the next day's return flight. Instead, because of a reported "mechanical problem," after the passengers disembarked that plane, it was taxied away from the terminal to a hanger for repair. Another Boeing 777-300er was positioned for the August 29 flight to Washington. This plane was already loaded with the 250 LADA paintings, including the very special one, and twelve members of an elite Special Forces team. Six members were in each of the two below deck baggage compartments. They not only were heavily armed but they also had a special breathing apparatus and arctic weather gear with them. This was done so if anything happened to the "Safe Live Animal" environment controls of the compartments, which include temperature, humidity level, and carbon dioxide concentrations, they would be safe. This team had brought the paintings from iSPY Gallery and LADA's studio to the hangar where they were loaded, unseen, into the belly of the aircraft. Additionally, the flight crew for this aircraft, pilots, navigators, and flight attendants were also members of the elite Special Forces team. Nothing would happen to this flight.

The Russian President, still unsure whether LADA and iSPY Gallery was the way the information was delivered to the United States CIA, had specifically ordered the Commander to ensure nothing would interfere with the safe passage of LADA and her companions. It wasn't for his concern for LADA, though there was that, it was that he wanted to make sure the information he was planting was received by the CIA and Special Prosecutor. It was part of his "Total Disruption Plan". His personal brainchild. Genius, he was sure!

The plane boarded right on time at 1:40 pm. Thirty minutes later, the plane's doors were closed and sealed. It had special clearance to immediately begin its taxi to the takeoff position. Other pilots in other aircraft wondered why this particular 777-300er was getting special clearance. But it was. All they could do was grumble a bit and wait their turn.

The 777-300er reached its runway. It positioned for takeoff and the engines began to rev. It increased in roar and quickly the large stretch aircraft powered down the runway. Its front wheel lifted off the pavement. It continued down the runway and then that most exciting moment happened as all aboard felt the rest of the plane's wheels leave the ground and the 775,000 pounds of aircraft, passengers, baggage, and fuel felt the first sense of weightlessness. They were airborne! The powerful GE90 engines thrust the aircraft forward and it started its climb.

The aircraft now began a slow banking as it reached 10,000 feet and turned toward the coast of France. In less than 40 minutes, it was out of French air space and headed over the North Atlantic. Four French Air Force fighter jets, unseen by the passengers, two several thousand feet below the jet and two an equal distance above the jet, which itself was now approaching its cruising speed of 554 miles an hour, would escort the Air France flight on its mission. The fighters would stay with the jet until it reached US air space nearly at Washington, DC. Each fighter jet would take its turn refueling from the Boeing KC-135 NATO Stratotanker circling the midpoint of the North Atlantic route. They would refuel twice, once going over to the US and once on the return trip to France.

The President of the United States, as usual for him, was unaware of this operation. Although he had been briefed, it hadn't meant anything to him anyway. His thinking might have been, "I have had that escort all the time. Must be some wealthy Sheik or something."

The flight was nearing its end as it approached the Washington Dulles Airport. The flight had been uneventful. Several times Etienne and Ninette had exchanged seats so the two women could be together. They talked about the intricacies that Nina would face setting up the show for LADA once they arrived. Etienne and Guy reviewed preparations for ensuring the safety of the team and the delivery of the particular canvas. Mostly, the individual couples and the separate men and women twosomes talked with each other about the fun they would have exploring Washington, DC, together. That is, once the painting was safely delivered to the CIA headquarters. Then it would be up to Alexei to do his magic, of which they had no idea how or what he would do to reveal the hidden information from the canvas. The lack of knowledge was okay with the four of them. The less they knew, the better and safer they were.

During the last thirty minutes, the plane's engines were fueled back. Eventually there were sounds of flaps lowering and the plane airspeed and altitude started to decline. The wheels dropping below the aircraft gave out a distinctive slow low groan and the airspeed dropped more precipitously. The engine speed was increased to make up for the wheel drag and the plane headed for a direct approach on the assigned runway. Again, other aircraft approaching Dulles had the same reaction as the ones on the ground waiting for their take off at Charles De Gaulle had: "Why is this Air France airplane getting the jump on all of us?"

The back wheels touched down, the plane glided along the runway for a few moments, then the front wheels hit. The reverse thrusters were engaged, and the plane seemed at first to fight the braking and reverse thrust. Then quickly it slowed, slowing more, and more slowly yet, it reached the taxi speed and turned right to a taxi strip, but to the majority of the passengers' surprise it was turning away from the terminal building. On the tarmac ahead and to the right of the taxiway stood two large black vans and several large black ominous SUVs. Armed guards were surrounding those vehicles.

Beside the vehicles were two large lift devices and two portable stairs. The stairs appeared to reach all the way to the front cabin doors. Quickly the outside machines and individuals began to position themselves around the plane. The engines were cut. The portable stairs rolled up to the right side of the plane and two of the heavily armed uniformed men climbed the stairs to the outside of the door. The passengers heard the baggage compartment doors open and the large lifts positioned under the aircraft raised to the now open front baggage compartment.

The pilot's voice came over the intercom and gave the same announcement in English and then French.

"Ladies and gentleman. As you can see, we have made a slight detour prior to reaching the terminal. We will be here only a short time and then we will proceed to an on-time arrival at our planned gate. A few of our passengers will be leaving us at this time as will several large crates stored in the front baggage compartment." This part of the announcement was then made in French.

The pilot continued again in English. "You will also see several heavily armed military personnel also departing the plane from the below deck baggage compartments. They have been there throughout the flight keeping some special cargo and the departing passengers safe, as well as us all. There really was nothing to fear and there still is nothing to fear. As you see with our direct approach, we actually landed nearly twenty minutes ahead of schedule even though flying into a rather heavy head wind." He now again repeated the message in French.

Back again to English, "Ah, as you see the baggage has been unloaded. Now the armed military men and women are departing." People on the left side of the plane had left their seats to lean over the other passengers on the right side of the plane to watch the action. The seven passengers in the business section descended the portable stairs to the SUVs. Moments later, with the SUVs and vans fully loaded, they sped off. The portable stairs and lifts were pulled back. The truck, which had a portable engine starter, restarted the airplane's engines. The passengers were instructed to take their seats for a safe taxi to the gates. The plane started to roll. It arrived at the gate at precisely 4:15 pm. Right on time with an incredible story for the passengers to tell.

35

Thursday, August 29, 2019
Moscow, Russia

SOPHIA'S PLAN

After leaving the President's camera view, what he did not see was the struggling woman regaining her composure. Continuing to take deep breaths, she realized she was a physical mess. She needed to compose herself before directing her team. She would head back to her apartment and change into a more appropriate, standardized, military dress. The shorter than issued skirt was changed and disposed of. She also changed the tight-fitting blouse and undergarments. There would be no attempt to distract her colleagues from the difficult, if not impossible, task ahead.

As she reached her apartment and began to unlock the door, it struck her. That was it exactly! It was an impossible task! A set up! There was no way her team could unlock this mystery in a month let alone twelve hours! The President knew this! This was not about recovering the materials. This was about exactly what happened today. Humiliating and demeaning her! Forcing her into a position where she could not defend herself from him and his evilness. She had to think and come up with a plan.

She set down firmly onto her cushioned couch. Her short skirt again displayed her long legs and most of her thighs. She couldn't care less. There was no one here for her to distract. No one here is leering at her. As she sat there, her plan began to take shape. First step, she had to change and head back to her office and assemble the team.

The military skirt she chose was the traditional length. It reached the top of her knee. The one she took off had been shortened six inches by her earlier that morning. Had she been caught in it by her superior officer she would have been reprimanded and court martialed. It had been used for one purpose only and that purpose had been ill thought out. She hoped her new plan would be more "fitting" for her now overwhelming needs.

Changed, with new makeup, an appropriate length skirt, and tightly buttoned blouse with a heavier material undergarment, she headed back to her office in the Kremlin to address her team with their assignment. It was just 10:00 am when she called them together. As she explained their orders, they looked at her incredulously. She had to be kidding! There was no way this could be accomplished. And she only gave them until 6:00 pm to do so.

They would meet at 6:00 pm in the commissary to assemble the full report. This was to be done over a hasty dinner of whatever was available in the cafeteria line of the commissary. Did they understand? They did. And her first steps in her quickly laid plan were accomplished.

She left them working and proceeded to do two things. She checked on the menu at the commissary for tonight's menu. She then took a cab several blocks away and walked in a couple of stores until she found the business. There she bought a small brown object and slipped it into her military purse. This she would use later in the plan. She retraced her steps and as she came through the last place of business, she spent some time looking before finding exactly what she needed for the meeting with the evil one. She purchased it for more than she wanted to spend. However, it would serve its purpose for that night only. She found the other things she would need and bought them. Then she headed out of the store to find a taxi.

Taking the cab to her apartment, as she got out, she instructed the driver to wait for her. She unloaded her purchases in the apartment. At the cab once again, she asked him to take her back to the Kremlin. The driver kept catching glances of her through the rearview mirror. Did men not understand that if they can see her in the mirror, then she could see them too? Men! They are all the same! She had been tempted to tease the man by hiking her skirt up her thigh and crossing her legs. That had gotten her into trouble earlier in the day and there was no way she would play that game again with this lech or any other. She realized she again was blaming herself . . . the victim. She had only thought of "playing the game" because she knew the type of person he was. Still, it was hard not to be angry with herself. Get over it, Sophia!

The taxi arrived at the Kremlin, and she exited it, paying the driver only the total on the meter with no tip. He got his glances at her in the car. Enough tip for him!

She hurried down the hall to the offices where her team was hard at work. They asked her where she had been as they were a bit annoyed that she had left and they were doing all the work on this impossible project. The entire time she had been gone they griped among themselves. She informed each one as they complained to her, independently, that she had to pick up some important items for the meeting she was ordered to have with the President that evening when she, alone, would have to deliver the report. To the men of the team this all sounded reasonable. They didn't have a clue. Typical men! The women of the team knew exactly what she meant. Most were concerned for her. A couple of others showed their hidden envy. How lucky she was. She felt it from them. If they only knew!

At 6:00 pm, knowing that there would be nothing for the team members to substantially report, they met in the commissary. She quickly led them to the line and had them choose their own meals. The office would pick up the tab. She was the last in the line and noticed not one of them had chosen what she intended to eat. It was known to be notoriously awful. And it was! That was good!

As they sat at the conference table in the small dining room a couple of them asked her if she was actually going to eat that gross food. The spaghetti in red sauce with some sort of hideous ground meat was known to be a stomach turner. She sighed and said for some unknown reason it sounded good to her. A lie!

She had each person give a report of what they had found. As each finished, they gave her their one page synopsis of what they had said. As expected, no one had found anything. What each person gave her was an unsupported assumption or theory.

Midway through the reporting, she purposely pushed her tray away from her and told them all they were right. The food she had chosen was disgusting! It particularly tasted and smelled bad this evening! No surprise to anyone. They all told her not to worry, as theirs wasn't much better. They could all die together of food poisoning tonight and save them from the wrath of the President. They all laughed . . . she just smiled.

The meeting finished at 7:00 pm. The men all wished her good luck. The envious female members of the team smiled and told her with a wink to "have fun tonight!" She smiled back. The other women express concern for her. They know she is in for a rough and unpleasant time as they had heard the rumors. She smiled at them too.

Back at the apartment, she laid out on the bed what she had purchased for that night. She then drew the hottest bath she could possibly stand. She stayed in the water until the last minute, rewarming the tub often. Her skin turned a bright red, the color she wanted. The water was not hot enough to truly burn her...not quite. She draped a soaking hot wash towel over her breasts building up the heat in her chest. Sweat beaded up on her forehead and she began to feel lightheaded. She didn't let it be too much and exited the tub just at the right moment. Releasing the drain to let the water out, she almost fainted. This was good, she thought. This is how it should be.

Moving to the bed, she pulled the light, flimsy, backless, green sequin mini dress over her head. The small dress skimmed her figure hanging from the tips of her breasts and tightly down her body to the flair of her hips and then just a few short inches down from the top of her perfectly formed long legs. Elastic spaghetti straps held the triangular bodice over each breast, revealing enough cleavage and chest to barely hide what was beneath. Her long neckline was ringed by a simple gold chain with small ruby colored beads. That was to ensure the attraction to her long feminine neck, which was hiding loosely under her mid-back length, long, natural blonde hair. Normally at work, no necklace and a tight military bun would hide this part of her natural charm. For this mission, this look would position the target where it needs to be. Loop earrings, open toe high heel clear plastic shoes and then the last of her attire for the trip to the Kremlin.

As she headed out the door with a small matching green clutch bag, she grabbed it off the peg and slipped on her heavy military raincoat. Although it was still nearly 23 degrees Celsius this late at night, she pulled the raincoat snuggly around her body covering as much of her as possible. Beads of sweat still formed on her forehead.

She found a taxi at 8:35 pm. She gave directions to the driver, who thought it odd that such a beautiful woman would be covering herself with a heavy military raincoat on such a warm evening. He noticed her beads of sweat and reddish tint and worried that she was perhaps sick. Still with the rank on the shoulders of her military coat he was not about to question her . . . she was headed to the Kremlin. It was odd, though.

Just then, he saw her in the rearview mirror, taking a small brown bottle out of her purse. She held it to her mouth, grimaced, and appeared to nearly gag. Moments later, even though the taxi was air conditioned, she opened the car's window just enough and appeared to drop the small bottle out of the car and onto the street below. No wonder she was acting so weird. She was on drugs! All these young people were on drugs. Even his son was. And this woman was obviously an officer in the military. No wonder our military was so sad. Good thing the man was the current President. He had changed that some over the years. He had more work to do. More work like ridding the military of people like this . . . this . . . druggie!

The taxi pulled up to the curb at the Kremlin. She exited and gave him a nice tip and said, "Thank you."

Well, that was nice he thought and changed his mind about this young officer. Maybe she was a little sick and that was medicine she was taking. "Perhaps I should watch myself over the next few days. I hope what she had wasn't contagious!"

His cab drove off. She walked through the secure entrance and headed for her office with just enough time. Although the security officers might have questioned why Sophia was wearing her military coat, once they saw her coming out to her office it was obvious to them. She didn't want other male eyes leering at her as they were now doing. The operator zoomed the cameras in on the front and back of her as she glided down the hall towards the President's office. Catcalls and whistles are a universal male thing. There were plenty of those going on in the security office that night. She almost felt and heard the cameras zooming in on her. She was sure this tape would be viewed the next day repeatedly, by everyone, including her own staff. So be it!

As she reached the outside security officer, she stopped. The beads of sweat were building and she felt the dampening areas on her back and underarms growing. She was glad the dress was both sleeveless and backless...backless down to just above her bottom. The two armed guards looked at her and smiled knowingly. This had happened before with many other young playthings of the President. They greeted Sophia by name and told her, while smirking, that they hoped she had a wonderful time. They continued to snicker and whisper among themselves as she walked on.

The President was waiting for her in his inner office. The guards released the electronic security latch and the outside office, with its hard granite stone entrance hall, was revealed. The same hall that she had to walk that morning. Fear was building!

She could feel the contents of the bottle working. She struggled to keep control. She knocked on the door and the President opened it. He greeted her in a loosely fitting cream-colored silk pajama shirt and pants. His eyes brightened with pleasure at what he saw. Clingy, yes. Slinky, yes. Extremely short, yes. No panty and bra lines, yes. Exactly as he had demanded!

"Sophia, you have listened well. I like what you have chosen for our meeting. Follow me!" He grabbed her arm forcefully and led her into another room. It wasn't truly an inner office as most people would expect. This office was a large bedroom. She was pulled into that room and saw the huge round bed in the center. The floor was no longer granite. It was a rich, most likely ancient silk rug from one of his defeated Caucasus regions. What a shame!

It was building, she could tell!

He looked at her with pleasure and surprise. His earlier toying with this plaything still had its effect. She was red with embarrassment and sweating from fear. He detected a slight grimace on her face as he reached with his right hand to grab her left breast and with his left hand to pull her to him for a forced hard kiss. Just then, it happened!

Gagging, her mouth opened wide, unable to hold it back any longer. She projectile vomited! The contents of the vomit hit the man's waiting face right on the nose and mouth. Scientific studies show projectile vomit travels at over 42 miles an hour. Once it's on its way, it's impossible to stop. A second loud and explosive retching happened and again the contents of the retch hit his open shirt and chest. A third blast hit his pants, right on his crotch and down his lower legs. As she began to retch for a fourth time, her eyes fell back in her head, as the fourth was released, her long legs melted and she slid down face first to the puddles of disgusting half-digested spaghetti dinner that were also now falling from his body onto the large puddles lying at his feet . Her beautiful hair was now completely matted. Remnants were spread all over her cheeks, lips, and forehead. She appeared to be out cold. Her last thoughts were "This is good. Target hit and eliminated. Military bearing fully back." Then she blacked out completely.

A completely shocked and disgusted President ripped the clothing off his body.

He used the shirt, what part he could find that was not completely covered, and tried to wipe the reeking vomit from his face. Throwing the shirt on the floor beside the motionless girl, he pushed one of the many emergency call buttons placed strategically around the room. Instantly, the door flew open with heavily armed security guards ready to handle the worst of situations. They never expected to deal with what they saw. There on the floor was Sophia, drenched in her own vomit. The smell and sight cause the security guards themselves to have to fight retching. One couldn't.

"Get that stinking thing out of here! Call the facilities people up here at once! I want this place to be scrubbed and disinfected, now! Call the medical team and hazmat to get that ugly piece of trash some place far away from me! I never want to lay eyes on her again! Now, damn it! Now!"

The President headed for the shower and remained there for over an hour. Meanwhile, the team did the best they could to get Sophia out of the room through the security door, retching and heaving themselves as they did.

The medical team arrived quickly. They loaded the young woman onto the stretcher covering her with blankets until they could have her cleaned up and checked at the hospital. It was some sight. A normally beautiful, young woman, with barely a hint of clothing on, soaked completely with her own vomit and sweat. Instantly, the medics considered food poisoning. They called ahead to the hospital to prepare to pump her stomach. They also alerted the security to close off the President's office area until it could be checked by hazmat. Lastly, they told security they wanted a list of everyone she had close contact with that day and where she may have eaten what was now the leftover of a very disgusting spaghetti dinner.

The ambulance, with medics and Sophia, raced off to the hospital, and the poison team was alerted.

36

Thursday, August 29, 2019
Washington, DC, USA

PAINTINGS ARRIVE AT LANGLEY

The entourage, two large black vans with 250 paintings inside, six large black heavily armored plated SUVs, one carrying LADA, Nina, Etienne, Ninette, and Guy, another carrying the Chief Investigator, Mrs. Smith, and two additional CIA colleagues, were both followed by the additional four SUVs with the French security personnel. Police cars in front led the convoy. Other police cars protected the rear. Side streets were blocked as they roared down the I 495 freeway. Those last four SUVs peeled off from the others once they reached the gates of Langley, CIA Headquarters. The four SUVs continued south on I-495 to Andrews US Air Force Base. There, the men and equipment were loaded onto a waiting British McDonnell Douglas/Boeing C-17 Globemaster III for the immediate turnaround flight back to Velizy—Villacoublay Air Base, home of COTAM, the French Air Transport Command.

The two vans and two SUVs were stopped at the gates. Inspections of the undersides of all the vehicles were performed to ensure there were no explosives. A quick search of the interiors of the SUVs was made, even though they were CIA vehicles. They checked the five passengers' passports in the first SUV as well as the driver's ID, even though he was well known by the guards. The same operation was performed on the SUV with Mrs. Smith, the Chief Investigator, the CIA colleagues, and the driver. Nothing was left to chance. All luggage was left in the vans as well as both Etienne's, Guy's, and the Chief Investigator's side arms. Mrs. Smith was allowed to keep hers.

Leaving the security gate, they drove to the back loading dock where the paintings were unloaded and their persons searched. Once security was assured the guests and the other SUV were cleared, they were all ushered into a high security conference room deep inside the building. Here they waited several minutes until the paintings were inspected. The inspection completed, Nina, LADA, Mrs. Smith, and the two CIA agents were escorted to the paintings. LADA and Nina selected the painting. Nina looked inquisitively at LADA. LADA just shook her head, and quietly putting her right index finger to her smiling lips whispered, "Shhh."

The other 249 paintings were loaded back into the van to be transported to the Kennedy Center for the Arts. The special one was transported under guard to a large safe that housed other important documents and items of national security. It would remain there until Alexei and Evalina would arrive a couple of days later.

Once back in the conference room, they all were feeling very relieved. Sitting and waiting for the next step didn't take long. A six-foot-tall, distinguished, gray haired man with military bearing, wearing a dark well-tailored suit, entered the room. The CIA agents, including Mrs. Smith, knew exactly who he was. LADA also knew. The others vaguely recognized him but were unable to put a name to the face. They later learned he was the US Special Prosecutor and a former Director of the FBI.

Without introduction, he congratulated them on fulfilling their mission. That task was now handed off to the CIA, FBI, and other agencies within the US Justice Department. He assured them that the mission would continue until complete. They would now be escorted to their hotel and for them to work on the project, of what he knew would be an outstanding show of the great artist LADA's work. He told them he was well aware of her work and that he had often admired the piece that was prominently displayed in the Oval Office at the White House. A painting acquired and loved by President Kennedy. Many of the Presidents he had served with admired the work too, all except the latest one. He then said not many of them knew of the importance of her work. He did. He appreciated it and the artist. Her work had for some time a large impact on the world. LADA, not known to blush, was turning just a little colorful. She was sure it was the room's heat.

He ended his talk. Just as the President of France did, he quickly left the room with many of their questions unanswered. The main question: what exactly had they delivered?

They sat there for a while discussing among themselves how strange their adventure had been. Everyone joined in except Mrs. Smith, the two other CIA agents, and LADA. As the discussions continued, suddenly the door opened again and two more civilian men and a mid-60-year-old woman, in a light knit wool suit with a white silk scarf that had odd circle designs of various shades of blue, walked into the room just behind the men. The men's actions showing a deference to her, obviously reported to her. On her face was a tight-lipped smile. Not quite a smirk but not really a smile. She and the two men, both of them dressed in dark navy suits with slightly different shades of red ties and white shirts, all sat down. She proceeded to examine everyone in the room before speaking. Mrs. Smith's eyes were directed to the table and avoided the woman's direct eye contact. Then the woman, with no introduction, spoke.

"Welcome to CIA Headquarters. Your journey has been long. It is just about over. Each of you will meet individually with one of our agents for a quick debriefing of your trip. Nothing difficult, I assure you. Routine questions. Then you will be taken to your hotel to set up what I know will be a wonderful art exhibit of this woman's," looking at LADA, "splendid works."

Etienne had started to rise to interrupt her. LADA, sitting next to him, took his hand in hers and pulled him softly downward. She looked into his eyes and almost imperceptibly to anyone, including himself, shook her head back and forth slightly with a nonverbal "No!" on her lips.

LADA knew who this woman was. She was responsible for many of the controversial suspected tortures "enhanced interrogation techniques" of a previous

United States administration. LADA also knew this was not a good turn of events, though she would keep it to herself at least for now. She, Evalina, and Alexei had considered, in advance, it might happen this way. So had the President of France, and his senior advisors and members of French Intelligence. They had been prepared. LADA had already taken the first step.

Troubled, Etienne and the others listened to her drone on about complexities and issues beyond most people's understanding, implying strongly, even beyond the understanding of those individuals in this room. She praised them for the actions and risks they had taken to deliver the materials. She assured them the material was in the "correct hands". The hands where they should be. Now it would be taken care of appropriately and safeguarded.

Without any warning, she got up, was joined by her two colleagues, and left the room to stunned visitors, everyone except Mrs. Smith, the two other CIA agents, and a knowing LADA. Over the last three years, those three CIA individuals were becoming used to this inhospitable and bizarre knee jerk action of that woman. LADA, herself, had witnessed this type of action over her entire . . . well almost entire . . . 90 plus years! This was not a good person!

37

Friday, August 30, 2019
Moscow, Russia

GETAWAY

Slowly her eyes opened to fog. Everything was blurry. There were noises she could not identify. A dark object loomed over her head. Her hand was touching something. Another hand? The cloud began to lift. There in front of her eyes was the kindly old face of her Godfather and mentor, Colonel General Dimitri Gorchakov, head of Russian Military Intelligence. He smiled down at her and said, "Child," he always called her that except when they were both in uniform and others were around, "what on Earth were you thinking?" This confused her. He looked at her and the confusion on her face and realized she at this moment did not realize what she had done.

"Eating that terrible food at the commissary." He gave her a knowing look however and continued, "Everyone knows the spaghetti is destined to cause food poisoning." Again, there was something else on his face. The smile is slightly incomplete. Perhaps a bit of worry?

"They pumped your stomach last night and will have the results of the evaluation later today. They will provide me with the reports as I have asked." He glanced around the room seemingly for no reason. She instantly picked up on this being his indication that the conversation may be recorded. That sent a shiver of terror running through her somewhat weakened body. She squeezed his hand to let him know she understood. She tried to smile. It may be video recorded too.

"They have decided that you are doing better and will be released in a couple of hours. I have asked my housekeeper to go to your place and pack a bag of clothes for you to change into. I think that will make you more comfortable leaving . . ." he underscored the word 'leaving,' "the hospital. Perhaps you would like to take a few days to go to your family's dacha to recover. Upon hearing of your being in the hospital, I have arranged for you to have several days leave to recover. The privilege of having a Godfather who is also your commanding officer." He gave her a big smile. Still there was a hint of warning.

"Thank you, surrogatnyy otets," meaning surrogate father.

He had become that to her after her father was killed during the war in Afghanistan in 1989, just before the Soviets left that country. He and her father were both captains assigned to the same division. Both had been on leave together with their wives enjoying the beach. That was the time when Sophia was conceived. Nine months almost to the day that the two men went back to the war, little Sophia was born. She never had the chance to know her father as he was killed by a sniper's bullet while eating breakfast with his friend Dimitri at their encampment.

Captain Karl Malenkov had just shared the news about her birth earlier that week with Dimitri. They had celebrated as best they could in the mountains of Afghanistan. A homemade brandy made from melons and bananas and sometimes grapes provided the questionable celebratory drink. Sometimes worrisome, as badly produced alcohol from unreliable sources could be highly poisonous. They knew this source and trusted it . . . somewhat. That was thirty years ago. Sophia was now a 31-year-old Major in the Russian Military Intelligence. A highly sought after branch assignment except in the location where she now served at the Russian President's Office. He had tried to keep that from happening. Although he was the highest-ranking officer in that branch, even he had his limits, especially when the lecherous eyes of the man had caught sight of something he wanted. He had. Her ending up in hospital was the result but not of HIS plan. The General knew this. Because he knew the truth, he had taken the necessary steps that morning.

The doctor entered the room and saw the Colonel General. He apologized for interrupting. He was assured it was not a problem. The doctor then said Sophia could go home to recover if she agreed. She did. Papers were signed and he left.

Moments later, the General's housekeeper came up with a bag for Sophia. The General excused himself so that she could change. He let her know that he would drive her and sent his housekeeper home. The General left the room and wandered down the hall to the nurses' station. There he chatted with the nurses. They had admired the stately, handsome General as he came to check on Sophia. He had been quite the talk. Now he was there with them, and they were able to completely enjoy the distinguished gentleman. Several even fleetingly fantasized that perhaps the brief encounter could develop further. It wouldn't. Although neither his wife nor Sophia's mother were still alive, his wife died of a heart attack while giving birth to their stillborn son, and Sophia's mother, despite the highest quality of medical care that Dimitri could find for her, had died of the Avian flu outbreak in 2017. The loss of both women, for whom he cared deeply, precluded him from wanting to share his life permanently with any other women. Other than the young woman he was helping now but that was different. Very different.

Still, he was a man, and he did like to playfully flirt. And he was doing so. However, this day the flirting was for show and purpose. The purpose was to ask if any stomach contents had come back from the lab and what they might have shown was the cause. He learned nothing had come back indicating anything out of the ordinary other than really bad food. His own suspicions were different. He thought he knew what had happened. This is why he was totally prepared with what he had in the car. A car specially designed to not allow for any sound or visual monitoring or any other means of eavesdropping on what went on inside the vehicle. A safe room of such.

They walked out of the hospital together. His arm around her to ensure she was steady on her feet. Surprisingly, she was. He had driven himself to the hospital that day, giving his chauffeur the day off. Sophia started to get into the front passenger seat beside where he would sit. Instead, he opened the back passenger door and insisted she sit there. The beautiful young woman with shoulder length blonde hair would emerge an hour later at the airport with much shorter dark hair. The flowing soft summer dress and sandals would be replaced with slacks, a blouse, and leather flats. Although still a beautiful woman, she would be completely changed.

As she entered the car, she found the additional bag on the floor space of the back seat. It was her special bag. The one she used for undercover espionage work. Her "spy bag". As he drove, he looked at her through the rearview mirror as she examined the contents and the added materials within it. Her lip, he could see, trembled a bit as the reality was beginning to strike home to her. He could tell she was fighting the misting of her eyes too.

"Dyadya?" Meaning uncle, that was her pet name for him. Today it was said with stress and sorrow.

"I know my child. There is no other way. You must leave the country quickly for your safety. You don't anger the Man that way. He holds a long grudge and his grudge as you know reaches far."

The tears could not be held back and began to fall. She knew this was not only the end of her military career but also her life in her home country. Then she realized she was not the only one in trouble. Dyadya would be in trouble too, for aiding her. She tried to say so, but he beat her to it.

"You must get away as fast as possible. I see you have already discovered the alternative identification and passports in the bag. You are now French, not Russian. You understand me?"

Sophia reluctantly nodded her head "yes".

"There is information for a Swiss bank account in there. You will need it to transfer funds to a bank account in Paris under your new name . . . a French bank. Once you have done that, in the next couple of days you are to use the second set of passport and identification to take a ferry from France to London and do the same to a second bank account in London under your British ID. Transfer the other third of your Swiss account to the British bank. Understand? One third to the French account, one third to the British account, and one third kept in the Swiss account."

Silently, the young woman's head bobbed up and down as the tears continued to flow.

"Child, I know this is difficult. There is no other way. They will uncover in the next couple of days the trace of the ipecac syrup you used to make yourself vomit. They will also piece together the video of your arriving at the Kremlin in a heavy winter raincoat and will deduce that you raised your body temperature in a hot tub so you would appear flushed and feverish." He obviously had already viewed the video and had seen her wearing the coat. "By asking your team they will figure you used the terrible spaghetti in the commissary to act as though it was food poisoning. You did very well, my child, but you will be found out. You must go. I will be leaving on a flight today too. My time is up. They will realize that I helped you, my child, and they will be after me too."

"I am so sorry, otets," realizing he was calling her "my child" and she just called him "father".

"I am taking a later flight two hours from now to Turkey. It will appear to be a pre-planned business trip. As soon as I arrive in Turkey, I will depart on a second flight to Spain. Once in Spain, I will also transfer additional funds from another Swiss account. In a couple of days, I will arrive in London and we will meet up again. I will be in contact with you through these people. He now reached over the seat and handed her a note with two names and a business address. The names were Evalina and Nina. The business and address were iSPY Gallery 1 Quai Voltaire 75007 Paris, France. Tell them that Yuri told you to find them. Do you understand, child? Yuri told you!"

Sophia, still fighting tears, said, "Yes, otets, I understand. I would be lying to you if I said I am not worried and scared for me and for you."

"We will be fine, my dear one, my child" . . . There it was again, "my child" . . . "These people will have a place for you to stay. Then, I have a special place already where we will be safe. You understand?"

"Yes."

"Okay, you must take time now to make yourself presentable for the airport. No one must suspect anything including seeing a troubled beautiful, young woman. One as beautiful as you Sophia would draw attention. That is not what we want."

She spent the rest of the drive doing as he had said. When she emerged from the car in front of the Air France departure check in, she was a transformed beautiful woman. She was no longer Sophia from the hospital. Her hair was short and black. The wig in the spy bag covered her natural blonde hair. The face looking back at her on her passport photo looked like her now but the name was not hers and neither was her new French address.

Her flight left on time, as did General Dimitri's two hours later. He made his connecting flight to Spain, shortly after she was landing in Paris and finding a hotel for the night. Their transition had begun. A new beginning for both.

38

Thursday, August 29, 2019
Washington, DC, USA

HOTEL ZENA

Once the team was completed, before they left Paris, Nina and Ninette asked Etienne if they could choose the hotel where everyone would stay. Neither wanted to stay in a large "American" type hotel. They would rather choose a small boutique European style. Nina also did not want the hotel too close to the Kennedy Center as she hoped enough distance separating where they were staying from where the show was taking place would give her a relaxing break.

Etienne checked with the Director-General and approval was given. The assignment of securing the hotel and their safety was given to the French Embassy in Washington and their "special security team".

The women found the perfect hotel: Hotel Zena! The hotel was built on a theme of "Female Empowerment . . . the first hospitality establishment solely dedicated to celebrating the accomplishments of women." Perfect!

The building itself was first built as a hotel in 1974. Over the years, it was renovated several times until it took on its new very modern and feminine theme look. The lobby, dominated by a portrait of honorable Justice Ruth Bader Ginsburg, was designed by Andrea Sheehan and produced by artist's Julie Coyle Studios using 20,000 hand-painted repurposed tampons. Its uniqueness honors Justice Ginsburg's life-long dedication to women's rights and equality and her humor. Another art installation features a curved wall layered with 8,000 protest buttons, representing generations of marches and events, promoting the feminist movement. It was a place to celebrate the women of this adventure, LADA—the aging Artist, Evalina—the entrepreneur and gallery owner, Nina and Ninette—the next age leaders. Ideal!

The "Portrait Gallery" in Hotel Zena's lobby also features the stories of female warriors. It displays artwork celebrating ten powerful women, in addition to Ruth Bader Ginsburg. Each woman made significant contributions in the struggle for Women's Rights and Gender Equality. Two pieces of art inspired by the Honorable Shirley Anita Chisholm, the first African American woman elected to the United States Congress are a portrait of her and a hanging installation constructed of painted folding chairs. They celebrate her powerful words: "If they don't give you a seat at the table, bring a folding chair."

"The only thing missing is a portrait of Josephine Baker," said LADA when told of where they would be staying by Nina and Ninette. "Perhaps someday, America would fully realize the gift they gave to France!"

The French Embassy secured the entire top two floors. It took some finagling and significant compensation to the already booked guests. Quite quickly, the cooperating staff of the property accomplished the task when the manager received a personal call from the President of France requesting her assistance.

All of the accommodations were suites. Nina and Ninette had suites in the middle of the 11th floor. On the side of Nina's suite was Etienne's suite. Between those suits was a door that could open to join the two rooms. It stayed open through their entire stay! The same was true with Ninette and Guy's suites.

On the other side of Etienne was LADA's corner suite. LADA's rooms were located between Etienne's and Mrs. Smith's suite. The chief inspector was housed directly across the hall from LADA. Two rooms remained open between his room and what would be Madame Marta's. She arrived the following day. Two days later the sandwiched rooms became the temporary homes of Evalina and her father Alexei.

Former "special" students of Madame Marta's occupied all the rest of the rooms on that floor. The floor just below, directly under LADA, Etienne, Nina, Ninette, Guy, Evalina, and Alexei's were also booked with former "special" students of Madame Marta and French visitors to Washington, DC. They had been a flight crew on their 777-300er. Security was in place.

The fact that the CIA was left out of the arrangements was not a misstep on the parts of either Mrs. Smith or Madame Marta. Both had apparently tried to secure that information, it appeared to their two agencies. Somehow, it seemed to have evaded both of them, though curiously, there were plenty of former "special" EFL students booked there.

The Russian Intelligence Agency was quite miffed. Hotel Zena was totally booked. They even tried to lease short-term space in "The Residence at Thomas Circle," an assisted living center. No luck. Ultimately, they took rooms at the Residence Inn by Marriott and the Westin Washington, DC, City Center. No direct observation and reconnaissance. And electronic monitoring of the rooms was out. The French security team ensured that was impossible by sweeping the rooms twice daily.

The CIA SUV carrying Nina, Ninette, Etienne, and Guy headed over to the Kennedy Center. There they released the driver to return to Langley. The luggage was delivered to the hotel by the other SUV. Ninette, Etienne, and Guy, having never been to Washington, were excited. Nina had been before, but never with the man she loved. On the trip to the Kennedy Center, Etienne used his phone's map. He found that the hotel was only a couple of miles walk from the Kennedy Center. A nice day. A good day for a sightseeing stroll later.

Nina wanted to ensure that the paintings had arrived safely. She touched base with the Kennedy Center's art manager about the show's setup. This was purely a social and security check. Tomorrow would be a recovery day. The following day, work would begin on the show in earnest.

While Nina was checking on the paintings, Etienne went to a private location, as far from the crowds as possible. Using his security scrambled satellite phone, he called back to Paris.

The call connected to the office of the Director-General d'Armee. He filled the Director-General in on the happenings at Langley and what he had learned from LADA, in secret, about the gentleman and woman at CIA Headquarters. The Director-General was not happy. The conversation ended with "I'll be back to you, Captain, with further instructions after I have conferred with the others and the President. Understand?"

"Yes, sir!" Etienne replied and the phone call ended. Etienne shook his head. There is more going on than we know! Then he went back to find Nina and see if he could help, which he could not. C'est la vie!

• • •

The four young people woke up early on Friday. This was a day to discover the real Washington. They met in the lobby and walked four blocks northwest on Connecticut Avenue to Dolcezza Gelato and Coffee. "Coffee in very quaint digs" is how it was listed on Google Maps. "Good news, they have croissants and espresso!" Etienne announced. The smiling group headed off for the day. Mrs. Smith and the Chief Investigator stayed with LADA. She planned to do some sketches of various sights on the Washington Mall. Perhaps she would run into the young folks at some point.

Dolcezza looked as they expected. Very euro. White porcelain subway tiles behind the Gelato stainless steel counter. Old brick walls painted white with black lettered menu attached and dark wood counter for the coffee and food service area. And, magnificent croissants, beurre, amande et croix au chocolat. They were at home. The women each had a croix au chocolat. Etienne, a purist, settled on the beurre croissant while Guy had an amande. Everyone had a dark rich latte, though Etienne was tempted to just get espresso. Ultimately, he was talked into the latte and was glad he changed.

It was close to 10:00 am in Washington when they finished. They decided to walk off the croissants. Heading down southeast along Connecticut Avenue, they saw the Whitehouse several blocks ahead. When they reached 17th street, they turned due south until they reached Pennsylvania Avenue. Turning right, they passed by the White House. It was just like the pictures they had seen. Nina had seen it before but every time she saw it again it gave her gooseflesh.

Again, they headed due south towards the reemerging Pennsylvania Ave NW and followed it all the way down to the white dome of the Capitol Building. The seat of government for the most powerful nation on Earth. More gooseflesh.

The couples walked around the Capitol Building admiring the height of the dome and the Statue of Freedom on top, a classical female figure. Under her helmet her cascading hair. "E Pluribus Unum " etched on the pedestal she stands on. Its statement reminded each of them of their own country's motto, "Liberte, Egalite, Fraternity." Such commonality between the two countries.

Funny, the two young ladies thought independently, how the figure of a woman is used to show strength, wisdom, and courage in almost all cultures. Men's images are usually used to show power, force, and dominance. Do these men of ours realize this fact? Nina and Ninette each looked at each other as if they could read the others' minds. Had they?

Walking down the north edge of the greenspace between the National Gallery of Art East Building, Nina turned to the others and asked if they could go in. They all without hesitation said "yes". This city, like Paris, is so full of historic spaces that they would not be able to cover them all in a year, let alone a few days. Each was thinking I have to come back again one day, Nina looking at Etienne and him at her. Ninette and Guy, doing the same.

They wished they could spend more time in the West Museum and all of the other museums on the Mall. The long trip, long walk, and worry told them it was time to head back to the hotel.

Ninette suggested they get back, rest, and try out the sundeck and pool on the top of the hotel for the afternoon. Then they could eat dinner somewhere. Perhaps even at the hotel or, suggested Etienne, at a French restaurant he had found online. The rest looked at him, sighed, and laughed. He did too.

Walking the mile and a half back to the hotel along 14th Street NW they passed the US Environmental Protection Agency, which reminded all of them of the issues that the world was facing with climate change. The Paris Accord had raised expectations that were quickly dashed by the current US President. He pulled the US out of those agreements. If he were using logic, the rest of the world couldn't see it. He was just being mean spirited as usual.

Then, passing the US Customs and Border Protection, they were reminded of another horrible crisis facing the world. Uncontrolled migration triggered by racism, ethnic cleansing, climate change crisis, water shortages, and human despair caused by violence and greed. It seemed odd to the four visitors that within one complex was the Customs Department, the Ronald Reagan Building and International Trade and the National Children's Museum. It seemed an odd combination of purposes.

It was a hot afternoon in late August when they finally reached the hotel. Agreeing to meet at the rooftop pool in fifteen minutes, the ladies went up to their rooms to change into swimsuits and cover-ups. The men needed to chat a few minutes about business and would join them at the pool.

Etienne and Guy went over to an isolated table in the lobby area and sat down. Here, Etienne filled Guy in on the private conversation he had with LADA after the CIA Headquarters meeting. He also told of his subsequent phone conversation with the Director-General d'Armee later that same day.
"This is a potential real problem, non?"

"Oui!"

The men ended their meeting with shared knowledge that at some time soon the Director-general would get back to Etienne with instructions on how to proceed. Until then, they both were not to reveal anything of what they suspected to anyone on the team, particularly not Mrs. Smith and Madame Marta. Heading to their rooms, they changed into bathing suits to then join their beautiful women on the roof deck for a cool dip in the pool.

Nina and Ninette were lounging on deck chairs when their men walked out onto the deck. Nina and Ninette were in very tasteful and only moderately revealing two-piece swimsuits. Enough revealing to attract the attention of all males by the pool and elicit the anger at being upstaged by the young women, particularly in the eyes of their husbands and boyfriends.

That changed when Etienne and Guy joined Nina and Ninette. Now it was just pure and undeniable envy and jealousy.

Broad shoulders with well-defined abs and strong taunt muscles over well-tanned bodies, the two men attracted every woman's eyes. Not only did these two handsome men have wonderful smiles on their faces as they walked the deck towards their ladies, additionally what attracted all the female faces at the pool and surrounding deck were the very small, tight Speedo swimsuits the men wore. They left nothing to the imagination, or better put, every woman's imagination was now in full bloom!

Nina and Ninette, noticing the attraction their two men were getting, looked at each other and chuckled. Obviously, the only beaches their men had been on were in Europe. Here in the US, most men wore those knee length baggy swimsuits. Ones that hid your body. Looking at most of the other men on the deck, that was certainly understandable. What amused Nina and Ninette more was how oblivious the two men were of the disturbance they were causing: jealous men on the deck and wishful thinking women!

When the men got to their ladies, Nina spoke first, "I see you both are armed and dangerous!"

“Pardon?” Guy replied.

“Look around you, Guy,” Ninette whispered. “Do you see other men who are as handsome as you both? And do you see anyone else with such strong muscles?” She and Nina were having fun with this.

“And do you notice how all the other men hide what they don’t have? They are less willing to show their true firmness,” Nina said, smiling and looking at what was not so hidden behind tight cloth on Etienne.

Now both men started to turn red. “This is not okay? We should have worn something else? Not our swimsuits?” Guy implored.

The girls both giggled nearly uncontrollably. Ninette broke the embarrassment with, “You are both dressed perfectly for us, and as you can see, all of the other females on this deck and pool as well. We suspect the boyfriends and husbands are less happy. But you are making many women very happy, especially us. Why don’t you give them all a big smile and wave? They will appreciate that.”

Guy looked at Etienne. Etienne nodded. They turned to their now realized audience of female admirers. They waved.

“Now, can we borrow your cover-ups?”

They all joined in a laugh together

The next day, Evalina and Alexei departed Paris for the meeting at CIA Headquarters.

39

Saturday, August 31, 2019
Paris, France

DETOUR

It was a beautiful morning in Paris. Light fluffy clouds floated high above the Seine River, left over from a fog of early morning. Evalina and Alexei loaded the taxi with bags and instructed the driver to go to Charles De Gaulle Airport Air France terminal. There they were to meet up with Jack from MI6 and Gaston from French Intelligence. All were scheduled on the same flight number that Nina and the others had taken just three days before. That would change.

As they got out of the cab, Alexei paid the driver. They headed for the door and check in desks. Jack, a slender man of six feet tall and Gaston, a shorter man but very solidly built, had been waiting for them to arrive. They walked up to Evalina and Alexei. Gaston spoke.

"There has been a small change. Check-in will not be necessary today. You are to follow us. Our car is waiting outside."

Alexei and Evalina looked at each other, not sure what to do.

"There is no worry. We will be leaving as scheduled. Perhaps a bit earlier in fact. More will be explained fully once we are onboard the aircraft. Our car is parked right outside with security watching it. Follow me." He then took Evalina's roll bag and Jack took the bag that Alexei was pulling.

Outside was a black SUV with two very heavily armed police officers standing watch. The four of them got into the vehicle, Gaston driving and Jack in the front passenger seat. Evalina, behind Jack and Alexei walking around the vehicle, entered the door behind the driver, Gaston.

"We are headed to a hangar where we will meet up with others. There has been a special flight arranged for us. There will be a slight detour from the original flight plan. One stop over. Perhaps for a day or so. Then we will resume the schedule by arriving on time at the CIA Headquarters. You will understand more shortly."

Alexei said in a firm but controlled voice, "Should we be worried?"

"Mas non," Gaston replied. "We will be traveling on a special aircraft and make a slight stop over for business. That is all."

Evalina and Alexei remained silent watching and wondering what was going to happen. A few minutes later, quite removed from the rest of the airport, the SUV pulled up to a security gate. The passports and identifications were all checked. A mirror on a long pole checked the underside of the vehicle. The car passed through the gate and headed for a large, unmarked hangar. The SUV pulled up to an open gate of the hangar and there inside it sat. The Airbus A330-200 aircraft of the President of France. Armed guards were surrounding the airplane, as did others stationed around the building. Gaston and Jack ushered the guests up the stairs of the plane as their bags were carried up behind the four by members of the Groupe de sécurité de la présidence de la République; the French version of the Secret Service. At the top of the stairs were more security members. Once fully inside the airplane, a familiar person came out of an office at the front of the plane. There they stood with the President of France.

"Welcome to my home away from home," he said with a smile, shaking hands first with Evalina and then with Alexei. "I hope you don't mind this slight departure from what I am sure would have been an enjoyable flight on the scheduled Air France flight to the United States. We thought you might enjoy the food on this aircraft slightly better." Alexei and Evalina were used to unusual circumstances, but this one was by far the most unusual.

"We will be preparing for departure soon. Until then please enjoy the comfort of the aircraft and this fine staff. I will join you again shortly to tell you why we have altered your schedule, only slightly. I think you will understand and perhaps enjoy it more fully."

With that, the President went back to his office and the four of them were led farther back in the aircraft to some luxurious seats. The aircraft was engaged by the tractor, which pulled it out of the hangar. The large blue, white, and red tail just fit through the hangar opening. Once outside, cables were attached to the huge Rolls-Royce Trent 700 engines and they were started.

Evalina glanced around the aircraft. There were several pods of lounge seats with coffee tables in between seats. She had not noticed the others when listening to the President. She had only seen him being overwhelmed yet again by his unexpected presence at yet another occasion. Now she realized there were others onboard too. She leaned over to Alexei and said, "Did you see the others? The Director-Generals d'Armee, of External Security, of Internal Security?"

Alexei nodded "yes". Only the Director-General of National Police was not there. There were a few others who also appeared to be senior advisors to the President. Noticeably, to both Alexei and Evalina, there were no representatives from the news media on board. That was strange.

"What do you suppose this means, Alexei? Should we be worried again for Nina and Ninette, and for Etienne and Guy? For LADA?"

"I think we will learn soon. I don't think they would handle things this way if the others were in trouble. This must be something more. Let's hear what the President tells us."

The A330-200 started to move. It proceeded to the taxi strip and on toward the runway. Both Evalina and Alexei settled back in their seats as a military steward brought them a glass of Dom Pérignon.

Evalina smiled at Alexei. "Well, papa, I think you are right. I doubt we would be served champagne if there was something to worry about!"

He smiled back but kept his thoughts to himself. "You are right, my daughter. Nothing to worry about for the others. But something is up. There is something to worry about, I'm positive." With that thought passing, he settled back for takeoff and sipped his wine.

As the A330-200, listed as "Cotam 001," lifted off the Charles de Gaulle runway, nearly simultaneously three other aircraft were taking to the sky too. They included "Royal Canadian Air Force VIP," the German "Konrad Adenauer," and the British "Royal Air Force VIP". All had listed false locations on their initial flight plans. Those flight plans would soon be amended to name one airport, Keflavik International Airport, Iceland. Each plane was escorted by four fighter jets of its own military. A special unannounced summit was going to be held that day. One that Evalina and Alexei would be attending.

Russian Intelligence, Russian Military, US Intelligence, and US Military were each alerted to the apparent strange happenings.

Headquarters of the Russian Military picked up on radar a strange phenomenon. Four fighter jets from Germany, France, Great Britain, and Canada lifted off runways at almost the same time. The jets were each circling over France near Charles de Gaulle Airport, Koln Bonn Airport in Germany, London's Heathrow. The ones from Montreal were already streaking eastward toward the Atlantic. They appeared to be escorting a wide body aircraft. But what aircraft and why? No public announcements had been made.

Now other wide body aircraft joined each of the flights of other fighter jets and they too began streaking westward toward the Atlantic from their own locations. The fighters and wide body from London were now over Ireland. What was going on?

The 60ish, thin-lipped woman sat behind her big mahogany desk. Stern faced as usual, her thin lips pulled tight. The papers in front of her were concerning. How is this stuff on the President being leaked? Where was the source? It had to be her counterparts in the Kremlin. They were the only ones who had the materials and videos. Although that was true, there was some kind of information secretly coded on a painting in the secure vault. Why hadn't her team of chemists figured out how to remove the paint and reveal what was there? At least, this could not be the videos! But what was coded on the painting? Why was an astrophysicist able to figure this out and not her team? And how did this artist, IKIA or DIKEA. Whatever the hell her name is, why was she able to create this method back during WWII and no one else able to figure it out? This doesn't make sense. Just then, there was a knock on the door.

"Come in, damn it!"

The Deputy Director and a Deputy National Security Agency Director entered her office. There were concerned looks on their faces.

"What?"

The Deputy Director answered, "Director." He would never dare to use her name let alone a first name. "There appears to be some very unusual activity taking place in France, Germany, Great Britain, and Canada!" He waited a moment for her to ask the question.

"What is so fucking unusual?!" Annoyed that the two agency Deputy Directors were making her ask the question. "God, damn it, tell me what is going on!"

"At nearly exactly the same time, from Montreal, Paris, Bonn, and London, four fighter jets took off from each location. That was 4:00 am Washington time. They each circled their respective airport air spaces for about ten minutes. Then, four separate unidentified wide body A300 series airbuses took off from those locations. They were joined up by the jet fighters as escorts. We can only surmise that these are the leaders of each of these countries. Where they are heading and why, we do not know. We are unsure that they are heading to the same place, but logic would tell us that it has to be the same location. It is so strange we thought we should alert you right away. We are trying to track them and anticipate the location where they might be heading. Right now, it is unclear."

The CIA Director was silent. She put her folded hand under her chin index and little fingers extended to her mouth in contemplation. The Assistant Director thought to himself, "Gosh, she reminds me of someone. Who? My God, it's the same pose as Dr. Evil from the Austin Powers movies!" He was mesmerized. Caught up in that thought.

Finally breaking out of that thought he added, "Director, there is something else we should inform you about. It perhaps relates to this strange event. The astrophysicist Alexei and his daughter Evalina, they missed their Air France flight this morning."

"What? Where are they?" she yelled.

"We are unsure. We had them trailed to the airport. Once there, our agents went into the check-in desk area to wait. The subjects never came through the door. We don't know where they went. They didn't make the flight."

Anger built in the stern woman. Her face turning red, she yelled again, "Find out what happened to them! Where they are! Report back to me as soon as you find out. And make sure it happens soon! You understand?"

Both men nodded their understanding. Then she told them, "Get out! I have to think!"

After they left, her mood turned even angrier. "Damn," she thought. "I'll have to bring him in too!" She picked up her phone and asked her assistant to get the Director of the FBI on the secure phone link. They needed to talk!

Just then a secure phone link to her counterpart in Moscow signaled a call. She took it and with building anxiety and concern, she heard him tell her that Colonel General Dimitri Gorchakov had apparently disappeared along with a key female associate, Major Sophia Malenkov. The counterpart asked if she knew anything about their disappearance. "Are they kidding?" she thought.

"No, I have not heard anything. Have they defected from Russia?"

"Presumably so!" Came a not too pleasant reply. A pause and then hesitantly, the voice at the other end added, "We believe he left with important security materials. Tapes of a kind." More hesitation. "These tapes could be bad news to OUR MAN and also to YOURS. You understand?"

Boy did she ever understand. More damn tapes. How many of these fucking tapes are there? These sick tapes had been the subject of many concerns of hers. She never suspected they would also be of concern for the Russian President too. There has to be more to this. Can she finagle this out of him?

"What is the subject of the tapes?" she asked.

"Private meetings of OUR PRESIDENT . . . and YOURS." "Shit!" she thought. He continued, "I understand from our conversation that you are unaware of the missing individuals and the materials in question, am I correct?"

"Yes, you are correct!" Just then her other secure line was blinking indicating the FBI Director was on the phone.

She told the Russian counterpart she would have to end the conversation now. She would let him know if she heard or found out anything. Tersely, their conversation ended. She picked up the other line.

"You called!" the gruff voice on the other end of the line said. Obviously, a bit putout that she had her office call him and then he was put on hold waiting for her. She had to think fast and ease the tension. She was, after all, going to need him. He was a straight shooter. A man of law. Willing to bend the law but not break it. He had helped a previous administration with that when she headed up the "Enhanced Interrogation Program". He was part of the team of Justice Department attorneys who found loopholes in laws to suggest that the torture she was conducting was just "enhanced interrogation".

Even with that, there was considerable effort on the part of the international community to charge her and others with "crimes against humanity". She was going to need his help again now, and this time his help might be a bit closer to breaking the law, something he would not do, she knew. Still, she would have to try.

"We need to meet," she told him. "Your place or mine. But one of the secure rooms."

"You come to mine," he said. "I've been to yours this week. I like the atmosphere better here!"

"What time?"

"Give me an hour. Let's say ten. I'll have the conference room reserved. Who else are you bringing?"

"Just me. And, just you too." Then she added, "Please." That's as much kindness as you will get, buddy.

"Ten then. Don't be late. I hate being made to wait!" He hung up.

"Asshole!" she screamed into the disconnected phone. She then slammed the phone down on its cradle.

Another knock on the door.

"What is it?" she screamed.

The Deputy Director cautiously entered. "All of the subject aircraft, as if on cue, suddenly changed directions. The one from Germany appeared to be headed for London. It changed to head due north along the Prime Meridian. Then an hour later took a nearly left hand, 90-degree change due west. The flight from Paris appeared to be on a course for New York. It suddenly turned due north along 15 degrees west Meridian. Likewise, the British flight out of London appeared to be headed towards Montreal. It, too, suddenly changed course. It then turned nearly due north on the 20 west Meridian. All of the support aircraft did the same as the aircraft they were escorting. They have all made additional flight corrections. We have plotted the new flight vectors and we believe we have their intended arrival location. It appears to be Reykjavik-Keflavik International Airport. Iceland."

"Shit! Why? Have we heard anything from the Secretary of State's office about something?"

"No, Ma'am," realizing his mistake, responding to her by a feminine gender reference . . . she hated that . . . he added, "I mean, no, Director."

Again, she took up the Dr. Evil pose. "Don't we have a NATO base there? A Naval air station at that airport?"

"Yes, Director." Not making the same mistake with pronouns again.

"Do we have anyone on the ground there?"

"I'm sure we must. I'll check. What would you want them to do?"

"Find out who is on those airplanes and why they are there?"

"How?"

"Oh, dear" he thought. "Big mistake."

"God, damn it! You figure it out! Get out and get it done!"

He turned and made a hasty retreat to the door before more of her wrath could come down on him. "God, I hate that woman!" he said to himself under his breath as he walked down the hall and quickly headed to the Ops Personnel Office. Sure hope they would have someone there!

The Deputy Director's hopes were dashed. Not only were there no CIA operatives in Iceland, there were no NATO forces other than those of Iceland's own Coast Guard, with three ships and four aircraft, one fixed wing and three helicopters. The last NATO country assignment ended on August 10. That was the US. The next assignment would not begin until October 1 when Italy will have the next four fighter jets at Keflavik. Until that time, the airspace is unpatrolled.

"Damn!!"

As the curse was leaving the Assistant Director's mouth in Langley, Virginia, another curse was happening in the air traffic control tower at Keflavik International Airport by air traffic officer Gunnar Egilsson.

"Hvad i fjandanum!" (What the fuck!) The air traffic controller said, having just learned that four wide body airplanes were headed for emergency clearance and landing one right after another. Following each of them, in between one and the next, were four fighter jets. A wing of four for each wide body. Sixteen fighters total! The first large jet now identified itself as "Royal Air Force VIP". The British Prime Minister's jet. The second incoming wide body was identifying itself as Cotam 001. The President of France's jet! Next in line was the German "Konrad Adenauer" Prime Minister of Germany's aircraft, and lastly coming in from the opposite direction the Royal Canadian Air Force VIP, that of the Prime Minister of Canada!

"Hvad i oskopunum!" (What the hell!) Instantly he picked up the emergency phone and notified the Coast Guard command. They quickly sent all of the armed guards possible including the National Commissioner's National Security and Special Forces unit. The President of Iceland and Prime Minister's staff were also alerted. They would be at the airport to welcome their unexpected visitors.

The lead plane's wheels touched down at 11:30 am Iceland time. The following fighter jets touched down one right after another between 11:35 am and 11:40 am. The second plane from France hit the runway at 11:45 am and again the four trailing fighters each landed within five minutes of the A330-200. The same thing continued for the next two wide bodies and was completed by 12:15 pm. All had taxied to the far end of the airport and what was the NATO and Headquarters of the Iceland Coast Guard military airfield facilities, Keflavik Naval Air Station.

As soon as the RAF fighters were refueled, they took to the sky to secure and guard the airspace near and around Iceland. The Director-General d'Armee picked up the secure scrambled phone on the French aircraft. His call went to NATO Headquarters. He spoke with the Supreme Allied Commander, a US Air Force general, to make him aware of the events in Iceland, He informed the Supreme Commander of the fact that these four world leaders were now in Iceland. The airspace above and around the country was being secured at the moment by RAF fighters. In a couple of hours, those fighters would be relieved by French fighters, then German fighters, and finally Canadian fighters. This was to continue until the work of the four leaders was completed. It should take no longer than two days but perhaps as short as a few hours.

As the French Director-General d'Armee was making this call, another officer on the British airplane was doing so with one of his friends of equal rank, the Deputy Supreme Allied Commander, also a British Army General.

Both NATO Generals were extremely unhappy to be informed this way and especially at such a late time in the event. The Supreme Allied Commander had already heard from his chain of command in the US military that something was happening. Had he approved it? When he informed them he had not approved the actions, the US Secretary of Defense was outraged.

Then the Supreme Allied Commander was dealt the final blow. The Chair of the NATO Military Committee, RAF Chief Marshal, had been informed. He had given on behalf of the Committee, which represents the 30 NATO Nations, approval for the air defense actions that were now underway. He had given this approval at 8:00 am in Belgium, 6:00 am Iceland, and 2:00 am in the US. It was now 12:30 pm in Iceland, the Chair had known this for six and a half hours and they were now just hearing about this! The US President, already unsupportive of NATO, would be furious.

40

Saturday, August 31, 2019
Keflavik International Airport, Iceland

FOUR WORLD LEADERS MEET

The four world leaders met in the French Cotam 001. The meeting was relatively short, lasting a mere three hours. Decisions were made.

They all concluded the current President of the United States, at best, was irrational and possibly unstable. They agreed that the Russian President, though stable, was ruthless. It was obvious that he held information about the US President. They agreed that each of their nations were being influenced by disinformation, which was coming primarily from Russia. They all had examples of Russia hacking into secure computer sites. They further all had proof of Russian attempts to undermine legitimate elections in their countries and to sow doubt through disinformation...outright lies. Lastly, they all agreed that Russia was successfully planting seeds of racial bias and hate using social media...all of it. They agreed to have their intelligence agencies work together and share information in order to fight these Russian actions. Their biggest concern was the political demise in the US, which was tearing apart this historic democracy. Most of it was caused by the Russian disinformation and supported, for political and monetary gains, by the US President.

The French President now revealed to the other members the fact that there was a painting that had information smuggled out of Russia that contained the damning information that aided the Russian President to control the US President and other world leaders. Although each of the four leaders in the room might have had some concerns about each other, they had nothing to worry about. They did have others within NATO to worry about, however.

The French President informed them of the rather unfortunate chain of events. The painting, which was to be in the hands of the special investigator regarding the Russian influence in the United States, was now, unfortunately, being secured by the CIA. The current head of the CIA, the person responsible for the "enhanced interrogation" activities of the United States. The information was now in jeopardy.

Evalina and Alexei were asked to join the meeting with the four world leaders. The President of France introduced them. He explained this was the team, along with the artist, who would figure a way to secure the information on the painting. This took Evalina and Alexei by surprise, something that seemed to be happening more and more often. "What did he mean by 'figure a way'?" they each wondered silently. "We already know the way . . . don't we? Is this the reason for the change in travel plans?" Alexei believed the extra step he and LADA had taken was even more important.

The world leaders expressed their gratitude to Evalina and Alexei. The meeting broke up as quickly as it began. Each leader went back to their own aircraft. Once on board, the planes taxied to the runway and took off in the exact opposite order as their arrival, each with their fighter escorts. There was one exception. The French President's plane followed the Canadian Prime Minister's back to Montreal. They had further work to do and needed Alexei and Evalina to be safe with them. There would be time next week for Alexei to work his magic.

41

Saturday, August 31, 2019
Washington, DC, USA

THE COVER

As the French Cotam 001 streaked through the late afternoon sky behind the Canadian wide body, the Director-General d'Armee called Etienne on the secure phone. It was nearly 1:00 pm Saturday afternoon in Washington, DC. He and Nina, Ninette, and Guy had been at the Kennedy Center since 8:00 that morning working...well Nina had...on the setup of the paintings with LADA and with the Kennedy art manager. They had gone through the painting list and the location map of the center placing where each painting would go. The basic layout of paintings followed a history timeline from WWII through to contemporary Russian times. The final painting, one of a set of duplicate images. The other copy was currently hanging in Nina's apartment on the Montmartre at 10 Rue Garreau. The location where the Martz couple would arrive in two days. It was a painting they would fall in love with. There was also one more set of duplicate paintings. This second set of duplicate painting, the most important of all!

The two couples sensing LADA tiring had decided enough work had been done for the day. The chief investigator and Mrs. Smith escorted LADA back to the hotel.

On such a beautiful day as this particular Saturday a walk and investigation of a new area of DC was in order. How about Georgetown? It was decided. A walk on the Rock Creek Trail, along the Potomac, from the Kennedy Center to the Georgetown Waterfront Park. That evening, they would find a nice restaurant for dinner. Wasn't there one where John Kennedy proposed to Jackie? Perhaps they could find that one. It was Martin's Tavern, right? Etienne called and made reservations for that evening at 7:00 pm.

Then, Etienne's phone rang. It was a secure phone call. They all stopped. The three others, knowing he would fill them in, walked away to leave him alone. They went down to the Potomac shoreline to watch the shells while rowers glided by.

"Hello," Etienne answered.

"Captain?"

"Oui."

"Listen carefully. Professor Alexei and his daughter Evalina are on Cotam 001 with myself, our President, and several other senior staff. We decided that we would not allow the Professor and Evalina to arrive in DC on the Air France Flight. Were you aware they had not arrived?"

"Non, I mean we just assumed they had. We have been at the Ken . . ." He was interrupted.

"No need to explain, Captain. They will arrive within the next couple of days. We stopped over in Iceland to meet with the Prime Ministers of England, Germany, and Canada. Our flight is trailing behind the Canadian Prime Ministers as we speak. We are headed for Montreal. It will be used as cover until we figure out all the plans. However, I need you to arrange for Professor K and LADA to talk with us later this evening. Perhaps around 11:00 pm. It must be in a secure location unobserved by others except for you, Nina, the Lieutenant, and the other young woman. Can that be arranged?"

"Oui, Director-General. On a secure phone. We will arrange it."

"Merci. Talk with you this evening. Au revoir." With that, the phone call ended.

Etienne joined the others and briefed them quickly. He then called the Chief Investigator using both his secure phone and Chief Investigators scrambled phone. He instructed the officer to have LADA at the French Embassy at 9:30 pm and that he was not to let Mrs. Smith or anyone else know where they were headed. The Embassy would pick them up in an Embassy car.

His next phone call was to the French Embassy secure phone number he had been given. He identified himself using the arranged code word. Etienne asked to speak with the Ambassador. His phone call was put through immediately. Without hesitation, the Ambassador arranged for the car to pick up LADA and the Chief Investigator at precisely 9:15 pm and he, the Ambassador, would also be in the vehicle to do so.

Etienne then called the Investigator to let him know the arrangements. That finished, the four continued their stroll and fun afternoon, assured that all would go well that evening.

42

Saturday, August 31, 2019
Paris, France

A NEW BEGINNING

Sophia woke up in the Hotel du Quai Voltaire. The room was small like most French hotel rooms. It was comfortable enough. The bed had been okay. The space around the bed, limited. Noise from outside through the single pane windows didn't bother her through the night. She had been exhausted. There was also a small closet, dresser nightstand, and desk. Her view was out across the Seine to the Louvre. Not a bad view for one night.

The hotel was also just a few doors down from the iSPY Gallery on quai Voltaire. "What a strange name for a gallery," she thought. It was also just two blocks away from the BNP Paribas Bank where she would open an account to transfer the funds. She would do the banking first, as it would close by 4:00 pm today. The gallery did not open until 2:00 pm and closed by 7:00 pm. Plenty of time after setting up the bank account to meet either Evalina or the other woman, Nina.

Sophia's new name according to the French Passport and other documents was Caroline Cadieux (meaning strong, little fighter). "Well, she was that," she thought as she considered the name. "Caroline Cadieux. What will you wear today, Caroline? Perhaps, as a fashionable independently wealthy young artist. That would be good." She had limited clothing with her. She had what was in the two bags she brought from Russia. They only contained two skirts. One a black leather mid-thigh mini and the other an ankle length blue with small white flower slit to mid-thigh. "Okay, so she liked to show her legs. They were good, shapely, and not often displayed in military uniform, except the one she had worn that day. Damn it! That did get YOU into trouble. Stop thinking like that!!!"

The leather mini could be accessorized with the black tights she had and a black short sleeve t-shirt. Black pumps with ankle straps. No jewelry. From her "spy bag," dark large square lens sunglasses from Prada with embellished temples. Those would finish the look. A mysterious and a completely stylishly changed young woman. The old Sophia turned into the new Caroline! Her choice was made. Blue with flowers would be used another day.

She slipped out of the panties and t-shirt she had worn to bed the night before and entered the bathroom. The bath/shower was a stand about two and a half feet above the floor. A round shower curtain pulled around it to keep most but not all of the water in the enclosed area. The tub consisted of a place to put your feet and indentations where you could sit your buns. The shower device was handheld. In most old French hotels, you hoped you were up earlier than the other guests were. If not, no hot water. Her water that day was lukewarm. Not relaxing, but certainly invigorating. Besides, sitting in bun indentations wasn't all that relaxing anyway.

She climbed down from the low roost of the tub/shower, reached the towel, and dried herself minimally. She wiped the mirror quickly with her hand and looked at the face in the reflection. "You will be changed, girl," she said to herself aloud. She left the bathroom and padded into the small bedroom.

Underwear? She looked in the bag. The ones packed by the housekeeper were what would normally be packed for a military army officer. Army issue! Ugh! She would have to go commando today. The tights would assure some sense of modesty. Same with the bra . . . braless for sure. A very appropriate look for a young French artist. Besides, freedom was nice. Perhaps she could get used to freedom.

Sophia, now Caroline, had been to Paris several times. She knew of the places to shop, large department stores on the north side of the river. The Galeries Lafayette, Printemps, and Samaritaine were all there. She had never stayed on the south side of the Seine where she was now. She would have to ask at the front desk for a suggestion. On her list to buy would be new clothing that fit the image of the new her . . . Caroline. She also would find makeup. Bold colors for expression. Makeup, especially bold colors applied in abstract ways can obscure facial features from being identified by facial recognition surveillance devices. They also had a shape-changing effect on the human eye that can prevent her from being recognized even by close friends. The trick would be the kinds of colors and the correct application. She was experienced and knew she could do this. But where to find what she needed?

She decided that the blue and flowered skirt would actually be handy today. What she wore yesterday would be discarded in the hotel trash and surrounding area trash containers as she came from the department store later.

Someone in the intelligence world always had to worry about how long it would take for them to be identified as gone and where they would have headed. Facial and body recognition, a major help in identifying someone, was aided greatly by identifying them though what they were wearing. Her clothing would have to go!

She put on the flower skirt, no black tights for now. She could wear the undies she had on yesterday and the shirt she wore yesterday too. Both were fine for the short time while she went to the store.

"I'll find a place to change into a new blouse after purchasing it at the store and discard this one on the way back to the hotel," she told herself.

She had some make up in her spy bag. Mostly subtle colors, unfortunately. Still, if she applied the lipstick heavily and the eyeliner with extended upswings at the ends and a bit too heavy on the eye shadow, she might just make it. The rouge would be heavy, which would accent her cheekbone line and make it appear that she was not quite gaunt. The sunglasses would have to wait for her later transition. The wig too would have to wait.

"If only I had a hat to cover my head." Although not perfect, on the small nightstand was something that might work. It was a bit dingy but not horrible. She picked up the 36" by 18" lace table runner. It could work as a scarf. She tried it on her head. Yes, it worked. It actually looked nice with the long flowered skirt. A good accent piece that hid some of her head shape and features, especially her long blonde hair, which she put in a ponytail under her new head cover. Perfect!

She had to wait until just as she exited the hotel to put it on, as she didn't want the staff to recognize it, though she thought they probably wouldn't anyway. Shoes were the ones from yesterday too. Those she could discard as soon as she left for the bank later that morning it was now 8:00 am.

Heading downstairs to the small breakfast room, she had a quick croissant and cafe au lait. After finishing quickly, she headed to the front desk. Fortunately, it was a different person at the front desk. A young woman.

She received directions from her about where to shop. Young women in Paris were always extremely helpful to other young women when it came to suggesting places to find good clothing and makeup. "Although you might be my competition, I think you should look your best" seemed to be their motto. This one said the place to go was the La Bon Marche, less than a mile from the hotel at 22, Rue de Sèvres. It was, to those that lived on the south side of the Seine River, equivalent to the Galeries Lafayette and Samaritan on the north side.

The directions were easy. Go east on Quai Voltaire to iSPY Gallery. Turn south on Rue des Saints-Peres until you reach Rue du Flour. Turn right onto Rue de Babylone and in two or three blocks, it will be on your left. "Tres simple!" Out the door she headed as she pulled the lace table runner over her hair and ears, shapes of ears are an easy give away about identity.

Arriving a short time later at the La Bon Marche, Sophia went to the cosmetic counters first. She chose several color sticks from Byredo. "The universal product. A multi-use stick to be used all over the face. Buildable coverage that is easy to apply and combine with other Byredo color sticks to contrast or enhance designed to be used easily, quickly, and instinctively while eschewing ultra-perfection; the intense color is blendable with fingers or brush."

"Now how much more like an artist can you be?" she thought. "Comes in finishes aligned to corresponding shades, encompassing lightweight, dewy, matte, and creamy textures suitable for cheeks, eyes, and lips. It was the creamy textures choice. The thicker, the better!"

The first chosen was one called "medium blue 457". It could be termed metallic turquoise blue. She also chose "469 purple stinger". The right name for this glossy purple blue lipstick. She loved the last one's name as it was perfectly fitting for her experience two nights ago . . . color stik 499, "sick pink"! She also bought a true lipstick from Byredo called, "worship her 119". That also seemed fitting for someone who had gotten even with a misogynistic egotist.

"Okay," she thought, "just one additional lipstick for now." 06-devil rouge, a satin lipstick by Kilian of Paris, a specially created harmony of marshmallow and orange blossoms. "Woman in Gold or Good Girl Gone Bad EXTREME". She was having fun. More fun than she ever had in Russia and especially in the army.

She had paid in advance for two nights in the hotel. That still gave her well over 6,000 euros available in her bag from what the Colonel General had provided. She wouldn't use it all today by any means. She had to use cash until the new bank account and transfer were completed. Hopefully, later today. Now she went on a clothing-buying spree. She had to buy those items she thought her new persona would like and wear. Caroline was a bit different from Sophia. She was kind of getting to like the idea of transforming into Caroline. Total immersion would take time. Shoes, pants, skirts, dresses, hats, and silky and soft feminine undergarments were chosen. What else, Caroline?

She checked her watch. It was now 1:00 pm. She had to get back to the hotel, finish changing, and head to the bank. With too much to carry, she had the doorman/security hail a taxi for her. He, like the taxi drivers in Russia, kept watching the young woman through his rearview mirror. "God!" she thought, "Men are alike all over the world!" Bags upon bags were unloaded at the hotel onto a small cart. She left some with the young woman at the front desk until after she took the first load up to her room. Giving the driver a nice tip, he had at least helped her carry the things into the hotel; she finished carrying things up to her room. It was now time to change for the second act.

43

Saturday, August 31, 2019
Washington, DC, USA

PRESIDENT FORD

There was still time for sightseeing before their dinner reservations at Martin's. The couples walked up Wisconsin Avenue Northwest. There on the left at the corner of N Street and Wisconsin was Martin's Tavern. The tavern had outside seating on N Street, or should it be cool they could eat inside. They would wait until their 7:00 pm arrival there to decide. They passed a chocolate shop, LA Burdick Handmade Chocolates. It sounded very euro, and they were tempted. The ladies decided that this evening's fun dinner might be enough for them. Both Etienne and Guy looked at each other with anguish. Both of their stomachs said that waiting until dinner might be a bit too long. However, they gave into their ladies and continued the stroll.

Two blocks ahead they came to Christ Child Opportunity Shop. Nina and Ninette stopped. Now the men did too, unsure what was going to happen. The two women looked at each other, nodded, and opened the door. Etienne and Guy looked at each other and each thought to themselves, "You have to be kidding . . . really?" They followed Ninette and Nina in. The store, a high-end consignment shop, supports the DC chapter of the Christ Child Society, which helps over 5,000 children in need throughout the area. A very noble cause. Etienne and Guy decided it was worth a look.

Interestingly, there seemed to be a quiet buzz in the place. No one was talking loudly but looking around and whispering to each other. It seemed strange and both Guy and Etienne were on alert. Nina and Ninette kept looking.

Finally satisfied that there was nothing here that they couldn't find at one of the good street markets or brocante shops in Paris, the women signaled to the men it was time to go. Out the door and to the right continuing up Wisconsin, bidding "Merci, Madame," to the clerk. No one said anything to each other about the strange atmosphere back at the store. Not one that was threatening. Still, it was different. "Perhaps it is hunger," the men thought.

They both saw it at once. Via Umbria! A small stylish Italian cafe and market. This time it was the men that opened the door and went in. The women looked at each other, shrugged their shoulders and they too entered. Etienne beat a route straight for the deli counter. Guy was right behind him. Nina and Ninette were not displeased with the place. It was a very cute store with hand painted Italian pottery. The kind sold in many stores in Paris. Shelves full of various olive and truffle oils Wine shelves with bottles from all over France, Italy, Spain, and even some from California. By far the thing that attracted both Nina and Ninette's eyes was just to the right as they had entered the store. Sitting on the wide plank old and stained wooden floor was the cutest azure blue Ape P50 single seat cab and open rear bed truck!

Nina turned to Ninette and said, "I want that!"

"Me too!"

The ladies, enamored by the find, didn't see the two men enter the store. They also had missed seeing those same men at the consignment shop minutes before.

Etienne and Guy were busy looking at the items in the display case glass counter. Cheeses of all types. Pre-made pasta salads in large bowls cooling and looking incredible. Ones with red and green peppers and others with olives. Some had anchovies, not the American type, but real anchovies that looked almost like small sardines. Guy was particularly drawn to the calamari salad. He stared at it longingly and came to a decision.

Etienne wandered over to the part of the counter where a clerk was talking with two men. Sausages that could be found at the outdoor markets in France lay before him. This was a great area of the store to find the snack to keep him happy until dinner that evening.

He was standing right next to one of the gentlemen when he overheard the shop clerk, a pleasant young woman, explaining the fennel sausage to the man. "Fennel sausage," Etienne thought, listening to her description. "That would be a good choice." The man next to him said he would take one. "Good, I will be next," Etienne thought and looked over at the man.

Etienne thought, "Gosh you could be a clone of Harrison Ford, the President in the movie *Air Force One*!" It was one of Etienne's and his team's favorite movies. Often played on the video at night when on duty at the station. "He even sounds like him!"

The two men took their purchase and headed out the door, passing by the two young women. The movie-President-lookalike nodded politely, putting his right hand's first and second fingers to his fedora. A kind of salute to the two women and left. The store clerk who was talking with Nina and Ninette about the small truck said, "Well, that was certainly exciting, wasn't it!"

Ninette asked, "Was that the actor Richard Gere?" She loved him in *Pretty Woman* and *Runaway Bride*.

"No, that's Harrison Ford. I hear he is in town to testify before congress regarding private pilot stuff or something." The shop clerk told them.

Just then Etienne showed up with his sausage and Guy with a small container of calamari salad and four plastic forks.

"You missed it, Guy and Etienne. Harrison Ford just left the shop. He nodded goodbye to Nina and me. Tres galant!"

"You're kidding. I was standing right next to the man. I thought, boy you look like a clone of the President in *Air Force One*!"

"You're right, Etienne. He did look like the President in that movie!"

Ninette and Nina looked at the men then at each other and simultaneously said, "Boys!"

44

Saturday, August 31, 2019
Paris, France

CAROLINE CADIEUX

Sophia panicked! She couldn't open a bank account! She had no permanent address in Paris or anywhere else in France for that matter. She needed an apartment lease, a utility bill, or a statement from an employer to prove she was a permanent resident. She looked at her new Caroline passport. It was there! There, of course, was an address. 12 Quai Papacino, Apartment 6 C, Nice, France. She had a French address! There were other documents too. Medical health cards, driver's license, and a note telling her that she was to go to any BNP bank. There she had a bank account under her new name and her address in Nice. She was to transfer the money out of a Swiss bank, EFG International. She had an investment account.

She picked up the British passport. There again was an address. 73 High Street, Cowes, United Kingdom. And she found a bank account document stating an account at HSBC in her name.

She had no idea how much money was already in these accounts, especially the one in Switzerland. Another reality hit her. The setting up of all this could not have happened over night! Her surrogatnyy otets must have been setting this up over time . . . a long time! But why?

The young woman was shaken by that revelation. She also was too worried about what it meant to focus on it now. She knew she had to go to a BNP bank and transfer money. How much? She would have to rely on them to tell her what was currently in her BNP bank account and what was in the Swiss EFG account.

How she was going to not seem like a ditz was going to be hard. Perhaps the new fashion look and the artist persona would work. It had too!

Still dressed as Sophia, she went down to the front desk. The same young woman was still on duty. She had what was perhaps her boyfriend with her. Her head was tilted, smiling at him, and playing with her hair. All sure signs of flirting as Sophia knew.

"Excusez-moi, Mademoiselle, can you tell me where is located a BNP bank? I have to open an account."

The young woman looked at Sophia only slightly annoyed for having to break off the flirt and replied, "Oui, mademoiselle. There is a BNP bank almost just around the corner from here on Rue Du Bac. Unfortunately, its closeness will do you no good today. All banks in Paris close at 1:00 pm on Saturday. I am afraid it is too late. It is now 1:45 pm. Banks will not open again for business until Tuesday at 9:00 am."

Somehow Sophia, still dazed from her encounter with the Russian President, had thought it was a weekday not a weekend.

"Today is . . .?"

"Saturday, mademoiselle."

"Oui, right today is Saturday. I knew that. Silly me."

Sophia turned and headed for the stairs going back to her room to think. The young front desk clerk looked at her boyfriend and made spinning finger signs beside the right side of her head. They both laughed.

The young man and woman were still together as the beautiful young woman, who was transformed into Caroline, descended the stairs. Dressed in a Kaba black leather baseball cap over short black hair, the 5' 10" Caroline fit perfectly in a black "Feisty as Fcuk" t-shirt, loosely draping over her split hem Shein SXY black leather mini skirt. Her long legs were just lightly covered with CETTE 30 denier semi-opaque footless jersey tights. Shoes were ankle strapped dancer's flats. Lips, highly glossed with the Byredo medium blue 457 metallic turquoise. Caroline had applied a light coat from the same color stick as eyeshadow and an accent to her jawline. The finishing touch was the metallic turquoise polish on her fingernails and toenails. The transformation was complete. And boy, did it have an effect!

Her sudden coming into view of the young man caused his mouth to drop. A rush of air left him as a whoosh. The young woman next to him, seeing Caroline and the young man's reaction, punched him solidly on the shoulder. All he could do was stare at Caroline and stammer. Caroline knew he was going to hear an earful as she pushed open the hotel front doors. "Well, that was a nice reaction," she thought and smiled.

She turned right along Quai Voltaire. Several expensive antique stores and galleries later she came to number seven, a women's fashion shop called Mes Demoiselles, My Ladies. She liked the styles, very feminine and casual. Soft looking materials with long dresses and skirts, jeans and blouses made of see-through antique lace fabric. "Hmm," she thought, "perhaps this is the look of the alternate ego for the current Caroline walking down the street. Later on the way back to the hotel I will stop here." Five doors farther she was there, 1 Quai Voltaire . . . iSPY Gallery.

A little nervous, she entered the door. The gallery was light—eggshell white walls and ceiling with black and white tile on the floor. Larger white tiles with four-inch black squares enclosed. Light gray-green chairs and sofas picked up the color in the limestone corners of the room. Most walls were sheet rocked, others were the eggshell color on stone. A very inviting space showing off the numerous varieties of art that hung on display.

A young woman about Caroline's age approached her.

"Bonjour, mademoiselle. I am Natalya. Welcome to iSPY Gallery. How may I help you? Have you ever been to the gallery before?"

"Bon après-midi, Natalya. No, this is my first time at the gallery. It was recommended that I visit with a woman by the name of Evalina. Is she here perhaps?"

"Oh non, I am afraid she is away for a few days. May someone else be of assistance? Perhaps I?"

"Well, I was told by my contact that I should ask for Nina if Madame Evalina was not available. Is she here?"

Natalya, shaking her head, replied, "Oh, I am so sorry. Neither one is here. Both are away in Washington, DC, with an important show of one of our artists. Are you an artist by any chance?" Seeing how the young woman was dressed and made up. Tasteful, but out there!

"Yes, I am," Caroline said. "I was told by Yuri that I should meet with one of them."

Natalya's smile left her face. "Oh, I see. Will you wait here a moment and let me call Evalina. Perhaps she would like to speak with you. Yuri is important to her, you see." Without waiting for a response, Natalya turned and walked away and into an office. "Interesting!" thought Caroline. She was considering walking away. However, through the office window, she saw Natalya not picking up the office phone. Instead, she picked up a cell phone out of a desk drawer and pushed the keys. A few moments later she was speaking.

"Madame Evalina, I am sorry to be calling you on this phone. However, you told me to do so if anything interesting took place, particularly regarding Yuri."

At the other end of the connection on another cell phone, Evalina replied softly, "Yes, Natalya. What is it?"

"A young woman. She says she is an artist. She looks like she could be. Anyway, she asked for you first. I told her you were not here for a few days. She, the woman, looked very disappointed. She then said that if you were not here, she was to ask for Nina. She said that Yuri had told her that she should speak with one or the other of you."

"Natalya, go and get the young woman and bring her into the office. Give her the cell phone and stay with her while I speak with her. Understand?"

"Yes, Evalina. I will get her now." She put the phone down on the desk and went to Caroline.

"Madame Evalina would like to speak with you. Will you come with me to the office? I have her on a cell phone there." This was said more as a directive than a question. Caroline followed Natalya to the office. She was handed the phone. Natalya moved as far away from Caroline as possible in the small space but stayed in the room. Caroline was a bit concerned but spoke into the phone.

"Madame Evalina, this is Caroline Cadieux. I am an artist and a mutual contact, Yuri, said I should speak with you."

"Listen carefully Caroline. You are on a safe phone. It is a scrambled phone. No one can pick up what we are saying. Do you understand? Just say yes or no."

"Yes."

"Are you safe?"

This Evalina person is asking me if I am safe? I am confused.

"Yes, I think so." More than just yes or no but no other way to respond.

"Where are you staying?"

"Hotel Voltaire. Just down the street."

"Yes, I know it of course. In a minute, I am going to speak with Natalya. She will arrange a room in a nice hotel where we house our guest artist. I am going to inform some people I am with . . . people who will assure your safety and security. Do you understand? Is that okay with you?"

Not knowing what else to do but to trust the person that her surrogatnyy otets had told her to trust, she said, "Oui, that sounds fine, Madame."

She handed the phone back to Natalya. Natalya listened carefully to Evalina. She then punched in numbers on the phone and spoke. She told the person on the other end who she was. They had a very special guest of iSPY Gallery and that they would like the very special suite of rooms for the guest. It was agreed. And Natalya said she would have the guest artist there shortly. "Merci" and disconnected the call.

She then handed the phone to Caroline saying, "Evalina wishes you to keep this phone with you. Should you need to speak with her at any time, just push one. It is set to speed dial her. OK?"

"Oui."

"Okay, let me tell the staff that I am going to take you back to your place and will return here shortly. I trust them all but no need in sharing with anyone where or why you are here other than to talk about possibly showing your work here at the gallery. Understand?"

"Oui."

"In just a few minutes, I will pull up on the sidewalk beside our doors. It will be a black Mercedes. I will take you around to your hotel and let you gather your things. I will leave you for about fifteen minutes to do so and then pull up right in front of the hotel on the sidewalk. Will that work?"

"Yes."

"Okay, while I get the car, you look around the gallery. Ask about our shows. Ask about the other artist. Look things over very inquisitively so that they think you are considering us. Don't go too deep into your style of art, unless you really are an artist." Said with a knowing smile. "Are you?"

"Non."

"Well, do your best to show them that you are. I'll be back soon." And out the door she went, leaving Caroline in the office alone for a moment, cell phone held tightly in her hand. Natalya said some things to the other staff and headed out the door. Caroline wandered out into the gallery and began her inquisitive investigation, not having a clue what to say or how to say it artistically.

The day before her visit, something fortunate had happened for her but not for someone else. The Commander saw no further reason to watch the gallery, thinking all LADA's paintings were now in the United States. His people had been re-stationed to increase observation of Evalina's house and Nina's apartment. No one was on duty near the gallery to observe this artist's visit there. The Commander had missed an opportunity to see a former Russian Military Intelligence agent in her new disguise. It seems his bad luck continued.

45

Saturday, August 31, 2019
Somewhere over the Atlantic Ocean

DEFECTOR

Evalina's cell phone had rung just as the world leaders meeting had broken up. She had stepped away for a short time to take the phone call. As the French President's plane streaked westward toward Montreal, she informed him and the others about the mysterious phone call she had received.

Both the Director-General de Armee and the Director-General of External Security called their respective headquarters. It didn't take long to learn that there appeared to be two highly positioned Russian military intelligence officers who were missing and suspected of defecting. This Caroline Cadieux could certainly be one of them. A major, 31-years-old, and an attractive female.

Evalina further informed them of the hotel where Carolina was staying. Within minutes, special teams of French intelligence were set up and in place at the hotel. They were in adjacent rooms and locations across the street. Although no one else could detect they were there, Caroline could, as soon as she arrived at the hotel. Her training allowed her to detect things out of the ordinary. Pairs of men at such a feminine hotel certainly was unordinary.

The agents were not to interfere with her in any way other than to ensure her safety, however necessary. They knew this appeared to be a very high-level defection. No other agencies, especially the Americans and Russians, should learn of this!

Sophia detected the teams. Now as Caroline, she was happy that they were there.

This was good.

At that moment, French Intelligence had no knowledge where the other Russian officer might be. That would soon change.

46

Saturday, August 31, 2019
Washington, DC, USA

MARTIN'S TAVERN

At 7:00 pm Saturday evening, August 31, 2019, Nina, Etienne, Ninette, and Guy were shown to booth 3 in Martin's Tavern. It was a beautiful fall evening. Etienne had to use some significant insistence to convince the other three travelers to give up and move inside. Etienne pulled Guy aside and told him that he would need Guy to guide Ninette away from the table when he gave a signal. Guy didn't understand but indicated to his friend that he would do so. Whatever the signal was, though he did not know what that signal would be.

The menus were delivered. They each ordered a glass of wine. The ladies both chose a white French chenin blanc. The men ordered cabernet sauvignon. After it was served, Etienne gave Guy a quick nod of his head to indicate it was time.

Guy immediately stood up and said to Ninette, "Ninette, I saw something interesting I want to show you outside before we order."

She looked at him questioningly and said, "Guy, what? We just sat down. Surely, this can wait?"

"No, Ninette. We must do it now before the sun is completely dismissed. You will love it. I am sure of that!"

Not hesitating further, he took Ninette's hand and almost yanked her out of the booth. They headed for the front door. Ninette in complete confusion looked back at Nina and Etienne and gave the familiar French shoulder shrug.

Etienne now looked at Nina. "Sweetheart, I don't have much time. There is something I must say before the two of them return." Now it was Nina's turn to look confused . . . and worried. Etienne continued.

"I know that we have only known each other for a little over two months. However, I knew the first time I rescued you, my little mermaid, that I had fallen deeply in love with you. You are the most beautiful woman I know. I love you." With that, he laid a small, dark blue two-inch cubic box on the table and opened it. Inside was a small diamond engagement ring of white gold. Running across the top of the band were four clear white diamonds, two on each side of a small red stone shaped like a heart. It was a ruby. Nina's birthstone. Her birthday, the same as the French Republic . . . Juillet quatorze, July 14.

She looked up from the ring to the handsome young man smiling at her and heard him say, "Nina, will you marry me?"

Without any hesitation, she replied, "I have been in love too with the handsome fisherman who pulled me out of the Seine two short months ago. This mermaid says, "Oui, Oui, OUI! Yes!"

While that was happening inside of Martin's Tavern, Guy was fluttering around stuttering and trying to come up with something interesting to point out to Ninette. He failed.

"Guy, I don't know what this is about. I am going back in to join our friends. It is nice outdoors but no different from when we came in and it is getting darker and I am getting cold and hungry." She headed for the door.

Guy tried one last time, "But darling, look at these beautiful geraniums. Have you ever seen anything as beautiful as them?"

Ninette paused. Looking at him, she started laughing. "Guy, you have to be kidding. Paris is the home of geraniums. They are on every balcony and windowsill in Paris. They keep the flies away!" Still laughing and shaking her head, she went back into the restaurant with Guy right behind.

As Guy and Ninette approached the table, they saw their friends holding hands. His right hand was placed under Nina's left hand. Guy did not see it, but Ninette instantly did. She rushed over to the other couple and started her own stuttering blubber. No one including Ninettte knew if it was a shriek of joy, cries of happiness, or what.

Now even Guy was aware something significant had happened. His police investigating skills kicked in. "You are engaged? Oui?"

The other three looked at Guy and laughed. Only Etienne said anything. Through laughter of his own, "Yes, investigator. Great police work!"

Now the maître d approached the table. In his hands was a bottle of 2010 Dom Perignon Champagne nestled in a bucket of ice and water. One of the servers was carrying four champagne glasses. He sat the first glass down in front of Etienne. The maître d uncorked the wine and poured just a small amount to taste. Etienne smelled the essence released by each small bubble and sipped. Then he signaled with a nod. A glass was poured for Nina, Ninette, and Guy and lastly he filled Etienne's glass.

Finished pouring, the maître d' now said to the young hand-holding couple, "Many long and wonderful years together to this beautiful young couple." Then, turning to Ninette and Guy he added, "and to their young friends too. Perhaps one day we will have the honor of serving you four again in celebration of a similar event?"

The four young people touched glasses. And just before the maître d' left, he took from the server the small bronze plaque. He placed it back on the wall below the windowsill. It read,

The Proposal Booth, where JFK proposed to Jackie

• • •

The French Ambassador's limousine pulled up to the front of the hotel right on time at 9:45 pm. LADA and the Chief Investigator had just emerged from the elevator. They scurried out of the lobby unnoticed. The chauffeur was trying to assist LADA into the back seat with the Ambassador. That was not needed. For a 90 plus year old, she was quite spry. She nearly jumped into the limo and greeted the Ambassador just as he was preparing to exit the vehicle on the other side and come around to greet her.

They met before several times at iSPY Gallery and shows of her work throughout Paris. Places such as the Musee D'art Moderne, Georges-Pompidou Center, Musée De La Légion D' Honneur, Musee Petit Palais, Musée Des Invalides, and the Elysee Palace. By now, he considered her an old friend. The trip from Hotel Zena to the Embassy took sixteen minutes. Had they been fifteen minutes earlier, they would have crossed Wisconsin Avenue Northwest just as the cab carrying Nina, Ninette, Etienne, and Guy had turned left onto Reservoir Road Northwest. As it was, the cab arrived at the Embassy fifteen minutes ahead and the four travelers were waiting in the lobby when LADA, the Ambassador, and the investigator arrived.

LADA introduced her old friend the Ambassador to her young traveling companions. Then they were ushered into a security room where only Etienne's security enhanced phone would work. He placed the phone call to the other secure phone in the hands of the Director-General d'Armee. Instantly, the Director-General answered the phone.

"Bonne nuit, Capitan."

"Bonne nuit, Director-General."

"Is Madame LADA there?

"Oui, Director-General. She is here along with Nina, me, the Lieutenant, the other young woman with us, Ninette, the chief investigator, and of course the Ambassador. "

"Merci, Capitan. Now, would you please hand the phone to Mademoiselle Nina? Have her and Madame LADA stay in the room. I must insist that the rest of you leave them alone in the room for special instructions. Understand?"

Perplexed but not willing to admit so to his commanding officer, Etienne answered, "Oui, Director-General."

Etienne handed the phone to Nina and asked that everyone except Nina and LADA exit the room with him, including the Ambassador.

Now it was Nina's turn to be perplexed. She started to say, "Etienne, surely you are to st . . . "

Etienne cut her off quickly, "These are our orders, Nina. We must obey. I am sure there is an explanation. Right now, they wish to only talk with you and Madame LADA." He smiled at her. She reluctantly nodded at his understanding and then gave him a small smile too. The others, except the two requested women, left the room.

Nina said into the phone, "Bonne nuit, this is Mademoiselle Nina. LADA is here with me. We are alone. The others are standing by outside.'"

"Bonne, Mademoiselle. Please put the phone on speaker so both of you can hear what we say. Can you do so?"

Although the phone was a bit different from her normal cell phone, after a moment, it was done. Both women could hear the others on the other end.
The Director-General told them that on his side of the conversation was himself, the President of France, the Director-General d' External Intelligence, Alexei, and

Evalina. He then proceeded to explain the troubling news from Etienne regarding who was in control of the painting. The Director-General confessed they were unsure how to proceed with the project. Each of the participants on that side, including the French President, expressed their concerns and each option they thought of had been tossed aside. Feeling a bit of despair over this, they confessed to the loss of the information, at best, held secretly and never being revealed, and at worst, being destroyed. Finally stopping, it was now LADA who expressed her thoughts and answers to their worries.

"Messieurs et Evalina, this is not a problem." She paused for a moment to let the words sink in.

"But Madame LADA, it is a problem. The information is in the hands of the wrong person. That person will keep it hidden. It will never come to light. In fact, there is every real possibility that it will be destroyed!"

"Bien!"

"Bien, but why?"

"Because she has the wrong painting!" LADA said. "Nina and I realized the situation and substituted a different painting. Besides, as Alexei knows, we arranged for this situation…him and me."

"But where is the good one?"

"Ah, a very good question. For now, it is Nina's and my secret . . . and partially Alexei's. One day soon, we will share it with you. For now, this is how we proceed. Alexei?"

"Oui, LADA."

"I want you to go to an art store and buy. . . ." She continued talking and telling him of an American solvent and several other chemicals including a small one-ounce bottle of Higgin's black India ink. He must be careful to keep the ink hidden until the proper moment of use. Once used, he must keep it hidden again.

"Do you understand, Alexei? You will be destroying a painting using the solvent and other chemicals. You will tell them it is my secret formula that was created during the occupation of France. Clearly, it is not. The India ink will give the impression you destroyed what the paint was covering. You will blame it on the damn American solvent and chemicals. This would never have happened with French paint solvents. Be outraged! You must do the great acting you can do. You have done it before. Oui? Remember a time long ago? You did it well then!" Her smile not visible to him over the phone came through in her voice, however.

Chuckling, Alexei thought back to the scene on the lakeside, long ago, when his Catherine had told him she was going to sketch him. Yes, he had acted before. He laughed audibly and everyone heard, including LADA. She knew exactly what he was thinking. She continued smiling to herself remembering that sunny day, and the "fun". "Catherine's fun."

"Oui, LADA, I can do this. Just as you have requested."

"Bien!" The old woman said. "Now Messieurs and my sweet Evalina, if it is not too much to ask. May this old artist return to her hotel and get some rest? It is well past my bedtime."

French President, Director-Generals, Alexei, and Evalina said, "Bonne nuit," to LADA and Nina. The phone call ended. However, before it had ended, they were ordered not to tell any of the rest of the team what had been decided. This, Nina knew, would be tough for her. It might even upset Etienne the way she had been upset when he had not confided in her about the fact that he was assigned as the team leader to escort her to the US. "I'm not sure I'm up to this spy stuff!" she said to LADA. Then she and LADA left the room to join the others.

47

Sunday, September 1, 2019
Langley, VA—CIA Headquarters, USA

THE CANVAS

On Friday night, August 30, it now appeared on recently changed flight records at CDG International and air traffic control records at Montreal-Pierre Elliot Trudeau International Airport, that a private Gulfstream V aircraft had traveled between the two cities. The aircraft's owners, Monsieur and Madame Desjardins, also one of Canada's largest art collectors, had apparently sent the Gulfstream to pick up a Parisian gallery owner and her father. The longtime friends of the Desjardins, Evalina and her father, Alexei.

The records showed the flight left Montreal that Friday morning at six, noon Paris time. It arrived in Paris approximately seven hours later, with strong tailwinds pushing it, at 7:00 pm Paris time. The return flight records again showed departure from Paris at 10:00 am and arrival back in Montreal eight hours later at 4:00 pm Paris time and 12:00 pm in Montreal. Coincidentally, this departure time was the same time as the Air France flight that Evalina and Alexei were supposed to board and further coincidentally the same time that a wide body Airbus 300 and four military jets had departed CDG.

The Gulfstream V has a top speed of up to 600 miles per hour and cruising speed of 562 miles per hour. Its range is 6,500 nautical miles. The cost of the Gulfstream V can range from slightly less than $6 million US dollars to over $13 million for a well-equipped newer model. The Desjardins' was well over the $13 million at the higher end.

Now, Sunday, September 1, 2019, the aircraft lifted off the Montreal Airport runway headed for another international destination, one on the same North American Continent. Its arrival was Dulles International Airport in Sterling, Virginia, not far from Washington, DC. On board were Evalina, Alexei, the two Desjardins, Jack from MI6, Gaston from French intelligence, and four very efficient flight attendants, two men and two women. The men looked as if they could "handle" themselves and Gaston and Jack figured they were flight attendants or bodyguards.

The Desjardins just wanted to say hello and congratulations to their old friend LADA and have an advance personal tour of the setup of her new show at the Kennedy Center. After all, they collected several of her pieces and those were now on loan for the show. They wouldn't stay long. Just long enough for "it" to happen correctly.

Two phone calls were made from the plane's air phone. The first call was to Nina on her unencrypted cell phone. Nina was told that Evalina and Alexei had an unexpected detour on Saturday to their friends the Desjardin, in Montreal, Canada. She was sorry to not have called the day before to tell Nina. Things just happened fast. After all, as Nina knew, these were not only old friends, but big art collectors and investors. How could they refuse the trip on the owner's private jet that had been dispatched for them? This did not explain why they had not contacted her on Friday. They must have learned of the new plan that day. It also didn't explain why they hadn't called from the plane on its seven-hour flight over the Atlantic on Saturday. They could have phoned then, like they were doing now. And, of course, they could have called on Saturday night from Montreal, which they hadn't. Fortunately, no one would think to question these concerns. Certainly not Nina. She knew what the plan was based on the conversation she had on the secure phone at the Embassy the night before. Guy and Etienne still had questions. They, however, knew that at this point they were not to question what was happening.

The second call was placed to Etienne on his encrypted phone, though it originated from a non-encrypted phone at Evalina and Alexei's end. It too could be picked up if people were trying. No one was. The message to Etienne was simple. Please have someone pick them up at the airport and escort Alexei on his trip to art supply stores. He needed to pick up important chemicals to be used on the special painting the next day, Monday. Second, Nina and LADA should join Evalina and the Desjardins at the Kennedy Center on Monday for a private tour of the show's setup. This was scheduled to happen while Alexei worked on the painting alone at the lab at Langley.

Business all being settled, he handed the phone over to an anxious Nina. There was only one other piece of non-business news for Nina to relay.

"Evalina, I have incredibly wonderful news!" She took a deep breath and then said with an excited voice, "Etienne asked me to marry him last night! We are engaged! He gave me a beautiful ring. White gold with four diamonds! Two on each side of a beautiful heart shaped ruby! My birthstone!"

The joy from Nina overflowed the phone line. Guy and Ninette put their arms around each other. Etienne beamed! A shirk of joy came over the phone and excited voices erupted with laughter and the happy sounds as Evalina told the news to Alexei and the Desjardins. Now each one was on the phone, one after another, congratulating her and telling Etienne, as the phone was handed back to him, what a lucky fellow he was. Of that, he was already so very sure!

The call ended with Monsieur Desjardin saying they would all go out tonight to celebrate! "It was settled!"

Indeed, there was a grand celebration that night. It was a good thing that the meeting for Alexei at the CIA Headquarters would not happen until 1:00 pm. It gave everyone an opportunity to recover from the grand excitement and fun the night before. Even LADA had stayed up well past her bedtime to celebrate. "Love is grand!" she had said and truly believed. In Nina and Etienne, she saw a young Catherine and Alexei. "The fun!" She also celebrated that night herself with the surprise she had in store for someone else. It will be revealed over the next few days. It was worth celebrating.

Although unable to find all of the chemicals that Alexei would need after arriving Sunday afternoon, Alexei, Jack, and Gaston had finally located the one additional necessary ingredient at Dick Blick Art, Holbein lavender oil, on Monday morning. They headed to Langley in the special SUV sent to pick them up at the hotel. Alexei would mix the chemicals at the lab inside the CIA complex. He was assured he could be alone as the process to remove just the over paint was to remain secret.

As was done when the others had delivered the paintings to the facility, the SUV was fully inspected. Identifications were checked, as were the materials that Alexei had in his leather satchel. The contents included pallet knives of various sizes, alcohol 70 % strength, white cotton cloths, cotton swabs, fine sandpaper pads, distilled water, a small amount of chlorine, acetone, and the secret ingredient, French Spike Lavender oil. A last ingredient had been pre-loaded into his fountain pen. In the tube of his fountain pen was the India ink. The small lever on the side of the pen, when held open, would let the ink drip out. Alexei had to use it at just the precise right time.

He alone was taken to the lab. Jack and Gaston had to wait for him in the lobby area. Neither was comfortable with that but had no choice. At the lab, Alexei was met by three people, the Special Prosecutor, the Director of the FBI, and the thin-lipped sneering Director of the CIA. He instantly did not like her. She was everything that LADA had said she was.

Courtesies followed but no small talk. He was asked if he needed any assistance to which he replied "no".

"Well, then," tight lips said, "we will leave you to your work. How long should it take?"

"About four hours is right, though you might check back in two hours to see how it is going. I should know by then if everything is okay."

The Special Prosecutor instantly said, "What do you mean you should know by then if everything is okay? Does this mean that something might not be?"

Alexei thoughtfully replied, "Everything in science, especially chemistry, is always open to potential complications. Not everything can be controlled. I am assuming that the canvas and paints are correct. I am assuming that the painting was prepared correctly. Any one of those not being true could cause a complication. I also must sand down carefully the outermost layers of the paint to try to find the right depth of consistency of the layer. Then comes the special chemical bath. It can only be allowed to stay on just the right amount of time. That takes careful monitoring by me. If the paint remaining on the canvas has reached the proper consistency, I must then carefully scrape off almost all the paint. As much off as possible. This is delicate work. The last step is to use a special formula that LADA developed back in the Second World War to wipe off the final layer carefully and slowly, revealing the coded message. And we must hope that the pigment used to code the message was not affected by the bath and rubbing. Anyone of these steps not perfectly followed leads to disaster. The destruction of the coded message below the paint. We are a long way from success. Appropriately, this is a true balance of art and science!"

"Let's leave this gentleman to the art of his science," thin lips said. As she and the others turned to leave, she swiveled back facing him. "How is it that an astrophysicist is the person working on a chemical problem?"

"Ah, yes, Madam, a very good question. My wife and I have been LADA's assistant many such times. I am not a trained chemist. However, I am a trained assistant of a very wise and intelligent artist. I supposed even she thought an astrophysicist might be able to handle the project with the proper remedial training." He smiled politely to her. And she left the room with a distinct "humph!"

Alexei studied the laboratory. It had a large shallow sink with a vacuum hood above it. The sink measurements were, he estimated, nearly 24 inches by 40 inches. Large enough for the canvas measuring 18 inches by 26 inches, once the frame was taken off. Next to the sink were several large trays. Each one appeared to be slightly larger than the canvas but smaller than the sink. Those would be useful for the chemical baths. There were goggles and respirator masks hanging on steel rods off steel backsplash plates. In fact, the whole room appeared to be stainless steel, similar to what one would find in a fine restaurant's kitchen, he thought, as there were the sounds of a slight rumbling in his stomach.

He pulled the goggles and respirator mask from his satchel and began to take out the chemicals and put them on the sink countertop. Once his items were assembled beside him, he glanced around the room apparently looking for any other useful item he might need. In fact, what he was doing was looking to see if he could find the many closed circuit cameras he knew were now focused on him. He got off the stool and proceeded to pull open drawers and look on shelves. Gave a shrug of his shoulders, the universal French sign for "oh, well" and went back to the stool and sat down.

He turned on the hood's suction and pulled a piece of paper off a spiral notebook he took out of the satchel. Holding the paper, he carefully placed it in the sink. Presto, it rose upward and quickly was fastened to the grid cover protecting the fan. There appeared to be enough suction for the necessary work so he would begin.

He placed the painting on the counter upside down and with a screwdriver and pliers, he managed to easily pull the nails out of the back of the canvas stretcher, which was holding the painting into the frame. Eight total 5-centimeter brad nails later, he turned the canvas back upright and laid it on its back in the sink.

God, he hated this! It was a beautiful painting of LADA's. Rich bright colors of the onion domes of the Kremlin, the long white office building with green roof and all surrounded by the red stone wall as viewed from across the Moskva River looking almost due north. The painting depicted the shadows and coloring in the sky and off the building of a setting sun to the left of the canvas. It was characteristically done in LADA's rich impasto style that had added a three-dimensional aspect to it. What a shame he was going to destroy it.

After putting heavy rubber gloves on his hands and up to his elbows, he took out a small scraper from his bag. He had on a lab coat but had second thoughts and went over to the Hazmat white jumpsuits folded up on the shelves. He had spotted those while looking for the cameras. Looking through them, he found a size he thought would fit him, extra-large, and tore open the plastic bag. Pulling open the zipper, which stretched from the neck to the crotch, he took off his shoes and slipped his feet into the ends of the sock part of the suit. After finally zipping the zipper back up and fastening the hood tightly over his head with the Velcro fastener around the neck, he again pulled the gloves back on and over the ends of the sleeves. For the most part, he felt he was completely protected.

Between the negative atmosphere caused by the suction of the vent fan and covering his body with the suit and gloves, there would be no worries about the toxicity of the lead and other heavy metal paints that LADA typically used. She was an old style painter. Heavy metal paints were mostly what she used.

He, Catherine, and Evalina had witnessed the deterioration caused to artists who were old style and continued to use heavy metal paints with no precautions. LADA was not one of those, however. She was very careful with her paints and her techniques so that she never came into close contact with the paint itself. Still, one could never be too cautious.

Alexei only wanted to use the scraper now on the largest blobs of paint to almost surgically slice the tops off. He was careful not to push too hard and too deep onto the canvas. He worked diligently and after nearly an hour he felt he had done all he could do with this technique. Next, he took a rather rough sandpaper block. Again, he rubbed very softly and proceeded to take off the next layer of paint and make the surface nearly perfectly flat. This process, though done with the same care, only took about fifteen minutes. He used a block of fine P120 sandpaper.

Following that, he used a P240 and lastly P400.

The traces of the pigments were still there, but only barely. It was now time for the first of the baths. That was actually a slight misnomer. Although the canvas would be wetted, it really would not be bathed. It also would not be scrubbed. It would be lightly soaked by a soft piece of linen, which he would moisten with the first chemicals, a mixture of a large amount of sterile distilled water, a very small amount of acetone, and an even much smaller amount of chlorine. The mixture of acetone and any amount of chlorine causes the creation of extremely toxic chemicals that cause a fatal fume cloud. Before mixing the chemicals in a small metal bowl, he was sure to double check the sink hood fan to ensure it was running on its highest level.

With each step, he did two other things. First, check his notes in the spiral notebook. Second, add notes of what he was doing. This appeared to any viewer that he was following the science, which he was. He was, however, setting the stage for the India ink to be added at the right time and appear simply as him writing in his book. No matter how many cameras and from what angles it would be viewed, it would look perfectly normal he hoped!

He could tell that a haze was formed as he mixed the three solutions together. It didn't take much. And he would not need much. Laying the linen cloth flat in the bottom of one of the large trays, he placed it in the sink while holding the mixing bowl up nearer the fan. Now he gently poured the solution onto the linen, making sure that he covered it entirely. Once done, he let it soak for a full five minutes to ensure it spread evenly over the cloth.

He laid the canvas in another pan. There was no need to remove the stretcher. It would actually help make sure that the linen completely covered the painting. Now was a critical moment. He had to lift the cloth out of the one tray and place it over the painting in the second tray while keeping all of his work under the hood. Carefully, he did so by tilting each tray against each other end to end with the other side resting on the edge of the sink. It was done. The linen covered the painting. He lifted it up close to the hood with his right hand. Holding it one handed flat on the bottom of the tray, looking like a waiter carrying a large meal to a table, he used his left hand to turn on the sink cold water faucet and completely rinsed out the other tray and the mixing bowl. After a few minutes of rinsing, feeling that the chemicals were rinsed away or at least highly diluted, and with his right arm tiring, he lowered the linen covered painting and tray into the sink. It had been five minutes of wetting. He would wait ten more minutes.

The waiting was difficult. What was that American saying, "A watched pot never boils." A French chef knows if you open the door to the oven the soufflé would drop. Still, he was "antsy". Wasn't that another American saying.

Time was up. His instructions now were to rinse the linen-covered canvas and all in the remaining distilled water. Pour it gently over the canvas. Gently, hell, he was going to ruin it anyway. Still, he knew he was playing the game. He did so. Let it soak for another five minutes then run the hot water over the whole canvas continuously for another five minutes. He did that too.

The notebook instructed him to pour off the water and discard the linen. He grabbed a hazardous waste bag and put the completely rinsed and suspected to be nontoxic now cloth into the bag and zipped it shut.

Now another very surgical action had to be done. He had to take a pallet knife and lightly scrape off as much of the remaining pigment and paint as he could. He diligently did so for another thirty minutes.

The two hours were up, and the door opened. The thin-lipped CIA Director and the tall, distinguished man, and the FBI Director peeked in.

"How's it going?" she asked.

"Seems to be going just fine. We will soon know for sure, as I have one more bath to give it. So far, everything has gone as the formula suggested it should. Check back in an hour and we will know for sure."

Again, a grunt from the woman and the door closed.

Alexei now laid the canvas into another tray. This time there would be little worry about toxic fumes. There would be the distinct and soothingly powerful smell of lavender, still he was told to cover the tray the canvas was in, and he knew why. He was to soak another cloth with the "spike lavender oil" and with drops of something else. Although he could not truly smell the lavender through his mask, he was sure that the laboratory had the odor of the south of France. He wished he were there right now soaking up the rays of the southern coast sun. Someday soon!

Thirty minutes later, it was time. Time for him to act. He unnoticeably let ink out into the solution of lavender oil. It had mixed thoroughly as expected. As he lifted the cover off the linen-covered painting, a look of horror was on his face. It was too expressive a look to not have been seen by the three observers at the other end of the closed-circuit connection.

Now they saw the man sink back onto the stool with a look and action of despair. This did not last long. He started throwing things around the room. He ripped off the ventilator. He took a cell phone out of his bag and dialed. Nothing. He tried again. Nothing. Now he apparently realized he was in a room from which he could not make a call. He ran to the door. It was secured from the outside. He banged and banged on it, yelling and screaming. The three observers raced to the lab room. Opening the door to his banging and yelling. Now he was muttering and in French of all things. Too fast for any one of the three, though two of them spoke fair French, the FBI Director and the distinguished gentleman. The woman kept loudly repeating and repeating, "What the hell is he saying?"

The FBI Director said, "I think he is asking to speak with LADA. Where is a phone he can use?" He was looking at her, as was the distinguished gentleman.

"How the hell do I know!"

"Well, it is your building! God, damn it!" the FBI yelled back.

Just then, a couple of other employees, hearing the ruckus, came out of the laboratory offices. The CIA Director yelled at them, "Where's a god damn phone? We need to call off campus!"

"You can use the phone in my office over here," a young woman said as she pointed to a door down the hall. "All you have to do is dial nine to get an outside line through the secure switchboard. They will ask you what the call is about and ask you for your identification number."

"What number?!" thin lips demanded.

"Director, I cannot give you my number. It is against the law and our own regulations. You will have to use your number." The young scientist said.

"God damn it! I don't have a number! I'm the Director!"

The young woman was now totally flustered and scared. She could not give the number to this maniacal woman, the Director, breach all security and end up prosecuted for breaking security and the law. On the other hand, she could disobey the Director and be fired! What to do?

Just then, both gentlemen stepped into the conversation. The first was the FBI Director. He said politely, showing the young woman his FBI Director's badge, "Miss, you don't have anything to worry about. I am here witnessing your assistance. I can assure you that no prosecution of breach of security will be pursued. You actually may be helping in a significant act of national interest."

The second distinguished gentleman now added, "I cannot reveal to you the full story, Miss. But as the Director has said, this is of significant importance to preserving the democracy we hold dear. I am an appointed officer of the Justice Department, and I too am a witness to your assisting the US Government."

With that, the young woman ushered the two men, thin lips, and a hysterical, hazmat dressed Frenchman into her office. She dialed nine and gave the officer on duty her number, dreading with worry that she had just made a mistake. She hadn't.

She started to hand the phone over to thin lips but was instructed to give it instead to the hysterical Frenchman. She did so and then was told to leave the area. "Gladly," she thought and nearly ran from the room and out of the laboratory area and then the building.

Then the next problem. Alexei needed to call LADA and had the phone in hand but he was dialing an international cell phone number. All kinds of alerts were set off and armed guards were immediately sent to the office where the phone call was being attempted. Of course, it was not being completed.

The voice of authority on the other end of the phone was demanding the name of the individual attempting to make the call. Alexei was overwhelmed by the questions, and though he spoke English well he was not nearly fluent enough to handle the barrage of questions being fired at him. He handed, almost threw, the phone at thin lips.

"Je ne comprends pas!"—I do not understand!

Now the CIA thin-lipped Director was yelling back at the official on the other end of the line. She identified herself as the Director and received the response back, "Yeah, right! And I'm the President of Russia!"

Just then, the armed guards burst their way into the office with guns aiming at all the occupants. It didn't take them long to realize that there before them was the Director of the CIA, the Director of the FBI, the Special Prosecutor, and a befuddled and hysterical Frenchman.

The leader of the security guards took the phone and identified himself to the officer on the phone line with all of the necessary identification information. Now Alexei was able to complete his call to LADA, but not before the Director demanded the name and rank of the individual on the other end of the phone. She left a trail of destruction in her wake and he knew he was going to be carried away by it.

Alexei made the call. LADA and he talked. She was appearing to calm him down. His hysterics ended. But on his face was the vision of despair. He turned to the others and said, "It is over. It is ruined. It cannot be salvaged. It is gone."

There were three distinct reactions by the other three. The distinguished gentleman known as the Special Prosecutor said, "Damn!"

The FBI Director said, "We will probably never know the whole story and how Russia interfered with the elections and hacked into so many important computer systems of our government."

Those two had looks of anguish on their faces, real disappointment.

Thin-lips, though her lips were too thin to really show it, smiled and said with a false sense of feeling, "Ah, boys, that's too bad. Oh, well. Can't worry about it now. What a shame."

The FBI Director thought to himself with a great amount of contempt, you got your wish you evil, cruel bitch! What I wouldn't agree to in the meeting you called, happened, just as you hoped it would. But it wasn't because of your actions, at least I think, and if it was . . . you will pay! And that, Madam, you can take it to the bank! I will find out!

They all went back in to look at the disaster. She knew exactly what the FBI

Director was thinking and perhaps the Special Prosecutor too.

• • •

The death viewing of the destroyed canvas did not take long. Heads shook. Chins rubbed. Curse words uttered. Then Alexei was left alone to clean up the mess. Outside the open door, two guards monitored his work. What was left of the destroyed canvas was loaded into a special plastic bag, which would be incinerated. The chemicals and solvents were also put into special containers that would be destroyed appropriately by the lab technicians. He closed up his satchel and he and the guards proceeded to the SUV, which was to take him back to the hotel.

Once the SUV left the premises of the CIA Headquarters, the next part of LADA's plan was put into play. He pulled out his non-encrypted cell phone and placed a call to LADA's non-encrypted phone. He knew the call was being monitored through earpieces by the driver and partner in the SUV, as well as back at the CIA Headquarters, just as LADA had planned.

"Yes, LADA, it is Alexei. I am so sorry for what happened. I followed the instructions perfectly. I have my notes and will show them to you when I return to the hotel."

"Alexei, dear one, you must not worry. Everything is okay. There is another special Presidential painting hanging in Nina's apartment at #10 Rue Garreau. All is well! But listen, chérie, we are not at the hotel now. We are at the Kennedy Center with the Desjardins. We can celebrate this secret. And I think the issue you had was that the spike lavender oil was not truly French spike lavender oil. No other will do. I am sure that has to be the problem!"

"Oui, I could not find true oil. It was an American made "French" spike lavender oil. I should have realized that Americans would only fake real French. Bonne! See you soon. Au revoir, LADA."

Alexei clicked off the call and then tapped on the bulletproof glass separating him from the driver and guard. The guard through the intercom asked what he wanted. Alexei gave them the new direction of the Kennedy Center, which they already knew from listening to the conversation. And off they went, Alexei with a smile inside; the guard and driver with a nod and smile to each other. They and the Director knew what she would do. She would see that the one at Rue Garreau would be destroyed too.

After dropping Alexei off at the Kennedy Center to join up with the others, the driver and guard headed back to HQ. The guard placed the call to the Director, as requested, to report Alexei's phone conversation. Unbeknownst to the two men, the conversation had already been reported to her by the Associate Director. She, in turn, had placed a highly classified and encrypted phone call to her counterpart in Russia, who had already informed the Commander, who had begun giving instructions to his men in Paris. The Commander's plan was delayed for two days with the unexpected arrival in Paris of renters of #10 Rue Garreau: the Martzes.

48

Wednesday, September 4, 2019
Paris, France

WORLDS COLLIDE

Mary was up early on their second day in Paris. Tom was already out the door to buy warm croissants for their breakfast. He left a note telling Mary so on the dining room table. Although she would have guessed where he was without the note. He had to have his morning croissant!

He pressed the digit code into the outside door and walked into the small vestibule shared by the backdoor to the restaurant next door. The front door to the restaurant was outside on the street. This one was actually leading to their back outdoor storage area where their trash containers were. Sometimes it was locked. Sometimes it wasn't.

A fresh French press of coffee was brewing on the kitchen table. Mary sat there with notepaper, pen, and notes she had made from earlier trips, along with something else. A small book on the table that she was leafing through and writing notes from it. The book by Jean-Christophe Napias with photographs by Christophe Lefebure, *Quiet Corners of PARIS.*

"Bonjour, ma belle chérie."

"Bonjour, mon beau monsieur."

"Finding interesting things for us to do today?" He sat down on the other side of the table from her and the mess of work she had in front of her. Pulling out a pain au chocolat and placing it on the small blue and white Lachaniette Limoges plate in front of her. "Pour mon amour."

"Merci monsieur. Oui, I have a wonderful day planned for us of all these small secret passages, courtyards, gardens, museums, historic houses, and other cool things like a Petanque area called Square Bomet. I thought what we could do is to wander the streets south to the Seine. We purchase a bottle of wine, a baguette, some cheese, perhaps one of those fennel sausages you like, some fruit, et walla . . . a picnic lunch watching them play. What do you think?"

"Sounds like a fun day. Let's get ready and head out."

As Mary and Tom headed out that day, they had no idea that they were being followed by two of the Russian agents who had been assigned to keep watch on the apartment, #10 Rue Garreau. The Commander wanted to know if these new arrivals were part of the Nina, Evalina, Alexei and LADA team. Unbeknownst to those two agents, they, in turn, were followed by two French agents. All four agents had the same objective . . . follow these Americans and find out their purpose for being at the apartment and relationship to Nina.

Two other Russian agents, also watching the apartment, had another assignment. Get the painting! They would be observed doing this and videoed to ensure they were successful with their mission.

"You know what is funny?" Tom asked.

"What?"

"Well in France the doors have all these locks that you lock when you are inside. A regular key lock. A deadbolt. Often another one like this one has a strange arrangement of metal arms that when you turn a handle of a knob also locks the door. But, when you leave for the day? All you have is the key lock. It's just funny that you are all locked in at night but no one is truly, fully, locked out during the day when no one is home."

"You are weird!" Mary said laughing and off they went on an adventure...having no idea what an adventure it was going to be. "Come on buddy boy, buddy boy!"

At a small cafe they sat at a small outside table and ordered deux cafe. Close by, at the corner of Rue Gabrielle and Rue Drevert, two sets of eyes of apparent tourists were on them. Further east on Rue Gabrielle were two sets of French workmen's eyes watching the ones watching Mary and Tom.

Finished with their coffee and "Merci Madame," the Americans headed south and out of the 18th. The next stop, the 9th Arrondissement, Square d'Orleans, was the past home of artists like Edouard Dubufe and writer Aleandre Dumas. It was just a short visit to the space to take in what Napias had described in the book. Out the entrance on 80 Rue Taitbout they headed, nearly colliding with the two Russians.

The walk so far, with stopping for coffee and all, had taken nearly an hour and half. It was approaching 10:30 am now. It was time to make a quick adjustment to all of Mary's desired locations if they were going to find a picnic lunch and the Square Blomet for watching petanque and lunch.

Mary and Tom headed southwest from the 9th arrondissement through the 2nd, 1st, across the Seine River on Pont du Carrousel and then along Quai Voltaire to Rue des Saints-Peres. It was on the way home, when they decided to backtrack their route that they were there at 1 Quai Voltaire, the address of Evalina's iSPY Gallery. At that location at 7:00 pm, the coincidence shaping the future happened.

Meanwhile, as Mary, Tom, and the four followers were huffing it towards the bottom of the 15 arrondissement, two others were making their move to enter 10 Rue Garreau. Their partners trailing the Martzes had phoned to let them know that everyone was heading south towards the Seine. Even if they would catch a metro back to the apartment, it would take a half hour to forty-five minutes, plenty of time.

The two men decided that it would be easiest to climb over the fence and wall in the park behind the apartment and then enter through the lobby backdoor, which they figured the restaurant would never lock. Their assessment proved accurate. It was still too early for the children to be in the park. The chain-link fence proved an easy climb. The stone wall was a little different. One man had to hoist the first up to the top. The first man then had to pull the other up while lying flat on the foot wide wall top. The one being pulled had to push hard with his feet into the wall trying to find a foothold and tore up the leather on the top of his shoes. The activity had a similar effect on the forearms of the first man. They were skinned.

The men dropped down the eight-foot wall and stooped quietly in the small back courtyard of the apartment listening and looking to see if anyone had seen them. Appearing no one had, they stood up and walked on tiptoes to the back door. Why, tiptoes? Who knows? They just did so because that is what they figured all burglars would do, even though it was broad daylight. Reaching the backdoor between the restaurant rear door and trash receptacles they found, sure enough, the backdoor to the vestibule shared by the restaurant and the apartment was locked!

"Locked!" the first one exclaimed. The second one shook his head. Then he proceeded to pull out a little bag in his coat pocket, his lock picks. Taking out a couple and moving them around inside the lock, it didn't take long until the door unlocked, and they were in the vestibule. Now he repeated the action again on the inside doorway. Both men climbed the stairs quickly to the third floor. They had not run into anyone . . . yet.

Less than ten minutes later, they came out with a small cloth sack about the size of a 46 cm by 46 cm painting and nothing else. When the investigators arrived shortly, it appeared to be a burglary, as items, including the Martz's clothing, were thrown all over. The second phase of LADA's plan was now in play.

• • •

On Wednesday morning at 9:00 am, while Mary and Tom were being followed, Caroline headed to the BNP Paribas Bank on Rue Du Bac. She had them access her account at the EFG International bank of Switzerland to transfer money to the French bank account. She was surprised to find, from the bank manager, that she already had 2.5 million euros in the BNP bank account in her new French name. Caroline showed no surprise to the manager of this fact. She then had him transfer another 2.5 million euros worth of the equivalent Swiss francs to the account. After that transfer, she still had twice the amount remaining in the Swiss account for her to do the same once she was in England. She would head to London the next day, Thursday morning. This afternoon she would call the General to inform him that she would be taking the Chunnel or ferry the next morning. Later in the evening, before it closed, she would stop by iSPY Gallery to talk with Natalya and leave a message for Nina and Evalina. That's when it happened.

• • •

They reached the Square Blomet. Inside a small park were four pétanque courts and a very small clubhouse. The gate was locked by padlock and chain.

"No way in," Tom said disappointedly to Mary.

"How about you ask one of the fellows inside the clubhouse how to get in, buddy boy." Smiling sweetly as she said it.

Now Tom spoke fair first, second, and third grade French, but asking this was a bit beyond his capability so he said through the screen window to two men pouring a glass of wine or perhaps something a bit stronger, "Pardonnez-moi, monsieur, parlez-vous anglais?"

"Mais bien sûr, tous les français parlent plusieurs langues. Seuls les Américains ne parlent qu'un . . . anglais. Une honte. Oui?" Then he replied in English seeing the lost look on Tom's face repeating what he had just said in French. "Of course I speak English. All French speak multiple languages. Only Americans only speak one . . . English. A shame. Yes?"

"Oui," Tom replied, feeling a bit foolish.

"Can we come into the park and watch you all play?"

"Of course you can. This gate is locked. If you go back out to the street and tournez a droit, I mean, turn right and walk along the street to the other side of the play field, you will find an unlocked gate. Follow the little path and it will take you to the benches over there," pointing to the benches tucked into the thick screen of bushes on the far side.

"You will not be able to play. This is a private club. Members only. But we welcome you to watch."

"Merci!"

"De rien."

And so Mary and Tom followed his directions and sure enough found a hidden gate. For the next three hours, Mary and Tom watched as the players coiled themselves, confined by what looked like plastic rings laid on the court, squatted before springing upward and lofting, underhanded, the four-inch metal balls, with fingers cupped over the ball, towards a small hard wood red target ball called a cochonnet . . . piglet.

Although not what you would call an exhilarating and exhausting form of athletic competition, it certainly was entertaining and often very humorous to watch, as Mary and Tom were doing.

"Wow, it is almost 5:00. Think we ought to start heading back to the apartment?"

"How about on the way back we stop off at Evalina's gallery and see what it's like. We came close to passing it when we crossed the river. Think you could find directions from here on your iPhone?"

"It's almost a straight shot north and the route shows it to be 41 minutes. I think they close at 7:00 pm. It's almost 5:00 pm now. We should get there with at least an hour to spare. Let's do it!"

Packing up the remains of the picnic lunch and saying "Merci" to the players, who all waved goodbye and said in English they hoped to see Tom and Mary again while they were in Paris, Tom and Mary headed off.

Not quite an hour later, they entered iSpy Gallery. They still did not know they were being followed.

Natalya saw them, recognized them, and came over right away.

"Madame et Monsieur Martz, bonsoir." She pulled out her iPhone and spoke into it in Russian and the translation was shown to them.

It read, "Have you been out of the apartment all day?"

"Oui," Mary replied.

It read, "Then you do not know of the break in?"

Looking at each other with a worried look on their faces, they turned back to Natalya shaking their heads, "NO" and replied, "Non."

Speaking into the phone once again but longer, Natalya showed them the phone when finished once again. It read, "Yes, I am sorry to say. Sometime this morning someone broke into the apartment. It was made a mess. I am afraid your clothing and things were disturbed. I hope you did not leave anything of value there. The police have been there all day. The only thing that appears to have been stolen was a special painting of LADA's, which Madame told me was painted as a gift for one of LADA's friends. I am so sorry to be the one telling you of this terrible happening."

"Tom, we should head back there right now. We can stop again here some other day. This is so sad. Are you sure you locked the door when we left?"

"Are you kidding? You know me. I'm Mr. Lock, check, and check again."

"Right, I remember you saying how strange it is that you can multiple lock the door when you are inside but not when you leave." Mary then indicated that she would like to speak into the phone to have it translate what she said into Russian for Natalya.

Natalya handed the phone over to Mary. In Russian, the translation of Mary's words read, "We are going to rush back to the apartment. We are sure we locked it when we left. We did not leave anything of value there. We carry all of our valuables with us in a special pouch Mr. Martz has inside his shirt. We are so sorry the painting was stolen. Is there anything you need for us to do, Natalya?"

After reading what Mary had said into the phone, it was Natalya's turn to speak into it. It read, "Thank you, no there is nothing I need for you to do. I will call the apartment and let the police know you are on the way back and will be there shortly. I am so sorry your stay has started this way. I know that Evalina and Nina will want me to do anything I can to make it up to you. Please let me know if you need anything from me."

"Merci, Natalya," Mary said. They turned and as they headed out the door a very strikingly dressed young woman in short black leather skirt, dark hair, glasses and bright lipstick, nearly crashed into Tom as he opened the door for Mary.

"Je suis vraiment désolé!" she said. Tom just smiled at her and said "Pardonnez-moi, Mademoiselle." Mary took Tom's arm and ushered him out the door laughing.

"What is so funny?"

"You, sir, and your long-legged young ladies!"

"What? She just about knocked me over. An old guy like me. It could have been fatal!"

"I'll fatal you. C'mon, let's find a metro and figure out the fastest way to the apartment. By the way, who do you think Nina is? Did you hear Natalya mention the name along with Evalina?"

"I did. I have no idea what she meant by that. Perhaps we will know when we get to the apartment."

While all this was happening, several other simultaneous things were taking place.

In Russian, one of the agents nearly yelled out, "My God! It's her!"

The other agent, also seeing the strikingly gorgeous young women enter the shop, turned to him, "What? And be quiet, you will attract attention!"

All of this was being observed by two French agents who had followed the two Russians as they were following Mary and Tom. Two more French agents, who had followed Caroline to ensure her safety, were now observing all four of them.

The first Russian spoke again, more quietly this time. "The young woman. The one in the short skirt."

"Yes?"

"That is Major Sophia Malenkov!! She is the Russian military intelligence officer who along with General Gorchakov have stolen military secrets!"

"Are you sure?"

"Yes, I'm sure! She was my commanding officer when I was in military intelligence three years ago. She was a captain then. Her hair was blond. She looked different for sure, but God I would not forget that body of hers! Even under a military uniform! She was spectacular! No doubt! That's her!"

The second agent pulled out his encrypted cell phone and made a call. The French agents following Caroline hearing what he was saying into the phone through their long-range hearing devices. The two agents following Mary and Tom, wondering "what the hell?"

"This is 532. We were following the subjects. They stopped at an art gallery. iSPY Gallery. Yes, I know, a strange name for a gallery. Listen, tell the commander. This is important. Tell him we just spotted Major Sophia Malenkov going into the same gallery. Yes, you heard me right. Major Sophia Malenkov. Yes, we are sure. 490 served under her (in his mind thinking what a wonderful choice of words that was) when he was in the military intelligence. Yes, he is sure!" Time passed. "Commander! Yes. Understand, sir! Yes, we will report back on both parties. Yes, sir!" He clicked off the phone. At the same time, the French agents listening to his end of the conversation were now making their own call back to French intelligence to report what they had heard. The second pair of French intelligence officers were also reporting back about what they were observing.

49

Wednesday, September 4, 2019
London, England

A phone rang in the Headquarters of British Military Intelligence on the desk of the commanding officer. He was a longtime adversary and good friend of Colonial General Gorchakov, formerly his counterpart of Russian Military Intelligence! He, General Gorchakov, was suspected of defecting from Russia along with one of his close associates and God daughter, Major Sophia Malenkov.

This particular phone number was reserved for calls from four people, the Prime Minister of England, the Director of MI6, the Queen of England and his old Russian friend Dimitri Gorchakov. He knew right away to whom he would be talking.

“Dimitri?”

“Da, how are you, Commander Bond?” Dimitri was always amused by his friend’s name, James, and always called him Commander Bond.

“Doing well. How are you? Is it true, Dimitri? You have defected?”

“Da, my friend. This spy is coming in from the cold. Not really much choice in the matter. All can be explained later. But this is the reason for this call, my friend!” Emphasis on “my friend”.

“Dimitri, are you safe? Where are you? Can I send in the cavalry?”

“Security assistance would be welcome, James.” Whenever he used the first name of the head of British Military Intelligence, James knew Dimitri was serious.

"Where are you? I can come with my men and pick you up. Are you out of Russia?"

"Da, my friend. I am close. Can you arrange for additional cover for my good friend, Major Sophia Malenkov? She too is defecting. I believe the French friends are already on the scene protecting her, but she will be coming to England in the next day or two. She will need protection here." He used the word "here" and James picked up on that but did not reveal it to Dimitri at the moment. "Can you arrange coordination with our French friends?"

"It will be done. I will talk with our friend as soon as we are finished. Where are you now? I will come and pick you up."

"No need to pick me up. How about taking a walk outside the ministry front door and go two blocks north and then east on Great Scotland Yard. Cut across Northumberland Avenue to Craven Passageway. Go through the passage to Craven Street and a bank of four of your red telephone booths, which the crazy Americans so desire for their homes. You will find a man there apparently talking on one of the phones. I think you will recognize him." The phone clicked off.

Rushing to grab his hat and coat, James headed out the door. As he passed by his assistant's office, he asked him to contact his counterpart at French Military Intelligence. He needed to talk with him directly in half an hour. Urgent!

"And I need two men to join me. Call downstairs and have them meet me at the front door immediately and make sure they are in civvies and armed!" Then he added, "Call MI6 and ask him to meet me in my office in an hour. Tell him it is urgent. He will want to be here!"

He headed down the stairs.

• • •

Paris, France

As James headed down the stairs, a phone call arrived at the office of the French Director-General for External Security. The assistant spoke directly to the Director-General and arranged for the telephone call in a half hour. The Director-General had a sense of what this call might be about. He had just heard from his own two sets of men of the mysterious young woman. They informed him the Russian agents following the Martzes saw her. Then the Director-General was told of those agents' side of the phone call to their Commander. They suspected the young woman was the missing Russian Military Intelligence officer, Major Sophia Malenkov.

This phone call the Director-General was to receive might be to alert him of the Russian defector, Colonel General Dimitri Gorchakov, found by his British counterpart. This was looking to be an incredible end of the day for French and British Intelligence.

Hopefully, if this is so, the Brits would feel as the French did. Keep the US CIA in the dark! No need for the tight-lipped witch and the crazy leader there, to be informed, at least not yet!

• • •

Moscow, Russia

The replacement for Major Sophia Malenkov knocked on the President of Russia's office door and entered. He would have to make a change. This intelligence officer looked like she could beat up all his former KGB associates with one arm. She had a slant forehead with heavy ridges above her eyes covered by hairy, almost furry, eyebrows. She was squat. Short large round stubbles for legs. The chest of a bodybuilder. And, at some time in her life, a really bad case of acne. This will never do!

"Mister President!" she said, coming to full attention and delivering a snappy salute. "We have just heard news from our people in Paris. Two of our agents following a strange American couple stumbled upon former Major Sophia Malenkov entering a Paris art gallery called iSPY Gallery."

"The two agents have split up. One is following this strange American couple," looking down at a paper she held in her hand, "named Martz. Thomas and Mary Martz. He goes by the name Tom. She has been known by several names but is now called just Mary."

The President of Russia had a completely puzzled look on his face and was thinking, "What the hell is this person talking about?"

She continued with her briefing, "The commander of the French district is on his way to Paris now to directly oversee the interception and arrest of this person, Malenkov." He also informed us that you are not to worry further. Both of the artist LADA's paintings have been destroyed! He wishes you to know he personally gave the order for them to do so. The CIA in America destroyed one and our men in Paris destroyed the second one, Mister President, sir!"

Now the look of puzzlement on the Russian President's face changed. He coughed and choked trying to get the words out before a loud, "He what?" echoed through the room.

Caught off guard but having heard that he had a bit of a temper, the squat Russian officer replied, "The Commander of Paris district is on his way to Paris to oversee the capture and arrest of former Major Sop..."

A visibly angry President interrupted her. "No, you idiot! Not that! The paintings. What did he say about the paintings?"

"As you requested, sir, the paintings will never reveal the coded messages on either one that you wished not to be revealed. They both have been destroyed, sir!" "Leave!" She stood still. "LEAVE! NOW!"

She saluted sharply and executed a smart about face almost running for the door, just barely keeping her appearance of a Russian military officer. Once beyond the closed door, she sagged and pushed out of her lungs a volume of air in a loud "whoosh". How do I get transferred from this?

• • •

London, England

James met up with his two agents at the front door. Both were large, strongly built young men. He quickly filled them in on the friend they would meet up with and who needed safe passage back to HQ. He informed them he did not know if there was any issue to be worried about but needed to make absolutely sure of the security for this person. He informed them that he wanted each one to go to a different door. They were to wait two minutes and then leave via that separate door and were to arrive at the junction of Craven Passage and Craven Street less than ten minutes later. One was to go down Whitehall to Strand and enter Craven Street from the northwest. The other was to go down Whitehall Place and enter Craven from the East off its junction with Northumberland Avenue. They were to hurry but not seem as though they were in a rush or anything out of the ordinary just in case the offices were being watched by foreign intelligence officers, which of course they knew they always were.

• • •

Paris, France

Mary and Tom arrived back at the apartment. It was now close to 6:45 pm. The outside of the apartment building looked relatively the same as when they departed that morning. However, there was a policeman standing by a police car next to the building and parked half on the sidewalk and half in the street. Behind it were two black Mercedes, also both straddling the sidewalk.

Mary and Tom attempted to open the door using the keypad. The police officer stopped them. "Personne ne peut entrer!"

"Pardon, monsieur le policier. Parles-tu anglais?"

Without responding, he pulled off his radio microphone on his collar and spoke in rapid French that neither Tom nor Mary could understand. They both did hear the words "deux" and "Americains" . . . two Americans.

"Vous pouvez entrer." He held the door for them.

The door inside at the foot of the stairs was also open and there were two more uniformed police officers guarding it. They signaled to Mary and Tom to go up the stairs. Climbing the three flights, at the door to the apartment, there was another policeman. The apartment door beside him was open. He motioned for them to enter. Once inside they saw that things were tossed around. Nothing appeared broken, just upended. Cushions off chairs and sofas, books pulled off the shelves. One thing was very noticeable. A spot next to the fireplace where a painting Mary and Tom both likedwas now missing, the painting!

"Mr. and Mrs. Martz?"

Turning to the voice at the doorway to the bedroom, Mary and Tom saw two men. One obviously dressed the way a young French investigator would dress. Euro tight dark suit pants and slim jacket, open shirt with no tie. Next to him stood an obviously American looking fellow dressed very well in American style. While the Frenchman was thirty-something, the American appeared late middle aged. He also looked familiar to both Tom and Mary, though neither said anything as neither could place why he looked familiar.

"Oui, yes!"

Seeing the hint of recognition in both Tom and Mary's eyes, the man said in English, "This is French Inspector Vanasse. I am Mr. Smith from the US Embassy."
Tom was just about to be "chewy chewy bar" as Mary called him when he

tended to speak too much. He stopped short when he felt the squeezing grip of Mary's hand on his. She jumped in with, "What can you tell us about what has happened here?"

Mr. Smith spoke, "The French police received a call from a neighbor who noticed two men appearing to slip out of the apartment with an oddly shaped bag. Although they tiptoed down the stairs, the creaky stair and door alerted the neighbor." This, of course, he was making up because everything the two men had done was being monitored by the French intelligence agency through the hidden video cameras.

"The American Embassy was alerted as we learned two Americans were renting the place while the occupant was out of the country. I was sent over to assist in the investigation, to interpret and to assist the two of you in any way I can."

"All this sounds logical," Tom thought. Mary thought, "Hmmm this is a bit suspicious. How would they know the apartment was rented? How would they know it was rented to Americans? And how would they know to alert the Embassy so quickly? And how come the person responding is the same "Mr. Smith" we ran into years ago in Restaurant Palette?" Hmmm! But she did not let on that she had these questions.

"I wonder if you would walk through the apartment with Inspector Vanasse and I to identify anything you think may have been taken of yours. We do apologize that your clothing has been disturbed. We assure you none of the officers or ourselves have touched anything. Also, perhaps you can identify anything you know is missing from the apartment."

The Martzes agreed to do so and began a meticulous search of the apartment with the two men.

• • •

Moscow, Russia

The President of Russia sitting at his grand Russian desk, a leftover from the Romanov dynasty, was deep in thought. "What did she mean they destroyed the two paintings? The damn videos could not be on paintings, only code could be and even that had never been proven by anyone. No one knew how to get to the code. Two of LADA's paintings destroyed! A national treasure like her and her work destroyed!! Why? How? And why did the CIA get involved? And damn it! I want those videos leaked out and not destroyed! This will take some time to sort out. Are the videos still around? Where? Who were these two Americans the Russian agents were following . . . the Martzes or Mertzes or whatever? Why? How are they connected?"

Now his thoughts turned to the second aspect of the report the frumpy officer had delivered. "They had spotted Sophia! Good! And the commander was on his way to Paris to personally apprehend her. Good! And perhaps that goddamn General Gorchakov!!" He thought about how he had used Gorchakov to leak and smuggle out the videos of the fool American President. Could it also have been Gorchakov all along who was leaking and smuggling other military and state secrets to the West? Damn him!!! Of course!! He would be perfect for doing so. But how? Much to contemplate. Poisoning may not be good enough for him!

He decided that it would be best to let the commander apprehend Sophia. They could learn much from her. He personally would take charge of that interrogation! That would be a pleasure to do. I hope he knows how difficult and ruthless she can be as he remembered that night with disgust. He would deal with the destruction of the paintings once the two defectors had been caught.

He needed some Vodka and a woman! But not the damn tree stump replacement for Sophia. The switch of that one from his office was also high on his agenda. So very much for the most powerful man in the world to think about. So much!

• • •

London, England

James and his two agents converged on the bank of red phone booths. No one was there. No one inside any of them. James looked around. Across Craven Street, a man, sitting at an outdoor table sipping a pint, waved at James.

"You two stay here," he said to his companions. He crossed the street.

Dimitri stood as James approached and motioned to a chair at the table. James sat and said, "Dimitri, I thought you would remain in the phone booth till we arrived."

"Ah, James, do you realize how foolish a man would look to Russian agents if he were just standing in a phone booth pretending to make a phone call. This is much better. No one will attempt anything on me even if they know I am in your country, which I can tell you they don't, or didn't until I called you." With that, he raised his eyebrows as if jokingly questioning his friend.

"And, I see you have brought two of your colleagues. Call them over. Let's have a drink together and celebrate my coming out party. Isn't that what you call it when a young virgin is introduced to the trolling young men at a party? I'm your debutante, James!" A big smile spread across his handsome Russian face.

All James could muster through his chuckles was, "Dimitri, if all the young debutantes in Russia are as beautiful as you, I understand why the young men would defect!" With that, he signaled to his compatriots to join them. Dimitri rounded up two more chairs and ordered three more pints.

• • •

Paris, France

Tom and Mary finished going through the apartment with Mr. Smith and Monsieur Vanasse. The only thing they were sure was missing from the apartment was the painting. They were asked to describe it. Although Mary, with her artist eye, was doing an excellent job, her description just did not paint an accurate rendition of the painting itself. Just as the two men were about to leave, Tom remembered he had taken a picture of the painting with his cell phone. Quickly, at least for him, he accessed it and showed the screen to Mr. Smith and Monsieur Vanasse. Both asked if he would email them a copy of the picture. They each handed him a business card. He took Monsieur Vanasse's first.

As he was talking, Mr. Smith said to both him and Mary, "Would the two of you be available for lunch tomorrow?" Looking at each other, and figuring we are on vacation, they both nodded.

"Sure," Mary said.

"Good. How about you come to the American Embassy at about 11:30. I'll make reservations at one of my favorite places. It is called Restaurant Palette." He smiled at both of them with a wink.

Afterwards, shaking Mary and Tom's hands the two men headed downstairs with the remaining police officers.

Mary turned to Tom, "If I told you, I would have to kill you!"

"Yep, need to know basis. This should be an interesting day tomorrow! For sure!"

"Are you hungry?"

"Me hungry? Is there ever not a time? Where should we go?"

"How about the restaurant just up the street to the left . . . hmmm, to the east?" said not too confidently. "It has a great view to the south," Mary smiled, "down the mountain to the city below. It is called something like Le Relais de la Butte. There is a big outdoor patio for us to eat and enjoy the sunset."

"You game to 'dismiss the sun'?"

That phrase they had heard from the maître d' at a hotel in Cherbourg, France, when they had escorted a university travel group on a trip to Normandy and Paris. The maître d' encouraged the couple, obviously in love, to take a walk on the boardwalk as the sun set. The university travelers were jealous that the couple was in love with each other, saying in reviews, "They always held hands like newlyweds on a honeymoon or something."

Too bad the other couples were so unhappy together! Tom and Mary weren't doing anything different from what they ordinarily did. However, Mary did feel it was a bit presumptuous that humans could feel they could "Dismiss the Sun"!

• • •

Paris, France

Caroline finished giving the message to Natalya about her going out of town for a day or two. She would like to keep the hotel room for a few more days, if that was okay.

Natalya assured her that there was no problem. Their conversation was quietly carried out in Russian inside the small gallery office.

Natalya said to Caroline, "Are you sure you will be safe leaving Paris? I mean I don't know anything really about what is going on but Evalina was pretty set that you were to be protected and kept safe."

"I should be fine. I am meeting up with my . . . " pausing to figure out how to describe the Colonel General, Caroline settled on . . . "Father. He is in London, and I am going to take the Chunnel over to meet him there. We will travel back here to Paris together."

Although the two women were in the office and spoke quietly in Russian, a man just outside the office window, appearing to be looking at a painting, was hearing every word. He spoke Russian too. He was the lone agent now following Caroline after the other one followed the Martzes back to the apartment in the Montmartre.

Sensing the meeting of the two women was about to end, he made a move to the door of the gallery. One of the other gallery employees asked if he was interested in the piece of art he had been viewing. He replied politely in not great French, "no, but I will think about it."

He left the gallery and went right, assuming she would head that way. He was wrong. When she came out, she turned left and headed west along Qua Voltaire. Peeking around the corner he saw her nearly a full block ahead of him. He hurried to stay up with her. Now she was aware she was being followed. He, however, was not aware that he was being followed by two other men . . . the French agents who were part of the team protecting her.

• • •

Washington, DC, USA

LADA had put into place the third part of her plan and it would arrive on the Russian President's office email the next day, Thursday, September 5. She would hit send that night when she was back at the hotel. Right now, she, Evalina, Nina, and Ninette were working with the Kennedy Center's art curator on the final touches to the placement of the paintings. The show would open with a grand gala on the 57th anniversary of the Cuban Missile Crisis, Oct 16, 1962 . . . forty-one days from now. A lot yet to be accomplished before that date.

The men, all complaining of hunger even though it was only 1:30 in the afternoon and they had eaten breakfast just five hours before, were sent off by the women to find something to eat. Men!

They wandered right next door to the Watergate South complex and grabbed some food and a glass of wine at Tazza Cafe.

"Etienne and Alexei, now that the painting was delivered to the CIA and unfortunately destroyed, how much longer do you think we will be assigned here? The opening of LADA's show doesn't begin until the middle of October. Do you think we will stay here that long?"

Alexei spoke first, "I know that you all might have to head home earlier than me. I am going to stay with LADA and my daughter until the show opens. It would be nice if everyone else is here to support LADA too."

Etienne took longer to respond, as he had to think through all the obligations the two police officers had. He thought the two Americans assigned to the protection force, Mrs. Smith and Marta, might go back to their normal US assignments soon. Jack and Gaston too would probably be leaving, heading home. Etienne now considered the fact that only he and Guy would be there to protect and assist LADA, Evalina, Alexei, Nina, and Ninette. Based on that fact, he felt he could build a reasonable case for Guy and him to remain on site.

"I think there is reason to believe that you and I, Guy, will remain with LADA, Alexei, Evalina, Nina, and Ninette." He explained his thinking to the group.

"I will contact the Director-General d'Armee today and see if I can persuade him. I will also ask if we can continue to be backed up by the Embassy security team."

"What about Jack and Gaston? Do you think you can talk the Director-General into extending their assignment too? That would be helpful."

"First, I will make sure that our assignment is extended. Once that approval is secure, then I will ask about them. I don't want to give the Director-General the option of considering extending them and not us."

"That makes sense. Spoken like a real leader . . . and a man in love!" They all laughed.

The waiter brought the items they had ordered to the table. Etienne had ordered the Angus Stack Burger as rare as they would legally cook it. It would be considered burnt in France. Guy ordered the Italian Melt Sandwich on a baguette. Alexei, the Marinated Veggie Sandwich on baguette. The other two looked at him questioningly.

"A man of my age has to watch his waistline! Besides, it looked good!"

After lunch, it would be approaching 8:00 pm in Paris. Etienne called the Director-General. It didn't take long for the persuasive young officer to secure the extension of his and Guy's assignment. Feeling that luck was on his side and that he was developing a rhythm in his argument, he asked about extending Gaston and Jack. Gaston was approved. Jack, the Director-General would have to get back to him. He would need to clear that with MI6.

"I think they will approve." The Director-General wished Etienne, "Bonne nuit, Captain. I'm sure the two young ladies and others will be grateful you are staying on, especially the young ladies. I too would have done what you did tonight at another time in my life." He hung up.

50

Wednesday, September 4, 2019
London, England

DIMITRI GETS AN IDEA

Dimitri, James, and the Director-General of External Security of France, Bernard, met by phone a little later than James had indicated he would call. The pints took a bit longer!

Bernard too was a longtime adversary of Dimitri's, but also a personal friend, as was James. Although most of the outward intelligence work was adversarial, the hidden work was not. Bernard suspected that much of the intelligence information leaked out of Russia had a high position as a source. Both he and James suspected for some time that it was Dimitri through a source known to them only as Yuri. To receive the kind of information that the source, Yuri, was passing through a Russian farmer and his wife, seemed impossible without an ultimate source such as Dimitri. The good news was now, for a time, Dimitri would be able to give both MI6 and French Intelligence extensive information, governmental, military, and personal about the current Russian leader. The bad news was the previous source of information would now dry up. The CIA would never know about any of this.

They talked at length about how Dimitri decided to defect and why at this time. When Dimitri finished telling his story about his God daughter, Major Sophia Malenkov, Bernard spoke.

"Dimitri, there has been an unfortunate turn of events." A worried look came over Dimitri and James' face.

"Go on, my friend. What is it?"

"We have been watching your God daughter and protecting her. All was going well but then . . . " He proceeded to tell about the LADA paintings carrying the information Dimitri had provided to Yuri. This obviously confused Dimitri because how could these videos and other information of this size and type be on a painting? He said nothing except, "Go on."

He was told about the young women Nina and Ninette. He was told about LADA's show in the US opening on October 16. He was told everything both he and James knew, including this strange American couple, the Martzes, renting Nina's place and the stolen piece of LADA's art. Then came word of the problem.

"Two of their agents, the Russians, assigned to follow the Martzes happened to see Sophia go into the iSPY Gallery. Although her appearance was greatly altered, one of the agents had served with her as his commanding officer when he was in the Military Intelligence before transferring to FSB. He recognized her somehow."

Bernard did not want to tell Dimitri what was said to the other agent and said over the phone, "I will never forget that body of hers even though it was covered in a military uniform!" He didn't see it necessary to tell a caring Godfather.

"The Commander of the French/Belgium division of FSB has left for Paris earlier, almost as this was happening. He informed his men he personally would be in France to arrest her and . . . " he paused . . . "You!"

Dimitri's worried look stopped. After a few moments he said, "Perfect! I have a plan. I will need the assistance of MI6, British Navy, and French Navy as well." He looked at each of them. "Want to hear the plan?"

51

Wednesday, September 4, 2019
Paris, France

TURN OF EVENTS

The FSB Commander of the France/Belgium district disembarked the plane at CDG. He had to take a private jet registered as one of the many oil oligarch's private jets. It, of course, was actually one of FSB's, as many of them are. As he walked inside the private jet terminal and showed the immigration agent his false passport, he was at this time Boris Smirnoff. He loved that the last name meant, "quiet, peaceful, and gentle". Hardly him at all!

Inside the lobby the two agents, who had broken into the apartment, met him. They did not say anything, just grabbed his bags as they were rolled in from the tarmac and carried them out to their parked Mercedes. Once in the car, the Commander finally spoke.

"Has the painting been destroyed?"

"Not yet, sir. We wanted to wait for you to make sure that is still what you wanted us to do. It is really quite a beautiful painting and we understand she, the artist, is considered a national treasure."

"I said destroy it! I want no questions from you about it! Do as I say! Understand?!"

"Yes, Commander. We understand fully. It will be destroyed tomorrow morning."

It was now close to 10:00 pm in Paris, 12:00 pm in Moscow. It had been a long day.

"Where am I staying?"

"Le Meurice, Commander. It is just across the river from the iSPY Gallery. It is a bit pricey, but we thought it would be . . ."

"Fine!" he interrupted. "Get me there quickly. I'm tired. Do we know what Sophia Malenkov is doing tomorrow? What have the others found out?"

"Interestingly, she did receive a phone call on a non-encrypted cell phone. It was from Colonel General Gorchakov."

The commander looked alert now.

"Really? What did he say?"

"He told Major Malenkov to take the morning 9:13 am Eurostar train from Gare du Nord to London St-Pancras station. He told her they could take care of business in London that day and return to France that evening by chartered fishing vessel from Dover Marina at 12:00 pm. They will take that hired fishing vessel to Calais, where they will board the Eurostar back to Paris the next day. She began to ask why they would not take the late Eurostar directly from London. He said he would tell her all tomorrow when they meet up. Something about needing to show her something in Dover."

"Interesting. Okay, contact our comrades who are watching her. Tell them to follow her to the train station but not to follow her on board. I will meet up with them at the Gare du Nord. They will be there ahead of me and purchase three First Class tickets. Two tickets for one of them and me to London. The other is to purchase a ticket only to Calais. He is to get off there and wait for a chartered fishing boat to arrive sometime early in the morning on Friday the sixth. The other will escort me to follow the young woman to her meeting with the General. We will wait for our chance and then capture them on board the fishing boat."

"But how will the one man know where the fishing vessel will dock? And, also, how will you capture them onboard a fishing boat?"

Angry, the commander replied, "First, you don't question me! Understand? Second, I am not sure at this moment how we will do it. It will be done. As for how the man will know where we will dock. He has all day in Calais to find out where private fishing boats dock. Now get me to the hotel. It is tomorrow already!"

They drove in silence. Both other men in the car felt very happy they were not going to accompany him on this trip!

While they were having this conversation, Evalina was on a secure phone with Natalya. She informed Natalya that while Caroline was out of Paris, Natalya was to secure all of Caroline's personal belongings and take them to Evalina's house. She was to put the clothing and other personal items in the same large guest room overlooking the park where Ninette had rehabilitated. Natalya assured her it would be taken care of, and the secure phone call ended.

Evalina now called Etienne and told him what she had asked to be done regarding the personal belongings to the mysterious woman. That had been arranged for the next day. Neither one informed the other of the identity of the young woman whose personal belongings were being moved. In fact, neither one knew. What they did know was this mysterious woman was to be protected and that order had come from the highest levels.

Etienne called the Director-General as soon as he had hung up with Evalina. The Director-General gave Etienne the name and information of the mystery woman. "Now this is a tres interesting turn of events!" Etienne said to himself. "Tres interesting!"

52

Thursday, September 5, 2019
Paris, France

TRAILING SOPHIA

The young mysterious Russian woman, Caroline, now Sophia again, woke, dressed, and had coffee and croissants in the hotel/guest house dining room. Hurrying out the door at precisely 8:00 am, she had an hour to get to Gare du Nord train station. She caught the direct number four metro from Odeon station, waiting only five minutes on the platform. The number four took her directly to the Gare du Nord, with no transfers and only nine stops. Purposefully dressed as Sophia, she knew she was being followed. Her Godfather had said he would be filling her in the night before on how the Russian agents had stumbled on her. He specified that she dressed this way so she would be easily identified and followed by them. The first part of his plan.

The agents had no trouble sighting her as she came out the hotel door. They had no problem following her as she looked exactly like she had when the agent who had been in her command had seen her in his previous military life. Only difference now, she was out of uniform and how he wished that body was out of civvies too. As they walked, he was describing to his partner what he was imagining. His partner was now engaged in letting his imagination flow too. Both so caught up in their visions, trying in their minds to remove each item of her clothing, neither one realized, once again, that they were being followed by two French agents.

Sophia stayed as prominently displayed on the station platform as she could. Not very difficult to do for this beautiful young woman. Although rush hour in Paris didn't officially begin until 9:00 am, already the metros were becoming busy.

The car she chose was full. She planned it this way so that her followers would feel they were obscure to her and make them believe they had not been spotted. This provided a bit of a challenge for the French agents. They choose the car directly behind the one the other three entered, Sophia and the two Russian agents. Everyone knew Sophia's destination. This was only a minor issue for the two Frenchmen.

The metro arrived on time for Sophia to stroll leisurely through Gare du Nord. She stopped occasionally at shops and made it as difficult as possible for her followers to keep hidden. She had purchased her ticket online the day before and at the last few minutes moving more swiftly, she rapidly moved to and through the border control lines. The Russian agents had to stop to buy tickets. Sophia was traveling in the first-class coach. The Russian agents were able to buy two first class tickets, one for the Commander all the way to London and one to the Calais stop. Unfortunately for the third, the only other seat available for him to London was a less comfortable coach class seat. This also proved helpful for the General and Sophia and made the General's plan easier. The Commander and this agent would be separated at just the exact right time.

They all rushed to the boarding. Sophia found her seat and settled in. The commander arrived just in time to get his ticket from the other two and rush through security. He found his seat four rows behind her and on the other side of the train. The other first class riding agent was two seats behind him on the same side of the train. This would make communications from this point on difficult unless they both left their seats at the same time. They could do so, but this might draw her suspicion.

The third Russian was several cars behind. He too was totally without communication with the other two. This also became a benefit to the General's plan. The two French agents, who had followed the four other passengers on the metro, had been replaced with two British citizens, a husband and wife, returning home from a quick trip to Paris to buy a baguette for dinner. They occupied seats near the economy class Russian. He was the target for the upcoming part of the

General's plan. A third British patron was seated in first class next to Sophia as had been also planned.

The first leg of the Eurostar began as the train started to move out of the Gare du Nord precisely at 9:13 am.

The Commander made another misstep when he decided to turn his cell phone off. It would serve no benefit until late tonight, he thought.

• • •

The President of Russia was sitting at his Romanov desk thinking about what havoc he could cause in the world . . . his typical morning mental exercise . . . when a ping came up on his private email. He looked at the sender's address and realized it came from his old friend, LADA. She was in America. Why would she be sending him an email? He opened it and read:

> I hope you are doing well. I, as you know, am in the United States with my friends from the Russian Gallery in Paris. We are setting up the paintings for my show that opens next month. It commemorates the long relationship between the Russian people and the people of the United States. A sometimes-troubled relationship for sure. One, however, that both countries seem to survive.
>
> The reason I am writing is to let you know that I have left a very special gift for you hanging in my friend's apartment in Paris. It is one that I made on my recent trip back to our country. I think you will love it! It is one of your favorite places. Hopefully, I can see that you get it on the day this show opens in Washington, DC. It will tie both ends of the artistic adventure together.
>
> In my thoughts,
> LADA

What an odd email! But wait!! She wrote "a painting hanging in the apartment of a friend!" Not one in the show in the USA. One from the apartment that is being destroyed???

He yelled to his assistant to call the damn Commander to no avail. The message came back to the assistant that the phone number could not be reached at this time. "Click!"

53

Thursday, September 5, 2019
Paris, France

COINCIDENCES

At 9:00 am, the Martzes had begun their slow walk to the meeting at the American Embassy with Mr. Smith at 11:30 am. Walking out the door and down the hill on Rue Durantin, their first stop was at Coquelicot, a small bakery and patisserie just a block from the apartment. This was their breakfast stop and would become so for several of the remaining mornings on this trip.

After the usual espresso and plain croissant for Tom and chocolate one for Mary, though she had debated about having an almond one instead, they started their adventure: finding a replacement black beret for Tom. He had given his old one to the partner of Mary's sister, Hank, on a previous trip when Hank had a bad cold. This, as with all of Tom and Mary's searches, would prove to be an interesting and fun challenge.

First stop, which they knew would be successful, Galeries Lafayette on Boulevard Haussmann, wasn't.

Mary and Tom went up and down the rows of clothing in the men's department. In broken French, they tried to explain to curious store clerks what they were looking for. All the clerks showed questioning faces but did hear the word "chapeau". They were led to racks and racks of hats . . . all brimmed hats . . . most like the English and Irish wear.

"What, no beret?" Again, trying to make the young clerk understand, Mary gestured by spinning her hand around her head and pointing to the hats brim and saying, “Non!”

They could tell the young woman trying to help them was holding back chuckles.

“Non, Madame. Nous n’en avons pas.” Smiling as she now spun her hand around her head and pointed to the British-looking hat with brim and shook her head “Non”.

“Merci, mademoiselle”.

As the young clerk walked off, Mary turned to Tom. “In the land of French berets, no berets? How can this be?”

“Remember on our first trip, our flight back to the US was canceled because the Air France flight couldn’t make it out of Chicago because of bad weather?” Mary looked at him and was thinking as usual, “Where is this line of thinking taking us?”

“Yes. So?”

“Well, remember they put us on another flight to catch a codeshare flight out of London on British Airways? Back when they did that sort of thing.”

Mary was now chuckling to herself because this string of thinking was so her Tom.

“Yes.”

“Remember that the Air France flight to get us to London just in time to make the connection to Chicago was postponed for half an hour, just enough time to miss the connection because of a ‘planned strike’?”

Now openly laughing. “Yes.”

"Remember also we went up to the Air France counter in Heathrow, once we finally got there and I was wearing my new French beret?"

"Go on."

"And the French Air France clerk informed us that they had already made arrangements?"

"Yes!" Now almost bent over in laughter.

"Well, the clerks said, 'Ah, yes. We French. That is what we do. We complain and strike. Complain and strike!'"

"Tom, where is this story going?"

"Well, then the Air France guy looked at me and shook his head saying, 'You give us French a bad name wearing that chapeau!' Remember?"

"Let's try Printemps," shaking her head and continuing to laugh.

With no better luck at Printemps, the Martzes headed over on Boulevard Haussmann to Rue Tronchet south past Place de la Madeleine and onto Rue Royale. This took them straight to Place de la Concorde. Turning right, or west, they headed over to Avenue Gabriel, the name of Mary's son and the street that the US Embassy is on. A sign!

They arrived at the front door precisely at 11:30 am.

54

Thursday, September 5, 2019
England

THE CHASE

Just as Mary and Tom arrived at the US Embassy in Paris, the Eurostar train, after a short stop in Calais where a very few passengers disembarked, including a gruff-looking man, pulled into Pancras station.

Sophia hurriedly departed the train and raced for the steps leading to the central station hall. She would meet up with the General there. The Commander, seeing her rush off, tried to stay with her. She was only carrying a shoulder bag and her purse. He was pulling a roller bag. Looking around his companion back in coach class was nowhere to be seen. He raced off after Sophia under the close observation of the MI6 agent who had been seated next to Sophia. Now two other MI6 agents joined the first, also following him.

As the chase took place by the Commander, the Russian agent in Coach tried to push past other passengers to get off the full train. He had no luck. Pulling out a piece of gum as he stepped onto the station platform, he looked around trying to locate the commander and the girl. He could see neither the good-looking woman nor his Commander. He placed the gum in his mouth and dropped the foil wrapper to the ground.

Just at that moment, he heard a voice.

“Pardon me, sir, but littering in England is a serious offense.”

He turned around to see two very large London police officers.

In the agent's not so good French, he said, "Je non comprends pas." Obviously said with a Russian accent.

The police officers pointed at the wrapper on the ground.

"Ah." And the agent bent down to pick it up.

"You will come with us, sir!" Each officer taking an arm.

Looking fully annoyed and not comprehending, he tried to shake the officers off. This caused them to be a little more forceful. His tension and anger mounted because he knew he was losing the woman and his Commander.

Just as he broke the grips of the two officers, two more Bobbies arrived on the scene. Now four Bobbies forced the man's hands behind his back and handcuffed him, cheered on by several onlookers, many of whom were taking videos with their cell phones. These videos later appeared that night on the BBC, French 24, Al Jazeera, CNN, and Fox News. Each told a slightly different angle to the story. The BBC, quite matter of fact. "A litterer apprehended for littering in the station started a fight with police officers. Several other police mates joined in the arrest."

French 24 had a panel debating, "Was this a justified arrest or the unwarranted harassment of a tourist?"

Al Jazeera, focusing on the apparent Middle Eastern appearance of the man and on outright racial discrimination.

CNN saw "an infringement of people's rights by the excess of video cameras in London that invaded everyone's privacy all the while they monitored their electronic information allure advertisements."

Fox News, "who cares about reality? We will tell you anything we want you to think. In this case, he was a typical worthless immigrant trying to take advantage of the upstanding and cultured white Anglo-British while disfiguring the station and trying to beat up the police who were just trying to assist him. Word is out that he is a Muslim!"

Whatever anyone would believe was irrelevant, as at that moment he was ushered out of the station to a waiting police van and disappeared into London.

55

Thursday, September 5, 2019
Paris, France

MR. SMITH

Mary and Tom walked up to the guards outside the front entrance of the US Embassy on Avenue Gabriel. Security at US Embassies has always been stringent, since 9/11, nearly impossible to get through. The first phase was the French Police. Once cleared by them, there were Marine Guards at a Guard hut. Beyond that, as you entered the front doors, more Military Police and metal detectors, a thorough search of any bags and the use of an electronic wand. And, of course, at each stage, you had to state and restate the purpose of your visit. Gosh, it was almost like having to restate your name and date of birth when checking in at the hospital.

Mr. Smith's name seemed to carry some clout, as each time the name was mentioned there was a slight nod and a pass. Literally at the last step one did receive a pass . . . an actual badge with the emblem of the Eagle of the United States on it and below in bold capital letters, VISITOR.

A nicely dressed young man came down a circular staircase in the inner lobby area. He walked over to Tom and Mary.

"Mrs. and Mr. Martz, I am Mr. Smith's assistant, Joseph Campbell. Mr. Smith will be down in just a couple of minutes to join you. He is with the Ambassador at the moment. Please follow me."

Leading the way, he led them into a nice living room. "Please make yourselves comfortable. Would you care for coffee, tea, or Perrier water?"

Both Tom and Mary declined the offer and sat down on what looked like an original Louis the XIII finely upholstered couch. Joseph sat down in a chair across a coffee table from them. It looked to be original from the same timeframe as the couch.

"How long are you staying in Paris?"

"Just ten days."

"It appears from what Mr. Smith has told me that the first couple of days have been interesting, perhaps a bit more exciting than expected?"

Tom began to formulate his response and reply but stopped short thinking, "chewy chewy bar". He looked over at Mary and nodded just enough to ask her to field the questions appropriately. She was good at it. No "chewy, chewy bar" from her. Just straightforward "yes" and "no" answers with just the right amount of extra detail to at least appear conversational. Tom could tell what she was thinking; however, "is this an interrogation, Joseph?" She would never say that aloud, but he knew she was thinking that. He was too.

"Yes, there was a bit of excitement yesterday. But it got us here to a nice meeting with Mr. Smith. By the way, does he have a first name? Is he just always called Mr. Smith?"

Tom laughed inside. A typical Mary response from her Jesuit University training. The Jesuits perfected it. Never answer a question outright, answer it instead with a question. Put the burden on the other guy.

Joseph stumbled with the answer but finally said, "Yes, of course he has a first name. It is Fred."

"Fred? We have a good friend named Fred. He lives in Kansas City. Perhaps they know each other!"

Joseph Campbell, eyes wide, shook his head in disbelief. What was she saying?

"Mrs. Martz, I'm . . ."

Mary interrupted him, "Where is your Fred from? Does he live anywhere near Kansas City?"

How was he going to answer her? "Well, you know Mrs. Martz, just because his name is Fred . . ."

Interruption number two. "You know all Freds know each other. Heck, you and I probably know a lot of Freds. Yes, there is Fred Townsend, who I mentioned. Hmmm, how about Fred Astaire, Fred MacMurray, you know from Disney's *The Shaggy Dog*, oh and *Flubber*. Of course, there is the young fellow from *Wonder Years*. My kids loved that show. Full of funny things that preteens go through. Do you have any children, Joseph? And of course, everyone's favorite Fred, Fred Rogers. You know, *Mr. Rogers*. Joseph, you looked bewildered. Is something wrong?"

This conversation continued this way for several minutes. Every time Joseph attempted to ask a question, it was answered with a question or misdirected down a different and confusing route.

Tom was dying with laughter inside, thinking how mixed up Joseph was becoming. He also noticed a familiar figure in the doorway. Mr. Smith had arrived a few moments ago and was listening to the conversation and he too was silently laughing. He broke the conversation with a "Uhhgh," and continued.

"Hello, Mr. and Mrs. Martz. Thank you for coming to the Embassy today. I hope that Joseph has kept you entertained until I was able to come down?" Turning now to Joseph, he said, "Thank you Joseph, I'm quite sure Mrs. and Mr. Martz appreciated their time with you, especially Mrs. Martz."

With that, Joseph, who had stood up as soon as he heard Mr. Smith's voice, hastily left the room saying a quick goodbye and wondering what on Earth had happened. The Martzes too had stood up.

"Please sit. We can chat here for a few minutes and then I'll give you a tour of the Embassy. Not many people have toured the place since 9/11." He indicated for them to sit.

He smiled at Mary and shook his head in admiration. "Have you ever considered a career with the CIA or in politics, Mrs. Martz? That was one of the best jobs of disabling an interview with non-logic I have ever seen. Joseph actually is pretty good at getting information from people. I think he may be needing a refresher course...or rehab. How did you learn to do that?"

Smiling back at Mr. Smith, she said, "Do you mind if I call you Fred? And while we are at it, why not use Tom's and my first names too? Mine's Mary. But I know you already know that. So, to answer your question. I raised five children Fred, two girls and three boys. Misdirection and answering with a question of my own was particularly useful with the boys. But I suspect you already know that too. I was schooled in college by the Jesuits. At Rockhurst University in Kansas City. But you probably know all that too. And you probably know that no one can make the illogic sound more logical than a Jesuit."

"Ah, I too was Jesuit educated. Georgetown undergraduate. And yes, they can use logic anyway necessary even if it is illogical logic."

All three began a nice conversation. Then the bombshell was revealed.

"I know you recognized me when we met at the apartment. My associate and I were Mr. and Mrs. Smith at La Palette Restaurant. What was it, perhaps five years ago? She is out of town right now on a trip with some close association to what is happening here the last couple of days. We of course are not really a married couple, as you suspected. And, yes, as I said in the restaurant, outdoor on the patio as I recall, I cannot reveal what we really do. But I feel pretty sure you have a good idea. And no, I would not have to kill you, but my colleagues would make it pretty uncomfortable for me if I did tell you."

Turning now to Tom, he said. "Mr. Martz, or Tom, you know you have been on our radar screen for some time?"

"What? How? I mean, what do you mean? You lost me. And I'm sure Mary too."

"It is a long story that actually begins with your great grandfather, a German immigrant back in the late 1800s. It really began to become interesting with your father, a Colonel in the US Army, assigned publicly in the Adjutant General Corps. Did you know that he had a special assignment his entire career in Military Intelligence? It started in World War II when he was secretly assigned to the OSS."

"You're kidding?"

"No. Someday we can meet again and go through all of his assignments that can be revealed. Some are not. However, I will skip to you now."

"Have you ever wondered why you are stopped so many times when passing through international airports?"

"Actually, yes, both Mary and I have wondered that."

"It started with the missing fingerprints. Let me change that, it really started for you and your brother in Park Forest, Illinois in 1953. FBI agents came to your home late at night and told your father that he and the family were not to have anything to do with the Stein family who lived next door to you. If you all didn't do as they said, his career in the army was over. Part of the McCarthy debacle. As I understand from the report in the files, your dad told the agents, in no uncertain terms, they could 'go to hell!' Gutsy move for a Colonel on a shortlist for promotion to General."

"You have to be kidding?"

"No, and unfortunately, it did put an end to his military career. Unfortunately, the times then were not much different than the political climate we have today . . . J. Edgar Hoover of then. The current President and his political lackey of today."

Both Tom and Mary thought the same thing at the same moment about that comment. They shared their thoughts with each other that night. It was good news. It pointed out just what this Mr. Fred Smith thought of the current President, the same thing they thought of him: egocentric, self-centered, sociopath.

"So later in life when you accidently burned off your fingerprints and could not have fingerprints taken for ROTC, from that point on your actions were watched even more carefully. Remember this was the 1960s and the turmoil with racial protests, the Vietnam War, the shootings at Kent State, which by the way, you announced in ROTC class."

"Wait, you know about that?"

"You were beginning to build quite a record in the files of the FBI. Let's just say under Hoover and the following leaders, many people were watched. Other agencies became involved when you traveled overseas, thus the meeting of you and Mary and me and "my wife" at the place we are going to have lunch today . . . La Palette Restaurant. Shall we go?"

Now the bewildered parties were Tom and Mary. This certainly was an eye-opening meeting. Over lunch it would continue to be more so.

56

Thursday, September 5, 2019
England

THE CHASE CONTINUES

The Commander now realized he was on his own. The associate was nowhere to be seen. He would have to handle this himself. He didn't want to risk bringing in the Commander of the British/Irish sector. The use of his men and him would lead to his taking over the assignment, and the glory when the two traitors were brought home would also be his. No, the Commander could handle this himself! And take all the credit! He was good at that.

Sophia and the General got into a Hackney Carriage line. They jumped the line and took the next one. The other customers waiting were not too happy with this. Then the Commander took the next one after that too. Again, the waiting customers were not happy. The commander just spoke in gruff Russian, and they all backed off. Once the General and Sophia were safely in the carriage, the driver asked where they wished to go. He was told the street number for a local bank.

In the second carriage, the Commander told the driver in very rough English, "Follow that car!"

Amused, the cabbie said, "As you wish, your Lordship!" He pulled quickly and with a jerk out into the traffic. A waiting black BMW series 550 black sedan pulled away from the curb moments later and the Commander was now followed.

The first stop for the General and Sophia/Caroline/Margaret, Maggie Bowsman as she was now listed on her British identifications . . . passport and driver's license—could she remember to drive on the wrong side of the road—was the

HSBC bank located at 31 Euston Road. The General asked the driver to wait. He told him it might take up to an hour. He would make it well worth his time and gave him a 100-pound note in advance. The two travelers got out of the cab and entered the bank.

The Commander also told his driver to wait. He did not offer the driver any incentive. This, of course, was not making the driver of the carriage very happy. Somehow, he would get even unless there was a big tip at the end of the trip. He sat there stewing. The Commander sat there wishing he had stopped at a restroom. He was after all a man over fifty!

It didn't take long for either of the travelers to make their transfers of Swiss Franc to British pounds. Each account now had the equivalent of 5,000,000 Euros deposited. The combined total of all accounts was a little over 25,000,000 Euros spread between two banks in Paris, two accounts in London at the same bank, a bank in Spain and the account that Sophia had in the Swiss bank. She was pretty sure the General had more there too. And had he done the same thing in his quick stop in Turkey? She was staggered by the thought!

The General and Sophia came out of the bank and got into the carriage. The General gave the driver two thousand pounds telling him he wished for the driver to take them to Dover, England, and the Dover Marina. "Not a problem!" the driver replied. Two thousand pounds for roughly four hours driving there and back. Plus, the mileage fare. Not bad!

The carriage driver with the Commander did not have the same reaction as they headed out on the A2. His fare finally in broken and heavy foreign accent told him that they were following the other carriage all the way to Dover. "Really?" the cabbie said. "There better be a good tip in it for me Gov'ner or you can get out right now and find another ride!" The Commander told him not to worry, he would be well compensated. "Don't lose that other cab!"

57

Thursday, September 5, 2019
Paris, France

REVELATIONS

Lunch with Fred Smith ended after several other enlightening revelations. Both Tom and Mary had been monitored for the last twenty years as they traveled. Fred had asked them if they did not find it odd the day when they first met, that a strange American couple sat down next to them and began a conversation. Mary said, "No," as that seemed to happen frequently with them.

"Like the strange independent movie producer of *Afternoon Tea at Midnight* in Amsterdam? Or perhaps the older American couple who sat next to you at the Le Concorde Restaurant Boulevard Saint-Germain?" His eyebrows lifted.

"You mean . . ."

"Yes, Tom and Mary. All were members of our team. That was before we were sure who you both really were. You seemed like the nice all-American couple you appeared to be. Although Mary, you don't like football, baseball, and basketball. Really? A bit un-American for sure. And being an art major in college. Hanging out with all the gay guys and of course J. Edgar was sure that all art majors were communist. And Tom, even though you were in ROTC you were not without your vocal concerns of Vietnam, your discussion with the history professor of moving to Canada. Your strange use of a passport to enter Canada when one wasn't used in those days. Lots of strange little things gave certain people pause about you. Still, you were removed from the watch list under the Obama administration's team's review of the lists."

"We would not have met up again had you not rented the apartment from Evalina and Nina. Someday I will tell you more about them. For now, let's just say that under the current administration the agency I am with is much like the FBI was under Hoover. Surprisingly, the FBI under the current Director, Christophe Wray, and a couple before him, Mueller and Comey, are surprisingly extremely well organized and led. Couldn't say that was true with the couple following Comey. And it certainly is not true with the current leader at the head of an organization called the CIA!" Again, his eyebrows lifted.

"Well, I have to head back to the Embassy. My car will be waiting for me out front. Can I give you a lift anywhere?"

"No thank you, Fred," Mary said. "We will just walk off this wonderful . . ." she paused, "and, heavy meal. Thank you. It has been very enlightening."

"You both take care. It has been fun getting to know you better personally and professionally. I think everything will go smoothly for you from here going forward." He smiled, shook their hands, and left the building, not unlike Elvis.

"Wow!" turning to Tom she continued, "Do you believe all that?"

"Wow is right. Yes, since he knew all the incidents he described, I have to believe it. Don't you?"

"Yeah, me too. Well, you know what Marcellous would say?"

"Keep your wick dry?"

Looking at him and shaking her head in disbelief, she said, "What?"

"You know, keep your wick dry so that it can go 'Boom' when needed."

"Do all men keep their wicks dry?" she asked, laughing.

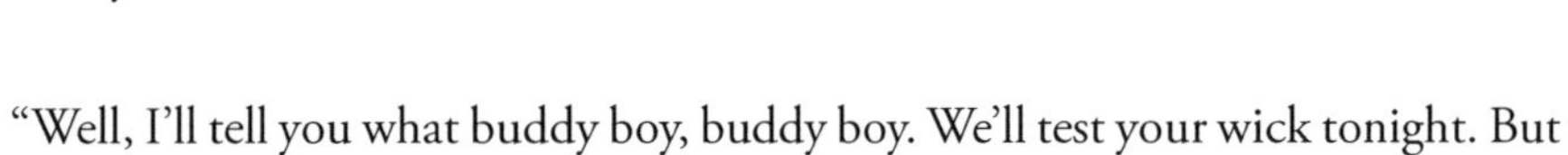

“Only to make sure it works.”

“Well, I’ll tell you what buddy boy, buddy boy. We’ll test your wick tonight. But I’m warning you . . .”

“Yes?”

“I won’t be keeping it dry!” she smiled.

“All right! But what would Marcellous have said?”

“Don’t get stuck with the Q!”

“Right!”

She took his hand and off they went for a late afternoon adventure.

58

Thursday, September 5, 2019
Dover, England

THE MARINA

The General and Sophia had arrived in Dover at the Marina at 3:30 pm. At some point shortly after leaving London, the Hackney cab driver had informed them that it appeared another Hackney was following them. The General said that he suspected they would be and to make it difficult but not impossible for the other cab to follow them. Pretty much driving as he normally would. Just don't let them lose the other cab. "Interesting," thought the driver. He and the other cabbie would stop somewhere on the way back to share notes.

He was with this distinguished older man and this "bird". Definitely not a "tart". The driver wanted to believe the woman was the gentleman's niece or daughter. Yes, that's it. A niece or daughter. "Can't wait to find out who was in the other cab. Wonder if the other bloke received the same amount. Three thousand pounds and the full fare for the ride too. A great day! And the young woman was nice to look at too. A bit of a 'jelly' young one for sure. Yes, quite a looker. The gent wasn't so bad looking neither."

The General and Sophia departed the carriage and found a fisherman and boat to take them safely back across the English Channel later that night. Leaving about midnight from Dover, they would arrive in Calais Marina between 3:00 am and 5:00 am. He agreed to their offer.

An apparent lurking crewman on the boat dock deck two boats away observed all of this.

The General, in almost Oxford English, told the boat captain that he and Sophia, now Maggie, his niece, would be back just before midnight to help prepare the boat for launching. The size of the boat allowed the captain, with their aid, to handle the boat by himself. No other crew would be necessary. They said they were going to get a bite to eat. Neither had had anything since breakfast. That is true with the Commander too. He definitely was feeling the hunger pangs.

The boat captain replied he would return sometime around 11:00 pm. He needed to take care of some things at home. Although the General had offered to buy him dinner, he refused. He would grab some food from home and catch a few winks. It would be a long evening ahead. Fog was sure to form on the Channel tonight and he wanted to be alert.

They shook hands and the General and Maggie departed for the restaurant the captain had suggested.

The Commander, having overheard the conversation, felt no need to follow them. He decided to find his own quick bite to eat. Just past dark, he would find a way to slip aboard the boat and hide. His takeover of the boat would be scheduled for some time mid-Channel. According to what he had heard from the travel plan, about 1:30 am or so. He was sure the boat would have somewhere on board where he could hide and surprise them.

He could assemble his carbon fiber handgun on board the boat during the time he would be waiting. Or, if he found a suitable private place beforehand, he would assemble it then. Interesting how modern technology allowed very powerful weapons to be produced that weighed nearly nothing. It could fire up to 2,200 rounds per minute with the proper feeding mechanism. His state of the art Heckler & Koch was just that sort of weapon. It had no metal parts. When broken down and dispersed inside his bags along with the bullets, no person or machine could identify there was a murderous weapon. It was invisible. He comfortably strolled away, backpack slung on his back, carrying his friend "Mr. Heckler" inside.

The boat captain observed the man from the upper floor of his nearby boathouse. He and the two men from MI6, which had trailed both Hackney Carriages to the Dover Marina, were now changing into comfortable clothing for a cold night at sea. Just as the boat pushed off from the dock, the two MI6 agents planned to quietly slip aboard the boat and hide until the right time. The boat captain, himself, was not a fisherman. He was, in fact, an officer in the Special Boat Services, the United Kingdom's equivalent to the US Navy SEALS. All three would be equally armed, as the Russian Commander, with their own high-powered weapons. That was also true of the General and Sophia/Maggie.

59

Thursday, September 5, 2019
Paris, France

ROGUE COMRADE

After viewing the meeting of Mary and Tom with Mr. Smith from the American Embassy, the Russian agent who had been following them, decided that following these two Americans was no longer worthwhile. He headed back to the location that he and the other Russian agent occupied, close to the apartment rented by Tom and Mary . . . 10 Rue Garreau. There, he would confirm how his comrade had destroyed the painting. The comrade had other ideas, however.

While the one trailing after Tom and Mary had followed them to the American Embassy, and then to La Palette Restaurant, his friend decided not to destroy the painting. He would never let his comrade or the Commander know this. He decided this valuable painting would be his own private property. "Let's face it," he thought, "this painting is too valuable to destroy. It is a product of a national treasure and it itself needed to be protected, as it too is a national treasure. It is my obligation, my duty, to do so, though one day I might sell it for a pretty price!"

Proud of the patriotic duty he was conducting, he, on his Vespa, hurried off to his own apartment with the bagged painting. He too was followed by French Intelligence officers. They had strong suspicions of what was in the bag and what he might be planning to do.

60

Thursday, September 5, 2019
Dover, England

STOWAWAY

Darkness fell in Dover about 7:10 pm that evening. The Commander made his way to the docks and acted as normal as he could. For the most part, everything was quiet. A heavy fog bank was just beginning to make it on shore. The crossing would be treacherous tonight. Not because of a strong storm, but rather because the air was still and heavy with fog. The Channel, a busy ship corridor, carried lots of freight cargo from the North Atlantic to the northern ports of France and Germany. Places like Hamburg, Bremerhaven, and Dusseldorf in Germany and La Havre, Deauville, and Calais in France. Their trip would be long and slow, as the captain would want to be sure to stay clear of ship traffic. Just to be sure, once on board, the Commander would find a life jacket and keep it with him. One never could be too sure!

The two men standing near a boat moored three docks away were turned the other way, looking back into town. Quickly, he climbed over the small fence blocking entrance to the pier and bent over, keeping a low profile. He climbed aboard the boat. Hurrying below deck, he looked for a safe place to hide. He didn't realize hidden micro-cameras were catching every movement.

The boat had two small sleeping cabins, one on each side of a small alleyway from the stern of the boat to the bow. Right at the foot of the steps below deck at the stern was the small galley. No place to hide there or inside the small cabins. At the bow of the boat was a small head. Surely, everyone would use the toilet before boarding. It was cramped quarters and would be a very bumpy ride being at the bow of the boat, but he could hold out there for a couple of hours until his takeover. That was all he needed once the Captain, General, and Major started coming aboard. Until then, he would stay comfortable in the midsection and assemble his weapon.

• • •

The President's assistant continued to press replay on the phone every minute trying to reach the Commander. The President's rage continued. Not only could he not reach the Commander, for some crazy reason no one could reach the men who had followed the Martzes, Sophia or had broken into the apartment. His contacts at the Russian Embassy in Paris were having no better luck. All working hard to reach the agents, they now feared they would find themselves looking at whales off the coast of Siberia! They would not be wrong . . . including the Ambassador.

• • •

The time was just after 11:00 pm when the Commander heard the Captain coming aboard the boat. Quickly, he looked around to make sure he had everything and the space looked unused. Feeling secure about that, he slipped quietly into the head, closed and locked the door. Although the red "locked" sign would be displayed, it would not be noticeable until someone actually tried to use the door. Those could only be the Captain, the General, and Sophia. He would chance that this would not happen at least until they were well out to sea, and he had them overpowered.

A little later, he heard the General and Sophia come aboard. There were murmurs but he was unable to make out what was said other than an occasional comment like "undo the mooring lines".

Now the engine started up. A bit noisier than he had hoped. No chance of hearing anything more. He sat down on the head and looked at his watch . . . 11:45 pm. The boat began to move. By his rough calculations, he would wait an hour and half for his move. They would be a good ten to fifteen miles from both shores. A good place for a surprise.

The noise for him inside the head became louder as the engine produced more power upon exiting the harbor entrance. The sea also seemed rougher than what the Commander had thought they would be facing on what had appeared to be a calm night. Perhaps he would have to adjust his timing of the take over a little.

Unbeknownst to the Commander, because of the slowness of the turn, the fishing boat was turning to starboard and not to port. It was moving toward the open waters of the English Channel between Portsmouth, England, and Le Havre, France. Portsmouth being the largest of the British Naval Installations and the place where part of the plan would take place.

The Commander, also because of the noise, could not tell that two Scimitar Class Fast Patrol Boats of the British Navy were now beside the fishing boat, one on each side. The boats, each with a crew of five and able to travel at 32 knots or nearly 40 miles per hour, were part of the British Rapid Response Squad. On board each boat were two navy frogmen trained as experts in rigging explosive charges to the undersides of ships, even in rough waters. Just over the horizon, a River Class patrol vessel was moving on a parallel vector. Measuring 90 meters in length, over 300 feet, and carrying a crew of 45 plus over two dozen Royal Marines, they would be a force no one would willingly want to encounter. Beneath the surface an Astute Class stealth submarine, launched out of Portsmouth, was waiting at the proper location.

From the French port of Cherbourg 2 VFMs (Vedettes de Fusiliers Marins) were launched. These boats, the newest in the French Navy, can reach speeds of over 40 knots, or 46 miles per hour. They were going to their station midway in the channel just on the French side of the invisible boundary line. They were back up for the British fast boats. Rigged out with two 12.7 mm machine guns and one 7.62 mm machine gun, they each carried a crew of ten. The each also had six fully equipped fusiliers.

"You might want to stand or sit at the stern of the boat now," the Captain said to the two MI6 officers, Sophia, and the General. "We are giving the lad in the head a bit of a go!" With that, the Captain began hitting full on every wave he could find either straight on or occasionally with a roll from port to starboard. The effect in the head was like riding a bucking bronco. Wave after wave, roll after roll for nearly an hour in the claustrophobic confines of the 6' 3" foot head. Any food the Commander had once had in his stomach was now deposited in the head. His head hurt, his insides hurt, his arms and legs hurt, his ears hurt. He was a total disoriented mess and looked it too.

Suddenly the noise stopped. Because of the ringing in his ears, it took a few moments for him to realize it had happened. The bouncing of the boat had stopped too. Now it was just small smooth rolling actions. They couldn't be in Calais already? Looking at his watch it had only been an hour! Still fifteen minutes from his takeover of the boat.

"Hello there. Are you still alive? You may come out in a moment but first it is my pleasure to inform you that on board with you right now are several members of the elite British Navy commandos. Sitting beside us are two fast boats with five crewmembers each and four more navy commandos. There also is a navy large patrol boat with two dozen more British Royal Marines. So this is what you will do. You will dismantle the carbon fiber weapon you brought aboard with you. You will drop each part, piece by piece, into the head to join the other filth you deposited there. You will then place your hands behind your head, unlock the door, and step out. Lastly, you have one minute to do this in or all of the on board members of the elite force will be required to fire their weapons through this door. Do I make myself perfectly clear? Or would you like me to repeat what I have said in Russian to you? You now have forty-five seconds to say yes and begin the process."

As these orders were being made, Sophia and the General made their way to the side of the boat where a waiting inflatable took them over to one of the two fast boats. There they made their way down below deck and out of sight.

"Thirty seconds!" The sounds of the military arms readying.

"Fifteen seconds!" Now the sounds of pieces of weapon falling into the basin of the head.

"Ah, that is good. We see that you have finished now."

"What?! There was a camera watching me the whole time?" The Commander looked around but still could not find it.

"You're close, but we don't have time for you to find the camera. We have a rendezvous to make. Unlock the door and put your hands behind the back of your head, fingers laced."

He did.

"Now, step out." As he did, all the onboard lights went out. He was in the dark as he felt rough hands grab him, pinned his arms behind his back and his wrist tied together with plastic ties. As the lights came back on, each of the men surrounding him had removed their night vision goggles and two of them were now securing his legs together with similar nylon straps around his ankles. Multiple automatic weapons aimed at him.

The head officer of MI6 now spoke, "Commander, you have two choices now. This boat will no longer be floating in less than ten minutes. You may accept our offer for you to defect. Or it will be our privilege to help you go down with this British Navy ship, which you have so kindly pirated. Which will it be?"

Totally disoriented, the Commander stammered, "What are you talking about? This is a fishing boat. At best, I was trying to apprehend two criminals . . . two defecting members of the Russian military. You cannot be serious. This is against international laws and treaties."

"Well Commander, you are wrong on several counts. First, this is a Royal British Navy vessel. It is used to monitor illegal fishing off the coast of Britain, mainly by illegal Russian poaching in our seawaters. It is only right that when you commandeered this vessel by force, we had to do what is necessary to stop your illegal act. That is piracy, sir! And that would be true if it were a civilian craft. Since you have tried to do so with a British military vessel, that is a possible act of war. If you were acting officially on behalf of the Russian Government. Were you?"

Mind still numb and disoriented from the rough treatment in the head with all of the bucking and bouncing, he fumbled for the right answer. To say that he was acting on behalf of his country would play into the idea of this being a government-sanctioned operation. At best, he would be causing a political bombshell. The most likely result . . . his ending up on an island off the coast of Siberia. If he said he was acting as an individual with no sanction, he could be shot as a spy or hanged or in prison for life. If he refused the offer of defection, he also could find himself Captain of a sinking boat headed to the depths of the Channel. Defection! How?

"Commander, we are now down to five minutes. We can wait no longer!" And at that moment, a whale of some sort rose out of the waters. No, the Commander now saw. It was a submarine! An Astute Class. The newest in the British fleet. "Your answer, sir! Defection or go down with this boat. In four minutes, it will be blasted apart. It will no longer be here. Will you no longer be here too?!"

"What about my wife and son?"

"We will see that they will eventually join you. You will be kept in a secure location for several months. After that, you will have a new name and identification. You and your family will be watched carefully, however. Time is up! Your answer?"

"Ok, yes. I will defect!" He would have to figure out what all this meant later. No time now.

With that, four large members of the assault team grabbed him by the arms and legs and carried him up the steps to the deck. There he was hoisted into an inflatable, and it bounced across the channel to the waiting British submarine. Once on the submarine deck, he was blindfolded and maneuvered down the ladder and ushered into a private room. There were two additional MI6 officers waiting for him. His interrogation would begin now.

On the ocean surface all members of the assault team and others were now safely on the fast boats that were racing away from the impending explosion. Prior to their exit, a hasty SOS message was sent. The panic in the voice of the Captain helped emphasize the horror that was to follow.

The message told of three passengers on the boat, two men and a woman. They had an argument. They spoke a language that the Captain could not understand. A guttural kind of sound. The one shot the other two but in doing so hit the fuel tanks with his shots. The boat was now on fire and the tank was too. The inflatable life raft was at the rear of the boat near the tank. Just then, the sound of gunfire could be heard, and the SOS signal ended. Moments later, according to other ships in the area a bright flash of light could be seen on the horizon. A few moments later, perhaps as much as thirty seconds later, a loud explosion was heard.

Ships in the channel from all locations turned toward the flash and sound. Based on what they had heard and seen, they doubted anyone would be found. They were correct. One boat, the one that was closest to where the incident had taken place, told of seeing what the ship's watch thought was a Humpback Whale in the area. He saw it shoot from the ocean. It appeared to be sitting on the surface for a short time and then quickly submerged. He had been drinking and was reprimanded by the ship's Captain for drinking on watch, especially in such a busy shipping lane. He was later fired, though he swore by his whale story.

There was an oil slick, and pieces of the shattered boat found. Even a life preserver with the ship's name was in the pieces. No humans alive or dead were there. Most likely blown apart with the explosion and fire. Food for the fishes, no doubt.

The British fast boats sped toward Portsmouth Naval Base. James and the Head of MI6 met Sophia and General Dimitri Gorchakov at the docks. Everyone was introduced to each other. Once that was finished, they entered a large BMW black SUV and headed back toward London. It would stop midway. There, Sophia and Dimitri would stay for a while.

"Dimitri and Major Malenkov, you realize that you will have to be our special guests in an isolated location for several weeks, perhaps a few months. Is that okay with the both of you?"

Looking at Sophia, he nodded his head slightly. She said, "Da. This is okay with me and you too, yes, krestnyy otets?"

General Dimitri Gorchakov nodded his head and said, "Yes, Commander Bond, this is fine with me too." They all started laughing except for Sophia who had a puzzled look on her face.

"I will fill you in later, Krestnitsa (Goddaughter). It is a joke between James and myself." Now she chuckled too as she caught on to the joke.

"No need, otets. I think I understand." The car continued its way toward London and their lives beyond.

61

Thursday, September 5, 2019
Paris, France

THE SWITCH

The Russian agent, after hiding the painting of LADA's in his closet, jumped on his Vespa and rode to the Place d' Aligre. A famous outdoor market of all things brocante. There, he hastily picked out a cheap print on canvas, about the same size as the LADA painting. Back on his Vespa, he rode back streets up to the 18th arrondissement and the headquarters for the two agents.

Once inside the building, he ran to the building's open courtyard. Taking the canvas print, he smashed it on the ground and stomped on the stretchers until they were broken and the canvas was ripped apart. He raced back inside to find something to burn it in. In their room, beside the small table that was close to the window that had allowed them to observe the apartment at 10 Garreau, he found it. The perfect container to burn the painting. A round metal trash can. It was already filled with cigarette butts. Why not add painting ashes to the mix?

Running back outside, he realized he needed one more thing. Lighter fluid or some burnable liquid. Nothing came to mind. Suddenly, he remembered. His comrade's bottle of Stolichnaya 100 proof Vodka! Going back inside to the apartment, he grabbed the bottle and headed back out. Pouring the entire contents into the metal trash container and soaking the print and stretcher he stood back, lit a cigarette, and threw the match into the container. It went out before hitting the liquid. He struck another match. Same thing. Finally, with the third match he lit he stood over the container and placed it into the container.

Whoosh!! Flames exploded from the container, shooting skyward. The bright yellowish white fire singed his eyebrows and hair. Patting his head, he put his burning hair out though burning his hands in the process. The can's fire was roaring now. It didn't take long for the image on the canvas to turn tan, then brown, and finally black.

He heard a Vespa pull up outside the building. Deciding to check to see who had arrived, he went into the building to the small vestibule and arrived at the front door as his comrade came in.

Looking at the man, the agent who had just arrived said, "What the hell happened to you?"

"What do you mean?"

"You look like you have been laying on the beach in Corsica. Your face is all red and . . ." Looking at him, "Your face looks funny. You have no eyebrows!"

Without another word, the man ran back into the apartment building and raced up the steps to the fourth-floor apartment. His partner was close behind. He tried to unlock the door but fumbled with his keys. Managing to finally unlock the door, he ran to the bathroom. Flipping on the light switch, he looked in the mirror. Sure enough, no eyebrows. Blackened hair too. Worse, the red skin on his face now had small areas that appeared to be blistering.

"Damn! It blew up in my face!"

"What did?!"

"The container in the courtyard where the painting is being burned!"

"We had better get you to the doctor to have them look at your face cause more blisters are appearing and some of the skin now has started to brown too!"

Calling a taxi, they went down to the front door to wait for the taxi to arrive. From his face, he started to feel pain from the flash of fire. In the courtyard, the container continued to burn. All the while, one of the French agents was observing the happenings from the location in the building next door. His partner, the other French agent, was at that moment breaking into the burned Russian agent's apartment. He had no trouble finding the stolen LADA painting. He stole it back. It would be sent to the recipient for the intended original purpose.

As the French agent left the apartment, he placed a note on the kitchen table. It had been typed on an old Jorsion typewriter. A common French typewriter of its time. The note simply read:

Your President thanks you for saving his painting.

:-)

62

Thursday, September 5, 2019
Washington, DC, USA

THE INVITATION

"Mr. M., the Ambassador from France, is on the phone. Can you take the call?"

The Special Prosecutor thought for a moment, wondering what this could be about. "Sure," he replied. His assistant let the Ambassador know she was putting him through to the Special Prosecutor.

"Mr. M, thank you. I know you are a very busy man. I am wondering if you and your wife could join me and my wife for dinner this evening here at the Embassy? I think you have met the artist LADA and her friend, Evalina's father, the preeminent astrophysicist Alexei. I believe you may have met him recently. They, along with their four French friends, will be joining us. I think you will find this to be a very informative and entertaining evening. I know this is short notice. Let me assure you that could not be helped. Recent developments today have made this possible."

The Special Prosecutor, being a very thoughtful and intelligent person, didn't hesitate. This had to be about the destroyed painting and the information it contained.

"Why yes, Mr. Ambassador, my wife and I would love to join you. It has been some time since we have enjoyed being at your Embassy. What time would you like for us to be there?"

"Would 7:00 pm be acceptable to you Mr. M?"

"I think that would be perfect. I will call my wife now and let her know of your kind invitation. We will be at the embassy at 7:00. Thank you."

• • •

The Special Prosecutor and his wife arrived promptly at 7:00 pm.

Inside the Embassy, already assembled were LADA, Evalina, Alexei, Nina, Etienne, Ninette, and Guy. They were waiting in a formal living room right outside the formal but intimate private dining room of the French Ambassador and his wife. They had been asked to be at the Embassy early to receive a formal briefing from London by Commander James and his French counterpart regarding an action taking place within the hour on the high seas mid-English Channel. They only learned that there was a possible defection of two high placed Russian figures and the arrest of a Russian agent. The same agent whose men had nearly killed Ninette and Nina during Pari Roller. They would receive an update later before they left the Embassy, the two men on the other side of the Atlantic had assured.

They knew the other guest that evening was the Special Prosecutor and his wife. None of them had any way of knowing how the episode taking place on the Channel had any connection to the information that was on the painting supposedly accidentally destroyed by Alexei. They just thought one was unlinked from the other and just a nice coincidence that an arrest was being made on the same night they were meeting with the prosecutor.

The French Ambassador had exited the room upon hearing that Mr. and Mrs. M had arrived. He greeted them warmly. There was small talk about the last time the Ms had been in the Embassy. It was 2008 when the French President had become the new head of the European Union. Could it be that it had been eleven years, they speculated? Yes, he was head of the FBI at that time. Reappointed to that position by President Barack Obama even though he was a Republican and first appointed by George W. Bush in 2001. Their hasty recollection closed with either the Ambassador of Mr. M saying something to the effect of, "My, times have changed!" All three agreed.

Upon entering the living room, the Ambassador introduced all the French citizens gathered. Of course, Mr. M had met Alexei and had briefly met the others except Evalina when the others first arrived with the paintings. It was helpful to be reintroduced to Mr. M and, of course, for the first time to his wife. The French members of the gathering would talk later among themselves about what a nice, warm couple the Ms were. Honesty and humbleness standing out as key traits they all observed.

After a short while, the head embassy waiter announced that dinner was ready to be served. They entered the dining room, tastefully decorated in French Provencal style. None of them knew that both the Ambassador and wife were from that area of France. The style was homey and bright.

Dinner was finished at 10:00 pm Washington time, and 3:00 am in England the next day.

The French Ambassador asked if the members of the dinner group, all but his wife and Mrs. M, could be excused, as there was an important discussion that must be held in a secure room by the others. Being used to these types of meetings neither the Ambassador's wife nor Mrs. M had a problem with this. They were assured the meeting would only last about an hour. The Ambassador's wife said not to rush, as she would give Mrs. M a private tour of their Ambassadorial private suite. This must be important business. Nina, Etienne, Guy, Ninette and others wondered why Mr. M would be included in an update on the arrest of the person responsible for the attempt on Nina and Ninette's life. But it couldn't hurt to have a prosecutor and former FBI Director included. So be it.

They entered the main operations area of the embassy and proceeded to the secure room, which had been used by all of them except Mr. M earlier in the week.

Two security officers of the French Embassy pulled back a curtain revealing a large four foot by six foot computer/TV flat screen monitor. They flipped a switch and exited the room.

Instantly, split screen images appeared on the screen. The largest image was of two men in their late 60s and a woman. Both men were obviously in good shape and handsome. The one standing close to a strikingly attractive young woman was perhaps more ruggedly handsome, a cross between actors Gary Cooper and Gerard Butler. Both he and the young woman looked very tired and were dressed in heavy sweaters and denim slacks. The gentleman with them was in a sports coat, open shirt, and nice lightweight sharply pressed wool slacks. The second image was of the French Director-General d' Armee. He was in military attire. What time was it there? 3:00 am in England and 4:00 am in Paris.

The gentleman in sports coat introduced himself and the other three on the screen. They were himself, Commander James B of the Royal Army Intelligence corp. With him was Russian Colonial General Dimitri Gorchakov; the four young people in Washington wondered if this was the person responsible for the attempt on Nina and Ninette. Next to him is Major Sophia Malenkov; perhaps she is the one. "I think most of you know Director-General d'Armee in the other half of the split screen."

Then he proceeded to allow the Director-General d'Armee to introduce the people in the French Embassy in Washington. Finally, all introductions completed, the Englishman spoke again.

"I am pleased to let you know of two important happenings tonight. First, both General Gorchakov and Major Malenkov have defected jointly to France and to Great Britain." Sounds of surprise rose from those in Washington, DC. All except Etienne, he had heard a little about a defection earlier that day.

"General Gorchakov will speak with you in just a moment. However, there is more. A little over two and a half hours ago, precisely located in the middle of the English Channel, the French and British Navies apprehended an agent of Russia who was trying to commandeer a British Navy vessel and kidnap these two people. The man who was stopped was given a choice that he had to make quickly. He too has decided to defect to the British. He has been arrested. He will be interrogated and held in isolation for several months. “

“I am also pleased to inform the two young ladies that though he had not ordered the attempt on your lives, the men who did make the attempt reported to this person. Therefore, he is directly implicated in the attempt by both British and French law. Appropriate trial and hopefully sentence will one day be doled out for the attempt on your lives.”

“The people on the boat all were blown up by an explosion set off by the Russian pirate. Unfortunately, there were no survivors. An associate of the Russian pirate was arrested in London earlier in the day. He will stay incarcerated at an unknown location until we are satisfied he has provided us with all the information we would like to receive. Then, we may give him an option of returning to Russia or defecting. We suspect, because of the failure of the operation, he will find it in his interest to defect. That’s also true for another accomplice who was apprehended just a little while ago on the coast of France near the town of Calais.”

“General Gorchakov, would you like to say a few things?”

“Yes, thank you, Commander Bond!” Smiling and with a nod, “First I wish to thank my two counterparts with the British and French Military Intelligence agencies for assisting myself and Major Malenkov in our defections. I have known that this would take place for some time and was well prepared. My colleague and God daughter Major Malenkov became aware of this only a few days ago. There is much too much to that story to share tonight. Let me just say, it has been a very trying, confusing, and difficult time for her. She is a very proud and loyal military officer. She is only doing this because of a hideous attempt on her well-being by the Russian President. He, as I am sure you all know, is a very corrupt and vulgar individual.”

“Let me also reveal to all of you and to her some of my past that only James and my French counterpart are aware of. For some time, I have been providing information to the British and French Governments regarding illegal and dangerous activities by the Russian President. " As he was saying this, a surprised look came across Sophia's face. "These activities and information have gone back for most of the years that this individual has been in office. I assure all of you that Major Sophia Malenkov had no idea of my actions or of the illegal actions of the President. That is, until recent times."

"Madame LADA, although you did not know who was providing you with the information that you have been encoding on your paintings, I am pleased to inform you now that I was your partner." A shocked but pleasant look came across LADA's face.

"I was passing the information to you through a distant cousin of Major Malenkov by the name of Yuri. Do you know of him?"

At that moment, Nina exclaimed uncontrollably but softly, "Yuri is my grandfather's cousin!" Suddenly the eyes of Nina and Sophia locked on each other... distant cousins! All the other eyes were on the screen and on Nina.

Then Evalina joined in, "And Yuri is my father's cousin. That means that the three of us, the Major, Nina, and myself are related by blood? Can this be true?"

The General replied, "It would appear so, though until this moment I doubt that any of us knew this! James, Director-General?" They all shook their heads "no".

Nina and Sophia both continued to look at each other trying to see if there was a family resemblance somewhere. Both were tall and very attractive women. Sophia was a few years older, but both were very athletic. Facially, although both were Russian, neither had the heavy eyebrow ridges that often were found on Russian women. Could be. For sure, there could be something there.

While everyone in all three locations were now amazed by the recent revelation, the General continued.

"Since we are in a very sensitive meeting, I am going to ask particularly for James, the Director-General, Mr. M, and the two young men with us to swear to secrecy what I am now going to say. Do I have your pledges?" The people mentioned looked from one to another and gave a "oh, what the hell" kind of nod.

"Good. Madam LADA, Professor K, Madam Evalina, I assume that you three already know of and are a part of the Order of Catherine. Am I correct?"

They nodded that he was correct. The others in the rooms in Washington, England, and France had a confused look on their faces, including Nina, Ninette, and Sophia.

"I can tell the rest of you have no idea of what I am referring to. Let me fill you in briefly."

"The greatest leader of the Russian people was a woman who lived from 1729 until 1796. She was the Emperor of Russia from 1762 until her death in 1796. You may all know of her as Catherine the Great of Russia. Evalina, I presume you may be named after her granddaughter. She was the daughter of Paul I who ruled for five years following the death of Catherine." Alexei's head was nodding "yes".

"It was during the rule of Paul I that the Order of Catherine was created. You see, she had been guiding Russia to a position of cultural greatness on par with the other great countries of the time, particularly France." The general nodded on screen to the position of the image of the Director-General. "The other descendants of Catherine realized her legacy was being corrupted and lost by Paul and the other Russian leaders of the time. Over the years, there was even a strong effort to paint the memory of Catherine not as an incredibly smart and good leader but as . . . well, a tramp and nymphomaniac with the most base of sexual appetite. She, however, did in fact have a very shrewd understanding of men and their attempt at control and misogyny. The characteristics of the current President of Russia, unfortunately. And, Mr. M, quite unfortunately of your own current President. Catherine knew how to combat these activities and use these men against each other until her death."

"What was lost when she died was the movement of Russia to one of honoring the people . . . the average person . . . giving them status and respect and many freedoms. Now, understand, she was not fully moving to a modern democratic state. Her movement was more to what was developing in England." Now he turned to his friend James and nodded.

"The ancestors of Catherine, and those close to Catherine in her court, formed a secret order, the one named the Order of Catherine. Its sole purpose is to preserve the effort of Catherine's to move Russia to a free society where every living Russian is honored and treated with respect and to provide for the culture and education of its citizens."

"I was introduced to the Order by Sophia's parents. Sophia's mother was, as each of you women, except for Madam LADA and the other young woman with you, is related to Yuri. You are the direct descendants of Catherine the Great of Russia." Nina and Sophia both showed on their faces that they were overwhelmed now by this revelation. Nina was openly crying. Sophia fought back tears.

"There is much more to talk about with Nina and Sophia about this. That can be done at another time. For now, let me change the subject just a little."

"Mr. M, I am sure you are wondering why you are involved with this. Well, for no better description, it's a family reunion. Let me now inform you of the why. You see, we are aware of the accidental destruction of a LADA painting that was delivered to the CIA. Doctor K, I believe it was you who was involved in that unfortunate accident. Correct?"

"Yes. Unfortunately, though, I tried to follow the directions carefully. Something went wrong."

The General now spoke directly on screen to Mr. M. "And you, Special Prosecutor M, were told that this canvas contained incriminating evidence against both the current Russian President and that of the US President. Information of collusion on many fronts as well as tampering with the US election process, the spread of misinformation leading to racial and political divide of the US people. This tampering and illegal activity included money laundering and breaking election prohibition of foreign payments to the US Republican presidential nominee's campaign and election. All lost! Is that correct?"

"Yes. This information could have been a vital part of the eventual prosecution of the laws that have been broken. For now, it would have been proof positive of the activities of the Russian President to influence and control our election process. It could have been extremely helpful to change election processes and to ensure enhanced security measures on our elections. Unfortunately, it is gone."

"Interesting!" the General replied.

A coy smile appeared on the old artist's face, which did not go unnoticed by the General.

He continued, "Let me put you at easy Mr. M. I have in my possession, actually in an undisclosed location at present but close by, flash drives that not only contain a small part of the original material but also additional video of the Russian President and the US President in . . . let's just say . . . extremely compromising situations. Copies of these tapes and the documents will be made available to you within the next few days."

The General now turned back to LADA, Alexei, Evalina, and Nina and spoke directly to the four of them. "Madam LADA, Madam Evalina, Doctor K, and Mademoiselle Nina, I find it very hard to believe that all the video and documents that were transferred to Yuri could have been coded in your traditional method Madam LADA on that canvas. Am I correct?"

No one responded but everyone in all the locations knew that the General was not going to reveal the fact that there must be a new way to transfer information via her art. However, there was.

"I'm sure Mr. M that if the information you were hoping to receive was not truly on the canvas that was destroyed, somehow, someday, that information will be additionally provided. Thank you all for your time in listening to me this evening. Both Sophia and I are grateful that both France and Great Britain have been so kind in assisting us with our defections. We hope one day, Mr. M, we can say the same for the US." The Special Prosecutor nodded his head in agreement with the sentiment.

"Director-General, do you wish to say a few words?" Commander James asked.

"I know it is becoming very late for all of us. Just a couple of quick additions to the comments already made by informing all of you of additional actions taken tonight in Paris."

"First, this afternoon while the General and Major were on their way to Dover, we trailed two other Russian agents. One was following the American couple, the Martzes, who are staying in your apartment Mademoiselle Nina. While he was trailing the Martzes, his partner was taking a LADA painting that was stolen from the apartment. We understand that it was a 'special gift' from LADA to go to the Russian President. Correct, Madam LADA?"

"Yes."

"The agent with the painting was told by the Russian pirate to destroy that painting. He understood it had copies of the information destined to the Special Prosecutor on it. We understand from you Madam LADA, the message on this painting was quite different. A rather vulgar message of 'fornication of himself' to the President in Russia. Is that correct?"

"Yes."

"Madam LADA, let me inform you and the others, your wonderful painting is safe. Our French agents stole it back after the Russian agent left his apartment. We understand he had intended to keep it for himself. Your painting and its private message will be safely delivered to the location at the office of the President of Russia in the Kremlin this morning around 9:00 am Moscow time. It is on a special DHL delivery truck."

"Lastly, the French President asked me to personally thank you this evening for the stunning LADA painting that was delivered to him at the Elysee Palace today. He understands it is an accurate duplicate of one hanging in the show there at the Kennedy Center in Washington, DC. He has found the appropriate location for it to hang.

"Since it is approaching 5:00 am here in Paris, 4:00 am in England, and 11:00 pm in Washington, I think that is all I have. I'm sure over the next few days, there will be more for us to discuss. I would wish you 'bonne nuit' but since it is now morning I will say 'au revoir!'" His image left the screen. The others said "goodbye" and the meeting was over, right on time.

63

Friday, September 6, 2019
England

SAFE HOUSE

Commander James left Dimitri and Sophia at their secure location. Although there were several military intelligence guards and MI6 agents on the property, they were alone in the manor house outside of the small town of Ashington, England, midway from Portsmouth to London and north of the Brighton coast. The property was a well-guarded two-acre estate with several outbuildings reconditioned to house the military guards and agents.

Believed to have been constructed in the early 1600s, the five-bedroom, grade II home with formal gardens typical of a country estate had easy access to London via the A24.

The interior was what would be found in a house of this age. Flagstone floors with exposed oak beam ceiling. A large inglenook fireplace and heavy latched oak doors. Although there were five bedrooms, Sophia and Dimitri took the two closest to each other. Each had a nice king size bed in it. In between their two rooms, a third small room had a single bed. This one would go unused, giving each person a bit of privacy.

After arriving at the home and settling in, it was now approaching full morning. Both too exhausted to sleep opted to take freshly made coffee into the family room off the kitchen. It was here that Dimitri filled Sophia in about the Order of Catherine, how he had learned of it from Sophia's mother and father, how the experiences of the Russian army in Afghanistan and the death of Sophia's father there had led Dimitri to be involved with the Order.

By noon, the story had been told and the questions were answered as best they could. It was all so unreal and complex for her to put her mind's arms around. It would take days for her to come to grips completely with what had transpired over the last week. For some reason, however, she was at peace with understanding that she was not truly a traitor to her country. She was someone, who by circumstances, had been thrown into a new role in assisting the Russia she loves to become the Russia that Catherine the Great, her ancestor, had envisioned. Helping to fulfill this vision could be her new mission. She was filled with excitement. Perhaps the same excitement that had inspired her parents and Dimitri, and her distant cousins Evalina and Nina, and of course this man Yuri.

64

Thursday, September 5, 2019
Washington, DC, USA

MUTUAL UNDERSTANDING

The Special Prosecutor left the Embassy with a desire to tell his wife what had happened in the meeting while she toured the private residence. He couldn't and she knew he could not and didn't push for information. He was grateful for the understanding she had over the years of the secrecy he had to maintain during his time as Director of the FBI and now in the role of Special Prosecutor. She was one very special lady. He was one very lucky man. It appeared from tonight that luck for him with the investigation had changed for the positive, as well as that for the nation.

As he drove back to their home in Arlington, he was lost in thought. She left him alone with them as she could see he was deeply in the thought world. She almost asked if he would like her to drive. Instead, she was comfortable watching him in the darkness of the night with the occasional lights of cars approaching, shining off his face. A good face. One of dignity and honor. One that would do, had done, and continued to do what was necessary to protect the country they both loved. They had sacrificed a lot in their personal lives so that he could do what was necessary. At this moment, she felt truly honored to be this man's partner, his wife. She would wait until later in the morning to give him this note she had received earlier in the evening for him from the artist LADA. Now there was a woman of true dignity!

65

Friday, September 6, 2019
Washington, DC, USA

ROYALS

It was after midnight when the chauffeured limos delivered the seven back to the Hotel Zena. Somehow, tonight's revelation made the place they were staying seem more coincidentally appropriate. A hotel that celebrated women of power and importance . . . all women . . . but for this night especially the descendants of the most important woman of Russian history, Catherine the Great.

The lounge was still serving, though the time was now approaching 1:00 am. LADA excused herself and headed to her room. She would have enjoyed staying with the young people, including Evalina and even Alexei, but being over 90 it was well past her bedtime. She needed her beauty sleep after all!

The friends were all rubbing it in now, teasing Nina about her royal bloodline. They spilled the teasing over to Evalina too. None of the young people had realized this before the General revealed the Yuri connection to Sophia. Then, the other connections were revealed too.

Etienne, Guy, and Alexei brought six glasses of wine and a bottle of Château Recougne Bordeaux Supérieur 2018 to the table. Once they sat down, Etienne raised a glass in toast.

"To our royal ladies and lady of the court."

"Etienne, stop that. Besides, Ninette is royal too. She is a distant cousin of Evalina's and mine."

The three men looked from one to another. Had they missed something earlier tonight? Then the women all started laughing.

"And to the fearless knights who protect weak and helpless ladies!"

Now things really started to break up in laughter and all pretense of seriousness was gone. It was just joy, friendship, and fun. In one hour, activities of a new day in Europe and Russia would begin.

66

Friday, September 6, 2019
Moscow, Russia
9:00 AM

The DHL delivery truck pulled up in front of the Kremlin. Guards with long poles and mirrors surveyed the bottom of the truck while others with Geiger counters entered the truck and scanned each package. That was easy. There was only one package. It measured roughly 64 centimeters tall, 89 centimeters wide, and 20 centimeters thick. A wooden crate. The address: My Dear Russian President, President's Office, Kremlin, Moscow. The return address was LADA c/o iSPY Gallery, 1 Quai Voltaire, 75007, Paris, France

The package was scanned with metal detecting wands and removed from the van then put on a special cart. The cart was rolled delicately to an x-ray scanner and viewed. It obviously had a painting inside. Areas of the painting were blocked by viewing by the traditional lead-based paints the artist had used. Still, it was a painting. There was nothing suspicious they could detect. It was wheeled up the ramp into the building and taken to the elevator. Arriving at the President's office after passing through additional extensive screenings, the President was notified of its arrival. It was now 9:15 am Moscow time.

• • •

Paris, France
8:15 AM

Tom rolled out of bed closest to the large lead glass windows facing the park. Mary was still sleeping. He walked softly out of the room to the kitchen and started the pot of water on the stove to make a French press of coffee. The leftover baguette from the restaurant dinner the night before would serve as breakfast. This was the fourth day of their trip. Nothing planned but he knew it was bound to be enjoyable and exciting, though perhaps not as exciting as the two previous days.

• • •

Moscow, Russia
9:35 AM

The Russian President's administrative assistant carried the package in. The President was excited to see what it was that LADA painted for him. The assistant with a small pry bar carefully opened the side of the crate and lifted the painting wrapped in several layers of bubble wrap out. Using a pocketknife, he now proceeded to cut the tape holding the bubble wrap securely and layer by layer removed it until the bottom of the painting was viewed.

On the back in oil paint, LADA had inscribed on the canvas:

A special painting from me to tell you how I feel. You will notice your image on the balcony. The light is on you. It reveals all.

LADA

"Interesting. What an interesting old lady. Very much my mother!" He looked around the office for the appropriate place for it to hang.

Behind his desk on the wall was the perfect space. It would hang behind him and as she put it, "Let the light shine on him"! Perfect!

He had his assistant remove the Marc Chagall oil painting of "Equestrienne". The painting depicted the image of a young, bare-breasted woman on the back of a white horse with a man's arms firmly around the woman. He liked this image, as it was a good portrait of the things of his desire. Women, a good mount, and power! Painted by a Jewish artist, though. It had been confined to storage until he found it. He enjoyed the image, imagining it was him . . . fanciful. It could go back in storage or perhaps move to his outer office area. Yes, the outer office. It would remind people of his "openness" to the Jews and to women, low as they were. Yes, that is the place.

• • •

Paris, France
8:35 AM

French President E. M. held the LADA painting in his hand. It was a beautiful painting. The note painted on the back of the canvas was interesting:

This is a special painting I have made for you and the people of my country, France. Like the Statue of Liberty, there are two. One in France and one in the United States of America. Within them, they both carry the light of the future. A light that will preserve freedom.

With my love and affection, LADA

"Interesting! Very interesting! Madam Delaunay, please have the custodian hang this painting in my private conference room. I want to share it with people. Merci."

• • •

Ashington, England
12:25 PM

Sophia and Dimitri decided to take their coffee mugs and stroll the grounds. This would be their home for a few days. They might as well learn the grounds. The air was crisp early fall. Fog which had been in the lowlands near the streams and ponds had long gone. Looking out the window earlier, it had given the country lands a soft and welcoming presence. Above the fog, the day showed to be a clear and bright English day. No sign of the frequent drizzle of fall. This day was going to be glorious in more ways than one, Sophia realized.

67

Friday, September 6, 2019
Washington, DC, USA

WHITE LIGHT

Mr. M, all showered and dressed for the day, went down to the kitchen. His wife was already there making scrambled eggs, bacon, and a grapefruit half, sectioned so it would be easy to eat. He smiled at her. She and he were a good team. Caring for each other was what they did well. It just came naturally. Today she fixed their breakfast, tomorrow he would. That is what they do, share.

He noticed beside his plate a small envelope. It simply had written on it:

Mr. M.

Special Prosecutor.

He asked his wife where it came from. She replied the artist LADA had slipped it to her as they all sat down for dinner. The two women were seated next to each other. "She asked me to give it to you this morning. That was all she said about it. I put it in my clutch purse. What is it?"

Mr. M opened the envelope. Inside was a small elegantly engraved LADA note card. A handwritten note in a beautiful script. He read it aloud.

Mr. M,

I am giving you one of my paintings in my current show at the Kennedy Center to keep safe for your country. It is my personal gift to the country that helped both of my countries, France and Russia, during times of great need. It has deep meaning in what it contains. The white light is important to the future of all free loving people. The Statue of Liberty stands for freedom for all. It was a gift from my adopted country to yours.

There is a duplicate of this painting and that light I am giving to your country. That duplicate painting, like the duplicate statue, is in Paris, France. It is in the hands of the French President, delivered to him today, as you heard last night in the meeting. I am trusting you and the President of France to preserve this light. One day you will both learn it provides you with what you need for the protection of freedom.

Sincerely,
LADA

Mr. M read it aloud again. Both he and his wife looked at each other questioningly. "What do you think she means?"

"I think we should go to the Kennedy Center today and see. It must be a painting of the Statue of Liberty. But what an odd note. It surely must be because of the French and English translation issue. Still the grammar is correct. I don't know."

The next year, an election took place in the United States. It was more than contentious. There was a full attempt to upset freedom and democracy. The Special Prosecutor had been armed with information on flash drives from General Gorchakov. Those flash drives even contained directions for how someone might initiate the attempted takeover of the free elections by storming the capital building should misinformation not prove successful in casting aspersions on a free and honest election. Every effort, it said, should be used to not allow the congress to count the electoral votes certifying the November 2020 presidential election. The documents on the drive went on to talk about the importance that an autocratic government needed to be established in the United States. It would become a full partner with Russia in turning the world away from democracy. It would move the world to one controlled by the elites of the world, especially two men . . . though truly only one who spoke Russian. The other, his fool.

The information was too overwhelming to be revealed before the election. The disinformation process was too far in effect to be stopped. The Special Prosecutor needed more specific information before he could go forward. He hoped there would be a time and a place for the truth to be unveiled. Above all, undisputed information would need to be found. It was. It was residing inside two paintings. Both paintings were of the symbol of liberty and freedom. One painting hangs in a private home in Arlington, Virginia, the other in the Elysee Palace in Paris, France.

• • •

In early 2023, once again a special flight of an Airbus A330-200 sped down the takeoff runway at Charles de Gaulle International Airport. It quickly met up once again with four French fighter jets. The fighters escorted the flight on its mission to the United States. This time, the flight did not use its official designation of Cotam 001. That designation was only reserved for the aircraft when the President of France was on board. The passenger list on this flight included four special guests of the President's: Evalina, Alexei, Col-General Dimitri Gorchakov, and his god daughter Major Sophia Malenkov.

Upon arrival in Washington, DC, they were escorted quickly to the Justice department. There they met up with the Special Prosecutor, the head of the FBI, and the head of the CIA. Other justice department officials and lab technicians joined them in a special room filled with computers and recording devices.

At the same time in the lower rooms of the Elysee Palace in Paris, a similar group was assembled. Joining the President of France were the Director-General d'Armee, the Director-General for External Security, the Director-General of the National Police, Nina, Etienne, Nina's parents, and a man named Yuri. This room too was filled with computers and recording devices and the investigators and technicians that used them.

At precisely 9:00 am in the United States and 3:00 pm in Paris, the small fingernail-sized devices were attached to the end of small threads woven throughout each of the paintings. Using the small devices, the thread was able to connect the computers located at the separate locations. Each canvas was the duplicate paintings LADA had painted of the Statue of Liberty. On both continents simultaneously, the devices began transferring the data that had been stored in the dark matter contained in those small thread-like filaments. The computer screens showed a continuous strong white light as the data downloaded. This white light continued for several hours.

When the two teams of investigators at both locations were finally able to sift through the hours and hours of data over several weeks, it was the verification needed to understand fully how the President of Russia controlled the other President, and so much more. It also showed how the other President had attempted to use the same process to control others within his own administration and his "friends" who were the leaders of other western countries. This data confirmed the reason why he had spirited off "classified and secret" documents to his personal Florida enclave. He could use that information to blackmail friends and foes. It could continue to build his wealth and power just as it had done so for his Russian mentor and handler. He had learned well, or so he had thought.

• • •

A question unasked and therefore unanswered for Sophia was why Dimitri was so caring for her? Her parents and Dimitri and his wife were close friends. He had told her that. Her mother had told her that too, many times. His wife, long dead, had died of complications during the birth of their stillborn son. She had heard stories of her own parents having trouble having a baby.

That changed following the R&R time both Russian officers had together during the Afghanistan war. The two couples had vacationed on the Black Sea coast and miraculously Sophia's mother became pregnant. Sophia was tall like Dimitri. Her mother was tall too. She never knew her father as he was killed in the war shortly after her birth. Pictures of the handsome young officer were of a man no taller than her mom. At best, 5'10". She always wondered, and even more now, could Dimitri actually be her father? Would she ever have courage to ask? Did it really matter? He treated her as his daughter. That love is what really counts.

Etienne and Nina were married at the French President's palace following the successful opening of LADA's show in October of 2019. It was a small civil wedding performed by the President of France himself. Close friends and relatives attended, including Sophia and Dimitri. Guy and Ninette's wedding followed shortly. They did not go back to the Kennedy's booth to become engaged, however. It happened the night of Nina and Etienne's wedding and was announced at the celebration that followed.

After the wedding ceremony and celebration, as Nina and Etienne lay locked naked in each other's arms, exhausted and totally content, Etienne spoke, "Can you believe, my love, all that has happened to us this year? Incredible, no? I mean everything! And today the President of France married us!"

She looked at him with a smile on her face.

"You want to hear something funny?" He went on without letting her reply. "Guy, at one point before we went to the US, said, "You don't think Nina is a Russian spy, do you?" I told him he was crazy! Of course not!"

Nina tilted her head slightly, raised one eyebrow and just kept smiling.

"Wasn't that funny?"

Smiling.

"I said, wasn't that funny of Guy to say that?"

Smiling.

"Nina, you aren't a Russian spy, right?"

Smiling.

"Nina. Right?"

She wrapped her arms and legs around his muscular body, pulling him into her, and said, "Let's just do it all over, and over, and over again!"

Smiling.

FINI

EPILOGUE

June 2019

BEFORE IT ALL HAPPENED

Tom woke up to the cawing of the crows. The alarm had been set for 5:30 am but had not gone off. He knew it had to be earlier. Mary loved to sleep with the windows and shades open even early in the spring and late in the fall. In the spring, she loved to wake up and listen to the birds. Through the summer into the fall, she loved to listen to "the bugs". The bugs hadn't begun to sing their "songs" yet. Too early in the summer for them to begin their courting in New Hampshire. But certainly not too early for the crows to do whatever crows do at 4:30 or 5:00 am in New England.

While lying in bed, he turned his head to Mary's side, the side closest to the windows. Sure enough, she was looking at him, eyes wide open and no sign of sleepiness. "Hi" he said, "listening to your crows?" Although he asked that question of her, he knew the answer. Yes, she had been listening to them but really closely watching him sleep. She loved watching him sleep. To tell the truth, he loved watching her sleep too. One of the many attributes they shared, looking at the other one and loving him or her deeply and unquestionably. He knew sleep had evaded her perhaps most of the night. Nights before "it" always did.

"Yep."

"What are they saying?"

"The usual," she replied. "Hey, this is my area!" "No, it isn't! It's mine!" "I'll tell my dad!" "Yeah, well I'll tell my whole family!"

Tom laughed but looked deeply at her. "You couldn't sleep, could you?"

"Not much," she replied. "You know how it is before these scans." He did. Every six months, a PET scan. Did the cancer grow? Has it spread? Is the current treatment working? What comes next? Options were becoming limited.

In December 2013, Mary had been diagnosed with an incurable form of breast cancer. A mastectomy of the left breast and hormone treatments, estrogen suppressants, had controlled the cancer until December of 2018. Five good years. More than the first doctors at Eastern Maine Medical Center had thought she would have. The first doctor at Dartmouth Hitchcock Medical Center (DHMC) had thought the same. "This is very serious; you may have a couple of years . . . perhaps less."

This doctor was considered a wonderful researcher. Bedside manner? Non-existent. Fortunately, Mary and Tom's son-in-law, Jason, a pathologist, found another doctor, Dr. Mary Chamberlin. Dr. Chamberlin had everything Mary and Tom needed for this part of their adventure together. She had compassion. She had empathy. She had a great bedside manner and the ability to convey difficult medical terms and treatments so a layperson could understand what was happening. But even more important, she too was a great researcher and scientist. She kept up on all the current medical knowledge of this type of cancer. If anyone could provide the treatments necessary to prolong a good quality of life for a patient with this cancer, they both knew in their hearts Dr. Chamberlin could.

Yet, despite this feeling about Dr. Chamberlin, every six months when the PET scan was ordered, Mary went through sleepless nights. This one had been no different. Monitoring of the cancer markers and blood work, white blood cell levels, red blood cell levels, and others had become routine appointments. But not the PET scan. "Cancer can't hide from the PET," Mary thought, "and neither can I!"

The PET was scheduled for 7:00 am. Nothing to eat for twelve hours, from 7:00

pm the night before. No breakfast, no coffee, only a sip of water allowed. Arrive at the hospital for pre-PET prep at 6:30 am. Park in the covered parking lot on the south side of the hospital. All the instructions were the same each time. This time, however, Tom had been thinking about making this PET appointment different, memorable, perhaps even exciting...a surprise. A surprise he did not share with Mary. It wouldn't be the right time until the meeting later that morning with Dr. Chamberlin. Then he would know for sure it was okay. Although he and Mary had discussed the idea ever since the 2015 adventure with Mary's favorite and younger sister Rita and her partner Hank, Mary had seemed much less enthusiastic than Tom.

The drive from #20 Pinewood Village to Dartmouth Hitchcock hospital was relatively easy and quick unless Hanover High school is in session. During times of school drop off and pickup and lunchtime, traffic on Lebanon Street can be problematic. At 6:30 am, the time Mary and Tom left home for arrival at the hospital at 6:45 am, not a problem. There was some traffic, of course, as DHMC and Dartmouth College itself are the two major employers of the region around Hanover and Lebanon, New Hampshire. There is only one major corridor to the hospital. South through Hanover Main Street to Lebanon Street and north out of Lebanon to the hospital on the same corridor, in that case Hanover Road. Both Hanover Road and Lebanon Street are one in the same, State Road 120. That's a funny quirk about New England roads that Tom had learned from his time at UMass in Amherst, Massachusetts. A road leading to a town is named for the town it is taking you to and that same road can be named for the town you came from if you are heading the opposite direction from your first destination. Therefore, Amherst Road leads from Belchertown to Amherst, and Belchertown Road leads from Amherst to Belchertown.

This June 25th morning, traffic was clear and the drive quick. Several hundred feet ahead as they drove, four deer crossed the road. They were headed from one forest area on the left side of the road to the forest area surrounding the hospital. Perhaps this was a good sign. A natural sign to say "put your mind at peace". As usual, Tom and Mary held hands. They did this most of the time as Tom drove.

He did most of the driving. She would tease him, she teased him a lot, about being a "control freak". He really wasn't, at least he didn't think so, he just liked to drive. Mary for the most part liked to look at nature. Again, they were very compatible that way. However, she did feel that she was losing some confidence in driving. They would discuss her taking the wheel for a short time and then finally decide they liked it the way it was.

They turned right at the stoplight, drove past the gas station and mini mart on the right side of the drive, and entered the long winding road to the hospital. The small lake, a rainwater holding pond, on the left side of the road offered another beautiful natural setting. The whole hospital grounds were beautifully laid out to offer a sense of serenity to the patients who sought treatments there. Of the four major universities that Tom and Mary had been associated with, Dartmouth Hitchcock Medical Center had done "serenity" right by their landscaping. However, they had a distinct advantage from the start, as DHMC is located in the natural setting of New Hampshire!

Tom turned left at the junction of the end of the entrance road and took the loop road around the hospital. Driving past the tall smokestacks, the gas storage tanks, and the heliport with the green and white helicopter sitting ready to take off for any emergency case in mid and northern New Hampshire, Tom always wondered to himself why they would put a heliport next to gas storage tanks. Were the tanks propane? Pressurized natural gas? Oxygen? A combination of tanks of all the above? He was sure smarter minds knew the reason. This was just Tom's natural way, thinking of the possibilities. A genetic and nurture trait he acquired from his deceased father, Col. Joseph Ray Martz, who retired after thirty-two years of military service and later became the State of Indiana's Director of Civil Defense and Office of Emergency Planning.

Instead of continuing to the entrance to the covered parking garage as instructed on the instruction sheet, he turned right into the entrance for the emergency drive and main east entrance to the facility. Circling back past the main east entrance was a parking lot reserved for cancer patients. It was outside but since it was a beautiful June day, not a cloud in the sky, and several yards closer to reception 3Z and on the same level, why not just park there? "So much for instructions," they both thought.

Dartmouth Hitchcock Medical Center is a modern structure having been built in the 1980s. It is the merger of Dartmouth College Medical Center and Mary Hitchcock Memorial Hospital.

The automatic doors to the east entrance opened for them. They turned right and proceeded down the long corridor towards reception 3Z at the opposite end of the long building. Sunlight streamed in through the glass-to-ceiling east wall. Walking past the first of two food courts at the facility, one on the east side they were passing and one on the west side of the complex, they continued toward the room where they would sign in and wait. Neither said anything as they walked. Holding hands, though, Tom could sense Mary's fear. She always squeezed his hand harder than she realized she was doing when she was fearful. He used to tease her about being a "fearful little bug". In his heart, he knew she was one of the bravest people he had ever known. When he would tell her how he felt, she would always reply, "What is my alternative? What else can I do? It's out of my hands. I'm just along for the ride." Still, she was scared.

Midway to 3Z he decided to try to help her relax. "I know you are going to have a good PET," he said. "Yeah, right. That's what you always say." She said this smiling at him. Her smile always melted his heart. It was a combination of true genuine joy and sometimes surprise. This time it was none of those. It was a smile of unsaid thought, "I sure hope you're right!"

She gave his hand a squeeze and he did the same back to her. Silently, they walked on. A quick right turn at a hallway leading to Emergency, and then a quick left turn down a long hallway leading between consultation rooms and imaging exam rooms led them eventually to one more set of quick right turns and left turn into reception 3Z. Tom thought to himself how odd it is that no hospital, old or new, has direct hallways to destinations. All hospitals are built with multiple hallways and turns. Some hospitals even need colored lines on the floor for you to follow. What does someone who is color blind do in those cases? His thoughts often slipped into those kinds of things, as he is dyslexic. "Have you ever tried to type in credit card numbers on a computer or any other requirement for streams of letters and numbers," he would ask people. "Try being dyslexic and doing it." Not easy. Oh, well, if that is the worst you have to deal with, flipping numbers and letters, that's not really so bad. Just double, triple check yourself every time.

Mary walked to the reception counter and gave the receptionist her full name and date of birth. The usual questions were asked. "Is your insurance still the same?"" "Yes." "Are your address, contacts, and phone number still the same?" "Yes." "Are the questions related to workmen comp and social security the same?" "Yes." "Take this iPad device and answer the questions and return it back to me when you are finished. Someone will come and get you when they are ready." Always the same. Pretty routine.

Tom had already sat down at a space that had two chairs separated from others. She went over to join him but almost immediately, a happy man's voice called out, "Mary." She got up and walked over to him. She gave him the requested date of birth. Tom had joined them. The technician said, "This should take about an hour and half with prep and all. She'll meet you back here at about 8:30 am." Off they went for another PET scan, the happy technician and Tom's Mary.

Tom passed the hour and a half wait as he always did. He walked to the west side of the hospital to Au Bon Pain for a paper cup of coffee and a toffee cookie. Their croissants were terrible. Too bready. Not at all a French croissant, which Tom would have preferred. He also would have preferred a porcelain cup for the coffee too. Paper cup and coffee is like wine in a plastic glass. Not right, just not right! Almost as bad as wine in a paper cup. That's even worse than coffee in one.

He took his paper cup of coffee and cookie to the southwest part of the hospital and climbed the two flights of stairs to the fifth floor. Interesting fact about the hospital is that the main entrances on both the east and west side are on the third floor of the hospital. When Tom had wandered around the hospital while Mary was in a breast cancer exercise group called Pam's Class, he had been down to the second floor. It seemed like the basement, but there must be another basement below that basement. He had never made it lower than the second floor. With coffee in hand, he opened the doors to the research office section and found his usual cubby hole area with two lounge chairs, a small table, and most importantly, a view out to the New Hampshire woods surrounding the hospital. A pleasant view to pass the long hour and a half until he rejoined Mary. Not nearly as long as the hour and a half she had to endure with PET prep and PET scan. He, at least, had a cookie and coffee and two spiders on a web outside the window to watch.

He could never wait the entire hour and a half before heading back to the 3Z waiting area. He always had hopes that her PET scan time would move quicker. It never did. Always an hour and a half later, she was brought back to him at the waiting room. It was true that day too. Here she came beside the smiling, happy technician, the same one who had come for her before. Pleasantries were exchanged, then Mary and Tom headed back the way they had first come to reception room 3Z. This time, they stopped at the small snack and coffee shop along the way to get coffee and a banana muffin for Mary. She had a thing about muffins. With her nerves up these days, that was all she could eat. Eating would come later and hopefully without fear and worry.

They sat in the coffee shop for just a few minutes so Mary could eat the muffin and drink the coffee. The space was filled with the usual assortment of people in a hospital. Hospital staff talking about the characteristics of a patient's diagnosis and treatments. The friends, but most likely family, of a patient undergoing those treatments. The patients themselves, like Mary, worrying and thinking about what those treatments would be like. And of course, the staff that kept the facility reasonably clean and the food bins filled with "nearly airplane" foods. The real foods were downstairs in the cafeteria. Food was generally good down there. The cafeteria was located on the west side of the hospital's second floor.

Finished with her nutritional breakfast of a banana muffin and coffee, Mary and

Tom walked the rest of the way to the second reception area of the day, reception room 3K, for check-in. Following check-in, she would be called for blood draw for a blood test and cancer markers, and then another hour and a half wait until the appointment time with Dr. Chamberlin to review the blood work and PET scan results. Sometimes following the blood work, if Mary felt up to it, they would find themselves downstairs at the cafeteria eating eggs, toast, and another cup of coffee. Tom would get bacon too, but not Mary. That was true this day. The day was nice, warm, and cloudless, inviting them to the outdoor tables on the patio so they could while away the wait time until the appointment with Dr. Chamberlin.

Forty-five minutes later, Mary did what she usually did, stood up and said, "Let's go to Dr. Chamberlin's office and see if we can push things along." She did this every appointment. "Waiting is driving me crazy." Mary was not one for idle time. She tried to fill her days and minutes with anything productive, challenging, or creative. Sitting and waiting was none of those. What she could never quite understand was that processing and reviewing the PET and blood work took time, especially if there might be a coffee break involved. Although one never knew if that was the case or not. Best to keep a positive attitude and think everyone worked as diligently as she did.

Tom had tried hard to get Mary to relax more, take things slower. Trying to stay active through the death of two sons in separate car accidents, working two jobs while putting herself through the rest of her college education, all the while being a single parent, for the most part, for her youngest child, had created this pressure to never let up. Perhaps being the oldest daughter, second in age, in a family of ten siblings had also created this drive. She was always the responsible one. Keeping the bigger, size-wise, brothers out of the ice cream in the freezer as her Mom had directed when little Mary was left in charge. Well, Mary tried, as she was expected to do.

After arriving at the office area of Dr. Chamberlin, Mary found the unit secretary. Mary explained that she was early for the office visit but perhaps things could be sped up. The unit secretary smiled, as she did each time, and said she would see what she could do. She also, for the third time that day, took Mary's vital signs, pulse, blood pressure, temperature, height, and weight. Nothing had changed from the two earlier times of taking vital signs.

A few minutes later, Mary and Tom were escorted to an open exam room to wait the final few minutes for Dr. Chamberlin. That moment arrived.

Nervously, Mary looked up as the noise outside the exam room indicated someone was there. A moment later, the door opened to a friendly face and Dr. Chamberlin entered the room with, "Hi Mary. Hi Tom. Mary, how are you doing?" She asked that each time with her usual smile. Mary replied with her typical answer to the question, "That's what I'm here to have you tell me," while trying to have her own worried smile on her face.

Dr. Chamberlin sat down at the small exam room table and opened her laptop. A few moments later, she said, "Well, your labs look very good. The cancer markers are down. Red and white blood counts are good. All blood enzymes look excellent. All in all, really good. It appears the alternation of two weeks on a high dose of estrogen, followed by four weeks of the estrogen suppressant appears to be working . . . very well!"

These words brought smiles to both Mary and Tom's faces. "What about the PET scan?" Mary asked.

"It hadn't been read and sent to me yet when I was in the office. Let's see if it's here...ah, yes, it is." A few moments of nerve-racking silence and then turning to Mary and Tom. "The PET is good . . . it's really good!" Mary and Tom's hearts jumped with joy. Mary said to the doctor, "It's good?"

"No," Dr. Chamberlin said, "No, it's really good! The cancer tumors look to have decreased in size and the one near the lung appears to have disappeared! This is good, really good." Mary had clutched Tom's hand firmly. This time the firmness was not out of fear. This time it was out of joy. The PET was not only good, as Tom had assured her it would be, it was really, really good!

A few more questions were asked and then Mary was ready to run from the exam room before anything could change her happy mood. Tom on the other hand had another idea based on one more question. He asked it.

"So, Dr. Chamberlin, does this good blood work and PET scan mean that Mary and I can go to Paris?"

Mary's jaw just about hit the floor. "What?" Mary asked.

Tom asked again, "Does this mean we can take a trip to Paris?"

Dr. Chamberlin broke into a big smile and said, "Absolutely. There is no reason that Mary cannot go to Paris. I highly endorse the idea!" Big smiles and hugs all around and out the door Mary and Tom headed before anything could change.

Nearly running to the parking lot, once outside the hospital door Mary stopped, looked at Tom, and said, "What brought that question on?"

Tom said, "Well, we've talked about it for some time ever since we got back from our trip in 2015 when we met up with Rita and Hank. I thought if you had a good PET, which I knew you would, why not celebrate by going to the city we love!"

"But you always think I am going to have a good PET."

"Yes," he replied, "But this time I just knew it would be a good one!" Mary smiled and squeezed his hand that she was still holding tightly. She pulled him close to her, kissed him firmly, and said, "Let's do it! We're going to Paris!"

ACKNOWLEDGEMENTS

I began writing our book on January 14, 2021, not quite three months after losing my co-author and love, Mary, to breast cancer. She had asked me to write the book for us. She first conceived the idea for the story when we rented the apartment in Paris in early September 2019. This trip took place thanks to two Mary's. My sweet Mary and her wonderful oncologist, Dr. Mary Chamberlin. It is to these two Mary's that this book is dedicated.

There are many others to thank for what we have written. I hope to not leave anyone out. I am sure that I will do so and wish to apologize to them now.

First, I must thank three wonderful young women who helped in so many ways with "The White Light Within". Tammy Lynn Harriman, my wonderfully gifted massage therapist who has kept me able to walk and out of a wheelchair. In addition to the deep tissue massages to treat the terrible transient muscle cramps and overly loose alternating with intensely tight joints. Tammy also had to be a sounding board to my story telling.

Kali Anderson McNutt, my former colleague and my volunteer editor. She, too, heard all of my stories over and over again. Both young women kindly listened, showed interest, and added greatly to the book. By the way, you will meet them as characters introduced in Mary's and my second book, "Between Two Doors: In Search of Colette". Tammy rides motocross and in the book will be the character Tammy "Green Hornet" Lynn. Kali has learned some mixed martial arts moves from her cousin Joel and will be Kali "Roundkick" McNutt. In book three, "The Author Goes Missing," they are the heroes who rescue him.

The third young woman is my Canadian friend and chief editor, Amelia Gilliland. A writer who is dyslexic and a naturally bad speller needs a great editor. Amelia is that and more. The order of my words is often odd. Correct spelling is nonexistent. Tom lived in Paris in 1st, 2nd, and 3rd grade and didn't learn US phonetic spelling. I mix French and English . . . look out! Who knows what language I created. Amelia and Kali both handled the task of order and translation expertly. You have just read the results of their dedication. I could not ask for better editors and friends.

Next, I want to thank all of my thirty or so beta readers for their gallant efforts to struggle through all of my misspelling, grammar mistakes, and sometimes odd word choices. The collective "post it notes" that they provided me with the original rough edits allowed for what was ultimately produced. Thank you: Patsy (Mary's old college roommate) and her husband David Reed, Jane Bancroft, Kristen Munroe, Bill Pettus, Don Kantor, Jim Woodward, Lisa Brown, my brother Wade Martz, Gwen Barlow, Mary's sister Rita Paul, Henry Hart, Laurel Stavis, Kristy and Jim Sanders, Ken and Deb Rozeboom, Fred Townsend (who gave us the title for the book by saying to me when I was angry at the world, "Oh, don't put negative thoughts out there in the universe. Only spread white light."), Doctor Mary Chamberlin and husband Jon, Cindy Ackil, Mary's and my daughters and husbands, Catherine Rieke and Jason Pettus, Sara and Jeff Passan, and many, many others. Thank you all for your frank criticisms and encouragement. You made this book possible. You also have helped me through these last two years without my Mary. She was a gift to us all. I know she is thanking you too. She lives on through these stories.

Lastly, Mary's and my stories are based on some real travel adventures and our imaginations of what could have happened. We believed travel helped us create and learn about others. Mary once said, "If I had a billion dollars, I would create a foundation for world peace!" "Really?" I said. "And how would you do that?" Her reply was simple. "I would provide a way for all students to have a travel abroad experience. That way, they would see that people of other cultures and countries are pretty much just like themselves."

That idea of Mary's was the impetus of the two of us setting up endowed "travel abroad" scholarships at UNC Charlotte, Husson University, and Indiana University. Proceeds from the royalties of this and other books are directed to those scholarships. Should you, after reading this and our future books, wish to help, we invite you to contact the giving offices at either Husson University or UNC Charlotte to help students fulfill Mary's idea. Since 2001 when the first scholarship was established, over forty students have had that experience, despite the two years when covid interrupted our ability to travel abroad.

I especially want to thank David Ter-Avanesyan for his incredible book design. The design captures the essence of the story. And watch for his future designs for the Sophia and Dimitri series and more adventures of Nina and Etienne.